CHARLOTTE BINGHAM

The ...
'A perfect escapist co...'
M...

'A perfect example of the new, darker romantic fiction . . .
a true 24-carat love story'
Sunday Times

The Nightingale Sings
'A novel rich in dramatic surprises . . . will have you
frantically turning the pages'
Daily Mail

To Hear A Nightingale
'A story to make you laugh and cry'
Woman

The Business
'A compulsive, intriguing and perceptive read'
Sunday Express

In Sunshine Or In Shadow
'Superbly written . . . A romantic novel that is romantic
in the true sense of the word'
Daily Mail

Stardust
'A long, absorbing read, perfect for holidays'
Sunday Express

Change Of Heart
'Her imagination is thoroughly original'
Daily Mail

Nanny
'Charlotte Bingham's spellbinding saga is required reading'
Cosmopolitan

Grand Affair
'Extremely popular . . . her books sell and sell'
Daily Mail

Debutantes
'A big, wallowy, delicious read'
The Times

The Love Knot

Charlotte Bingham

BANTAM BOOKS

LONDON · NEW YORK · TORONTO · SYDNEY · AUCKLAND

THE LOVE KNOT
A BANTAM BOOK: 0553 507184

Simultaneous publication in Great Britain by Doubleday,
a division of Transworld Publishers

PRINTING HISTORY
Doubleday edition published 2000
Bantam Books edition published 2000

1 3 5 7 9 10 8 6 4 2

Set in 11/13pt Palatino by
Phoenix Typesetting, Ilkley, West Yorkshire

Bantam Books are published by Transworld Publishers,
61–63 Uxbridge Road, London W5 5SA,
a division of The Random House Group Ltd,
in Australia by Random House Australia (Pty) Ltd,
20 Alfred Street, Milsons Point, Sydney, NSW 2061, Australia,
in New Zealand by Random House New Zealand Ltd,
18 Poland Road, Glenfield, Auckland 10, New Zealand
and in South Africa by Random House (Pty) Ltd,
Endulini, 5a Jubilee Road, Parktown 2193, South Africa.

Reproduced, printed and bound in Great Britain by
Mackays of Chatham plc, Chatham, Kent

In loving memory of Mopsy,
whose gaiety, beauty and charm lightened many
a dark creative hour,
and who will always be remembered by
the author of this book.

Prologue

The awful truth was that it had happened, and it was real. And the worst of it was that it could not be given to the servants, or locked away in an attic as a piece of outdated furniture might be. It was there, and strangely immoveable. It. The baby.

As she stared at her grandchild, the woman thought with some relief that at least 'it' was a girl, and as such did not really matter. It might have been a little more difficult to give away a boy, a grandson, but to give away a girl presented really very little difficulty.

'See that it is given a good home. Make sure that it is looked after properly. I have decided that my daughter will be buried here in London. Normally she would be taken back to the family estate, but her father wants nothing to do with her. He has cut her out of his life entirely.'

'You cannot cut people out of your life when they are already dead, surely?' Lady Angela could feel herself burning with a kind of biblical indignation, yet only her blue eyes reflected her inner fury. 'We are all deserving of forgiveness. Let him who is without sin cast the stone, and so on and so forth?'

But this pious reference was lost on her listener who continued as if she had not heard a word.

'Your friend has paid the price of her own foolish misbehaviour, and that is all that can be said on the matter, Lady Angela.'

'Had she been a boy her behaviour would have merely been called *sowing wild oats*. Had she been a boy Society would have easily forgiven her, if not condoned her.'

'But she was *not* a boy, Lady Angela, and nor is this poor creature here. You must be not just very young but also very foolish if you expect justice in this world for women, my dear.'

Whereupon the older woman swept out, while Lady Angela clenched her elegantly gloved fist and raised her eyes to heaven as if she could see her friend somewhere beyond the ceiling, as if she was calling silently to her that, though everyone else might have disowned her in her misery, she at least had not.

Moreover, Lady Angela did not care how very young or how very foolish she was: she *did* expect justice, and what was more she was determined to see that at least a little bit of it was shown to her poor friend's baby.

Part One

Stepping Stones

When you have gone away
No flowers more, methinks will be . . .

Yanagiwara Yasu-Ko

One

1900

All the time she was growing up in one of the poorer districts of London, Leonie had no real need to fuel her deep desire to better herself. She had only to pass the door of the women's workhouse at St Pancras and feel the shiver that ran down her foster mother's arm into her own small, plump hand to know that *not* to better herself would be more terrible than she could imagine.

Once, when Mrs Lynch had cause to actually go into the workhouse on some errand for the vicar – Leonie could not now recall exactly what it was – just the sight of those rows and rows of women seated on hard benches, their plates of stale food in front of them, the look of despair in their eyes, was enough to scare the living daylights out of her. Had they been swinging from the gallows their fate could not, to Leonie's lively mind anyway, have seemed more terrible, and her foster mother's murmur of 'They're dying a slow sort of death' was not just a muttered remark to Leonie, it was, without any doubt, a dire warning.

So much so that there was actually no need for

5

her mother to add, 'Mark my words, that is a place you do *not* want to end up, dear.'

Leonie was the last of the Lynches' ten children, and quite different from the rest, being tall, and blonde, with unusually bright turquoise eyes. She had been fostered by Mrs Aisleen Lynch when she was only a few days old. The money her arrival had brought into the Lynch household – where not even Ned Lynch's regular Covent Garden porter's wage was quite sufficient to keep them all – was most gratefully received. It was not only gratefully received, it was well spent, for Mrs Lynch was a good woman. She might be poor, but she was clean. Indeed her front doorstep positively glowed with the scrubbing that she gave it shortly after her husband left for work in the early hours of each morning, not to mention the whitening that she gave it with chalk. And the nets at her window were washed as regularly as the steps, just as the geranium that sat behind them was watered daily and its bronze pot polished.

To be clean, to see her children clean, her house polished and food on the table was all that Mrs Lynch desired of her life. Her cleanliness, her freshly chalked step, and her whites, were her pride.

No-one is so poor that they cannot be clean, was an often repeated maxim among the residents of Eastgate Street, where chalk-white steps were respected and doors had no locks. So were Ned Lynch's words to his children, said just before he carved their precious Sunday roast: *To be poor and be seen to be poor, is the devil all over* – a saying which

Aisleen herself always only just tolerated, secretly thinking that, for some reason that she could not name, it did not sound entirely nice.

What Aisleen Lynch had never told Leonie, however, was that as a baby she had arrived at number fifty-three quite out of the blue on a dark rainy night, through the auspices of Aisleen's friend Mrs Dodd, a nursing sister, who ran a private home very near to, although not in, London's Harley Street.

Mrs Dodd and Aisleen had become friends while attending the same convent school in Streatham. Aisleen had married a good man who, through no fault of his own, had been robbed of his business, but who fortunately, by dint of his great height and knowledge of the Covent Garden markets, had eventually been able to find work as a porter, his days spent not in adding up columns of figures and noting sales, but carrying great weights on a tray placed on the top of his massive head.

Aisleen's friend Mrs Dodd, on the other hand, had married a man who was the right-hand man of a particular kind of doctor. It had not been long after her marriage that Mary Dodd, with one eye on the housekeeping accounts, had suddenly, and wisely, appreciated the need for a certain kind of nursing home for the daughters of the nobility and gentry who had not made a timely visit to that self-same doctor for whom her husband worked.

Upon this realization she had persuaded her husband to invest his already considerable savings in a large house where such unfortunate young girls could come, for a fee, and in the most discreet circumstances deliver themselves of their 'mistakes' – those same small 'mistakes' to be farmed out by Mrs Dodd herself to families willing and able to bring them up. Naturally this would be in return for a regular and much needed stipend provided by the girls' families, or the fathers of the infant mistakes, that stipend being well above the cost of the child's keep and therefore very profitable to the foster parents. Thus was the unfortunate babies' survival ensured.

This particular night, and Aisleen would always remember it, Mrs Dodd had arrived with a young lady whom Aisleen had immediately taken to be the young mother in question, until her friend had made it clear that the unfortunate young mother had in fact died in childbirth, and that Mrs Dodd's *companion*, as she was discreetly referred to, was none other than the dead girl's best friend, determined on seeing for herself that the baby was delivered into a properly respectable home, where the poor child might be supposed to have some sort of chance in life.

It was obvious from the first that the young lady, so extremely fashionable in her bustle caged high at the back, her bonnet ribbons glistening with the raindrops from which her coachman had been unable to shield her, had been from the highest circles, for she moved and spoke with a delicacy and tact not usually to be found in Eastgate Street, where good humour and a need for survival jostled with the kind of insecurity and directness that this young lady could never have known.

It was not only her manners that had remained in Mrs Lynch's memory. Used as she was to seeing only drab stuffs and black dresses in Eastgate Street, she would always remember how the light had shown up the beauty of the material of that grand young lady's dress, with its particular combination of stripes down the side, and spots on the elaborate panniers, not to mention a great spotted bow placed atop the cage to the back of her. And of course her hat had been an exquisite confection of flowers and ribbons, those same ribbons tied beneath her pretty, delicately moulded, if rounded, chin.

At once, on entering the Lynches' front room, she had commented most appreciatively on its furnishings.

'Mrs Lynch, you have a very pretty room here. I can see for myself that you cherish your home and your family.'

At the time the young lady's voice, to an ear all too used to the sharper voices of Eastgate Street, had sounded exquisite to Aisleen Lynch; as exquisite as her fingers had looked as, having carefully removed one of her gloves, she shook Mrs Lynch's hand (a most unusual gesture in one so gently bred, to say the least) and smiled at her, sadly, solemnly, her eyes once or twice straying to the baby in the shawl that Mrs Dodd held only a few steps away from them both.

'This is my friend's baby, Mrs Lynch, but my

friend is now, alas, dead. It is a baby girl, and as such would have been completely unwanted by either her father or her grandfather, a man who, believe me, although he is titled is no gentleman. There are very few girl babies from the wrong side of any patrician blanket that are wanted, I fear. Sons are different, they are needed for the Empire, but not girls. Girls do not count.'

Aisleen had always remembered this particular statement, first for the firm, proud, almost disdainful look that had accompanied it, and second for the astonishment that she herself had felt that any young woman coming from such a privileged background should have taken it upon herself to bother to ensure that the future foster home of her poor friend's baby was all that it should be. And then that she should have been so readily prepared to acknowledge an illegitimate baby as such, when most young ladies, even should they have found the courage to visit Eastgate Street as she had done, would have evaded the issue, was extraordinary to say the least. But, as Aisleen was to find out, Lady Angela Bentick was a very unusual person.

'I promised her, I promised my dearest friend – I gave her my word that in the event of her not surviving her terrible ordeal I would make sure of a good home for her unborn child. And I asked to come and meet you so that I could be assured that the poor baby will be brought up in a loving home. And now, on meeting you, I *am* reassured. You are a good woman, Mrs Lynch, and will take care of her.' She turned to the baby for a second and gave it a long, loving look before turning back again. 'She does need a name, though, does she not?' she said, as if the thought had only just occurred. 'When I think about it, I rather think her mother was favouring Leonie.' Again she had turned aside to dab her eyes with a handkerchief, the reality of what had happened obviously suddenly overcoming her, but she continued after a minute: 'Mrs Dodd, here, is to take care of the rest. Goodbye, darling little baby.'

She had kissed the top of the baby's head most tenderly, and then she had fled back to her carriage, and to her very different life.

The vicar had duly christened the baby Leonie, for her dead mother's sake, and Mary for Mrs Dodd's sake, and that had been that, until just this last week, when Aisleen Lynch had suddenly become aware that it was no longer at all suitable for Leonie, being now seventeen and quite finished at the convent where she had, courtesy of an old friend of Aisleen's, received a free education, to stay sitting around in Eastgate Street doing nothing but embroidering blouses and running errands for her foster mother. With this realization upon her, Aisleen had sat down to write to her old friend at the private nursing home, and then awaited a reply with her usual patience, knowing that such was Mary Dodd's character, and indeed her supreme sense of duty, that it would not be long before she responded.

In the event, the reply was followed by a visit

11

from Mrs Dodd herself, grown stoutly fat and wheezing just a little as she sat down in the Lynch front room. Having accepted a cup of Aisleen's best tea, she gazed appreciatively at the plate of home-made seed cake that her friend was offering her.

'I don't know that I should, not really. But if you insist.'

Which of course Aisleen did.

Tea and cake over, there was a slight pause, during which time Mrs Dodd's eyes took in the furnishings of the room, Aisleen's new shawl, and the canary in a quite elaborate cage on a stand.

'You have all of them off your hands at last, Aisleen dear,' she stated.

'Leonie will be the last to go,' Aisleen agreed, and she gave the particularly comfortable sort of sigh of a woman who knows she has fully discharged her duties as a mother and can now look forward to a future where she will be taken care of by at least a handful of the children whom she has struggled so hard to bring up. 'She'll be down in a jiffy,' she added, and sighed again, but this time in pleasant anticipation, because she knew that Leonie had been upstairs ironing and goffering her best navy costume, not to mention her underclothes and petticoats and matching hair ribbons, and that by now she would be sitting waiting with some impatience for her foster mother to call up the narrow, bare, wooden stairs to her to come down.

Of course Mrs Dodd, as one of the child's

godparents, had taken a preliminary interest in Leonie as she was growing from babyhood into childhood, but, as is the way of things, in these last few years prosperity and a burgeoning business had prevented her from visiting Eastgate Street, and so it was with some interest, verging on the nervously expectant, that she turned as Leonie entered the living room.

No sooner had she seen Leonie Lynch, tall, blonde and wearing a costume of navy blue with a sailor collar in perfect taste, than her feelings of nervousness were replaced by a strong desire to laugh delightedly. Indeed Mrs Dodd found herself putting her hand to her mouth to stop herself saying something too extravagantly praising (so bad for young girls) of her goddaughter's beauty.

She had, of course, given the progress of time, quite forgotten the beauty of the mother, quite forgotten her arrival at the discreet private house where young ladies were delivered of their illegitimate babies by expert medical men who, very often, if they were friends of the girl's family, or had some other connection, would give their services for free.

But now she was shaking the hand of Leonie Lynch, and the tall young girl was curtsying, and there was so much about her that was natural and beautiful that Mary Dodd found she did actually remember Leonie's poor young mother from seventeen years before, and her beauty, and her delicate ways. She imagined that the mother must have had turquoise eyes as this girl had, and even that she was as happy-looking as her daughter, but she knew, given the awfulness of the situation, that the latter at least must be impossible, and her memory must be deceiving her.

She turned to Aisleen.

'Upon my word, she is a credit to you, dear, really she is. I cannot have seen her since she was – well, hardly more than twelve, I am all too ashamed to say, but being so very busy at business as what I have been these last years, it has been more than hard for me to get out to you here.'

'She is a credit to the nuns, dear, not me.' Aisleen gave a shrewd nod towards the window as if she could, at that very moment, see a troupe of the good sisters passing by the glass. 'Nuns are ever so much better at education, I always think, than what normal folk are.'

'And they knew quality when they saw it,' Mrs Dodd stated, with an approving nod of her own towards the window as if she too could see a group of hurrying sisters in their purple habits and white veils.

'I love Sister Agnes and Sister Therese,' Leonie agreed, but shyly, because she knew just how much depended on this meeting with her godmother. But since there had been a considerable pause during which both the older women had sipped their tea she had felt emboldened to make some comment.

Both women now turned to her and nodded slowly. 'You can't do no better than a convent,' Mrs Dodd opined. 'And all that sewing and that – so good for girls. Never mind that most of them are French or Irishy, they're still the best.'

Having been advised to say as little as possible, and leave everything to her foster mother, Leonie only smiled, and instead Aisleen spoke for her foster daughter.

'We *was* thinking of nursing as an occupation for Leonie, but the uniform, you know, and so much to pay for in the first three years if she is to go to a decent training establishment.'

Despite the canary cage, the new tablecloth and the shawl with the lace insets, Mrs Dodd could well appreciate that to pay for nursing training and a uniform would be too much for the Lynches. Any help for their youngest foster daughter would have to come from outside. She herself had no children, and now that she saw how grand and beautiful her goddaughter had become she suddenly no longer felt the lack of them. Now was the time, she could see, for Leonie Lynch's godmother to come to the forefront and help guide the girl's future into a safe harbour.

'Course, dear. I understand, it's out of the question . . .' Her voice tailed off, as her thoughts raced ahead.

Mary Dodd was now very wealthy. Not wealthy in the way of Lady Angela Bentick, of course, not *privileged* and wealthy, but she was very well cushioned, and nicely set up too. She still had her own nursing home, despite her husband's unfortunate demise. But although the nursing home was most respectable, it was not at all suitable for Leonie

Lynch. The type of girls that were taken into the home would not be at all desirable company for a young innocent girl fresh from a convent.

Oh, they were upper class all right, those girls, but they had all but been abandoned by their patrician parents to grow up half stable lad and half hoyden, with the inevitable result that her nursing home was rarely if ever, alas, empty.

Lady Angela on the other hand had her own hospital, very proper, where military officers of all ages came for operations and recuperation from every sort of wound or illness. Lady Angela had accompanied Leonie to Aisleen Lynch's house. Lady Angela was therefore the person to whom, Mary Dodd determined, she would now turn for advice and help.

'Leave everything to me,' she told Aisleen. Not wishing to raise hopes, she said no more, neither mentioning any names nor making any promises.

After she had left, with all the usual injunctions, and departed in a hansom cab back to the West End and her nursing home, Leonie turned to Aisleen.

'How was I?'

'Every inch what she could have hoped or expected, I should have thought.'

Of a sudden Leonie threw her arms around her foster mother's neck.

'Oh, if only something could come of this, Ma. If only!'

'There is so much to think about, is there not, when a young person is involved?'

16

Lady Angela Bentick looked across at Mary Dodd. That she had spared the time to see her visitor alone in her office they both knew was an unusual concession, but behind this mutual appreciation of the moment there was another deeper appreciation. There was no doubt at all, in either of their minds, that Mrs Dodd was an equal rather than an inferior of Lady Angela. They understood each other really very well, not by virtue of their social class, but through their work, both of them having to deal with human suffering daily, sometimes hourly. They were alike too in temperament, since neither was conventional, and both had been forced to become businesswomen.

In fact, they understood each other so thoroughly that when Lady Angela's blue eyes stared across the top of her desk at Mary Dodd they stared not down at her but into her, searching, as always, to do not what was easiest, but what would, in both their opinions, be right.

Following a long silence, which Mary Dodd had no intention of curtailing, Lady Angela spoke again.

'How has she grown, my dear friend's child?'

'Tall.'

'Yes, well, she would be, all the—' She filled in what would have been the moment when she mentioned Leonie's true surname with a little cough. 'All her mother's family are tall. And dark – very dark, usually.'

'No, blonde, with turquoise eyes.'

'Turquoise? Surely you mean blue?'

17

'No. Turquoise, Lady Angela, pure turquoise, like the sea in Italy, now I come to think of it. Really lovely.'

Lady Angela hesitated again. Leonie's mother had always refused to reveal the father of her child, but the idea of 'turquoise eyes' rang a bell in her head. She frowned and thought about it while a good minute went by, a minute during which Mary Dodd's own thoughts ran back to the past, to the days shortly after they had travelled together to Eastgate Street in Lady Angela's carriage to deliver little Leonie to her foster mother. For both of them it had been a time when their lives were at a crossroads, before they had each, in their own way, taken firm steps towards independence, towards gathering the reins of their lives into their own hands.

Lady Angela could not have been more than eighteen when she had thrown over the traces. After a dutiful London Season and presentation at court to please her mother and grandmother, she had displeased them by remaining stubbornly unengaged. Not so very long after delivering her friend's baby into the hands of the good Aisleen Lynch, she had announced to her father that she wanted nothing more than to enter Florence Nightingale's profession and to spend her considerable inheritance on a nursing home, and this at a time when, in the highest circles, nurses were considered only marginally better than prostitutes.

But Lady Angela was not to be deterred. She wanted to minister to the sick. She wanted to improve conditions, not just for the patients, not just to alleviate their suffering, but to better conditions for the nurses themselves, so that the reputation of nursing in general would improve, would become what it should be – respectable.

It had become a passion with her, this desire to help the sick and the injured, to restore people's bodies, and with them, their minds – so much so that her family feared that from being too independent of spirit she had now become quite unhinged.

After much controversy, and a considerable length of time during which her father held her a virtual prisoner in the country, he had, at long last, relented, and Lady Angela, against all advice from her truly shocked family, had been allowed to leave home and do as she wished.

As it turned out she had spent her inheritance wisely, buying a large, elegant house near Buckingham Palace, and setting about converting it into a nursing home with all the usual facilities, so that it became in effect a hospital which also had that particular kind of comforting country house ambience so reassuring to the sick and wounded coming in from abroad, or nearer to home. Here the wounded officer could be made better in surroundings that would be familiar to him.

Still thinking about turquoise eyes, Lady Angela was called away by one of her senior sisters, leaving Mary Dodd to look around her and appreciate the kind of environment that made a stay in 'Sister Angela's Nursing Home' a most particular experience, and one it seemed to Mary Dodd which could only make the lame walk, the sick heal.

Here the kind of bright decoration made fashionable for some time now by the influx of young American heiresses marrying into aristocratic circles had long ago made its entrance, so that there were no gloomy pot plants or dire stags' heads, only bright and comfortable chintz curtains and covers, and flowers in great blue and white vases.

So homely was the atmosphere that a newly arrived patient would have the sensation of staying in the home of a relative rather than booking into a hospital. Indeed there was nothing institutional about any of the surroundings, and even a visitors' book laid out on the table, a page from which, Mary Dodd knew, if she was so indiscreet as to read it, would more than likely read like an index from a book devoted to the scions of great houses who had been nursed by Lady Angela.

'Very well,' said Lady Angela on her return, 'now we must resume our thoughts together. What is it that *you* have in mind for Miss Lynch, Mrs Dodd?'

'As her godmother I would like to be Miss Lynch's patroness, so that she may enter your nursing home as a junior nurse.'

They both knew what this meant. Mrs Dodd was prepared to pay for Leonie's considerable uniform and for her keep during her training, and to hold herself responsible for her in every way. If Leonie disgraced herself, if she let down her training, or was in any way found wanting, Mrs Dodd would be called upon to take her back. If she behaved herself she would stay under Lady Angela's patronage and be privileged to do so.

'That is very generous of you, Mrs Dodd. And you are quite sure – despite everything – that this could be rewarding?'

'Despite everything' meant that Leonie Lynch, 'despite' being brought up in Eastgate Street, could pass as a young lady from a rather more sophisticated sort of background.

'I think that when you meet Leonie, Lady Angela, you will be, let us say, pleasantly surprised, really I do.'

'Gracious, Mrs Dodd.' Lady Angela sighed and suddenly put one long-fingered, white hand to her forehead. 'Do you know, I can remember that awful week so well, even now – despite its being seventeen years ago. And I remember Mrs Lynch being the only ray of hope at that moment. I remember thinking, the moment I met her, that she was a very good woman, and that we could trust her to bring up my poor friend's child. We did what we could, did we not, and there was nothing more we could do, was there?'

To Mrs Dodd it seemed that, of a sudden, Lady Angela was once again the worried young woman from years ago, her eyes reflecting all the old agonies she had suffered during that terrible week of indecision and grief.

'Lady Angela, I have to tell you that my friend,

Mrs Lynch, poor though she may be, is not the same as her neighbours, not by any means. Indeed, had it not been for her husband being tricked out of his business by unscrupulous loan sharks in the City, who added clauses and forged signatures and goodness knows what else, her own marriage would have been set against quite a different background. She would have had servants, and a silver tea set, not to mention her own carriage, but he was tricked, Mr Lynch was, and Mrs Lynch stood by him, as a good woman should. I would always have stood by my late husband, even had he lost his business, or I know not what.'

Lady Angela cleared her throat as a churchgoer might when the vicar's sermon had gone on a mite too long.

'Bring Miss Lynch to see me next week, and we will discuss this matter further. But say nothing, if you please, of our connection. She must not know I knew her mother. That would not be right.'

Although she was possessed of a calm temperament Lady Angela now found that she felt oddly excited at the idea of seeing her dead friend's grown offspring, and yet at the same time part of her, although admittedly only a very small part, was in dread that the young girl might turn out to be not quite the thing, and prove to be a social embarrassment.

Mary Dodd curtsied to Lady Angela and hurried off, her smart street clothes in their excellently cut dull cloth and her feathered hat disappearing into her opulent carriage watched by Lady Angela

22

from the window of her downstairs room.

'What a curious world it is,' she remarked to her secretary later.

She stopped precisely there, for to go any further would be to be indiscreet, and if there was one quality which even Lady Angela was aware that she possessed in full, it was discretion. Without it 'Sister Angela's Nursing Home' would not be the undoubted success that it was.

Only a few days later Leonie Lynch was delivered to her godmother's house, where Mary Dodd was waiting for her in some excitement. Having no children of her own (and since she had assisted in the birth and placing of so many unfortunate mistakes her reluctance to become a mother was surely understandable) Mrs Dodd was looking forward to the pleasure of transforming her goddaughter into precisely the kind of daughter that she, in an admittedly fairly wild flight of fancy, would have liked to have had. Under interrogation she would have had to admit that she had ambitions for Leonie Lynch, and that those ambitions did include marriage to someone prosperous.

It was for this reason that she watched Leonie step out of the Dodd carriage with some fascination. Leonie had always been a pretty child, but now, seen from above, it was apparent that she was quite, quite beautiful, and what was more she stepped like a lady, she walked like a lady, she stopped and looked around the street like a lady. And, too, the manner with which she wore her velvet-collared coat and simple hat made them look a hundred times better than they were.

'My dear, how marvellous that you are here. Step this way.'

Mrs Dodd led her protégée up the stairs towards her bedroom, a light and airy room whose windows gave on to the chic-er aspects of London's West End, where she could watch carriages arriving and decanting other young ladies more richly dressed than herself.

'One step at a time,' Mrs Dodd told Leonie, as she saw the young girl gazing down, obviously already mesmerized by some of the sights below them. Beautiful women stepping up into coaches, while dowagers stepped down from them, their gloved hands held by their coachmen. Gentlemen in their immaculate cutaway tail coats, grey and black striped trousers, grey top coats, spats, boots, gloves and – despite the warm spring weather – black furled umbrellas. 'One step at a time,' Mrs Dodd repeated.

They both knew what Mary Dodd was trying to say, and a sudden look from Leonie's turquoise eyes told Mrs Dodd that the girl might be well brought up but she was not stupid, and the warning not to try to take too big a step would be not just heard but heeded.

This was most reassuring to her godmother, and yet at the same time Mrs Dodd could not help hoping that Leonie would not turn out to be too intelligent, or that if she was she would be wise enough to hide this particular attribute, for while a nurse at Sister Angela's would be expected to be good, and ladylike, to be patient and gentle, clever she must not be.

If she turned out to be sufficiently stupid to show that she was clever, she would have no prospects at all. Any chance of success in English Society depended entirely on a girl acquiring an aura of gentle innocence and gracious stupidity.

'Now, dear, elegant though you undoubtedly are, we must dress you to fit your new role, for although you are to be trained as a nurse you must look, at all times, like a lady, or you will have no prospects. Our first visit will be to my good friend Madame Chloe, the costumier.'

The 'costumier' was an old acquaintance of Mrs Dodd who went under the fashionably Frenchified name of 'Madame Chloe'. She too had grown stouter than she would have probably wished, but, perhaps in compensation, more prosperous than she could have ever dreamed of either.

'Mrs Dodd!'

Madame Chloe would never dream of addressing her old friend in anything but the most formal terms, especially in front of her own assistants and mannequins, girls that she liked to keep 'under her thumb' and treat as, in her opinion, all girls should be treated – strictly.

'Madame Chloe.'

Madame Chloe seemed to swim towards Mary Dodd. Despite the similarity of their backgrounds she and Leonie curtsied to each other, and then Mrs Dodd sat Leonie beside her on the small upright red velvet 'duenna's sofa' that was placed in one of the windows of Madame Chloe's first floor rooms.

'This is my goddaughter, Miss Lynch.'

Now Madame Chloe, having observed the formalities for the sake of her staff and her own sense of what was fitting, nodded and smiled at Mrs Dodd in silent congratulation as she turned Leonie's pretty head from one side to another, examining her really quite perfect profile with evident satisfaction.

'Well, well,' she said finally, bending slightly sideways and speaking behind her hand, 'we shall take great pleasure in having the dressing of this beautiful young lady, shall we not, dear?'

'Yes, indeed,' Mrs Dodd murmured, and she too smiled, because considering they had grown up together the formalities that they used in public were all a bit of a charade, albeit one that they both hugely enjoyed. In front of the world at large they were careful to behave quite differently from the way they would be to each other in private life when Madame Chloe was 'off duty' and went round to her old friend's house, usually late of a Sunday afternoon. At these times they would take tea together and have a great laugh, not to mention a most enjoyable talk about the old days.

'So, now, it is time to begin.' Madame Chloe clapped her hands, and into the room stepped the first model. 'Here we have a walking costume.'

As soon as Leonie saw the model, took in the cut and the cloth, the hat, the gloves, every fine detail of that costume, she wanted to rip the girl's clothes off and put them on herself, but instead she sat very still in her home-made navy blue dress with its formal little sailor collar, and her small hat which sat atop a head of rich, thick blonde hair, as Madame Chloe pointed out all the tailoring details of the coat and skirt.

It seemed hours, but was most likely actually not more than one, before Leonie was at last allowed to try on Mrs Dodd's choices of day dresses and coats and skirts, not to mention two evening dresses, and a cloak.

'Is this part of my uniform for Sister Angela's Nursing Home?'

Mary Dodd laughed such a rich laugh that, although she felt embarrassed at her own ignorance, it could not but remind Leonie of frankly indulgent things like dark fruit cake and port, and the velvet interiors of jewel boxes, and the red leather, pliant and buttoned, that made up the seating in the Dodd carriage.

Leonie's turquoise eyes turned to Mrs Dodd. The enquiry was genuine, for she had never expected to be indulged by her godmother in quite this way, and certainly not so soon. She had expected to have to work hard at her nursing for what she was being given, but doubtless the price that she would have to pay for such luxuries would come later?

'These clothes are for when you are *off* duty!'

This time they both laughed, understanding exactly, together, and for the first time, that Sister Angela's Nursing Home was only a stepping stone to something much, much more exciting.

Any time that is not spent on love
Is wasted.

Two

Dorinda Montgomery sighed impatiently. She hated the way her husband, Harry, always disappeared the moment their train or boat arrived. She really disliked how he seemed to delight in going off at that precise second in search of something quite negligible like a newspaper or a buttonhole. It was so intensely irritating to watch him strolling off in the opposite direction that she always, and immediately, felt like screaming. Not that Harry would notice if she did scream, of course. She could scream and scream and scream if she wished, and he would remain totally unimpressed. All he would do would be to look in the opposite direction until such time as she had stopped screaming, and then resume whatever conversation they happened to have been having before she started to yell.

Life had not been good to either of them since they had married two years before. Each of them had been a disappointment to the other. She because she could not settle to a quiet life in the backwaters, and he because he could not learn to make ends meet, which meant that they had spent the first two years of their marriage in small, run-down boarding houses in Jersey or the Scilly Isles or France, while Harry tried to make up his mind how his life should go – and, sometimes, but not so often, Dorinda's too.

Finally, unable to bear it any longer, Dorinda had packed up their suitcases and gone down to the harbour, purchased two tickets, sent for a porter, had the suitcases put on the first boat to England, and stepped up the gangplank, in company, as she had fondly imagined, with her husband Harry. But no, a few minutes later, back down the gangplank went Harry, and disappeared.

At first Dorinda tried not to react to his absence, but just stood forlornly waiting for his return, as time ticked on and on, and on. With no further sight of her vanished husband, up and down went Dorinda's small, elegant foot, tapping with impatience.

He was *meant* to have gone for the wretched *Morning Post* without which it seemed he could not start his day, but as it was he seemed to have gone *altogether*. Various whistles blew, and blew again. Another man hurried up the gangplank, and for a few seconds her hopes were raised, only to be dashed again as she saw that the man whose outline she had been following was someone quite other than Harry Montgomery, although wearing what had seemed like an identical suit.

Dorinda leaned anxiously over the side of the ship and stared up and down the quay below them. Any minute now the gangplank would be pulled up and she would be quite alone.

'Harry!' she started to call frantically. 'Harry!'

Inevitably there was no reply, and as she started to move towards the gangplank, hoping to delay the boat by running down it to find her slowcoach of a husband, a hand pulled at the base of her tight-fitting jacket, and a voice said in her ear, 'It's no good. The gangplank is about to come up. It's too late!'

'But my husband!' Dorinda cried, and without turning she shook herself free and plunged off in the direction of the gangplank. 'Harry!'

In the event the voice that had spoken from behind was right. It was too late. The gangplank had been raised, and all made ready for the ship to sail from the harbour. Now below her for the first time Dorinda could see her husband strolling – literally *strolling* – towards the ship, and then, seeing it was indeed moving off, starting to increase his speed, but far, far, too late, until finally he was left on the quayside, waving to Dorinda, as if he had suddenly changed his mind about sailing with her at all.

'Oh, what shall I do? What *shall* I do?'

She turned away, but as she did so she found her way blocked by a tall, sophisticated man with greying hair, informally if impeccably dressed in a tweed suit with half belt. His eyes attempted solemnity as he raised his boater to her and bowed politely.

'In the circumstances, madam, your husband being left on the shore, surely the only answer is to accept an invitation to lunch with myself?'

Dorinda, who had been just about to burst into tears, promptly stopped.

She stopped for many reasons. First because she suddenly realized what a complete bother it was to burst into tears – such an effort really. And then to have to put cold flannels on her eyes, that too was a nuisance. Next, she was not quite sure that she really cared that much about leaving Harry on the shore anyway. He had been nothing but a prize idiot, going off like that at the last moment, and just for a newspaper.

As a matter of fact, the realistic part of her applauded the fact that for once her dire warnings, warnings that Harry always seemed to so enjoy ignoring, had left him where he so richly deserved to be, not only high and dry, but upstream and without a paddle. For, she realized, turning, he had left not only his suitcase with her, but his Gladstone bag containing a great deal of what was left of their money.

Having decided not to burst into tears, and after an appropriate if quite short pause, Dorinda smiled suddenly and brilliantly at the middle-aged man who was still holding his jaunty straw boater in a gallant salute.

'I have a private cabin. May I invite you to take luncheon there? It would be so nice to be able to make up to you for your terrible distress.'

Dorinda knew that she should not accept. She was a married woman, and married women were not expected to take luncheon alone with men in their private cabins. But Harry had proved such a crashing ass, never listening to a word she said, and not minding too much about how she felt about anything either. Therefore, instead of saying no which of course, in the normal way of things, she would have done, she heard herself say, 'Thank you, I should be delighted.' And the dreadful thing was, she *was* delighted, not least because, in a somewhat lame attempt to save every penny of their money for their longed-for journey to England, Dorinda had not actually eaten properly for many days.

'I have just ordered enough lobsters to feed a party of six, so the thought that I am to have a guest is too delightful.'

'Lobsters! I adore lobsters. But . . . what shall I do with my luggage?'

'Why, Mrs . . . ?'

'Montgomery, Dorinda Montgomery.'

'Mrs Montgomery. And I am Gervaise Lowther.'

'What shall I do with my luggage?' Dorinda asked again, as if a man who could have the foresight to order lobsters for luncheon must surely have the same kind of command over suitcases.

They both stared at the suitcases. With the exception of the really rather new Gladstone bag, all the Montgomerys' luggage was pretty shaming, and shabby. It was not the kind of shabby that was acceptable either, not worn down with genteel age, just worn down from only a few years' existence because it had been so very inexpensive in the first place.

Gervaise Lowther stared from it to Dorinda, and back again to the luggage.

'I tell you what, Mrs Montgomery, why don't we leave it here, just for a while . . .'

'Not the Gladstone bag. That I will take with me.'

Dorinda, ever practical, quickly picked up that particular piece of luggage.

'No, perhaps not that, but the rest can surely be left?' Gervaise Lowther's eyes swept over the Montgomerys' suitcases in such a way as all at once to make them seem like just so many brown paper parcels containing clothing for the poor and needy. 'As a matter of fact, why not have a porter come for it and put it in the hold? And we will take ourselves off to my cabin where I hope we may enjoy our luncheon in peace and quiet.'

She was a married woman, she was going to lunch, quite alone, with a stranger, but suddenly Dorinda could not have minded in the very least.

She turned her most dazzling smile on Gervaise Lowther and taking his arm as if it was the most natural thing in the world, the other hand firmly gripping the Gladstone bag, she sauntered off towards his private cabin.

Afterwards, long afterwards, Dorinda would, privately, put down her fall from marital grace to too much wine, and the rocking of the ship, both of which, combined with the starvation to which she had, due to lack of funds, subjected herself in the previous days, had meant that, after several glasses of champagne and the most wonderful luncheon she had ever eaten – lobster mayonnaise being just the entrée – she had succumbed to Gervaise's obvious charms all too terribly and beautifully easily.

At that particular moment, however, all she felt was blissfully happy, for such is the effect of hindsight that what has given an individual nothing but pleasure and delight at the time, can in retrospect need a more moral, or understandable, explanation.

So much so that, with the passing of the years, Dorinda could even persuade herself that she had felt sorry for Gervaise, that he needed comforting. Or she would feel moved to pity for the poor innocent that she had once been – on board a ship for England, all alone, still only twenty, starved with hunger, and with an uncaring husband. Tears of sorrow for her young self would easily well up into her large, violet blue eyes, but if sorrow for herself developed over a distance of years, at the time, in reality, she took nothing but delight in her situation.

The truth was that she would never have married Harry Montgomery had her pushy mother not made it quite plain to her that if she did not she would make her become a stenographer, or put her in a convent, and not even as a nun, but as a domestic. Since neither course of action was in the least appealing to such a spirited young girl, Dorinda, half French and half Celtic as she was, decided to take a sanguine view of her future, and married the dull and unappealing Harry Montgomery.

Over lunch with the sparkling Gervaise

Lowther, however, her more wild and romantic side re-emerged. Besides revelling in the delicious food, she found she was quite able to enjoy herself without her husband, and, what was worse, cared about neither her future nor her past, and only for the present delectable moment.

The fact was that Gervaise Lowther was perfectly wonderful company. Not only was he urbane, and reasonable, he told her stories, and he laughed and joked, and – even more impressive to Dorinda – he knew everyone there was to know in London Society.

From the very start, inexperienced as she was, Dorinda realized at once that her lunching companion rubbed shoulders with the kind of people she had only read about in that same wretched *Morning Post* that had caused her husband to miss the boat. Gervaise Lowther referred to people in the highest circles in such a casual and amusing way that it seemed to Dorinda (all too conscious of her own provincial background) that just by lunching with him she was already curtsying to royalty.

'One thing so often leads to another, do you not find?' he asked her, laughingly, after they had not only lunched, but – inevitable when two attractive people have eaten and drunk so well – made love.

Dorinda lay against the mountain of pillows that seemed to her to be so terribly essential to the kind of lovemaking that she had just experienced and nodded, quite unable to speak. The past uncountable minutes had been extraordinary.

She had been awakened to lovemaking, indeed passion, of the most wondrous kind, of the kind that made her realize just what she had been missing in the past two years.

'Should we, I wonder . . . again?' she asked him, drowsy as a bee on a summer afternoon.

Gervaise Lowther looked down at her and burst out laughing.

'My dear, I only wish that we could, but the white cliffs of Dover are approaching. We will be arriving within the hour, and you surely need to take some rest after your activities, really you do!'

'Oh dear, oh dear, oh no, oh well!'

Dorinda clutched the sheet to her but insisted on kissing him nevertheless, a kiss that could have led to more and more, and more and more, had he not straightened up, laughing, and shaken his head.

'No more, my dear. You must rest.'

'And after I have rested?'

'Like every other lady – you dress. But can you—' He looked at her suddenly alarmed. 'I mean, can you dress, without your maid?'

Of a sudden he seemed far from sophisticated. Indeed, he looked panic-struck, and it was immediately obvious that if Dorinda had expected him to help her it would have been hopeless.

In two seconds flat Dorinda understood what was required of her and quickly replied, 'Oh, yes. I have done so before, although I really don't like it,' and this despite the fact that she had never even realized, until that minute, that no real lady ever dressed herself. That was definitely not something her mother had told her, stupid woman.

'Well, well, well, you are certainly a young woman rich in many talents if you can dress yourself too.'

'Yes, but you will have to help me with the laces on my corset.'

Gervaise Lowther, forty-five, man about town, experienced lover, racehorse owner, friend of the Prince of Wales, bon viveur, sighed with relief and lightly touched Dorinda's cheek with the tip of his finger.

'That is not all I will help you with, my dear. I shall also help you have your luggage thrown into the sea. After which I would advise you that you are going to come and live with me in St John's Wood, where I have a house, which shall be yours until further notice, that notice being dependent on your being as good a girl as you are at the moment, which is to say – very good indeed.'

Dorinda frowned, and thought, *How strange.* She quite imagined that she had just been bad. She looked down at her wedding ring. She knew she was married, but just at that moment she could not even remember what Harry Montgomery looked like. Or rather, she could remember what he looked like, but not what he was actually *like.* Nor even what clothes he had been wearing that morning when he had strolled off in search of the wretched *Morning Post.* Nor even quite how his voice sounded. Her meeting, so out of the blue, with Gervaise Lowther had swept all those details

40

from her twenty-year-old mind, and what was more the mere mention of having her own house had swept everything else out with them too.

She gazed out of the window at the sea. She was going to have her own house! It did not seem possible. After all those dreary months and weeks in run-down boarding houses, she was going to have a house in a place called 'St John's Wood', wherever that might be.

'Can I also have the use of a hansom cab when I want?'

Gervaise turned round and stared at his newest mistress.

'Have the use . . . have the use of . . . of a hansom cab?' He opened his mouth to laugh at such a notion, but on seeing Dorinda Montgomery's innocence of expression he quickly smiled instead. 'You are not going to use a hansom cab,' he told her gravely, watching as he did so the expression of happiness fading from her eyes, 'no, no hansom cab for you. You are going to have your own carriage and your own horses, and dresses and ball gowns, and some jewels, not the best, but some fine ones none the less. Provided you go on being as good as you are now.'

'Why are you doing all this for me?' Dorinda asked, having duly kissed her thanks to him.

'Because you are beautiful, and you please me, why else?'

For a second just a tiny part of Dorinda had hoped that she might be going to hear that he loved her, but since her husband – tiresome Harry

Montgomery – had never once told her that he loved her, not even when engaged in *intimacies*, Dorinda knew not to expect too much. And so having smiled her appreciation of Gervaise's compliment she lay back on the pillows and fell resolutely into a blissful sleep.

Duty is unyielding until it
Comes to love unbridling.

Three

Mercy Cordel would have been astonished had she known what a good daughter to her father, a good stepdaughter to her stepmother, a good sister to her brothers, she had been, for the fact was that she considered everything about her life at Cordel Court in a remote corner of Somerset as being really her good fortune, possibly because all her relatives had told her so, and many times.

Of course she knew herself that she was fortunate in being born both aristocratic and rich. Even as a child she was grateful for knowing that she was destined to follow a certain kind of life, a life in which she had grown up, that she had come to accept as being not only her lot, but the lot of every other daughter born into an old family who still possessed a large estate, and a town house in London.

She also knew that she would grow up to know all the sons and daughters of those other fortunate aristocratic families, children who like her had been confined in their parents' country homes, given ponies to ride, lakes to boat on, and woods in which to roam.

Sometimes when Mercy was on her own and

both her brothers were away at their schools, she would dream what it must be like to be a boy and be sent away. She could not imagine ever being allowed the freedom that her brothers enjoyed. Free to go anywhere on the estate, free to use their brand new bicycles and venture as far as they wished, free to meet whomsoever they chose for shooting, and go hunting without a groom. At these times it seemed to her that the world was closing in on her, instead of being large and exciting as her atlas told her that it was. It had been terrible for the Cordel children to bury their beloved mother, after she had died from typhoid fever – caught while staying at Hurst Castle where she had been invited for a Friday-to-Monday – but when, very shortly afterwards, their father married Lady Violet Mancer, a widow with no children, Mercy came to realize that she had indeed found that rarest of all beings, a truly kind second mother.

Mercy was not pretty, she knew, but her stepmother was so kind and so sweetly encouraging that she always made Mercy *feel* pretty. And all the time Mercy was growing up she felt that if she just tried a little harder she could make the miracle happen and that by just thinking and praying one day she would wake up as beautiful as her stepmother, who always said, *Will is everything. If you will something enough – it will happen.*

But Mercy was not content to leave everything to the power of her will. She knew that she needed God's will too, so she also prayed, daily, in the little chapel which was situated up two stairs and hidden behind the great fireplace in the first floor reception room at Cordel Court – although sometimes she did find herself stopping to wonder what she was praying *for*. A beautiful life, certainly; to marry someone she truly loved, naturally; to be good, of course; but also, in so many other ways, she knew that she was praying to be rescued from just *being*.

Very occasionally Lady Violet would join her at prayer, and they would leave the little private chapel together, Lady Violet with her slender arm around Mercy's waist, and Mercy, as always, lost in admiration, listening to her talking of so many things: of the outside world, but most of all of the need never to relinquish her faith in God.

But all that was in the past. Now it was growing near to Mercy's seventeenth birthday, and she was to be taken up to London for only the second time in her life. London – where she would put up her hair for the first time and be fitted for dresses for Ascot and coming out balls; sent to Busvines for her riding habit, for hats to the top milliners; measured for elaborate gowns for every kind of occasion, and naturally for a presentation dress for her Court curtsy to the monarch. But most of all she was being sent to London to hope against hope that she would find herself a dashingly handsome husband, and be married by the end of the Season.

'Head up, Mercy, my dear, just so, very good, shoulders exquisitely straight, just so, just so.'

That was what Mercy found so excessively generous-natured about her stepmother. She never ceased to help her and her brothers, Henry and Humphrey, to become better people, correcting them in the kindest possible way, advising them in the most tactful tones. Yet neither did she relax any of those rules for herself, applying them assiduously to her own life. She did everything to the best of her ability, running her husband's three homes with tact and efficiency. Just to see her beautifully dressed figure, its hourglass shape almost breathtakingly elegant with its tiny, tiny waist and its long trail of graceful skirts, was for Mercy to take heart and realize that if she tried harder she too could become like her stepmother, elegant and beautiful, but most of all fun. Because the truth was that Lady Violet made every occasion that she graced delightful. It did not matter if it was something quite routine and dull, she would turn it into an occasion of gaiety, and long before Mercy rounded the corridor and entered the room where her stepmother was busying herself she would hear the echo of laughter from everyone around Lady Violet. She brought fun and music, beauty and lightheartedness to wherever she was, to the extent that Mercy had to struggle to remember her own mother's qualities compared with this stepmother whom she and her brothers so adored, not to mention her father, Lord Duffane, whose face would light up the moment Lady Violet came into sight.

'Just watching her trip down the Great Walk

gives me hope for the world,' he murmured, every now and then, to his only daughter, and they would both watch with admiration that wonderful figure swaying in front of them.

'Beauty is very important, is it not, Papa?'

Mercy posed the question with feelings somewhere between dread and anticipation, and in the certain knowledge that she would never be so.

'It is everything,' Lord Duffane murmured in reverential tones. 'Beauty in a woman is like honesty in a man: it is everything.'

Mercy wanted to say, *But what happens if you are not beautiful? What happens if God and nature and your ancestry have made you very much less than beautiful, if your profile is very much less than Greek, and you are small in height, and although slim not possessed of Step-maman's wondrous grace?*

But her father was too stern for Mercy to dare to ask these questions of him. He did not think that girls 'counted', which is to say that, although Mercy knew that he loved her, he could not possibly be expected to love her the way he loved his sons. It was just a fact, like the sun coming up in the morning, or the moon and the stars coming out at night.

Before going to London with her stepmother in the family barouche Mercy stood in front of the cheval mirror in her small bedroom and stared at her reflection, determined to be as heartless and realistic about herself as she knew that Society would be about her.

I am small and slim, but not at all pretty. This has to

*be faced. I have nice eyes, but not much else. My nose is
too big, and turns up, my lips are not full enough, and
my profile is much less than Grecian. So I shall just have
to work on my personality. I shall have to work so hard
on it that it shines through my eyes and I shall just have
to hope that someone in some ballroom or at some tea, or
at the opening of the Academy – someone somewhere
will look into my eyes and see my potential as a person.
For not only am I no beauty but my hair is a very dull
colour, being brown and not blonde, and my skin
although pale is not quite the marvellous bright white
that Step-maman's is. No-one will write a poem to my
beauty, I fear, but even so, please, please, God, help
someone to fall in love with me!*

Mercy felt much better after putting herself
through her own personal honesty test. She felt
she could face the world without wearing a
heavily veiled hat from fear people would reel
back in shock at her lack of looks. She felt that in
seeing herself as she truly was, in facing up to the
world as she was and not as she would like to be,
she had somehow made strides, put her best foot
forward.

'What shall I say if people ask me for my opinion
on art? I cannot remember what you advised.'

They were in the coach on the way to London.
Lady Violet turned her brilliant brown eyes on her
stepdaughter.

'No-one – no *gentleman* – will ask you such a
question,' she said with her usual mixture of
wry humour and hauteur. 'To begin with, the
gentlemen beside whom you sit at dinner, or with

whom you dance in the ballroom, will not want to know what you *think*. No Englishman ever wants to know what is going on in a woman's head, he is only ever interested in what is on his plate. And that being so, you will find that the only person asking the questions and making the conversation, as the saying goes, will be you. And we have been through that, have we not? We have been through what to ask? And whom to ask it of?'

Mercy nodded obediently, and then stared out of the window. She was well aware that she was having a nervous crisis about going to London, about coming out into Society, about everything, and it was foolish to continue with this conversation as Lady Violet's slightly stern reaction and her quick turn of the head to stare forward had just made clear.

Lady Violet went to London for the Season every year. In fact she had been to London for the Season every year without interruption since the age of seventeen. It was obvious that it was not in the least bit interesting for her to talk about what Mercy might or might not say at dinner. She already knew every social grace there was to know. She knew exactly how to provoke and question, how to tease or put at ease, any gentleman, anywhere. Mercy knew this because her father had told her so.

'Your stepmother can bring out anyone she chooses. People flower in her company. I have never seen her stumped with a personality of the day, not once,' he had told Mercy many times, which, since Lord Duffane was so very shy himself, was, to him, a heavenly gift in a wife. 'You can see her having drawn the shortest straw at dinner, sitting next to some fellow whom no-one else has ever seen laugh, or become interested in anything except his gun or his fishing rod, and within seconds Step-maman has taken him on and he has become as playful as a kitten with her. She is a remarkable woman, believe me, Mercy, remarkable. The Prince of Wales adores her – everyone adores her.'

As the daughter of a peer below the rank of earl Mercy was the Honourable Mercy Cordel, Cordel being an old Norman name, tracing back to 1176, but she was not an heiress, as her mother and step-mother had been. Both she and Lady Violet, not to mention Lord Duffane, knew that whoever married her must want her for herself, and not much more, for she had no inheritance.

'Oh don't worry, little sister,' Henry, her eldest brother, had teased her. 'You will break hearts in the ballroom, I promise you, if only because you dance like a dream and you have beautiful eyes. There will be no gilt chair with your name engraved on it because of too much use. You will dance every dance, until finally you are waltzed off into a conservatory and proposed to by some handsome masher.'

But Henry was her brother, after all. Just the eldest brother whom she adored, and for whom she would do anything at all, and sometimes had, risking all to steal jam from the kitchens for him and Humphrey when they were little, not to mention ice creams on a hot day, and tomatoes from the greenhouses when they were fishing and not wanting to leave their rods, although she too, it had to be admitted, longed to bite into the fruits' fragrant, warm, scented middles.

'Life is very special at Cordel,' Henry would say, sighing and looking round dreamily at Mercy standing beside him on the river bank when he fished.

Although they were cheerful words, they were somehow sad too, for Mercy always felt that he sensed life would not always be as it had been for them when they were children. She imagined that Henry wanted to stop them all somehow from growing up, wanted everything to stay just as it was, a sort of permanent Maytime. A time when everything is just out and the green is at its greenest and the blue of the sky pale and kind, and the sunlight warm but not scorching, and just watching ducks snatching at midges, or horses eating the sweet new buttercup-strewn grass, was in itself a fulfilling pastime.

But now there was no time left any more for any of those things, her brothers had long ago left home for their regiments, and Mercy's hair was already put up. And not just her hair, her portmanteau and all her stepmother's luggage were put up too, in the back of the family carriage. Now moments from a past life that would never come again – fishing with her brothers and running through the fields to steal apples and pears for them from the orchards – ran through her mind as she followed Lady Violet into the old barouche with its much faded coat of arms on the door and its equally faded coachman and 'boy', both of whom had been in family service for longer than perhaps even they could remember.

Mercy leaned out of the carriage and waved to 'her friends' which was to say those of the kindly older upper servants who had gathered on the steps to wave goodbye to her. They knew, as she did, that she had to find a husband, that now was the beginning of the end of her days of innocence at Cordel. Quite as much as her father and step-mother they wanted 'Miss Mercy' to marry well, if only to prove to everyone that having grown up at Cordel Court, where *they* had all grown up on the estate, would stand for something in *that London*, as the folk in Somerset called the capital. For London to all the people who lived in or around Cordel Court was not just another world, it was another country. The housekeeper had never been to London, but the butler had, although only once, on a train. It stood for something, though, in the servants' hall. It meant that Tallboy was cosmopolitan and could stride about with a man of the world air, and be believed.

'Welcome spring, welcome my favourite time of the year, the start of the Season, the start of fun and gaiety. At last!'

Lady Violet turned to Mercy after she had made this speech and as she did so it seemed to Mercy that her stepmother's unaffected happiness was perfuming the air. She followed her garlanded announcement with laughter, for no reason that Mercy could see, so that Mercy realized with a little jolt that perhaps her stepmother did not love Cordel Court quite as much as Mercy herself, for if she did why would she look so thrilled and excited at leaving it?

Soon the talk was of dresses for the coming Season, something about which Mercy knew nothing at all, having only a riding habit (and then only because it was found in the attic and dusted down for her re-use), some cotton dresses for summer – 'dreadfully old fashioned' as her step-mother had been the first to admit – and some tartan wool costumes cut again from old outfits of her grandmother's, and also retrieved from Cordel's endless upper floors. Up in those attics you never knew what you might find, but somehow if you outgrew your winter coat, or had need of a petticoat, something *was* always found. The last few winters Mercy had managed to make do with cloaks from an old trunk, venerable garments that had great brass catches at the throat and were so heavy with fur lining that she some-times felt that she was growing up stooped from the weight of them.

'I must be the first to admit that although we have had some nice dresses made for you, and some pretty hats in Bath for day to day events, for your coming out dress we shall have to do just a little bit better, I fear. I myself will be going to Worth in Paris for my Court dresses – the Prince of Wales does so hate to see anyone in anything twice, and one never knows quite what is to happen during some of these Friday-to-Mondays one is asked to where as many as fifteen changes are required. But at least for you, Mercy my dear, we need not be so extravagant. You are after all only going through your first Season.

'We can choose you some beautiful creations from Madame Chloe in Dover Street, yet with no needless extravagance, which would never do. Madame Chloe is very clever and adroit, and her costumes and dresses will be quite sufficient for a debutante. No-one, no debutante, must ever look too extravagant, my dear. It gives the wrong impression to the young men. They start to imagine that you are an heiress, and you, alas, are not.'

Strangely for a girl as romantic as Mercy, she genuinely liked this very practical side of her stepmother's nature. It recognized life for what it was, which Mercy found somehow reassuring.

From listening to her stepmother as she grew up over the last few years she had garnered a shrewd idea that the world was not an easy place to inhabit, and that being a young girl was a hazardous business, not to be regarded lightly. If Lady Violet told Mercy 'this is how it is' she believed her, and all the more because she was so very down to earth sometimes. It made her realize just how much she owed her stepmother, and how lucky she was that Lady Violet was so practical and easy to talk to about really *anything*. In fact Lady Violet was so much her friend in every way, she could not imagine making or needing any new ones.

'But,' Lady Violet continued, 'that is not to say that we are not going to see to it that you make a great match, because we are. The Season and coming out can be difficult, and sometimes even a dangerous time for a gel, but – and you must bear this in mind at all times, Mercy – there is and always will be a chance that a man, a man from a most suitable background, perhaps even a hand-some rich man, will fall in love with you. It does not happen often, for as you know wealth is usually attracted to wealth, but it can occur. And does. Why only last Season Lady Caroline Scaradale walked off with the heir to the Duke of Stonner – three castles and a London square, not to mention railways in America and Canada, and so on, and so on. This is the kind of thing that can happen. I do not say it will, but it can!'

Lady Violet gave a gay laugh and pointed to the signpost.

'Only another one hundred and fifty miles and we shall be in heaven, Mercy dear!'

Mercy had been to London once before, but only for a family funeral, so she had only really seen the inside of Browns Hotel – where she had been put up with her brothers because their London house was being redecorated and the interior of St George's, Hanover Square, before they were swiftly returned to Cordel Court in the family barouche. So now, longing though she was to lean her head out of the window and stare at the elegance of the carriages, and when they went

57

through the Park at the ladies and gentlemen of fashion on their beautiful mounts, passing and repassing each other, she knew she must not. However, she could see from out of the corner of her eye that sometimes the fashionable folk were halted in little groups, chatting, and sometimes they were walking sedately, but wherever they were the sunlight caught at the decorations on their riding habits or the feathers in their elaborate hats.

Of course no-one of fashion ever stared at people of fashion, and people of fashion only acknowledged greetings from their equals, or from old family friends. Mercy knew this because she had managed to obtain a very modern book of etiquette, which she had spent the last months reading again and again, and again. From this little booklet, discreetly despatched from a Bath bookshop which specialized in sending young ladies books in plain wrappers, she had learned everything there was to learn about etiquette and the Court. Of course there were some things which she knew instinctively, which could not be taught, but other things . . . like staring ahead, for instance, which was so different from life in the country where to ignore someone – anyone, really – would mean setting up a rift that could last for centuries.

'And here, at last, we are – and as always when I reach London, even after two long days of travelling, and all the changes of horses and so on, I feel eighteen again!'

Lady Violet stepped out ahead of Mercy to be

greeted at the entrance of the Duffane house by their newly hired London butler, for the redoubtable Tallboy did not like the capital and hated to be asked to leave Cordel Court.

He was not alone. Lord Duffane too hated London. And since, now that he was older, he relied on Tallboy so much for his day to day needs, he was loth to force him to come up to town for the Season knowing that Tallboy missed his life at Cordel Court and his nightly port (actually his lordship's but that was by the by) but most of all his cronies at the old inn in the village where he appeared with a regularity that was much appreciated by the landlord.

'My lady. Miss Mercy.'

The butler bowed and Lady Violet and Mercy stepped into Lord Duffane's town house with some relief on Mercy's part, for it had been a long, long journey from Somerset and she did not have the same sense of happiness at arriving in the capital as her stepmother.

Not that she was dreading her first London Season, by any means. She was, in many ways looking forward to it, but she was already missing the family's pug dogs – not to mention her dear old mare, Grandy Girl. Mercy was no great horsewoman, and she did not hunt and had no wish to do so, but she did like to trot round the countryside on Grandy, and she loved a fast canter uphill, sometimes even daringly jumping a small stream, if Somerset's clay soil was not too hard, or too muddy, for Grandy Girl's thoroughbred legs.

'New hall boy, new butler – the place seems better already,' Lady Violet murmured as she swept ahead into the panelled hall where, since the day had turned suddenly chilly for the time of year, the servants had rather touchingly, Mercy thought, lit a fire to welcome them.

'Well, there we are, Mercy, here is your room. It has been redecorated for your coming, you know – such a kind papa as you have! And my suite is below you, of course, but you know that.'

Mercy did not, yet she did not say so, for her stepmother's assumptions, she had found, were best left just as they were. Mercy had noticed that it always bothered her to be interrupted and to be asked questions if she was on what Lord Duffane called 'one of Step-maman's conversational runs'.

Lady Violet stared around Mercy's newly allocated room with approval.

'I chose the cretonne myself, and if I may say so I think it catches the light just beautifully.'

With another gay laugh and a wave of her hand Lady Violet left her stepdaughter, passing two of the lower servants who were bringing Mercy's trunks up to her room, and went below to the first floor where her own suite had been made ready for her occupation. And where, Mercy knew, her innumerable trunks and hat boxes would already have been opened and the contents laid reverentially in cupboards and drawers by Smith, her devoted maid.

Mercy looked round the beautifully decorated room, at the cretonne at the windows, at the velvets on the chairs, at the tapestry on the *prie-dieu*, at the richly dressed bed. It was all so different from her really rather run-down room at Cordel Court, where the furniture was throw-outs from guest rooms and her bed only a little better than a truckle bed, nothing having been changed there for many years, and certainly not since her mother died.

As she stood in the middle of this new and glowingly sumptuous room Mercy could not help wondering how she looked in the middle of it. The room was dressed so beautifully that it was plain even to her that it showed up the poverty of her clothes, just as her stepmother's elegance and beauty showed up the poverty of her step-daughter's demeanour and allure, and Mercy saw, yet again, just how difficult it was going to be for her to attract the right husband in the short months ahead. What rich Sir Galahad would want a mouse like herself? She was a bookworm, not a hunts-woman. When left alone, without her brothers to bully her, Mercy preferred sewing at her tapestry by the fire in winter. Or, in summer, sitting under the apple trees in the orchard reading poetry, or playing the piano in the saloon. She infinitely preferred these occupations to sharing luncheon baskets with the men on her father's shooting parties.

But this was all hopeless as far as Englishmen were concerned, and she knew this, again, from her brothers, and of course Lady Violet. 'Englishmen think of girls as boys in girls' clothes. As long as you know that, you will never be disappointed.'

Mercy stared out of the window. She was determined to begin as she meant to go on. She must not be a timorous mouse afraid to go out on her own, afraid to face the fashionable world which lay in all the streets around her. She would go for a walk in the Park with her new maid. She would see at close quarters those delightful ladies on their beautiful thoroughbreds, glimpsed from the carriage, and afterwards she would sit under a tree and, having smuggled a book out, she would sit and read it well away from any danger of mockery – for no-one in the family except herself read books. It was unknown. Her father boasted of it a great deal, always saying heartily, if anyone so much as mentioned reading, 'No, no, no, never read a book in my life.'

He had said it very often while Mercy was growing up. Sometimes she would have preferred it if he had found something else to boast about, but there it was. The Prince of Wales did not read, so as a consequence none of the men did, nor were they likely to do so. It just was not done. To be sporting yes, to be bookish, absolutely not.

'Mademoiselle Mercy, we should not be sitting ourselves 'ere, I think, huh?'

Lady Violet had passed on her 'bulldog' as she called Clarice, her old French maid, with strict instructions to guard Mercy every minute that she was in London. They had walked through the park together from Mayfair, and, it being fine, Mercy had seated herself beside the Serpentine.

'We must walk, Mademoiselle Mercy, and not sit

with a book, huh? It is not *convenable*, so we go back to the 'ouse, soon I think, or Lady Violette will be very hungry.'

'*Angry*, Clarice, not hungry. Lady Violet is rarely hungry and if she is she would never say, and you and I both know she is never angry. But still. Oh, very well.' With a small sigh Mercy stood up again, knowing that Clarice had a better idea of London and the conventions than she herself. 'It is a pity that sitting with a book in the Park is not proper.'

'There are many things that are not *convenable* in London you will find, Ma'mselle Mercy. Most of all in the Park. You may ride in the Park, but walking is not ladylike at all – *n'est-ce pas*?'

'I am afraid I shall not be doing much riding along Rotten Row. You know I am frightened of any other horse except Grandy Girl, and it was too expensive to bring her up to town for the Season, Papa said.'

As they talked they were making their way briskly back towards the Park gates, but they were forced to stop in order to let a horseman on a large, dark bay gelding canter slowly past them. He was beautifully dressed in tight riding breeches and an exquisitely cut coat, his shiny top hat set on a handsome head of dark hair with just a little touch of grey to the sides – which meant that he was no longer a young blade but a man of the world, and possessed of a natural, elegant seat on his horse.

'I can tell everything from the way a man sits his horse,' Lord Duffane would say, and although Mercy was no huntswoman, she knew exactly what he meant. The way a man sat his horse proclaimed sensitivity, courage, temper.

Glancing back towards the horseman who had just passed them Mercy imagined that he had to be courageous, for the horse was not an easy ride. He also had to be at least even tempered, for he was sitting his mount with patience, but although he had kind hands she wondered whether he would be the same with humans for, as she had sometimes observed, men who loved horses were not always the kindest of characters. Sometimes indeed you could hardly reconcile the man and his horses with the man and his family and friends. So although she went along with her father a little, she did not agree with him wholeheartedly. She knew very well from the gossip of the county which reached even Cordel Court while she was growing up that seeing a man on a horse was not the whole picture, at least not as far as a woman was concerned. So she did not turn to look at the rider again. Indeed, she forgot him.

At the beginning of the twentieth century there were already cars to be seen in the capital, although the old Queen would have none of them. And while the Prince of Wales might be proud of his new 'motor stables' and many of his friends the same, for the most part the old order of the horse still reigned in the fashionable streets of London, where no man would be seen walking to his club in anything but the smartest clothes.

This Season it would be a high collar and a wide

cravat tied not in a bow but in a knot so that the effect was less artistic. A waistcoat, a long frock coat, a curly-brimmed topper – not so tall as it had been this, following the tone again set by the Prince of Wales – and of course a thin, graceful walking cane for town, with perhaps a family crest engraved on the handle.

Mercy had already noted all this as she sat in the family carriage, before being once more decanted with Lady Violet onto a London pavement.

'Come, Mercy,' Lady Violet commanded, and her stepdaughter, smiling dutifully, followed her up the steps of the discreet brass-plated establishment in front of them.

Mercy should have been concentrating on dresses and the excitements of the balls ahead, but instead she was annoyed with herself, for she had running through her head a poem that she had learned which began *My Love in her attire doth show her wit, It doth so well become her.*

The poem would not go away, and it was somehow shocking because the poem ended in a way that – well, in a way of which her stepmother would certainly not approve: *But beauty's self she is when all her robes are gone.*

It was always the same, Mercy found. Whenever she wanted to be correct, something particularly *in*correct, or *in*appropriate, or in this case *fast*, came into her head. It sometimes happened in church. It sometimes happened when she was helping to prepare a charity tea at Cordel Court. It was as if there was nothing, but nothing, better that her mind could find for itself to do than to turn itself towards something which it quite definitely should not.

'Mercy, this way!'

Lady Violet beckoned, and Mercy promptly obeyed, followed in her turn by Clarice looking at her most grim and carrying a Gladstone bag of great antiquity, its gold clasps wrought in a complicated cypher and its handle much decorated, giving it the look of a respectable Englishwoman who had been overdressed by an Italian. It was always known as 'ze casse' by Clarice.

The interior of the small house into which they walked was most discreetly set about on the first floor with sofas and chairs. No-one could have known it was a shop, which is what it was. Neither could they have guessed that it was frequented by the mothers of debutantes unwilling or unable, due to monetary problems, to dress them at Worth in Paris. Lady Violet preferred to visit such places in person, not liking to be disturbed at home by visiting mannequins and other inconveniences.

As soon as they entered, Clarice, who obviously knew the form, held back, and stayed downstairs on one of the hard hall chairs guarding who knew what – although from the look on her face it might well have been her ladyship's jewel case hidden inside the large old faded Gladstone bag.

In welcoming Lady Violet and Mercy, Madame Chloe sank to really quite a deep curtsy, although Mercy noticed that her small dark eyes were alive with the kind of determined observation that misses nothing that may be of use to a woman committed to the business of clothing the daughters of the well-connected for the London Season.

The two visitors were shown to a sofa. Lady Violet, herself so magnificently dressed that she was quite obviously not in need of the dressmaker's art, nodded to Mercy to sit beside her while Madame Chloe clapped her hands and the first of the mannequins appeared from behind a piece of curtaining.

Madame Chloe's eyes had rested approvingly on Lady Violet's elegant ensemble before summoning her own mannequins. There was no doubt at all that her ladyship was a challenge to Madame's art. Lady Violet always looked magnificent, whether mounted on one of her thoroughbreds – sweeping hunting skirt allowing just enough boot to show, plumes in her hat, fine leather gloves – or walking through Cordel Court, closely skirted, her high-collared lace blouse showing off her long neck, her French pocket watch pinned to her breast.

But now, in London, and that morning most particularly, she so far surpassed anyone's expectations of a fashionable woman of a certain age that people turned and looked as they passed her stepping from her carriage, or stopped and, quite frankly, stared from the other side of the road at the vision she presented.

And yet that morning she was dressed only in a walking dress from the previous season, although only the most knowledgeable and the most fashionable would have known it. Her hat was a wide saucer of white with red flowers placed at the front, the hat itself tilted most carefully low, towards her nose. Behind the flowers at different angles rose two white wings made of the same material as the saucer, looking a little like birds' wings. Her rich, dark brown hair, brushed out from the sides for a bouffant effect and beautifully arranged by Clarice, was shining and full, and caught up at the back into a large chignon fastened with combs, themselves concealed not just by the hat but also by the high red collar of the coat, which was lined with thick guipure lace, rising behind and falling to the front into wide lapels, also faced with the guipure. The full length buttoned red coat, interfaced at set intervals with the same lace so that it formed a pattern down the front, fell nearly to her feet. The shoulders of the coat were wide, and there were deep lace cuffs to the sleeves. The whole effect was magnificent, and Lady Violet's slender, hourglass silhouette set it off to perfection.

But this was last year's fashion. The whole outfit had been, metaphorically speaking, only thrown on for a little morning's shopping, and all too soon, Mercy knew, it would be put to the back of Lady Violet's London wardrobe, to be replaced by something a great deal more up to the minute. Besides, it was now April. Lady Violet must have worn this coat upwards of a half a dozen times. It had, as she had remarked a little ruefully to Mercy that morning, 'had its day'.

She did not know why, but as the first of the costumes were paraded before them Mercy could not concentrate on the clothes that were being shown to them so expertly, but found herself instead feeling really very sorry for the young girls who had to sweep out from behind the red velvet curtaining and show off the latest of Madame Chloe's designs.

The dresses might be really very pretty, but the girls themselves were pale, and thin, and obviously quite as young as herself, or perhaps even younger. Instead of looking at the gowns Mercy fell to wondering how they had come to model Madame Chloe's clothes, and if they had ever had a square meal in the last months, and whether it was right for such very young girls to be used in this way, to show off dresses to people of fashion when they should probably be still at home with their families.

Because Mercy's mind was quite caught up with these thoughts, she missed Lady Violet nodding towards the dressmaker and saying, 'Yes, yes, we will take everything so far, provided you can assure me that the fittings will be at home, and that my stepdaughter will not be passing every other housemaid dressed in the same thing?'

'Oh, Lady Violet is so amusing always,' Madame Chloe said, but she did not laugh or smile. Instead she lowered her voice and added, 'They are all for your approval and your approval alone, my lady, of that you can be assured.'

'I remember that dreadful incident last Season, when the Duchess of . . . well, we all remember that, do we not? It was a perfect scandal.'

But Madame Chloe had already raised her hand and shaken her head before Lady Violet had finished and her expression had become one of such pain that for a second or two Mercy was quite sure that she was going to be unwell.

'That was due to a very unfortunate incident. I do assure you, my lady, it would be difficult to describe to you my deep feelings of sympathy for poor dear Monsieur Worth. It turned out that there was a grudge involved, spies from England . . . a seamstress with a grudge is worse than a poisoning wife, I always say. So near to the seat of power, too easy for them to accept money, temptation everywhere.'

'As there so often is, Madame Chloe. Too often!'

'The copy was made in great secrecy, but not here, my lady, I do assure you. I as much as anyone worship at Monsieur Worth's shrine, but even Monsieur Worth can be copied, as my lady well knows.'

This last was said with a hint of steel, for Madame Chloe knew that Lady Violet would shortly be off to visit the House of Worth for the greater part of her own new season's clothes.

As the mannequins continued to glide past them in what looked to Mercy like mouth-watering gowns, Lady Violet kept making a little 'hah' sound, very brief and light, at this or at that costume or dress. It could not be translated, but it seemed to satisfy both Madame Chloe and herself, as if they both knew what she meant by the sound, and were of one accord regarding her reaction.

'There are some very bad people about, Madame Chloe,' Lady Violet went on, indicating with the brief raising of a finger that one of the mannequins might be allowed to approach so that she could stare at the material of her gown through a small eyeglass.

'My lady, if we knew the whole, we would doubtless be unable to step out of our houses.'

Again the 'hah' sound, this time followed by a nod of approval at both the mannequin and the dressmaker.

'Quite so, quite so. You may send the last three costumes and dresses to the house for my step-daughter. I am pleased to think that you will fit her out very well, Madame Chloe. I myself am off to Paris for fittings.'

'Of course, my lady. No-one does Monsieur Worth so much credit as you, my lady – indeed I always think—'

Precisely what Madame Chloe always thought was lost for ever to everyone but herself, as the very last of the mannequins, modelling the ball gown of blue silk that had won Lady Violet's approval, promptly fainted. And, as if fainting in front of the company were not embarrassing enough for all concerned, she hit her head as she collapsed and blood started to pour from her temple onto the floor, before Lady Violet's amazed and objecting gaze.

Mercy sprang to her feet and went at once to

help. Oblivious of the blood she cradled the girl's head in her lap, while Madame Chloe saw fit to do nothing but wring her hands and apologize to her stepmother, more sorry about the sight to which she had been subjected (blood! so unsuitable for her salon!) than for the unconscious young girl with the wound to her head.

'Mercy! I think we must leave. And at once! Such a pity. I had hoped to lend you some jewellery to try against some of the materials. Always such a good idea, I think.'

In between her ministrations Mercy glanced up at her stepmother, who was standing by with a look that was actually saying *Stand up at once and leave her*, a look which Mercy had no hesitation in pretending not to have noticed.

'If Madame Chloe would be so kind as to call a hansom I will personally see her to a hospital.'

'Your dress, quite ruined!' Madame Chloe looked down at the skirt upon which the still unconscious girl lay. 'I must make it up to you, Miss Cordel.'

'You are not Florence Nightingale,' Lady Violet said, lowering her voice. 'It is not suitable for you to accompany this girl.'

Yet they both knew that the case was a lost one, for since the age of six or seven Mercy had run a small animals' hospital at the back of the stables.

Here the grooms would bring her wounded birds, and animals of all kinds, and here she would spend days and weeks nursing them all back to health, only to keep some of them secretly as pets in her top room at Cordel Court where not even the servants ventured, for the maids never even bothered to dust her rooms, her brothers being the important children, and she being regarded by both upper and lower servants more as a friend to them than a member of the family to be waited on. They knew that Miss Mercy would always be willing to help them when they were short of a pair of hands, and it had to be faced that during her growing years she had finally become more a part of life below stairs than she ever had above them.

'I must do my Christian duty as I see fit, Stepmaman,' Mercy murmured, holding her own lace-edged handkerchief to the girl's temple.

Lady Violet gave a tight little sigh which was edged with impatience. Everyone at Cordel Court had always bowed before Mercy's *Christian conscience* – and very dull it was too, Lady Violet privately thought – and even her stepmother did not dare come between Mercy and what she thought of as her duty. It was a fact.

'Oh, very well, if you see it as your Christian duty, but take Clarice with you to wherever it is. I must change before noon. I have a luncheon which I must attend – the highest personage requires me – but there, if you must go with this girl, I have Mildred at home to help me dress, so do not fret yourself on my account.'

They both knew that 'the highest personage requires me' was code for the Prince of Wales's commanding her attendance at some perhaps informal occasion. Mercy, looking up at her step-mother, smiled briefly.

'Of course, Step-maman. I perfectly understand.'

Lady Violet swept out, leaving Mercy surrounded by a clutch of young mannequins hurrying towards her with newly wrung out cold flannels and bandages for the poor wounded girl, whose head was still lying in Mercy's bloodstained lap.

Eventually the hansom cab arrived, and Mercy and the rest of the girls helped the still uncon-scious sufferer into the hansom, where she lay against the leather upholstery, murmuring unintelligibly.

Mercy directed the driver to the only hospital she knew – Sister Angela's Nursing Home, a place where Mercy herself had once been operated on as a child for poisoned tonsils, and which she remem-bered only dimly for its pretty name and the kindness of the nurses into whose care she had been delivered whilst her parents holidayed on their yacht in the South of France.

'This is it, ladies,' the cab driver called up to them, opening the door, and he helped the young mannequin down from the cab, draping her arm around his neck, and then handing her over to Mercy and the maid.

The driver was paid by Clarice, who followed Mercy up the wide stone steps of Lady Angela's establishment and through the polished mahogany doors murmuring 'Mon dieu, mon dieu' but, happily, still clutching Lady Violet's precious Gladstone bag.

'Ma'mselle Mercy, this is enough, *enfin*?'

Poor Clarice must have said this a dozen times, and each time Mercy smiled at her kindly, but firmly. She indicated to one of the more senior nurses that she wanted the young girl admitted at her own expense, and watched while two young men carried her to a room which was more like a room in a private house than anything any ordinary person would associate with a hospital.

The young mannequin, who now looked barely in her teens, lay on the bed, her eyes unseeing, but before lapsing once more into deep unconsciousness she said what sounded like 'My lord, my lord'.

'She is very pious, huh?' Clarice asked, of no-one in particular, from the corner of the room, as Mercy waited for some attention from a doctor, or at least a senior nurse.

Mercy took one of the poor girl's hands in her own cool one.

'There will be someone to help very soon.' No sooner had she sought to reassure the girl thus than the door was opened by a tall young nurse wearing an immaculate uniform: long white apron covering a long dark dress, and a hat of stiffened organdie delightfully perched on her head of beautiful blonde hair. The whole simplicity and purity of her uniform somehow seemed to set off her astonishing beauty to an even greater degree than if she had been dressed in something more sumptuous.

She curtsied to Mercy, and smiled. Mercy was amazed, for the nurse's beauty was such that it had to take away the onlooker's breath. But it was her eyes that were the most astonishing. Mercy had never seen eyes of quite that colour before. As deep a blue as the sea in Italy, or at least how she had always imagined that the Italian sea would look.

'I am Mercy Cordel. My stepmother, Lady Duffane, was choosing some costumes and ball gowns for me when this poor girl fainted and hit her head on the corner of a table as she fell. She is in quite a bad way, I am afraid.'

Leonie looked down at the young girl on the bed and then put out a practised hand to feel her pulse.

'She is suffering from a very bad blow,' she agreed. 'We will dress the wound, and watch her very closely for the next few hours. Would you like to come back this evening?'

'I will certainly call back, nurse, but can you tell me how you think she will go on?'

Leonie looked down at the prostrate girl.

'It is difficult to tell. She is not conscious at the moment and the wound looks quite deep. The wound we can dress, but the damage she might have done with such a blow to the temple we cannot yet tell. Blows to the head, as you may appreciate, Miss Cordel, vary to such a degree. She has very thin skin, as you can see – the veins show straight through to the surface. There is very little cover for the poor child, very little to cushion such a blow.'

Mercy knew that the nurse could not be any more than her own age, and so when she referred to the patient as a 'poor child' it meant that she must agree with Mercy that the girl was indeed yards younger than she was meant to be taken for. In other words, Madame Chloe, like so many dressmakers and people who made their living from fashion, employed girls who should still be at home with their mothers, girls who might, even now, be being sought by their distraught parents.

'Clarice, if you might wait outside?'

Mercy, always conscious of gossip among the servants, waited for the maid, still clutching the Gladstone bag, to go outside the room, closing the door behind her.

'Miss . . . ?'

'Miss Lynch, Leonie Lynch.'

'Miss Lynch, I am interested in what you have to say, very interested. You see,' Mercy lowered her voice even more, 'I too think this girl is in fact a child. I do not think she should be working for Madame Chloe—'

'Madame Chloe? Is she a mannequin there, at Madame Chloe's?'

'Yes. Why? Is she known to you?'

'Yes, indeed, Miss Cordel. My godmother, Mrs Dodd, is a close acquaintance of hers, and besides, I have only recently been purchased some costumes and gowns there.'

The two young women stared towards the bed, and then looked up at each other.

'Of course any expenses will be paid for by myself,' Mercy said suddenly, as if she wanted to distract from the way she imagined both their thoughts were racing – the guilt they both undoubtedly felt at the idea that this girl, hardly more than a child and probably employed for sweatshop wages, had only recently been showing off gowns which they themselves were about to wear with pride.

'I do not think that such very young girls should be used in shops,' Leonie volunteered, suddenly finding herself wondering whether she really wanted all her costumes and gowns after all, whether they were not in some way contributory to the suffering of the poor patient in front of them.

'God knows, nor do I,' Mercy agreed with sudden vehemence, adding wryly, 'but then, Miss Lynch, in case you had not noticed, God, when He came down to earth, did not come down as a woman.'

For a second the nurse looked shocked, and then she smiled.

'I fear you are right, Miss Cordel.'

'And I also fear Clarice will be keeping my stepmother waiting.'

With a sudden rush of conscience Mercy had realized that Lady Violet's jewels were in the case which Clarice was so faithfully guarding, and that her stepmother was some ten minutes away across the Park. She fled back to the hansom cab in company with Clarice, but too late. When they arrived back at the Cordel family mansion it was to find a note from Lady Violet.

Your absurd bleeding heart has meant that I had to lunch with the future King of England minus my jewellery! VC

Mercy sighed. Happily, she would be out again at Lady Angela's before her stepmother returned, and then Lady Violet would be out to dinner and an opera before Mercy herself returned. With any luck they would not catch sight of each other again for some long while, by which time Lady Violet would doubtless have quite forgotten the incident and would be on to some new item of interest – such as who had the eye of the future king, a now middle-aged man in poor health who nevertheless, by all accounts, still appreciated women.

'Step-maman will be sure to have amused the Prince of Wales by now, and that is all that matters!'

With that reassuring thought Mercy took herself off to her room and her books.

'There is no good news, I am afraid, but then there is no bad news either.'

Miss Lynch looked across at Mercy before they both looked down at the poor young girl on the bed.

To Mercy – and perhaps she was being fanciful, she certainly hoped so – she might not be worse, but she certainly looked much paler, and although Mercy could see her breathing was regular it also seemed to her that the breaths were more shallow, which she remarked on to Miss Lynch.

'I am afraid I really rather agree, Miss Cordel, and I said as much to the doctor, but' – she hesitated, her eyes suddenly wary, as if she was wondering whether she could trust Mercy – 'but you know how it is? Doctors are not in the habit of listening to nurses, which is strange, for we spend more time with the patients than they do. We observe more of their actual physical condition from hour to hour. We notice tiny changes which are all-important.'

Once again Mercy felt the inward helpless feeling that had been so familiar to her when she nursed animals, when try as they might there was nothing more that they could really do.

'We have been trying to find out if she has some sort of family, but so far it appears she has not,' she told the young nurse.

'Miss Cordel . . .' Again the nurse hesitated, but seeming once more to think that she could trust Mercy, she went on, 'I think a great many of these girls – and they are often country girls – are lured to work in these couture houses. I understand certain women make a practice of meeting them on the big London stations when they arrive in the capital, and of course, being innocent, they are duped into going along with the women, who offer them free lodging in return for going out to work in all sorts of dubious capacities.'

'Miss Lynch, I too am only just up from

80

Somerset, and quite likely to be as ignorant as this poor girl here!'

'But not as likely to be bought by the promise of a few dresses, I would have thought.'

The nurse laughed and Mercy laughed with her, looking down at her own shabby coat which was only just holding together. 'I could do with some, though, as you can see! As a matter of fact, I often think I could be bought with just the promise of a case full of books.'

Leonie caught on to the game straight away.

'And I with flowers, so many flowers, great banks of flowers,' she said, sighing just a little. 'I must tell you, though – and I know you will not be upset by this – I do not like to think that the girls' employers might be in league with such women. I cannot think that they would be, can you?'

'No, of course not. They would not be in league, but they might, if they had to do with the clothing trade like Madame Chloe, they might hire girls who had already been trapped into some terrible situation.' Mercy's eyes were full of indignation at the very thought. 'Mannequins come from every walk of life. Some are young widows needing to keep themselves, some are, as you say, young girls fresh from the country who have lost their way somehow.'

Leonie stared across at the slender young woman in her faded countrywoman's clothes, and could not help remarking to herself on the sincerity of expression in her large eyes, eyes that did not

81

drift over everything in a deceptively dreamy manner as Leonie's had the habit of doing, accepting life, if, she hoped, nevertheless undeceived by it. Miss Cordel's eyes were quite different. They were searching for something rather wonderful and magical to happen, for life to wake up and prove that it could be beautiful. Unlike Leonie, brought up in Eastgate Street, Mercy Cordel was obviously innocent and naive to a touching degree, but not affectedly so. She was just, as Leonie's foster mother might say in her down-to-earth way, *as innocent as a kitten, dear, or as mad as a bat – and I sometimes think there is no difference.*

'Miss Lynch, I am not, as you are, a nurse—'

'Nursing, I am *nursing*. Not yet a *nurse*, by any means, Miss Cordel.'

'But I *have* nursed, at home, in Somerset, where I come from. It is very uninteresting to talk about oneself, and I only do so with your forbearance because, you see – well.' She began again. 'Well, once I had to nurse a young village girl whose mother had died in a farm accident, an accident in which the girl herself was knocked unconscious, and for many days it seemed likely that she would die. After about a week, I really did not know which way to turn, and it was an embarrassment too, because my family had not wanted to take the girl in, and I had to bribe the servants who had hidden her condition from them, all of us fearing that the estate manager would send her to some asylum or institution for such cases, where she would assuredly die from lack of attention.

'So we kept her out of sight in one of our cottages, but in our village was one of those old witchety women. I expect you know the kind? She had no end of remedies and potions and a good record of curing, I might say. At any rate I went to her, and she directed me to the girl's feet. To put ice from the ice house on the girl's feet was what she told us; and so that is what we did. You can imagine, it took two footmen to carry the lead-lined box to the cottage which was some few miles away! And all this without my family discovering! Well, it worked, Miss Lynch. Truly. It took some time, but the girl was sitting up and drinking broth within a few hours. Had I not seen it for myself I would have said it was some sort of exaggeration. But just as keeping feet warm can stop a patient's condition declining, it seems that sometimes cold works too, and can bring them out of a state of unconsciousness.'

Leonie stared down at her patient and then across at her visitor. The sister in charge of the younger nurses was off eating her supper. It would not be difficult to fetch a bowl of ice from the outer room near the kitchens, and it was certainly, surely, worth a try?

Perhaps seeing her hesitating, Mercy went on, 'The fact is, Miss Lynch, you see, that the Ancient World believed that much that goes wrong in the body, or needs putting right in our heads and hearts, is linked to the feet. There is much mysticism associated with the foot in ancient medicine, and Granny Lovelace – she was this witchety person – used to make poultices of herbs and all sorts of things that made people's headaches and pains disappear, all through applying them to the feet.'

'I am prepared to try anything for our patients, even if people do laugh at me. What does it matter? Wait there, Miss Cordel, if you do not mind, and if your maid is not going to fall asleep in the hall, would you help me?'

'Willingly, Miss Lynch. But after that I really must go. My brother is being allowed a few days' leave before returning to his regiment, and I must be at our house to dine with him.'

'I perfectly understand – Lady Angela too is a stickler for punctuality.'

Together the two girls applied the ice to the soles of the unconscious girl's feet, but with no discernible success, and a great deal of effort on their part.

'It might take a few hours of constant attention.'

Miss Lynch looked at her small gold fob watch, a much treasured gift only recently given to her by Mrs Dodd.

'You must go, Miss Cordel.'

'I will come back tomorrow.'

Leonie nodded. 'You have given me hope, at any rate. There is nothing worse than clinging to nothing, but once one has some sort of slim thread, things do not seem so black, do they?'

Mercy waved from the door, and, since she was already late, fled to find Clarice waiting outside.

After she had gone Leonie stared out of the

window at the sight of her climbing into her family carriage, closely followed by her primly dressed maid.

'What a charming girl,' she remarked out loud to her unconscious patient. 'Let us just hope that what she has recommended may help to bring you awake.'

She turned her attention back to her patient, and stood applying ice to her feet for the next hour or two, hurrying backwards and forwards with fresh bowls once she knew that there was no senior member of the nursing staff likely to observe her indulging in such an unorthodox form of cure.

She was about to cross the hall once more for fresh ice, her last effort for that night, when she heard heavy breathing and smelt the strong smell of cigars coming down the wide polished staircase. The footsteps descending towards her were as heavy as the breathing, and the smell of cigar smoke grew stronger and stronger until it seemed to Leonie that she might start a coughing fit from just breathing the now clouded air. She could not reach the door which led to the kitchen passage without attracting attention, so she shrank back against the wooden panelling, praying that she would not be seen. Fortunately, in the half light that came from the outer lights, and the hall light that was way above them, the man did not seem to look up, perhaps more occupied by keeping his cigar alight, by putting on his hat, by opening the side door which led out to the back street and through which, the rule was, only

Lady Angela came and went by night or day.

As he passed within a few feet of her Leonie's terror increased and she knew at once who was going out of the door to the street. The future King of England, Emperor of India and Defender of the Faith, a man who, once crowned, would accept the Sword of State, and the homage of bishops and peers. A man so powerful that, had he seen the young nurse flattening herself against the panelling, it was in his power to do anything that he wished with her. But what he was doing at Sister Angela's Nursing Home late in the evening, she dared not even think.

Four

Dorinda's mouth would have dearly liked to drop open, and stay open, when she followed Gervaise Lowther into the St John's Wood house that he had insisted was to be 'hers' from now on. It was *so* charming, so *mignonne*, so *soignée*, so everything that she had ever wanted a house to be. It was as if Gervaise had, before he met her, had the house designed just for her, Dorinda Montgomery, with no-one else at all in mind.

American wallpapers, flower-strewn and delicate, silk-lined curtains, not a wretched potted palm in sight, nor a stag's head; everything so up to date; and such chintzes! Chintzes such as she knew, from the periodicals that were available even in the provinces, were even now being taken up by the most fashionable, so that the rooms echoed not stark Victorian ideals and morals but gaiety, and – above all – cosmopolitan attitudes.

'*Mais c'est tellement chic! C'est – ador-*able!'

Dorinda turned, and, since the housemaid was busy hurrying out to the hansom cab to help the hall boy fetch in the luggage, she felt quite able to kiss her lover on the lips. Not too much so as to be embarrassing, just briefly; enough to make him realize that she appreciated him, but not so much that he would not wonder whether she had perhaps cooled a little. For Dorinda was already mistress of the art of keeping a man at a sufficient distance to intrigue, but not so far that he would become bored and take off for fresh fields. It was the greatest fun, and, what was more, she knew now that in this ability lay her future. Not with Harry Montgomery – and goodness knows she had been forced to practise just such wiles on even him – but with much bigger fish, fish so big that soon it would be her photograph, along with the others, that the shopkeepers would be hawking in all the London windows. It would be she for whom everyone would stand upon chairs or park benches when they heard she was passing.

Gone was the dull old wifely routine, the subservience, the poverty; from now on she would be a leading member of the *demi-monde*, that select band of beautiful young girls and women who were kept in total luxury by everyone who was anyone, including the Prince of Wales.

'A man has a wife,' Gervaise had said during their stop for lunch and a change of horses on the way to London, and as he spoke he had drawn straight lines with the tines of his fork on the white, linen tablecloth, 'and his wife has given him a son, and once that has happened, they have their separate lives. She has her entertainments, and he has his *petit amour* who entertains him informally and pleases him. In return he gives her a house, a fine carriage, horses, jewels and clothes, and they

88

both observe the one golden rule, which must never ever be broken – discretion!'

Dorinda might be only twenty but she well understood what was what when it came to rules, and regulations, and indeed who was what. Even with her mouth full of the most delicious chicken pie and sipping at a white wine of whose delicacy she had never before dreamed, she thought that Gervaise's contract, his bargain, as it were, was the fairest, nicest bargain of which she had yet heard. As a matter of fact she was quite sure that she was getting the best of it, and that she must quite definitely not let him know! Poor fellow. He must be mad! Or else his wife was so terribly dull that it was almost unimaginable. But no, it seemed not.

'My wife is the sweetest, kindest, most sensitive of creatures, but she has been quite ill, and so – well, it is not possible for her to entertain me as she has previously been able. We were married when she was barely seventeen, and after three children . . . it is not possible – her doctors forbid. She finds her pleasures with friends and entertainments of all kinds, and we love each other devotedly. But you understand – ahem.'

Dorinda understood 'ahem' very well already. 'Ahem' had been awfully boring and dull with Harry who, apart from everything else, was recently proving to be much more interested in collecting rare butterflies than in keeping his wife entertained. Dorinda, withering away in yet another boarding house (accommodation that she frequently referred to as 'boring houses'), found that by the second year of her marriage she had come to know exactly how one of her husband's wretched butterflies felt.

She felt as if he had pinned her, lifeless and dry, to some hideous little piece of backcloth with her name in Latin underneath it – *Dorinda Montgomerius Rare Blue, Guernsey*.

Whatever her feelings might be, her mother had been most unsympathetic.

In all seriousness, she had wondered when Dorinda sighed and looked forlorn. What had Dorey expected of marriage? Happiness? Love? Surely not. She was not some housemaid with foolish ideas scraped from some penny booklet, was she?

Dorinda had been forced to admit that she was not a housemaid – although, when she came to think of it, she realized that she might have quite liked to be a housemaid, in a real house with other people to talk to, rather than a lodger in a boarding house. Indeed, as the weeks and months crawled listlessly by, with nothing much to think about, and certainly nothing to which to look forward, and she listened to Harry snoring his way through the dull, long, unmoving nights, she came to see that she was actually becoming just like a housemaid who read penny booklets, for she longed with all her heart for a life outside her own trivializing existence – in short, she wanted *more*!

'My dear, here is your maid, Blanquette.'

Dorinda eyed the curtsying maid sharply. She was not *so* young that she did not know that to be able to trust your servants meant everything to a person of affluence. And then of course, having been brought up in the Channel Islands, she knew the 'French' very, very well. She knew half-Frenchies and whole Frenchies, she knew Breton from Parisian, and Parisian from the Loire, and the whole boiling lot from a southerner with his sometimes unfathomable accent, and often very mixed Mediterranean origins.

Blanquette, when Dorinda had cross-examined her swiftly in French, turned out to have been brought up to be a nun, and had run away rather than face having her hair cut. A dim look to her face was balanced by a sly expression in her eyes, and she had a soft voice which belied that same shifty glance. Dorinda made up her mind at once that not all her servile manner, nor her foolish face, would allow her to trust Blanquette an inch, and what is more – half French though she might be herself – she thought it a very good thing for Holy Orders that the girl had been too vain to become a nun.

'You speak very pretty French,' Gervaise said, sounding just a little surprised. But then, remembering, he laughed and said, 'But of course you would! The Channel Islands.'

'Not at all,' Dorinda told him, smiling, 'nothing to do with the Channel Islands, everything to do with being educated in Paris. An academy run by nuns – *enfin!*'

She waited a second, her eyes drifting up the small pretty staircase of her new house, its walls decorated by charming lithographs of eighteenth-century women with dreamy expressions wearing large hats or becoming ribbons.

'Of course, of course.' Gervaise took her silent point, which was meant to prompt him to an unspoken understanding, and gestured to her to go ahead of him up the stairs, which Dorinda did with some delight.

Upstairs was as charming and as appropriate as downstairs, with only one disappointment. Dorinda dismissed the maid at the door of her boudoir, and gestured to Gervaise.

'This will never do,' she told him sorrowfully.

Gervaise looked around the bedroom with its matching dressing room off, its screens and its mirrors, its gilt and its gold, its pictures of cherubs partially clothed, its rounded velvet-covered furniture, and then into Dorinda's reproachful eyes.

'My dear, is there something you do not like?'

'*Cher Monsieur Gervaise*, blue! Never, never, never for the boudoir. Blue is beautiful but it is not the colour, let us say, of – *love*! Rose or lemon, or deep red, particularly deep red, but although I love dresses in blue, and cloaks in blue, and leather in blue, never, never for the bedroom. It makes the gentleman feel brrrrh – cold!'

Gervaise was humbled.

'But of course! Change it at once! No wonder—' He stopped, remembering his last love, and realizing all of a sudden that the deterioration of their relationship, his ardour cooling as it had, might well have been due to something as simple as the colour of a boudoir. He sighed.

But then seeing Dorinda smiling, her hourglass figure, so slender and so appealing, he forgot all about Louette who was now posing as a French governess in a vastly grand palace in Oxfordshire, and turned instead to the beckoning charms of the late afternoon sun playing on Dorinda's rich chestnut coloured hair. And what with her violet blue eyes and her charming full lips and small retroussé nose, he became extraordinarily interested in helping her divest herself of her clothes, while she chattered on about the benefits of rose colours in the boudoir. Or perhaps a French grey contrasting with a pale yellow?

Whatever the merits of either, not very long after it seemed to Gervaise that, blue or no blue, he was in heaven.

Not many days later Dorinda too was in heaven, but of a rather different sort, as painters and decorators, milliners and costumiers, tradesmen of every description, came pouring through the door of her chic little house in St John's Wood, while at the livery stables only half a mile away stood her very first carriage pulled by a pair of dark bay horses, with her 'coat of arms' about to be painted on the door that very week.

'But do you have a coat of arms, my dear?' Gervaise had asked her mildly, if perhaps a little impolitely, puzzled.

'Oh, yes. It is very ancient . . .'

'And it is?'

'A heart rampant with two cupids supporting!'

Gervaise had thought this so funny he had ordered the coach painter to design his new mistress something just such as Dorinda had joked about. Two cupids, discreetly clothed, at angles to each other with ribbons tied with love knots linking them, the two holding bows and arrows, with a pierced heart in the middle, and Dorinda's family motto underneath being inscribed as *She Who Loves Wins*, or as the coach builder translated it *Vincit Quae Amat*.

It was all the greatest fun and it seemed to Dorinda that every morning when she woke she was about to embark on some new and utterly enthralling adventure, an adventure so lovely that she could not believe that her life had changed so dramatically in such a very little time, and all because of a newspaper.

Sometimes, after her maid had brought her a cup of chocolate in the early morning, she would pick up her hand mirror and stare at her lovely face and thank it for what it had done for her life, not to mention her beautiful body.

This morning, shortly after she had performed this singular little ceremony – a ceremony which had started to take on something of a religious ritual – she was interrupted by Blanquette scratching on the door and calling to her.

'It's all right, Blanquette, you may come in. In England we never knock on doors.'

But despite obeying her mistress Blanquette's fluster became more pronounced as she announced in total bewilderment, 'There is a monsieur below, madame, who say 'ee is your *mari!*'

As she said *'mari'* Blanquette crossed herself as if the very mention of a husband required extra help from the Almighty to protect them both from such a devilish phenomenon.

'You must tell him,' Dorinda said, after a slight pause as her blood too ran just a little cold, 'that I will be down in a minute.'

Blanquette backed out again, and as she did so Dorinda flew from her bed and locked her bedroom door. Whatever happened she was not going to allow her husband into her new boudoir, now palest lemon and a beautiful French grey. She dressed herself in double quick time, managing her corsets and everything else as she had always used to do before Gervaise came into her life, and pinning up her hair really very adequately. But this time as she stared at herself in the mirror she was determined that no Harry Montgomery was going to defeat her. She was now a proper lady living in St John's Wood with her own carriage – just about to be embellished with her own coat of arms (sort of) and her own pale blue leather interior, and her own dark bay horses with silver trimmings on their bridles setting off their beautiful dark bay heads.

'Harry.'

Dorinda said her husband's name as if it was a pebble she was dropping into a pond, a pebble whose waves she would note with interest but which would undoubtedly, before long, sink to the bottom without a trace.

'Dorinda!'

Harry said his wife's name as if he had been having hysterics for the past week, as if he had been calling it, over and over again, becoming more and more despairing when there was no answer.

If Dorinda had ever loved her husband, even a little bit, she could have felt sorry for him at that moment, but Harry was so cold, and had always been so indifferent to her welfare, not caring in the least if she was always in rags and forever trying to make ends meet in boarding houses, that not even her initial mild affection had survived.

'How are you, Harry?'

Something in her manner stopped him from being as angry as he wanted, she thought, and then from the look on his face she quickly realized that it was nothing to do with her manner but everything to do with her new clothes. She must be looking magnificent compared to the mangy drab that she had been when he last saw her trotting ahead of him onto the boat for England, for he suddenly seemed unable to think of what to say next.

'I am . . . very well, Dorinda.'

Dorinda waved one jewelled hand towards a beautifully upholstered sofa, and her husband sank into it, it seemed to her, most thankfully.

'May God forgive me, Dorinda, but I do not

know whether I am on my head or my heels. One minute I have a wife, and the next minute – after hearing that Gervaise Lowther had acquired a new mistress by the name of Dorinda Montgomery – I have no wife, but am visiting the one I thought was my wife – in, of all things, another man's house! It is not a matter that I can take lightly, Dorinda, I do assure you. But I can forgive you if you come home with me now. I find that I can do that.'

Dorinda's large, usually good natured violet blue eyes suddenly seemed to glitter, matching the light catching the colour in her large new oval sapphire ring, a ring which Gervaise had sweetly presented to her only twelve hours earlier because he felt so sorry for her not having any jewellery whatsoever, aside from her dreary little wedding ring.

'I can not and will not come home with you, Harry Montgomery, for a very good reason and that is—'

But quite suddenly Dorinda was distracted. She sprang up before she had finished speaking and going to the drawing room door she opened it just as suddenly, in time to find Blanquette with her ear to it. Whereupon, in impeccable French and in words that she knew that Blanquette would understand all too easily, she ordered the young maid below to the kitchens, where she was to stay until such time as Mrs Montgomery rang for her.

'Where was I? Ah yes.' Dorinda reseated herself on the sofa and began again, her summary dismissal of the maid having left Harry wordless.

'You were just saying that you thought I ought to return *home* with you, Harry. Well now, that is a very interesting proposition, particularly in view of the fact that I am, now, *home*. This is my home now, Harry, and since you have never once provided me with anything even amounting to a hovel in which to hang up my hat, I can only tell you with the utmost sincerity that while I would very much like it if you *had* provided me with a home to which I could return, Gervaise Lowther has provided me with not only a home, as you can see, but furniture and a carriage and horses, and clothes, as you can also doubtless observe, and a beautiful box at the Opera which I can use whenever I like, not to mention accounts with all the best shops – opened in my *own* name – all in return for the other thing that you have never given me, Harry Montgomery – and that is love.'

'I hardly think that a fair accusation, Dorey. I married you, after all. I did marry you. Who were you before I married you, may I ask? I will tell you. You were the impoverished daughter of a widow, and she herself was running a seaside lodging house. You were hardly a catch, Dorey, my dear, hardly a catch by any means. You were lucky to catch *me*, in fact. Everyone said so at the time. Everyone on the island said you were lucky.'

Dorinda sprang to her feet and stamped one of them good and hard, clenching her hands in a fury.

'How dare you! How dare you – you, you – oaf! What sort of person do you think you are, coming into my house and insulting myself and my mother in that way? You who have never cared an oat if I came or went, if I was in rags or starving, just so long as you did not have to do a hand's turn, or work for so much as an hour a day. You who only wanted to spend your days chasing butterflies and your nights drinking wine and falling asleep over the card table. You are an inebriated imbecile at best, and a cold hearted fish at worst, Harry Montgomery. Gervaise Lowther on the other hand is funny and kind, and I find I can love him. Whereas you – you I have never loved, and now I hate!'

It was a truly extraordinary sight (but very satisfying) to see Harry white in the face, his lips trembling, fetching his walking stick and hat from the floor where he had laid them. He who had once been so pompous – and on really bad days, when he was suffering from too much wine the night before, quite bad tempered and waspish – was now standing looking at her as if he would like to take the walking stick and use it across her back, but could not because he was in her house and she was under the protection of another man, and there was not a jot that he could do, not a tittle or a jot, Dorinda realized with relish.

He walked to the door using his walking stick as a gentleman should – to walk, rather than to beat his wife – but he turned when he reached the door and announced in his cold, dry voice, 'This is not the last of it, Dorey, I do assure you.'

'Oh, but it is, Harry, I assure *you*.'

'He will never marry you, Dorey. You will be

thrown aside as all women such as yourself are, and end up in the back streets, gin-ridden and unable to make your way even to the poorhouse.'

'I really do not think it is anyone else's business except my own where I *end up*, as you call it, Harry. Really I do not. Certainly it is no longer your business.'

'I shall divorce you, of course.'

'No you will not, Harry. You have not enough money to divorce me, but I now have plenty of my own to divorce *you*, and I do assure you I can, on the grounds of total cruelty and neglect. Anyone, any judge, will hardly have heard me make my case before the whole court will be sobbing in sympathy for me, and not for you, Harry. Not for you who neglected and disdained me, even putting collecting the *Morning Post* before my well-being and protection! If you ever want to blame your wife's leaving you on any one thing, the straw that broke this particular camel's back, Harry, was just that. You actually cared more for your wretched newspaper than you did for me. No wonder I took up with Gervaise who is kind and considerate and has given me everything I have ever dreamed of.'

'You have the mind of a housemaid.'

'I had rather have the mind of a housemaid than a heart of stone, Harry Montgomery. And with that, sir, adieu!'

Dorinda herself shut the door behind him, and she did not bother to watch him walking off down the street, past her carriage and her matching dark bays, perhaps even past the hansom cab that would be bringing Gervaise to luncheon and other delights with her.

Blanquette's face appeared at the top of the stairs leading from the basement.

'Madame called?'

'You know very well that I did not call, Blanquette.'

Dorinda stared down at her maid, realizing with gratitude that she was really rather ugly, and therefore unlikely to attract Gervaise.

'Bring me a glass of red wine,' she commanded. 'I find I am feeling very anaemic.'

'Ah! Le bon vin rouge! Tout de suite, madame, tout de suite!'

After Blanquette had left her and she had drunk the wine, Dorinda stared at herself in the mirror above the fireplace in her delightful new drawing room.

'The cheek of him coming here, and after all this time!' she told the Dresden figures on the chimneypiece. 'The utter, utter cheek of him. I shall tell the servants in future to deny him entrance to my house. Good gracious! Carrying on for all the world as if he had been married to me!'

After she had laughed out loud at this Dorinda dabbed her wine-stained lips with her lacebordered handkerchief in front of her drawing room mirror and shook her head. Really! What were husbands *coming* to? Calling without leaving a card? Barging into one's house and demanding to see one? Anyone would think that they owned their wives, like an African chief or some such. It was both shocking and appalling. Besides, anyone who had taken ten whole days to find his wife certainly did not deserve for her to want to go back to him.

Quite frankly, she hoped she never saw him again. Certainly seeing him just for those few minutes this morning had brought back the most unpleasant memories, memories that served only to remind her how very, very fortunate she was to be where she was now.

Oh, but the time! Any minute now Gervaise would be arriving back at the house, and she not changed into the very newest of her dresses, the most delightful dress, a dress which she had just had delivered from Madame Chloe in Dover Street.

Dorinda skipped up the stairs to her newly decorated boudoir, calling to Blanquette to follow her and singing at the top of her voice the French National Anthem, which somehow served to satisfy both Blanquette and herself, being of a rousing nature and at the same time easy to sing while your dress was being pulled over your head and your stays tied.

'The first thing we have to do, my dear, is teach you to ride. That is the first thing.'

Gervaise had dined so well he was disinclined to go anywhere after dinner. Really, there was little doubt but that Dorinda, his new and beloved mistress, was a pearl among the many pearls of her kind that inhabited the many discreetly fashionable houses in St John's Wood. Not only was she wondrous in the boudoir, imaginative and sweet to a point that was well beyond any normal Englishman's dreams, but she was also brilliant at supervising the kitchen, claiming that the art of the cuisine and the art of the boudoir were as closely entwined as ivy on a tree.

'My grandfather told my mother that if a man tasted a woman's food and disliked it, or was bored by it, or found it dull, there was no point in his taking her to bed!'

Gervaise found himself agreeing with Dorinda's grandfather wholeheartedly. Had he tasted Dorinda's food – or at least the food that she had directed the cook to prepare – he would have had no hesitation in inviting her upstairs within seconds of finishing dinner.

Nevertheless the menu that night had been really quite light – consommé with rice followed by fillets of sole, tomatoes stuffed with veal, tiny roulades of lamb cooked with rosemary and served with a juice of red currants, and wild duck roasted with tiny parsley potatoes and a green salad.

And to finish, a confection of meringue with a crème anglaise, and a compote of fruit, and – on the cook's insistence – something called *laitance de hareng à la diable*. ('*Urgh*, what is this?' Dorinda had demanded to know, at which the cook had assured her that all meals in England ended in this way, especially in the houses of the aristocracy. Dorinda had again muttered her personal sound of disgust, but allowed it.)

'How shall I learn to ride, Gervaise? I have no riding horses.'

'I have been offered the use of a very nice ladies' hack, a bright bay gelding, a most comely creature. A sweet and reasonable ride, I have been told by someone who knows a little about ladies' hacks – and so that is how we must start.'

'Where shall we begin?'

'In Rotten Row, my dear, in the early morning. I shall take you myself, and you will be quite safe with me.'

Dorinda smiled down the dining table at her lover. He was really so sweet and protective, and handsome too. But a warning voice ran through her head when she thought of someone who loved her teaching her anything at all.

Alas, the voice she could hear clearly in her head was her mother's at its most sensible.

Never allow a man who imagines that he loves you to teach you anything, not a single solitary thing. Not even how to tie the laces on your boots. The moment he loves you, for some reason I have never understood, he feels quite free to treat you like a galley slave while he plays the Roman. You can do nothing right, and the less you can do right the more you find you do wrong, and the more you do wrong, the crosser he becomes, until enfin – you would both like to kill each other, and that is the truth!

'Gervaise.'

'My dear.'

One of the things that was so utterly delightful about St John's Wood was that the women allowed the men to smoke their after dinner cigars in the dining room, and did not mind in the least, it seemed, if the curtains smelt in the morning.

But then, life in St John's Wood was altogether such a pleasant contrast to being fashionable, and being seen to be fashionable and correct by the *haut ton*. And there was an end to it. Although of course, ultimately, a man could not do without both sides to his life. His public life with his wife and family was one thing and his private life with his mistress another, the one balancing the other quite exquisitely, as Gervaise now realized – to his own immense delight.

His wife and family were happy with him as a husband and father, and blissfully ignorant of how he spent those leisure hours when he was not either with them or dancing attendance on the Prince of Wales. He was happy. His mistress was happy. As far as he was concerned his world was altogether a happy place, outlined as it was on the one side by the boundaries of convention, and on the other by his own insistent desires.

But of course, a major part of the balance in his life could only be kept if he was able to teach Dorinda to ride, and not just to hack, but to jump her mounts so expertly that once winter came he could take her away to his Leicestershire hunting box, where she could be out all day with him, and although of course she could never be invited by any of his friends to their houses in the evening she would be there in the hunting box whenever he wished to visit her after tea. Or before dinner, and after dinner too, if he was lucky.

'*Gervaise!*'

Gervaise liked the way that Dorinda said his name. She did not precisely speak with a French accent yet it seemed to him that she did, for she did not pronounce her words in the same way as his completely Anglo-Saxon wife, nor did she move or smile in the same way. Her manner, her expression, everything about her was lighter and quicker. Quickness of speech and lightness of touch seemed to be her hallmark, and her hands always seeming to be darting about, as if she was anticipating his boredom and changing the subject, or her dress, or her manner, before he could tire of whatever it was she was saying or doing.

'Gervaise,' she said again, returning to the subject in hand while she managed to also look reproachful. 'You know how much I owe you, you know how much I love you, but I must remind you that I am not first in your life. You have another life which is very, very important and which is not going to be important enough if you take it upon yourself to teach me to ride. No! I must insist you be a good boy, yes? You must be early at the Foreigners Office—'

'Foreign Office—'

'Exactly! This is it! To do your work, and then to go riding with me, but only when I am good at it, yes?'

It was almost more than Gervaise could take

in. Imagine having a mistress who was both passionate and amusing, but also ambitious for him. Who wanted him to do well at the 'Foreigners Office', who had, in short, *serious* intentions for him. Not just his wife (that was after all part of her duties – only to be expected) but now his mistress too wanted him to become Foreign Secretary, it seemed.

Gervaise half closed his eyes, but then opened them again.

'But who will teach you to ride, my dear, if not myself?'

'Well, there must be a man who can teach me, yes? Perhaps some friend of yours? Perhaps Lord Crosstitch? You were mentioning him . . .'

Gervaise hooted with laughter.

'Crosswaite. Robert Crosswaite! Capital. I will ask him. He is a bachelor and has less on his mind in the early morning than a married man.'

Dorinda smiled at her lover, and as she did so the candlelight caught the marvellous dull red of her garnet choker, with its matching ring and bracelet, with which dear Gervaise had presented her, just before he had to call for his opera cloak.

'There was so much that I wanted to tell you, Gervaise, but I am afraid you must hurry, my love, or you will be late for supper and the ball.'

He kissed her goodbye and later waved up to the window like a little boy being sent off to school. Dorinda watched him climb into a hackney cab, folding his hat and pulling his blue silk-lined cloak around him. She could reflect very happily on the past weeks that had brought such a change in her fortunes. She would like to think that she had brought as much happiness to Gervaise – perhaps more, who knew? – as he had brought to her, but she was too wise to think that he would think of *her* in terms of any future.

She had not been married for two years to a feckless, uncaring good-for-nothing without learning that a man's interest in a woman could last ten minutes, ten hours, ten days or ten years, and whichever it was, Dorinda knew that in her position she was bound for uncertainty. She was a ship in a bottle bobbing about on the waves of life. If she was not to end up, as Harry Montgomery had predicted, in gin alley, she must become more powerful, in her way, than any protector could possibly be. It was just a fact.

But first, as Gervaise had said, she must learn to ride. But not just learn to ride – she must learn to ride beautifully and to hunt brilliantly. That way she would attract just the right amount of attention from just the right kind of interested and interesting gentlemen, so that if, and when, Gervaise tired of her, or she of him, she would be famous enough for it not to matter.

One thing on which she was determined was that she would never ever see, or be within walking distance of, gin alley. Much more likely that Harry, with his silly preoccupations and his pride and conceit, would end up destitute and living in the poorhouse.

Tomorrow she would be on her way, buying

riding skirts and any amount of attention-seeking clothes for Rotten Row. Soon she would be trotting out on a bright bay gelding in . . . she paused, thinking of the colour. Of course – her favourite blue, with matching plumes. She smiled at just the idea. She would stun them. She was determined on it.

In another more correctly fashionable part of London, in that part which the oldest families travelled to and from during the Season, life was not as easy as it would seem to be in St John's Wood.

Mercy stared down the table at her step-uncle, Marcus Stanton. He was such a strange man, part gossip, part friend, partly too correct, partly too incorrect, and yet, with it all, she always felt she could ultimately trust him to say or do the right thing, although why she could she did not exactly know.

During her childhood he had sometimes seemed to Mercy and her brothers to be a permanent guest at Cordel Court, staying for months at a time, and helping his sister, Lady Violet, tolerate the English winter. He was tall, like his sister, and despite being middle-aged he was still immensely good looking, but unmarried, and likely, Lady Violet always said, 'sadly to remain so'. An accident in childhood had precluded marriage, but Mercy had never dared to ask her stepmother why, any more than she would have dared to ask her father if he felt sad when his favourite horse was shot.

'My dear, I fear you have the most extraordinary competition in the ballroom this Season,' her step-uncle was saying when Mercy returned her thoughts to earth. She watched him as he took a large helping of pudding and stared first with satisfaction at his plate, and then down the table with less satisfaction, or so it seemed to Mercy, at his mousy step-niece. 'There are beauties of every kind, and so many to choose from! Lady Elmont's daughter, Mathilda, Lady Soutine's niece, Amaretta – although she might not count as she is slightly foreign with a strange accent. There are considerably fewer heiresses, the Americans having discovered what appalling husbands titled English gentlemen make – or no, I lie, there is one coming over with the Duchess of Marlborough for a short season, I hear. Well, well – at any rate it is doubtless all a tremendous challenge to your maid and your dressmaker, not to mention my sister.'

He had already begun his pudding. Mercy had refused hers, for the truth was that she found her appetite had fled once 'coming out' and 'doing the Season' was mentioned. It seemed to her that even as she watched her step-uncle ladling what appeared to be mountains of meringue and fruit and cream into his mouth she could feel a hard chair sticking into her 'sit-upon' and hear music playing, but feel no white-gloved hand on the back of her ball gown.

'I expect Lady Violet is doing something about your hair and dresses, is she not?'

He had finished and was now wiping his ripe over-red lips on his napkin even as he lifted his wine glass yet again.

Mercy remembered how her brothers, back at Cordel Court, had nicknamed him 'Marcus Mighty Mouth' as he passed them to take his sister in to dinner if their father was out visiting someone on the estate, or attending to his duties as Lord Lieutenant of the county.

'He only comes here to eat,' they would say, 'he can't do anything else. That's all he's good for, bridge and eating.'

'Yes, she is doing something,' Mercy agreed in a low voice, and found herself praying that she would die before she reached a ballroom, or the presentation rooms at Buckingham Palace, or drove to Ascot, or took to the dance floor with someone, anyone, who would dance with her.

'Still, at least you have my sister to present you at Court, that is a blessing. She will guide you in every way. It will be a dream come true, mark my words.'

He smiled down the table at Mercy.

But Mercy thought that it would not be a dream so much as a nightmare. She had heard all the stories, as all young girls of her age and position had, about girls who while walking backwards from the Queen tripped over their trains. Of dresses that had caught up at the back, unbeknownst to the wearer, thus exposing her pantalettes to the amused and interested Court. She had been told of dowagers who had dropped their tiaras where no-one would want to drop anything. Of the Prince of Wales's inability to miss a single presentation because it meant that he could eye the new Season's crop of debutantes and make a note of those he might wish to see again after they were married and had, in the accepted manner, given their husbands sons and heirs.

'Above all, do not let it prey on your mind. The secret of a successful London Season, believe me, is to relax and be yourself – enjoy yourself.'

Mercy nodded blindly down the table through the candlelight, because to relieve her tension she had put her mind elsewhere – with Nurse Lynch at Sister Angela's Nursing Home, as a matter of fact. With the beautiful young nurse who might or might not, by way of ice on the feet, be helping that poor young mannequin back to consciousness.

'Forgive me, my dear, but you seem somewhat preoccupied.'

'Oh no, not at all, not at all preoccupied,' Mercy lied.

'I expect you are tired. I am awaited at the opera, of course, so I know you must be feeling tired.'

And Mercy knew it was incumbent on her to withdraw from the dining room, and did so, making her way without pause up to her own room where she sat down suddenly on her bed and put her head in her hands.

She was a mouse, not a ballroom star. She was plain, not a beauty. How would she ever survive what was ahead of her?

And yet, as she found herself twisting her

handkerchief around her fingers in a fever of tension she knew, from what had happened that day, that she was quite wrong. The condition of the poor young mannequin was what mattered, and how Mercy Cordel was pulling through these first days away from Somerset was not important in the least. What mattered was what had happened to that other country girl, not whether or not Mercy Cordel found dancing partners or a husband in her first London Season.

Reluctantly she went to the cheval glass in the corner of her beautifully furnished bedroom, and stared at herself. Turn this way or that, do what she could, she was still unable to deceive herself into thinking that she was a beauty, or could ever be. Her hair was brown rather than blonde, her eyes grey rather than blue, her mouth, though generous, not full lipped, her height small rather than Junoesque.

She needed no convincing of her coming fate. She knew that she would end up without a husband or an engagement to announce, and would be sent back to Cordel Court like a parcel marked *Return to sender*. There she would fritter away her life between her books and her horse, while pretending to herself that she was of use to her family by sewing and helping out with all the thousand and one things that were always needing to be done in a large country house, until finally she would die unmarried, even her gravestone proclaiming the failure that faced her in the coming months.

'I know I shall care so much, feel so humiliated,' she thought, as she turned away from the mirror. 'But I shall just do as I have always done. I shall pretend that I do not care and that way I will survive. I shall think of what really matters, and what really matters is not to do with me, it is to do with other people's lives, people's deaths – other people matter, not myself. I must be like that nurse, think less of myself than of other people.'

But as she heard the fashionable carriages passing under her window, and as she thought of the people inside those carriages, witty, good looking and above all rich, Mercy knew that she did care, very much. She was too honest not to realize it, and so she found herself kneeling by her bed and praying, first for the girl in the nursing home, but second for herself, that she might somehow survive the coming months.

Five

Dorinda had always, but always, suspected that her life had been destined from the start to be somehow very special. Perhaps it was because she had so disliked her mother that she had finally become convinced while she was growing up that she would one day be transported from the place where she was – a dull grey-tinged boarding house inevitably filled with spinsters and bachelors whose only purpose in life seemed to be making up a four for bridge – to fulfil a special destiny.

It was also because of the inevitable attentions of all those occupants of that self-same boarding house that she knew she was quite beautiful. They were always telling her she was, and it had seemed a bit of a pity not to give in and finally believe them.

The point being that from the time she was small, Dorinda had realized that people turned to look at her when she passed them. It was something which she took for granted, and enjoyed. Her mother, who did not really like anyone else being beautiful, said, often, that it was only because of her hair and her violet blue eyes.

'It is the contrast in your colouring, Dorinda,' she would say, flatly. 'You have your father's hair colouring and my eyes. It is the contrast, that is all. And since your looks are nothing to do with yourself, but everything to do with *le bon dieu*, you will not become conceited about them, if you please.'

Dorinda did not care for the last part of that oft repeated sentiment; every time she saw the words forming on her mother's lips, she would skip away from her. Sometimes she would find herself running towards the sea shore which bordered their garden, towards the beaches and the tides, the sighing winds and the noisy nagging cries of the seagulls, all of which helped to drown out the sound of her mother's voice. Dorinda knew very well that it was always her mother's intention to drag her down, to make her ordinary. The ground was where Dorinda's mother wanted her only child's feet to stay, and the ground was what Dorinda had every intention of floating above, whether it be on a horse or in a well-sprung carriage.

And here she was, stepping down from just such a well-sprung carriage as she had dreamed of so often, towards her first riding lesson with Gervaise's friend Lord Crosswaite, whom she could see, even now, waiting for her at the entrance to the livery stables, himself immaculately attired in the latest riding clothes.

'Lord Crosswaite.'

He bowed, but not before Dorinda had seen the expression in his eyes change from impatience (*Lord, this is going to be a dull morning*) to one of amazement and fascination. Dorinda did not blame him in the least. She knew she was looking perfectly at her best, which was to say very, very good indeed, but she did not know this because of having looked in any mirror. She knew it from looking into Robert Crosswaite's eyes.

'Mrs Montgomery.'

He bowed and kissed her hand in the French manner, for which Dorinda immediately gave him good marks.

'I am so looking forward to you teaching me everything you know . . .' a slight pause, and then, 'about *horses* and *riding*, Lord Crosswaite. Mr Lowther tells me you are expert in the hunting field and always follow your own line, whatever that might mean!'

Dorinda gave a little ripple of laughter and Lord Crosswaite too laughed, although she had not really made a joke, and really they were both laughing because it was a sunny morning, a beautiful day, and Dorinda was wearing such a becoming riding habit, close-buttoned, long-skirted, in her favourite blue, her curly-brimmed, short-topped, shiny ladies' topper sitting forward onto her forehead in just the way the fitter at Busvines had told the famous 'Skittles', Lord Hartington's great love, to wear hers.

Skittles had made herself famous riding not just in Rotten Row but also in the Bois de Boulogne, where crowds would gather to watch her pony chaise with its matching pair of black cobs and its two grooms on coal black cattle behind.

117

'It is so kind of you to offer to help me, Lord Crosswaite.'

By this time, Dorinda was standing on the mounting block and a groom was holding her hireling's head, and she was being helped by his lordship into the saddle. From behind her Dorinda could hear just the slight suspicion of a sigh as if her teacher was enjoying some secret pleasure, and then they were away, Dorinda's mount walking sedately beside that of Lord Crosswaite.

The two of them headed right into Rotten Row. It was a great deal too early in the morning for many of the fashionable to be about, something for which, Dorinda confided to her companion, she was only too grateful, since if she was to take a 'flyer' she would rather do it with a smaller than a larger audience.

'It is the most perfect sensation,' she went on, 'to be out on a morning such as this with a beautiful creature such as this, and a lovely way to see London too.'

Robert Crosswaite was obviously not used to this ingenuous view of the fashionable life, but seeing Dorinda's smiling delight in everything, and how prettily she already sat her mount, he too started to look about, at the trees with their tender green, newly come out in time for the Season, and the occasional carriages and hansoms that he could see across the Park, but most of all at Dorinda whose genuine, innocent delight was so very refreshing after the demeanour of more fashionable ladies, so many of whom, it had to be faced, often gave their male companions the impression that they were more than tired of the Season before it had really begun.

Of course Crosswaite did not know that Dorinda had sent for a ladies' side saddle and had been practising sitting on it for some days now, one leg forward over the pommel, one down to the stirrup, back straight, eyes always ahead.

'Mrs Montgomery,' her *pilot* Lord Crosswaite told his friend Gervaise a few hours later, 'is a natural on a horse. Once she has her own mount, she will become as famous a sight in Rotten Row as the Empress of Austria in the hunting field. I predict it.'

As a matter of principle Dorinda had actually no intention of not becoming famous, and so after that first expedition with her kind young pilot she went out regularly, at first with him, but then, after a few weeks, with another, and yet another, and yet another, all of whom, the gossip of the clubs being what it was, having heard that if they rose early enough they would find themselves escorting a new and fabulous beauty who went by the name of Dorinda Montgomery. An early morning beauty, a stunning woman on a horse – the combination was enough to lure all the most fashionable men to rise before they really liked.

Of course Gervaise was nothing if not proud of Dorinda's swift progress, and as a consequence was soon encouraged to buy her a stunning liver chestnut mare of her own.

If it had not been vulgar Dorinda would have

kissed her lover straight away when she saw 'Glitters' being led up in the livery yard, but as it was she contented herself with murmuring, 'My, my, but she is a very pretty thing, is she not?'

'I thought I must have it right. I was not sure, but I thought I must, because she is exactly the colour of your hair,' Gervaise said proudly. 'Why, you could be sisters!'

'She will look very much the thing with my Dorinda Blue riding skirt set against her shining liver chestnut colour, will she not?'

'I hear "Dorinda Blue" being bandied about all over town. In such a short space of time, my dear.'

'Do you mind, monsieur?'

'Monsieur' looked down at Dorinda. He did not mind at all. He was proud of taking her up as he had, but he was also realistic. Once a young woman was being talked about in the clubs it was only a very short space of time before her name came to the attention of the Prince of Wales, and after that, of course, anything could happen, and usually did.

And so he found himself, for once in her company, falling silent.

It was difficult for Mercy to slip off anywhere with Clarice, not that she was not adept at sidling out of doors, and in through them again too, but because Clarice was such a clumsy old thing, forever walking about in squeaking shoes, or standing still and hiccuping when she was meant to be creeping, quiet as a mouse, after Mercy.

This afternoon, two days after their late afternoon visit to Sister Angela's Nursing Home, Mercy was sure that it would be quite safe to slip off to see how the young mannequin was progressing. She was aware, however, that if she should dress in any of her new town clothes – those clothes that had arrived from Madame Chloe's Maison de Couture – she would be noticed, if not by her stepmother, at least by one of her stepmother's friends. They would all be calling to leave their cards; friends who, over the last two mornings, had been 'looking Mercy over' for their sons, and had, by their lack of enthusiasm, made it all too clear that they thought their sons could do really better than Miss Mercy Cordel.

For this reason, in order to visit the nursing home once more, Mercy made sure that she was dressed in her coming-to-town shabby Cordel Court clothes, and insisted Clarice wear shoes that for once did not squeak.

Having guarded against all exigencies she slipped out of a side door into the street and walked off in the direction of a hansom cab. Once safely round the corner she jumped into it, followed by her maid, and sat well back. London was so small, with so many eyes to see you, she knew that she had to be careful. She also knew that Clarice, for all her disapproval of such activities as reading novels in the Park, had given her full support to Miss Mercy's interest in the poor young girl.

'It is what Christians must do, huh?'

Mercy had to agree it was just what Christians should do, although not usually Christians of her class and age. For the truth was that nothing had interested her more, since coming to town, than the incident at Madame Chloe's establishment.

Not that Madame Chloe was unkind. *She* was not unkind, but the whole fashionable system of using innocent young girls was cruel. And the whole idea that she could have been taken off to some public hospital and abandoned, with no-one to take an interest in her, aroused Mercy's deepest feelings of disgust at the way a so-called Christian society conducted itself.

Of course, nothing had altered very much. She had been the same at Cordel Court, and doubtless when she returned there, assuredly still very much a spinster, her attitudes would still be unchanged. She would still be all set to rescue some lame dog, or some stray or waif, and nurse them in some lonely cottage, far away from the prying eyes of her family who so strongly disapproved of her involvement with such things or such people.

Not that they were unkind, or uncaring. Their attitude was that once they took up with more than their usual charitable concerns – namely the Church, the Church Orphanage, the Church Old People's Trust, the Church Committee for the Settling of Waifs and Strays, and the Church

Benevolent Society – they would have too much on their hands.

'So many depend on Cordel Court already,' her stepmother was always murmuring to Mercy. 'It seems to me that if we take on one more person we shall be like the famous boat that took on one too many to crew, and promptly sank.'

Mercy longed to ask which 'famous' boat it was that had been so over-crewed it had sunk, but her stepmother was always gone before she could frame the question, rapidly walking away from her, glancing at the tiny French watch pinned above a pocket of one of her fine lawn blouses, her quick light steps echoing down the stone-flagged floors of the old house, a small terrier at her heels.

'Miss Mercy, we are here!'

Mercy jumped down from the hansom, thankful that although she was no heiress she did at least have a small income – *girls' pin money*, it was always called disparagingly by her brothers who had considerable inheritances from all sides – from her mother's estate. But, disparaged as it was, the money was enough to allow her to pay for ribbons or medicines or lace or, as in this case, hansom cabs, without having to resort to asking for charity from someone else.

She was so anxious to know whether the ice had been of any benefit to the patient when she saw Nurse Lynch she forgot to greet her.

'How is the poor creature? I am sorry I have not been back before this, but I have had to—' Mercy stopped. It was no good. She would have to confess. 'I am to be presented at Court, and really there is so much fiddle-faddle to everything, what with the dresses and the costumes – oh, it is so fatiguing and tiresome really, and then the dowagers and the duchesses come in to take tea with my stepmother and look me over, and go away again quite resolved that they can do better for their sons! It is such a thing to be a girl, and not at all pretty. But then – you would not know about that, would you?'

She laughed, and Leonie coloured slightly. She did not think of herself as beautiful, although to be truthful she did not think of herself as ugly either, because that would be plum stupid.

'I am such a plain Jane, I shall doubtless spend all Season on a spindly chair and then be taken home to Somerset to help look after the house, consigned to one of those little sewing rooms that the upper maids use in winter, and allowed out only to help pick and bottle jams and conserves in summer.

'But never mind. I am sure I do not, for the very idea of marriage sometimes seems to me to be rather horrible. I have seldom met a really happy married woman, excepting my stepmother of course, but then she is the exception to most things. She is beautiful and clever and kind, and that is more than you can say of most people. But all this is by the by, and how selfish of me to rattle on when I see this poor child is still not conscious. Oh dear, so the ice did not work the miracle, in this case?'

The nurse was still as tall and blonde and beautifully turquoise of eye as Mercy remembered her from a few days before, but now as she stood on the other side of the bed shaking her head she was also clearly miserable.

'I tried what you suggested, but it was to no avail. I am afraid, Miss Cordel, she is dying by inches, as Lady Angela and the doctors agreed only this morning. Apparently there is nothing to be done now, except to wait, but not, alas, in hope.'

Mercy's large, honest, innocent eyes fell on the young girl lying on the bed, and as they did so she could suddenly see the truth of what Leonie Lynch had just said. She had not seen much of death, but she had seen enough to know that there was a look that came upon people, as if they were already not there. It was like watching someone gradually, little by little, disappearing into the distance, until they were at last – gone.

Looking across at the young nurse, Mercy could see now that while she herself had been a witness to death some few times before – even helping to lay out her own mother – Leonie was feeling helpless and frightened by what she was witnessing.

'I will stay with you until the end,' Mercy told her, immediately understanding the scene before her.

Together the two girls sat in sad, sorrowful silence on either side of the poor young mannequin's bed, each holding one of her hands, until eventually, as the afternoon light faded into four o'clock, the poor innocent on the bed gave one little last gasp, a few little quick breaths, and then was gone from what for her had, undoubtedly, been a sorrowful world.

'Oh – God rest her!'

'I will help you.' Mercy looked across at the nurse, who was standing staring down at the bed as if she could not believe what she had just seen. Mercy knew just how she felt, although she herself was quite calm, having witnessed such a scene before. 'It's all right, I know what to do. I have had a little nursing experience, on my father's estate in Somerset. You would be surprised how much goes wrong in the country – or perhaps you would not,' she added, turning away to help fetch such things as she knew would be necessary.

After informing Lady Angela of the demise of her patient and the unhappy necessity of calling the undertakers, Leonie expected Mercy to go. Instead, she turned to Leonie and said quietly, 'Why don't you fetch your cloak and come with me to a tea room near here? We have Clarice with us, she will see we are not disturbed. It will be perfectly proper, and no-one will miss me until dinner. I can change in a second into an evening gown with Clarice's help, so it will not be of great matter if we have twenty minutes of some sort of refreshment together, will it?'

Leonie was grateful, but never more than when she walked into the tea room and saw other people sitting behind pretty china eating cakes and scones and chatting. Life was still life. There were still such things as tea and cake, and gossip, and fashionable accessories, and maids who sat at tables by the door and sipped tea and ate buns while their mistresses ate cake.

'My stepmother would not wish us to be here, but there it is. Sometimes there are events which necessitate refreshment, and somehow . . .'

Mercy looked firmly at her new friend and Leonie tried to smile, although feeling very low indeed, and only really able to see the face of the poor young girl on the bed.

'I somehow feel it is my fault,' she confessed in a low voice. 'That I could have done more.'

Having ordered tea for all of them, Clarice included, Mercy said firmly, 'We all feel that, I assure you. There always seems to be something that we could have done more, that we should have done more, but the truth is that there is no such thing as "more", only what has been *done*. That is the acceptance that has to be faced, I think.'

'How old are you?'

'Seventeen, eighteen at the end of June.'

'You talk as if you were much older.'

'Yes, I know,' Mercy agreed ingenuously. 'My brother Henry used to say I talked old when I was born. As a matter of fact I think it is more to do with having grown up in such an isolated place as Somerset – having to be so much on my own. I think that helps one to grow up quickly. Also, I was always with older people when I was young, and that makes you older too, I find.'

Leonie thought back to Eastgate Street and her mother, and all those grey-faced creatures in the workhouse she had passed so often, sitting, row upon row upon row, not moving until they were brought their filthy gruel, and then how they grabbed at their bowls and ate faster than any starving animal.

'I think growing up in London is ageing too,' she said, after a moment, and she could not help thinking how different in every way their two childhoods must have been.

'Of course it is. London is so very direct, is it not? You pass beggars and fashionable ladies and great carriages and the poor carts almost at the same moment, but no-one feels responsible for each other, do they? That is the first thing I noticed when that poor girl fell and hit her head – no-one was willing to be responsible for her, and no-one – aside from you and Lady Angela of course – was even a little bit interested, whereas in Somerset someone would have tried to take an interest – although, thinking back, perhaps not *always*. But at all events, I know I would!'

'Did you find any of her family? She must have some relations, do you not think?'

Mercy stared across the table at Leonie.

'Well,' she said sagely, 'she must have once had, but I have asked a little bit – of Clarice, as a matter of fact – and she has told me that all the fashion houses, to which she has been accompanying my stepmother for many seasons now, are always taking up young girls, too young girls, who are usually . . .'

She paused and sipped her tea, not quite knowing what to say, not wanting to shock her companion, knowing that country life had made her more than a little earthy.

'They are usually "fallen",' Leonie put in, matter of fact and straightforward as always, this also being a side effect of her upbringing in Eastgate Street. 'I too have made my own enquiries, of Mrs Dodd, my godmother, you know? She has known Madame Chloe all her life, and it seems there is little to be done. Madame Chloe merely provides employment for these girls, when and if she can, during the Season. There is little else she could do. She is not a rich woman, and really without people like herself the girls would be in a poorhouse. It seems that they are actually seduced into their way of life by wicked women who offer them dresses and then dope them and pass them on to young aristocratic gentlemen. Afterwards they are thrown aside and have to take work wherever they can find it. Sometimes they simply go on with that same way of life – and well you may know the rest. It is most unfortunate.'

Mercy did not like to say so, but having not been brought up in Eastgate Street she did not 'know the rest'. But she thought she could guess, because fallen women were fallen women, and everyone knew what happened to fallen women, they died of excesses. Or took to drinking gin, or had babies and had to give them up to foundling hospitals, and that kind of thing. It was all very sad and, as Leonie said, most unfortunate.

'I always think it could happen to any of us, do you know that?'

Mercy stared at Leonie. She had such a beautiful face, such delicate features all brought together in one extraordinary, fascinating whole by her wondrous turquoise eyes. It was a pleasure to stare at her, even though Mercy was actually staring for quite other reasons.

'That is a very – honest thing to say. An extraordinarily honest thing to say, Miss Lynch.'

Leonie nodded in agreement, because it was.

'I know, I know. But it is true, is it not? Any of us can be led astray. Sometimes it is by the dresses, and sometimes it is by something even more powerful.'

'I do not think, with all my best will, and all my best imagination, that I could be led astray by *dresses*.' Mercy smiled with sudden impishness. 'But that is because I am not really worth *dressing*! I always think I am a little bit like one of those unfortunate house owners who, try as they may with furniture and paintings, with marble statues and gilding, and with plasterwork of the most exquisite kind, can not make their houses look any better than they are. Really, they are better not to try, just to leave them unvarnished and plain.'

'You have honesty and kindness that is far better than beauty,' Leonie told Mercy, feeling oddly sorry for her. 'Beauty is just something you are born with, and goes quite soon too, I hear! Better to be kind than beautiful.'

'Not,' her new friend confided, 'alas, when it comes to the marriage mart, or even just finding partners in the ballroom. I am very much afraid that beauty is the first lure there.'

'And the second?'

Mercy indicated to the waitress that she should take their tea bill to Clarice, who had charge of her money.

'The second, Miss Lynch, has everything to do with that which Clarice is even now handling on both our behalfs!'

They both rose from their seats, Leonie with an anxious look to the clock.

'I must not be late back.'

'I hope I will not have got you into trouble. I always seem to be getting people into trouble, I don't know why.'

Leonie smiled suddenly, probably for the first time that afternoon. She liked this small, slim young girl with the wry manner. She was not at all like most of her type. She did not make Leonie Lynch from Eastgate Street feel as if she was from a different class, or inferior in any way, as some young women could not wait to do. She had no airs and graces. Rather the reverse – she seemed to think that everyone in the world was vastly more interesting than herself.

'Oh, and I should tell you I will be happy to pay for the young girl's funeral, Miss Lynch, not just her stay at Sister Angela's Nursing Home.' As Leonie followed her outside to the street, she added, 'I could not bear her to go to such a terrible end as a pauper's grave, not after seeing her that morning, so fresh-seeming, so young. You see, I have such a conscience about the whole thing. I fear she must have fainted because she was starving. I will pay for a service and the funeral. It is the least I can do, since I will be wearing the dresses which the poor child was forced by circumstances to model. If you send to this address' – she scribbled on a piece of paper from her maid's bag as they stood outside in the now rainy street – 'I will come whenever it is arranged. I rather fear, you see, that despite the work she was being paid to do she might actually have been starving.'

Clarice shot a large black umbrella up over both of their heads as they stood talking on the pavement and Leonie took up this point.

'You are quite right, Miss Cordel. She *was* starving, and that is why she died. She had nothing in her to help her regain consciousness – the doctors said as much to Lady Angela. Her flesh was literally hanging from her bones, the way one sometimes sees horses in the back streets. Too awful, don't you think?'

Mercy's kind young face saddened at this, and the expression in her eyes grew sombre.

'It does not bear thinking about, does it? I shall come whenever you send to me for the funeral. It is important, I always think, that no-one should go to their grave unmourned, particularly not such a young person. Au revoir, Miss Lynch!'

She turned and gave a wave which seemed suddenly, for no reason that Leonie could think, to have a hint of both courage and sadness in it.

*   *   *

132

'Where have you been?'

Her stepmother stood at the top of the staircase resplendent in a yellow evening gown, with a wide black velvet ribbon studded with diamonds at her throat. Evening gloves, exquisite hand-made evening shoes, the whole adding up to a look that spelt style, breeding, class, money, power, influence – everything indeed that the poor young girl whom Mercy had just seen through her last moments on earth had not, and would not ever have had.

'Thank heavens anyway that you had the sense to take Clarice with you, wherever you were, or your reputation would be ruined for ever!'

Mercy looked up at her stepmother. She was so beautiful.

'You look wonderful, Step-maman!' she told her.

Lady Violet smiled, radiantly, at Mercy's words. It was as if a thousand electric lights had come on at once, and were lighting up the hall.

'Well, at any rate, all is well.'

Suddenly she did not seem to want to know where her stepdaughter had been, and no longer had any interest, which was probably just as well.

'You dine in again tonight with Lord Marcus. I know you find him vastly entertaining, as everyone does.'

As she passed her Mercy thought how funny that was, for possibly the only amusement to be had from Lady Violet's brother was the very fact that he was *un*amusing. However tired out by the events of the day, she said nothing, but went on up to her bedroom, wishing in some strange way that she was back at Sister Angela's Nursing Home, where such things would seem not just superfluous, but faintly ridiculous.

She must change for dinner, but as she did so, with Clarice in close attendance, she was less interested in being entertained – or not – by Lord Marcus (who to her way of thinking seemed to be using her father's house in order to save on his own expenditure) than in thinking of her new friend. Mercy knew that her stepmother would not approve of such a friendship. She would say that Miss Lynch was *not quite the thing*, and steer Mercy towards some more suitable acquaintance with another girl about to step out into her first Season, but Mercy could not agree. She was resolved to be firm about this new friendship. She did not care that Leonie was perhaps not of the same upbringing, or of the same background. She knew she was good, and that surely was all that mattered?

The note said, *It is all arranged. Come at eleven o'clock on Wednesday – tomorrow – when I will meet you at the Church of the Holy Angels, East Sheen. The vicar leaves much to be desired, but he has agreed there will be music. LL*

There was not a shred of what the old Cordel great aunts and uncles would have called 'a goer' in Mercy's blood. She was, and would always remain, she knew, within the moral and mental outlines of her upbringing, but overriding all this was a sense of realism.

Long before she really knew about such things as deprivation, she was aware that there was a whole world, and a rather more important one perhaps, that moved and lived outside the small Society in which the Prince of Wales and his set revolved around each other in what sometimes seemed – to Mercy anyway – to be a constant, wearying, fashionable dance.

And so, having read Leonie's hand-written note, she hurriedly made arrangements for Clarice and herself to leave the following morning free for the mannequin's funeral, forgetting that she had also agreed, long before, to be 'looked over' by the Dowager Duchess of Clanborough, a formidable woman who was keen to meet Mercy as she had an elderly unmarried son whom she had long been trying to pass off on some unsuspecting debutante.

In their haste to rearrange everything, however, Clarice and Mercy forgot to take the note with them, hurrying off in a hansom cab to collect Leonie Lynch before going on to the service in East Sheen.

Inevitably, an hour after they left in such a hurry, the Dowager arrived as arranged and Mercy was sent for by her stepmother. Her room was found to be empty but the note was discovered by a house-maid, who brought it – with a somewhat excited expression – to the attention of Lady Violet, who, having read it herself, was forced to exercise the most exquisite self-control, as for a few terrible hours she lived with the idea that her stepdaughter might have run off to get married to some appallingly unsuitable personage. It did not occur to her that Mercy had in reality gone to attend the funeral of an unknown mannequin.

Although they could not have known it, as they crossed the park in a hansom together, Leonie and Mercy passed Dorinda riding out on her new brilliantly coloured, hair-matching, liver chestnut mare. They might have given her a glance, but certainly no more, for the Park that morning was crowded with the fashionable, and the less fashionable, not to mention the *demi-monde*, all anxious to be seen by each other and everyone else at their sparkling seasonal best. For in May and June London was the best place to be, and everyone, all over the world, knew it. The Empire was still the Empire and the world worshipped the English, for both their style and their elan, and nowhere were those qualities to be seen to a greater degree than in those months of early summer in London.

But as the hansom pulled over the river and turned right along the side of it, making its spanking clip-clop way out past elegant Regency houses to where various dukes and other noblemen kept up their shooting lodges, and Richmond Park lay basking in the early morning sunshine, and on towards a small church which stood conveniently not far from the main cemeteries that served the city, both girls' thoughts centred on the less than fashionable occasion ahead of them.

'Good morning, good morning.' The vicar was in brusque mood, and Mercy was very glad that she was wearing her best clothes – new clothes, as it happened. They were clothes such as the poor girl had no doubt often modelled; smartly fashionable for mourning, black close-fitted jacket, wide skirt, the whole set off by an immense hat.

Leonie was also dressed in newly purchased black, for formal mourning was, and always would be it seemed, a large part of their young lives. Being fitted for such clothes was as important as for any other ritual.

'Any more relatives of the deceased?' The vicar stared over their heads as if a trifle disappointed at such a poor showing of mourners.

Mercy answered, suddenly stern, 'No, we are her only mourners, vicar,' in her best clipped tones.

It was the Cordel coming out in her, and she knew it. Yet she could do nothing about it. It was there, always, that Cordel bit of her, even when she did not want it – she was always aware of its being ready to be used, although only for certain importunate people who seemed to her to lack grace or understanding.

'Do we pay you now, vicar?' Leonie put in, equally suddenly, all innocence.

Mercy, realizing at once that she was trying to be impertinent for the same reason that Mercy had been, refrained from looking at her friend, while all at once surrendering to an urge to give an imitation of one of her great aunts. This entailed staring straight ahead past the vicar, not wanting to take advantage of what she knew was going to be his disconcertion.

'Payment after the service will be quite time enough, I find,' came the frosty reply.

Seconds after that the service began.

Leonie could not concentrate. In some ways it was because she was too used to funerals. Not because the nursing home had many fatalities – far from it, as a matter of fact – but because she had grown up in Eastgate Street where, it sometimes seemed to her, there had always been someone about to go to heaven, and whoever it was, however little time they had spent in the street, all the neighbours had always attended their funeral.

As Leonie's foster mother said sometimes, 'Not least because of the wake, dear. They do like to mourn, of course, but they come to keep warm and for the food too, you know. Stop that, and no-one would come.'

Aisleen Lynch had always been in the habit of making small pies and custard tarts for these occasions – occasions when discreet amounts of both tea and sherry were ladled into cups (half of them usually on loan from someone else because a cracked cup was a mortal sin in Eastgate Street) and pallid cheeks became well flushed as a result of the much needed refreshments.

So death was just death in Eastgate Street, no more to be particularly remarked upon than new life, and sometimes greeted with rather more relief than the sound of a baby's first startling cry, heralding as it usually did yet another new mouth to feed.

'I chose "Away in a Manger" for one of the hymns, because although it is a Christmas hymn I did think it might have been one of her favourites,' Leonie told Mercy, as, after the service, they dutifully followed the simple coffin to the churchyard. 'And I chose a white coffin, because although she was not quite a child she seemed to be hardly more, don't you think?'

Mercy nodded. She did not need to be asked to think, as it happened, because she had much to think about at that moment. The funeral, the coffin, Leonie's lovely singing voice – rather more lovely than Mercy's own – but most of all Clarice's face when she realized that they were required to go on to the churchyard, for, as she hissed to her young mistress before they both climbed into the waiting hansom after Leonie, 'I 'ave jus' remembered that the dowager duchess were coming thees morning!' All these thoughts were more than enough for Mercy as they returned to London.

'Will it be all right with your stepmother, do you think, that you have come?' Leonie asked anxiously as they parted an hour later.

'Yes, of course,' Mercy said in as reassuring a way as was possible, given that her heart was already thumping twice as fast as normal just thinking of the anger that she must have incurred.

'You mean no, do you not?'

'No. I came because I wished to, and for no other reason. Let us be glad that the poor little

139

mannequin had the three of us to throw earth upon her coffin. I will call and see you soon at Sister Angela's, you may be sure.'

'You are in trouble—'

'No, no, not at all. Please, it is of no matter.'

Leonie waved the hansom goodbye, although the occupants could not have possibly seen her, and then walked slowly back to Mrs Dodd's house. She could not imagine what would happen to Miss Cordel now that she knew she had been expected to be at home, and she could only hope and pray for her.

Once more Lady Violet stood at the top of the stairs and looked down at Mercy and Clarice, but this time she was not in full evening dress, and certainly not in a good mood.

'Follow me to the drawing room,' she commanded Mercy.

Clarice muttered *'Mon dieu, la pauvre'* under her breath and sped away to the upper reaches of the house where she could, and doubtless would, stay out of Lady Violet's way for the rest of the week.

Mercy followed her stepmother into the elegant first floor drawing room with its light turquoise paint and its gilded paintings, its immense flower vases and its *florions*. Mercy did not know what florions were exactly but she knew there were a great many within the decorative patterns of the plasterwork of the room because Lord Marcus had told her so.

'What do you mean by this?'

Lady Violet produced the note that Leonie had sent round to Mercy the previous day. Staring at it for the second time, Mercy realized suddenly why there was such an atmosphere in the house, why her stepmother was white to the lips, Leonie's was a message that could so easily be misinterpreted.

'I can explain, Step-maman.'

'I would imagine that you will have an explanation,' her stepmother said tightly. 'I can not imagine, however, what you *will* explain. I will be immensely interested, as you may know, since I have had to explain your absence – albeit with your maid, thank the Lord – to the Dowager Duchess of Clanborough who, you may also imagine, was more than surprised to find that you were not at home as expected. I passed off your absence as a medical emergency, your having had to have been rushed off to Sloane Square with a bad tooth. Now, you may now pass off your excuses on me and I will see whether or not to believe them.'

Mercy took a deep breath, as well she might.

'To begin at the beginning. This note is from Leonie Lynch, a nurse at Sister Angela's Nursing Home. Do you remember when the mannequin passed out at Madame Chloe's?' Mercy could see that Lady Violet hardly could, for the simple reason that it was such a very trivial occurrence. 'Well. As it happens, I went to Sister Angela's with her, and afterwards I – well, I kept on visiting her. Not for long, though – and always with Clarice, of course. Because, well, I felt so sorry for her.'

'Your wretched lame ducks again – you silly gel.'

141

How and when will we cure you of your bleeding heart?'

There was a long silence as her stepdaughter stared up at her.

'Quite so,' Mercy said, suddenly icy, because of a sudden she had become once more 'Cordel' and remembered that her stepmother was *not* a Cordel. It was only for a second or two, but it was enough, and, oddly, she saw that Lady Violet had perhaps remembered it too. For some reason she stepped back, and sat down. Mercy remained standing in front of her, since she had not been invited to sit, but preferring to do so anyway, as it happened.

'Continue.'

'The young mannequin. She was unconscious to the last, alas, and subsequently died. Today was her funeral, the expenses for which I had undertaken myself, from my pin money, because I felt not just sorry for her but in some way responsible, since it was I for whom she was modelling the ball dress – the one which she collapsed in, if you remember?'

'Yes, yes, yes, I understand, but oh the boredom of it, Mercy! But thank God at any rate that you are at home. Do not let us refer to it again, shall we? All is well, and now we can just get on with the Season and its delights. But I do beseech you, Mercy, while in London, forget about your conscience, forget about your lame ducks, and *smile* a little! You look like a wet week in Wensleydale, I do assure you. No-one is going to want to dance with you, you know.'

Mercy stared at her stepmother, but not for long, because this was all so like her. Just as you thought she was going to explode, she smiled. And the moment would have passed. She had always been like this, reassuringly so, one minute all thunder and lightning and the next back to fun and laughter, bringing some colour to Mercy's pallid cheeks.

It was only when she had left the room 'late for luncheon, my sweetest, with a certain personage for whom no-one must be late, but he will forgive me, I know, for he always does!' that Mercy at last sat down, and rather abruptly, for she had suddenly realized that had she not had an adequate explanation for Leonie Lynch's note she would have been ruined.

If she had been out without Clarice, or somewhere that could not be substantiated, and word got out – as 'word' via the servants had a habit of doing – she would have been sent straight back to Somerset, and there would be no chance of her ever being able to marry within her own class. She would be considered damaged goods, and those goods would be confined to the schoolroom to teach any small children who had been left – as children were wont to be – to grow up at Cordel Court, or to the linen room or the still room, and no-one would have even cast a look in her direction again. Overnight she would have become 'poor ruined Aunt Mercy, you know, such a scandal and in only the first weeks of her Season. No-one would touch her.'

That night Mercy knelt by her bedside and prayed for the young girl upon whose coffin she had thrown earth that morning, but what she could not get out of her mind was the tall man in the impeccable black hat who had appeared from nowhere at the burial in the cemetery.

Tired out at dinner by Lord Marcus and his fascination with gossip and trivia, Mercy fell asleep, forgetting as she did so that for one second she had seemed to recognize the dark looks of the man in the churchyard.

Six

Dorinda had caused a scandal. She had not meant to, but the truth was that she had. The fact that she had caused a scandal by doing nothing more than riding out with Lord 'Crosstitch', as the poor fellow was now permanently nicknamed, was not exactly her fault, and to give him his due Gervaise was the first to acknowledge this.

What happened was that she had been riding amicably, and for her really rather beautifully, in Rotten Row, when they had stopped to greet a friend and ardent admirer of 'Dorinda Blue', as Dorinda was now known throughout fashionable London.

Unfortunately the friend tried, for some reason best known to himself, to muscle in on Lord Crosswaite's position by the railings, at which his lordship, being a man, and so naturally ready to see insult whenever or wherever even vaguely possible, dismounted from his horse and prepared to throw a punch at him.

On seeing the really quite flattering little incident suddenly turning ugly Dorinda did as she knew all fashionable young women must at such a time. She promptly, and quite beautifully, fainted.

Naturally this had an immediate effect upon the two men who turned their attention away from each other and towards her. But without any doubt whatsoever, it also caused a stir among those who were riding in Rotten Row. News of the incident eventually reached the ears of the Prince of Wales despite the fact that he himself had not been out that morning, on account of feeling not quite the thing.

Although really very set in his ways now, it seemed that His Royal Highness had suffered through just too many scandals of his own to want any more within his circle, and so he had sent for Gervaise, and the conversation had quickly turned upon the reason for this too public argument.

'Is she very beautiful?'

'Yes, Sir.'

'And her name is . . . ?'

'At this time, Sir, everyone calls her 'Dorinda Blue' because of the colour of her riding habit. It is a colour that I have to say suits her chestnut hair quite admirably. It is a kind of—' But His Royal Highness was already bored and so, in dread, as everyone was, that the heavy eyelids might continue to droop, Gervaise had quickly finished, '—the kind of blue with which men dream of surrounding a woman with red gold hair, you understand, Sir. Dorinda Blue's eyes really are quite dreadfully fascinating.'

Nowadays his stocks and his shares, his yields from railroads, his friend Sir Ernest Cassel who was making the royal mistress Mrs Keppel rich

146

beyond even her own husband's dreams, were of far more interest than love-making to the future King of England and Emperor of India.

But so romantically sincere did Gervaise sound that the royal eyelids suddenly reverted to their less drooped position and he nodded, saying in his guttural accent, 'Red gold hair is always charming in a woman, I too find. You must bring Dorinda Blue to one of our little supper parties, after the theatre. I should be charmed to meet her.'

A flash of the rubies on his plump fingers, a nod of the balding head, and the great figure had turned away, his mind already on something, or someone else. As to Gervaise himself, shortly afterwards he made his excuses and fled back to his town house, his wife, and his children, wondering with something of a sinking heart what would be the result of taking Dorinda to one of 'our little supper parties'.

Supper parties after the theatre were traditionally all-male affairs, and the women who were brought in to make them more 'amusing' were chosen because they were known to be more availing than the wives and the daughters, the aunts and the nieces, of the men who attended these discreet gatherings. Yet, beautiful and amusing though they might be, they were also the kind of women that Gervaise well knew the female members of his family *avoided*, even with their eyes.

Over the previous twenty years the Marlborough House set, which the future King of England had long dominated, had been rent apart by feuds.

Some whom the Prince of Wales had counted on as friends had proved to be very far from so, and, as happens with any group who start out young together, not many of those who had been happy to sow their wild oats with Queen Victoria's son and heir in his salad days now remained in the same set to lighten the dullness of his late middle age. Instead, to take the place of those companions of his youth, there was 'Little Mrs George', as Mrs Keppel was known.

She was always at the centre of everything that was modish, and thought to be a cool-minded individual who had helped to calm His Royal Highness, providing among other things charming conversation, bridge, and a regular and apparently enjoyable little domestic interlude in the late afternoon when he called on her for 'pleasure and tea'.

None of this was, as yet, of the slightest consequence to Dorinda, who on this particular afternoon had been happily engaged in the redecoration of her suite of rooms until a carriage drove up to the front door and deposited an enormous bouquet of malmaisons in her small hall.

As soon as she saw them, knowing the male sex as she was just, it seemed to her, beginning to do, Dorinda's heart sank. Large bouquets of flowers, most especially expensive malmaisons, were not normally sent by a lady's lover without reason. What more did Gervaise want of her?

'There is to be a little supper party, and His Royal Highness . . .'

Dorinda was not so provincial that she did not

know of 'little supper parties' and how 'the Jersey Lily' had met His Royal Highness at just one of these, thereby insuring her social success until, most unfortunately, she gave birth to a 'mistake'.

Breaking the rules could not be forgiven, and so after that Society had been forced to turn their backs on her charming company and beautiful face. In her turn Lillie Langtry, like many another of her kind, had been forced by financial circumstances to take to the stage, which she did with great aplomb and considerable success.

It had all been most regrettable, really, but it had to be said for the Prince of Wales – Dorinda's mother had hinted in veiled terms – he did not, as some men might have done, abandon his Lillie from Jersey after the birth of her *petite betise*. Far from leaving her in the lurch, he took a large party to attend the first night of her play in the theatre, thus ensuring her lasting success in her new career. So, all in all, from this and other generous acts, Dorinda knew that 'Bertie' was a good man.

Yet she still dreaded meeting him, and there was a good reason for this. She knew that 'meeting' the Prince of Wales would not entail just shaking hands. Normally, for a woman like herself who had, by force of circumstances, become a member of the *demi-monde*, this would not have mattered. Indeed, it was considered to be the ultimate compliment. But it was different for her, despite her change in status from wife to mistress.

She stared down the table at the reason for the

difference, who was at that moment sampling what appeared to be a particularly satisfying glass of claret. Her enchanting, handsome Gervaise. He was so naughty, and yet so brilliant! She could not lie to herself about him, she adored him, and the thought of perhaps turning him in for the ageing Prince of Wales was not even a tiny bit appealing to her. Dorinda did not mind that she was not Gervaise's wife – in fact she rather thought that she had the much better part of the amorous bargain. She enjoyed her status and freedom as his mistress a great deal more than she could or would, it seemed to her, enjoy being his spouse. She just did not want to be passed on to the future King of England at the moment. It would be – well, muddling.

But being a shrewd young woman Dorinda also knew that it was her duty to be much less than truthful to her lover, or else he would not remain her lover. Her mother had always told her that men did not like the truth, in any form whatsoever. They did not like sentimentality. Most of all they did not like displays of emotion.

So, having waited until Gervaise finished his wine, Dorinda murmured, 'I should be happy to attend a supper party whenever His Royal Highness commands me.'

Even as she said it her heart was sinking and she suddenly saw that she might have a future that did not include her beautiful Gervaise, who fascinated and entertained her, spoilt her and cosseted her, but included instead a not-so-young prince.

Gervaise stared down the table at Dorinda. For his part her words were something he, in truth, had dreaded to hear. He did not want his Dorinda Blue to join that long line of ladies who could not wait to display their physical charms to delight the future king.

Nor did he wish that same future king to pick on his adorable mistress as his next *amour*, but what could he do? There would be a scandal within his set should he refuse to take her to supper. He realized, sadly, that he might lose the current delight of his life, for much as he loved his dear, kind wife, for him Dorinda Blue was something quite other.

Leonie was standing still in the hall of the nursing home, pausing for a few seconds between checking on patients and thinking of nothing much at all, other than that her feet were aching at the end of a long day, when the fat gentleman with the cigar passed her once more.

She could not believe the bad luck of it. For here she was again, cowering in the dark shadows of the hall as he trod heavily by, the smoke from his cigar mingling with the quite overpowering smell of his eau de Portugal. It was strange, and at the same time most unfortunate, that this very important personage always seemed to pass Leonie when he was making what was obviously meant to be a *discreet* exit from Sister Angela's. It was as if fate kept throwing her in front of him, as if he was meant to meet her, which she very well knew that

151

she was not, for the Prince of Wales did not meet young women like Leonie socially, and they certainly did not meet him.

At last she heard the hall door close behind him. Feeling more than relieved, not to mention amazed, that he had in fact exited into a hansom cab of all things, Leonie hurried off into the wet spring night. Happily, Mrs Dodd's house was so near to the nursing home that it was easy to just shoot up an umbrella and run through the light rain to her godmother's front door.

As she ran through the London rain Leonie thought of the Prince of Wales, for she was almost sure that it was he who had passed her both times. So sure was she that as the rain splashed around her buttoned boots and off her large black umbrella she fell to wondering what it was that had brought such a distinguished personage to the nursing home.

As she ran on, the rain beginning to dampen her coat, she fancied that, despite the scandals that had dogged him in previous years, the Prince of Wales must probably be a very kind man who had taken to visiting some especially sick friend. She knew of course that she would probably never find out the true reason for his presence at Sister Angela's, for it was not the kind of place where people asked questions. The unspoken rule at Sister Angela's was that what was, just *was*, and no-one was encouraged to say anything about what happened there, not to each other, not to anyone, perhaps not even to themselves. Once they had hung up their stiff white starched aprons and hurried off into the evening everyone knew that whatever had passed there had passed, and discretion was all that mattered.

Reaching Mrs Dodd's front door at last, Leonie put up her key to the lock, but before she could turn it the housemaid had already opened to her. She smiled at 'Miss Leonie' as she was known in the Dodd household, and Leonie, shaking her umbrella, smiled back at her as she stepped into the hall. The maid took the gamp from her, the hall light playing kindly on the servant's crisp uniform, her tidy hair, her polished shoes.

'Thank you, Mavis.'

Leonie had not yet become used to the felicity of having a maid open the door to her on any night, but on such a cold rainy night as this it was particularly welcoming.

'My dear, Leonie, my dear.'

Mrs Dodd's expression of greeting was full of her usual good humoured kindness, but when Leonie stared up into her godmother's small, boot button curranty brown eyes she realized that she was more than worried about something, she was most anxious. She could see as she mounted the stairs towards her that Mrs Dodd's colour was heightened, and her costume of dull maroon with black silk lacings appeared to be a little too tight for her, because her breathing was a great deal faster than it normally was. Leonie privately feared that she might be going to have an attack of the 'pulps' as palpitations were called in the Dodds' household.

'My dear, come quickly. Come up at once, to my sit— to my drawing room. Would you come?'

Leonie could only wonder as she dutifully trod up the patterned stair carpet to the first floor what it was that was worrying her godmother. What could she have to talk about that was so urgent?

'It was Madame Chloe, my dear. She came round, only an hour ago, and she told me of your – well – *excursion* with Miss Cordel. How you both took it upon yourselves to look after this young mannequin. And Leonie dear, alas, that Lady Violet has taken a strong dislike to you on this account!'

Mrs Dodd put a small, plump hand to her lips and there was a pause as she swallowed hard, while Leonie, in her turn, realized the implications, possibly endless, behind the words.

For a second or two Leonie saw Eastgate Street looming once again, a front door with a step whitened weekly by chalk, a geranium in the window, but also a bed shared with her foster mother's visiting children, and no crisply uniformed maid opening the front door to her, no warm fires in every room, no endless steaming hot water, no beds warmed with a ceramic brick, no cool linen sheets.

'The whole disaster turns on the fact that the Duchess of Clanborough had to be put off. She was there, waiting to look Miss Cordel over. It was too awful. It seems that because of this incident Lady Violet has threatened to withdraw her custom from Madame Chloe and to induce her friends to do the same should you be seen, you know, nursing people together, or whatever it was that the two of you were intent upon doing.'

Mrs Dodd's handkerchief was now dabbing her lips.

'Oh dear, oh dear, Leonie, we cannot have this any more, dear. You must know that you are not one of *them*, dear. You are – well, you are – well, you know, dear . . .' Mrs Dodd's handkerchief conducted some unseen orchestra now. 'Well, dear. It is difficult for you to understand, but you are one of *us*. Although . . .' she paused, her mind struggling towards a newer and more difficult thought. 'Although of course to us, to your foster mother and myself, since your mother was from the aristocracy, you are one of *them*. That is very true.' After a long pause while she swam slowly towards this last thought, and then on to the next, she began again. 'But you see, dear, *they* do not know anything about your *mother*. They would think of you as simply one of *us*. And that being so – and this is so important to know, dear – they could not possibly accept you as one of *them* D'you see?'

Exhausted with what was, to her, the ultimate statement on Society and its rules – the *them* and *us* of it, as it were – Mrs Dodd collapsed on the sofa behind her, and waved her handkerchief about her face.

'I should hate to let you down, in any way at all, my dear godmother.'

Her godmother looked across at Leonie and nodded in sad agreement.

'Oh, I know that, dear. It is just that this is such a hard lesson to learn, most especially for you, coming as you do from Eastgate Street, and yet not *originating* from Eastgate Street, having been fostered by dear Mrs Lynch the way you were.

'You see, dear, I really do understand that it is really rather awkward for you in many respects, but nevertheless I must ask you to repeat this valuable lesson to me, so that we may both know, once and for all, that we are, as Lady Angela would say, *as one* on this.'

Leonie frowned, and after a small pause, she said, 'They, the aristocracy, are *them*.' At this her godmother nodded with satisfaction, as if she was listening to a singer hitting top C. 'On the other hand,' her goddaughter continued, '*we* are "them" to them. And *not* us.' Again came a nod of satisfaction. 'We have to remember that just as we are them to *them*, so they are *us* to themselves.'

Mrs Dodd sighed.

'Just so, exactly. We are not *them*. I knew you would understand. This is just how it is, dear, and must always be accepted. The *them* and the *us* of Society. Once understood, never forgotten, Leonie dear.'

Leonie nodded, again in agreement. She quite saw that she *must* never forget. Nor must she ever put a foot wrong again. She sighed inwardly. It was a pity. She had liked Miss Cordel so much, but there it was. It had to be accepted. She was one of them, and Miss Cordel was 'one of us'.

There was not the smallest regret on Mrs Dodd's

side, and she now nodded, satisfied that her protégée and goddaughter had seen the error of her ways and would never again mistake persons such as Lady Violet or Miss Cordel for her equals.

'Change into your Chinese tea gown, dear Leonie, and we will take supper together in front of the fire, here. Just the two of us, all cosy and nice. And then you will oblige me by reading to me, perhaps, dear? I have to say that the dear nuns' elocution lessons certainly paid off. You have such a pretty voice, although doubtless that is – well, it just might be something that you inherited, too, dear, from your mother's side. Voices are inherited, I believe.'

Mrs Dodd, despite her lecture on the *them* and the *us* of Society, loved to refer to Leonie's mysterious parentage, knowing as she did that her poor dead mother had been from an aristocratic background. Such had not been the case with Leonie's foster mother, Mrs Lynch. She had been less than impressed by her foster daughter's aristocratic blood. Indeed it often seemed to Leonie that her dearly beloved foster mother was more than a little embarrassed by this sad fact, seeing that side of Leonie as a hindrance to 'getting on'.

'We don't want any of your la-di-da ways around here, little Miss Lynch,' she would say if Leonie objected to anything that any of her older brothers and sisters might be doing. 'There's no point in being an aristocrat if you ain't got no castle, as my dad was always saying. No point at all.'

It always seemed to Leonie that Mrs Lynch had a deep suspicion of the aristocracy, considering the upper echelons to be much worse than they should be, and loose in their morals. But, worst of all, loose with their money, a sin in her mind in anyone, but most of all in the very rich.

'What you want in a rich man, to my view, is someone with an impecunious way with him that will not set the noses of others out of jointure, and will not neither put it in the minds of others to cut off his head. When you see a rich man you don't want someone to say *I wish I was him*, you want to say *How nice to see such a nice man with gentle ways not behaving like a Rajah*, that's what you want.'

All this oft repeated wisdom from her childhood ran through Leonie's head as she walked up the stairs to her bedroom to change. For a moment she despaired of her particular position in society. Neither fish, nor flesh, nor good red herring, but a half and halfer who would never, truly, fit in. By the time she reached the corridor outside her bedroom she was seeing herself as a motley figure, the top half blonde haired and turquoise of eye, the bottom half all serge stockings and heavy boots.

And yet she was never far from being able to be cheered up, and there was no doubt that the thought of a delicious and soothing supper in front of the fire with Mrs Dodd was very inviting. Also, she liked to hear about the mother she had never known, although she had realized that she must have been a bad girl, or she would not have given birth to Leonie.

Of one thing Leonie was quite sure and that was that she did not want to be *like* her mother, always described by Aisleen Lynch as 'a poor patrician creature, God rest her, who made a mistake in life only to pay for it with her death.'

For her part, as she waited for Leonie to return, it occurred to Mrs Dodd that such a sensible girl as Leonie would never do or say anything to hurt her friends or acquaintances in any way, much less – in the case of poor Madame Chloe – their trade. It would have been, Mrs Dodd decided as she helped herself to an evening cordial with a dash of fortification slipped into it, it would have been Miss Cordel who became involved with the unfortunate young mannequin.

All that insistence on taking her to Sister Angela's Nursing Home, that was Miss Cordel, not Leonie. Leonie would not have wanted to make a show of herself in that way. Over the years Mrs Dodd had observed it to be an unfortunate characteristic of aristocratic circles that they would, and did, find it necessary to repay Society for its undoubted munificence to them by trying to do good wherever, and whenever, possible.

Or as her friend Madame Chloe had said, somewhat pithily, 'forever sticking their noses where they shouldn't and making it harder for the rest of us lower mortals to get on with our lives, God help us!' No, Mrs Dodd told herself, she knew that Leonie had too much *sense* to have made a fuss about such a worthless girl as the mannequin most likely was, a girl of no consequence, a girl who was only one step up from the streets; a bad girl, undoubtedly. A foolish girl, assuredly, up from the country and bound to fall into trouble. It was Miss Cordel who insisted on taking this most unsuitable young person to Sister Angela's Nursing Home. Such a committed act of spontaneous and impulsive charity would not have been forthcoming from a former incumbent of Eastgate Street. The narrow street where Leonie had received her upbringing was not given to crying over worthless little mannequins, girls who often came to London already in a parlous state, who would alight from trains all innocent and stupid, only to be bought by the first man or madam who met them at the station. Coming from Eastgate Street Leonie did not suffer from a 'bleeding heart', she had seen too much of poor people to feel sorry for them, been too poor herself. It was only people who had never been poor, who lived off the earnings of others, who kept trying to make those same others' lives better. Unrealistic to a fault, that was the aristocracy.

Mrs Dodd sat back, staring into the fire. Her fortifying cordial had made her feel much better. A crisis had, thank goodness, been avoided. She felt most strongly that all would now proceed smoothly, Leonie would become a right hand of Lady Angela, and she would live to be proud of the little orphaned girl whom she had placed that cold and rainy night with her friend Mrs Lynch in Eastgate Street.

Upstairs in her heavily draped bedroom with its

mahogany bed and large, inlaid mahogany cupboards and dressing mirror, Leonie stared at herself thoughtfully in the large looking glass.

This part of London, this new part that she now inhabited, seemed to be full of so many pitfalls. Thanks to her upbringing she had thought she knew a little of how to go on, but now she realized that she had known nothing at all, and it seemed to her now that everywhere she turned there was some new pitfall to be avoided, some new way that she should not behave, some new place where she should not be, and all of these hazards not really hidden, but waiting to pounce.

As she stared into her undoubtedly beautiful turquoise eyes, Leonie chided her mirrored reflection severely. She must be more careful. She did not want to jeopardize whatever future she might have by putting one of her slender feet on the wrong path and earning herself an ignominious or shaming dismissal from Sister Angela's Nursing Home.

Eyes down, girl, from now on! she instructed herself, before changing into the fine Chinese tea gown so recently purchased for her by Mrs Dodd.

She turned back once more to the long mirror and sighed, this time with pleasure in the beautiful tea gown that was now affording her so much welcome relief from her underclothes and the whalebones of her corset, not to mention the starch of her uniform.

Yes, it is eyes down from now on, Leonie Lynch. And that means right down. Wherever you are. It does not matter where you are, you have seen nothing – most of all you have never, ever seen the future King of England on a private visit to Sister Angela's and taking a hansom cab home. Not ever!

As to Miss Cordel, and here Leonie sighed to herself, she would have to continue on her lonely way. To be presented at Court, go to Ascot, attend evening balls – in fact do whatever girls from her impeccable background did during their few months on the 'marriage mart', as Mrs Dodd and Madame Chloe always called the London Season – and that would be that.

It was quite clear to Leonie that it was impossible for herself and Miss Cordel to go on being friends, or even acquaintances. It would hurt too many people. Besides, if Leonie was realistic, Miss Cordel had really no need of her. Once the Season swung into life she would have a hundred friends from whom to choose. Their circumstances were far too far apart – whole worlds apart. As far apart as Sister Angela's Nursing Home and Eastgate Street, really, now that she came to think of it.

And not only that – and here Leonie smiled at her image in the mirror – she was enjoying herself far too much.

Her resolution not to be friends with Miss Cordel any more was just as much to do with that as it was to do with any generous feelings towards her godmother and mentor, Mrs Dodd, and not to admit as much would be really very wrong.

Leonie's life was as grand as she would ever

want it to be. As a matter of fact it was twice as grand and luxurious as she had ever dared to imagine it could be. She had no wish to meet some aristocratic or other gentleman and marry him. The guiding rule of her life was that *she did not want to be like her mother* and die in childbirth. What she wanted most in the world was to be like Lady Angela – elegant, beautiful, and unmarried. She did not want to be dependent on some man who would betray her, as she realized her own young mother – whoever she had been – must have been betrayed. Leonie wanted only to come back to her godmother in the evenings, to go on wearing fashionable clothes made by Madame Chloe and bought by Mrs Dodd. In other words, she wanted to go on enjoying life at just the level she had now reached.

She loved her godmother, albeit that she had funny ways of being and doing. She loved being in this part of London. And Leonie was quite sure, more sure than she had ever been of anything, that she did not want *more*.

More was what she sensed when she heard that old gentleman coming downstairs smoking his cigar. *More* would be deeper and deeper curtsies, taking her into deeper and deeper waters, and the higher she flew, Leonie instinctively felt, the greater could be her fall. Most of all, more than anything, the memory of those wretched women in the poor house kept her from ever wanting to fall anywhere, except, as she thought she had now fallen, on her own two elegant feet.

Happily Mercy Cordel did not know of the resolution made by the girl whom she had come to think of as her friend. Indeed, if she had known, it might have been difficult for her to register any emotions concerning it, for it seemed to her that she had never felt so cold – what she herself always called 'inside cold' – nor longed so much to be somewhere, anywhere, other than where she was at that moment, seated on a gilt chair at yet another ball – it seemed like her thirtieth – behind the beautiful and ever fascinating Lady Violet.

The coldness, Mercy knew, sprang from the inescapable realization that she was a social failure. It was not as if her dress had not been carefully chosen, nor her hair beautifully arranged. The dress she was wearing was perfect for her in every way. She knew this because Lady Violet had particularly selected it to go with her brown hair.

Coral and brown are perfect together, my dear. Mercy could still hear the voice of her stepmother – as Mercy had come down the stairs to muted applause from the servants. *Perfect, my dear, perfect. You will dance all evening and your feet will never touch the ground!*

The servants had applauded again, knowing that Lady Violet was the acme of elegance and beauty. Being so proud of their mistress as they were, they liked to applaud both her and her pronouncements on semi-state occasions such as departures for balls.

'Oh, Miss Mercy, I just do not know how it must feel to be you,' one of the maids had said this particular evening, while handing Clarice the hairpins to fasten diamond stars into the back of Mercy's raised and coiled hair. 'Every evening when we see you dressed and ready for yet another ball, I think you must be in heaven, you must really!'

If only that little maid had known just how much Mercy longed to be her at that moment. Wearing yet another dress that seemed to her to turn her skin the colour of putty, Mercy was all too aware, after endless balls and routs, that she was doomed to failure in the ballroom, whereas doubtless the young maid, on her monthly day off, probably went home to her 'beau' and was the greatest success possible in whatever she chose to do, or wherever she chose to go, on that most special, and treasured, of days.

Lady Violet turned to Mercy and said, rather too loudly Mercy felt, 'Do not worry, Mercy, my dear, there will be a dancing partner along quite soon. I know there will be. Quite, quite soon. It is just rather trying for us all, the wait and so on, do you know? Just so trying, waiting for a partner to put his name in your card, dear. I do so hate you always having to sit among the chaperons. If only you had a brother with whom you could dance, what a difference that would make, would it not? But there, your brothers are with their regiments, and nothing to be done.'

It was quite clear that Lady Violet, unlike so

many who chaperoned the young, had decided to take each ball as a great event of enormous interest. Not for her the bored yawns and the surreptitious glances towards some timepiece of the other chaperons and dowagers who sat upright and eagle-eyed watching for the time to pass. Rather, she preferred to take a lively interest in who danced with whom, and as of that minute who did *not* dance with whom.

'My dear, did you see?' she said suddenly to Mercy from behind her fan. 'Lord Haskett is taking Miss Bouverie de Blanche into the conservatory. And she hardly yet out!'

Mercy did not look up. She preferred to stare at her feet rather than observe this minor sensation of the London Season. She did not want to be taken into any conservatory. Nor did she want to dance, really. She just wanted to go home and read a book, but to admit as much to anyone, anyone at all, would be to earn herself a reputation as a blue stocking, and it was bad enough being a brown mouse without being known as a blue stocking as well.

'Might I see your card, Miss Cordel?'

A young officer glanced down at Mercy's card with momentary interest as she and Lady Violet passed him on their way to find some lemonade.

'Of course,' said Lady Violet, immediately speaking for Mercy, and at the same time giving the officer her most dazzling smile, a smile which was instantly and quite understandably returned in kind. 'Show Sir Perry your card, Mercy, my dear.'

Mercy held up her card for the young man to

write in it. Her mother had left her a gold bracelet attached to which was a small gold pencil, for just the use to which she now fervently hoped the young officer would put it, namely to scribble his name in her card.

Oh, please, please, God, help him to just put his name in my card. Just one name in it, for once, please!

The young man, handsome and slim with dark hair almost as polished and black as his boots, glanced down at the card, and seeing it quite empty of any other names looked briefly at Mercy – without his eyes lighting up, it had to be admitted.

Nevertheless, he did seem to be about to make use of the precious little gold pencil when Lady Violet said, 'As everyone knows, my stepdaughter has weak ankles. That is why her card is always so empty, nothing to do with her appeal. Too annoying for her, would not you say?'

The officer glanced down at Mercy's quite elegant little feet and looked momentarily put out.

'How too, too tiresome for you!'

'Yes it is, too tiresome,' Mercy agreed miserably, hardly able to believe her ears.

'In that case might I ask you for the pleasure, Lady Violet? Seeing that Miss Cordel is not quite up to it?'

'Sir Perry! How amusing you are, to be sure! Good heavens, I am not a debutante, you know, by any means.'

'Yet I know you will say yes, for you are quite as fresh as any here tonight.'

'It is not done, Sir Perry, and you very well know it.'

Lady Violet laughed, pretending to be shocked, but hugely enjoying the moment.

'Then it should be done, Lady Violet. There are none as beautiful as you dancing. I promise you, once on the floor you will be the toast of the Season yet again.'

'Oh, dear. Well, if you insist.'

As Lady Violet, head held high, presented herself on the ballroom floor, to the open astonishment of all present, Mercy once more settled back on her wretched little gold chair, her cheeks flushed with the embarrassment of it all.

She sat down in a flurry, making sure that she was behind a large pot plant where her continuing failure to find a partner would be hidden from the majority view. Little wonder she had not enjoyed any partners at any of the balls, if her stepmother had given out that Mercy had weak ankles and could not dance. What a cruel thing to go round saying. She could hardly believe it. But then, since she loved her stepmother, it seemed to her that she must have said this to protect Mercy in some way. That would have to be it. Lady Violet would have felt nothing but protective towards her stepdaughter. Indeed, Mercy could well remember how embarrassed Lady Violet used to be for her, and anxious to point out how Mercy could improve her dancing and deportment. How she should hold her head, and so on. Constant improvement had been the theme of Mercy's upbringing and she had always, until now, been most grateful. She had always seen Lady Violet's side of things, which was that Mercy, because of her lack of looks, had to try *harder*.

But, as the dance wore on, and despite trying to be reasonable, the miserable thought *would* keep coming back that Lady Violet had announced that Mercy had weak ankles less to help Mercy out of the embarrassment of having a blank card than because she herself was bored to ribbons with sitting it out for yet another ball with the rest of the chaperons.

It had to be faced that Mercy's beautiful young stepmother could not wait to take to the floor.

Mercy sighed inwardly. Whatever the reason Lady Violet had spoken as she had, there was no getting away from her own lack of social success. If she was to be honest, given her dull looks, she was really unsurprised to see that Sir Perry was finding Lady Violet infinitely more interesting and amusing than Mercy Cordel, who it must be said was hardly going to turn a head even on the brightest evening. She had been a failure at the start of the Season, and now, as Ascot approached, she was about to be a failure at its end.

She would be returned to Cordel Court, an unwanted parcel, destination unknown – except it *was* known. She would become part of the vast team of unmarried women who serviced old houses, unmarried women whose feelings were supposedly put on the shelf, like their marriage prospects, whose frustrations with life and its endless greyness would manifest themselves in occasional fainting fits, or endless miles of tapestries.

To take her mind off her feelings of ignominy and embarrassment, Mercy switched her thoughts back to the undoubted glories of Cordel Court. To the birds and the trees, the flowers that would even now be blooming in the warm May night, the dawn chorus to which she loved to awaken. She thought longingly of how quiet it would be there at this moment. No wretched orchestras, or elegant young men, and above all no utterly miserable young girl sitting it out on a gilt chair of incredible discomfort, fanning herself while at the same time keeping her eyes from straying in any direction. Around the old house there would be just nature, straggling and struggling, beautiful and bold, but understandable too somehow, certainly to her, in a way that London and its Season was not.

'My dear Miss Cordel, might I have the pleasure?'

Mercy looked up at a tall, dark man, older than Sir Perry, because, although he had the same kind of thick dark hair, his was greying at the sides. He also had dark eyes but with an older, more bored look to them. Yet altogether the face was very handsome, and what was better, it was smiling down at her.

'I am sorry, really, but I don't think so. I mean I don't think I can give you the pleasure, because I am not really dancing. Indeed I have been sitting on a gilt chair for so long now, I think I have probably forgotten how to dance at all.'

'Oh, and why is that?'

'Because,' Mercy replied with her usual candour, 'my stepmother was so mortified, quite properly of course, that I had not been asked by anyone – not for the whole Season, and certainly no-one here tonight – for the pleasure of any dance that it seems she has given out that I have weak ankles. So should I leap up and prove to Sir Perry, with whom she is now dancing, that my ankles are perfectly all right, I will make her out to be telling some sort of a lie, albeit a kindly meant one.'

The tall, dark, older man looked towards Lady Violet and Sir Perry, his expression thoughtful for a second. They undoubtedly presented a fine sight together, Lady Violet being so tall and elegant and the young man quite the same.

'Sir Perry is a brilliant dancer, we must give him that at least! And being a hereditary knight he is obviously intent on being dashing and courtly, and who can blame him for that either?' he asked, but he turned back to look down at Mercy in some amusement.

Mercy nodded, yet, determined as she had suddenly become to be frank, she could not let go of her point of view. If she had to remain seated for yet another ignominious evening, watching everyone else enjoying themselves, she might as well be truthful about her situation, and that would be that.

'Oh, yes, you are quite right, he is a brilliant dancer,' she agreed. 'But, do you see, Sir Perry was my one chance to remove myself from this wretched gilt chair? My first and only chance for the whole Season, a Season in which I have been not just a complete failure but almost, I think, a famous one, if there can be such a thing.'

He laughed again, and looked at Mercy appreciatively.

'If you truly can not dance, I shall be forced to join you on a chair, and pretend to be a dowager chaperone, for there is no-one else in this whole room with whom I would rather dance at this moment, I promise you.'

'Oh but I can dance.' Throwing care to the winds, Mercy sprang up suddenly. 'I can dance all evening, I assure you, and what is more I love dancing, more than anything in the world, except swimming in the sea.'

'In that case, as I see you are walking perfectly, will you please do me the honour, Miss Cordel?'

'How do you do?'

'John Brancaster. Quite well, thank you.'

He bowed, smiling, instantly affectionate, almost paternal, and they began to dance. Mercy knew at once that everything was going to be all right again, and she no longer wanted to swap places with the little maid who, earlier in the evening, had helped to put up her hair.

'You dance beautifully, if I may say so?'

'You are very kind.'

'It is not said to be my first virtue, Miss Cordel – kindness.'

Mercy smiled up at him. 'I thought it was a girl's place to be modest, Mr Brancaster, not yours!'

'Touché. Men are deemed to be braggarts, are they not?'

In the back of her mind just actually who 'John Brancaster' might be was even now coming back to Mercy. He was not unknown, she realized, as she moved gracefully around the ballroom with him.

John Brancaster was a renowned sportsman, a huntsman, a man about town, unmarried, and very much a person around whom much talk centred, the interested being more than fascinated by why he still remained, or indeed how he still remained, a bachelor. And this despite his being rich, sporting, a godson of the Prince of Wales, and altogether very much in demand in the ballroom and the hunting field, and on shooting weeks.

'May I say that your first name, Miss Cordel, is very unusual, is it not?'

Mercy gave a small sigh. She was all too used to both the question and her own answer.

'I know, it is rather strange, but on the other hand, when you hear the reason . . .'

'Which is?'

Mercy hesitated. 'It is quite a – shall we say *inti mate* story, Mr Brancaster.'

'I am a man of the world, Miss Cordel. It will remain with me, I promise you.'

'Well, it seems that when my mother was presented with me by the doctor in attendance at my birth, she said just that.'

'Mercy?'

'No, Mr Brancaster, not "Mercy?", but – *Mercy!*'

He threw back his head and laughed at that, and

Mercy saw that he had good strong white teeth, which was always attractive in a man, not to mention a most amused laugh, the laugh of someone who found life endearing, but absurd, who thought that life should be challenged, and enjoyed, and wanted more than anything to ... *live*.

As the dance came to an end, Mr Brancaster carefully picked out the pencil from Mercy's bracelet and scribbled *Mr John Brancaster* over the space left for the next dance too, because as he said to Mercy, 'I am not going to be so amused by anyone else present, and at least, being older, I have the good sense to know it.'

And so they danced the following dance, but etiquette forbade more than two, and they parted at the close, Mercy to return to her chair, although not for long.

Happily, as she soon discovered, once danced with by *one* man she was soon taken up by *all* men, which meant that for the first time ever the evening ended on a successful note, despite all her worst forebodings. She could hardly believe her luck as she glanced down at the names now scribbled on her card. And she knew just to whom she owed this 'luck'. Mr John Brancaster.

When Lady Violet signalled that they would be leaving, Mercy hung back from collecting her cloak, leaving her stepmother to sweep ahead of her to their carriage, hoping to catch sight of Mr Brancaster and thank him for his kindness.

The men too hung around, waiting for cloaks and top hats, for carriages, wives and daughters

– all the usual reasons, and many another too.

Mercy, not finding Mr Brancaster among the stragglers in the hall and feeling oddly disappointed, went out of the great marbled hall with its sparkling Italian chandeliers and down the wide steps into the street.

It was only as she made her way towards the Cordel family coach that she realised just where it was that she had seen John Brancaster before.

Dorinda knew what she was being prepared for and deep down inside she could not help feeling just like a nice plump chicken being made ready for the oven. No different from one of the many dishes that Signor Lambrusco, the famous chef, was probably preparing for yet another supper party to entertain the future King of England. And his *sous chefs* would be chopping and basting, mixing and stirring as hard and as fast as Blanquette, the dressmaker and the hairdresser had stirred and mixed, as it were, all the many and beautiful adornments for Dorinda's first supper presentation.

Earlier in the day Dorinda had received a Mr Tarleton, who had come round to the house armed with leather and velvet boxes containing a whole new set of jewellery.

Gervaise had not wanted anything too spectacular for what was, in effect, Dorinda's entrée into Society. On instructions from his client Mr Tarleton had therefore designed a delicate dog collar of pearls and Indian sapphires.

As Gervaise had explained, 'The blue of the sapphires is not *quite* Dorinda Blue, but it is beautiful none the less, I think.'

And the blue *was* beautiful, almost matching the violet blue of her eyes. And what with earrings and a ring to match the dog collar, and a most delicately designed stomacher of small diamonds and pearls, Dorinda knew that she was going to look at her most beautiful. And yet still her heart sank, and she wished herself somewhere other than going to supper with the Prince of Wales.

The truth was that she was desperately nervous. Indeed she fidgeted so much that the hairdresser introduced into the household by Blanquette to help her produce something very spectacular in the way of a coiffeur, dropped the hot curling tongs with which she had been coaxing Dorinda's hair into a confection of curls, narrowly missing burning Dorinda's magnificent silk-clad legs.

'Oh, I am sorry, ma'am, really I am. I would not have such a thing happen for the world.'

Blanquette frowned at the hairdresser. 'Careful, careful,' she warned. 'Madame's *jambes* are monsieur's pride!'

There was a few seconds silence as the remark seemed to hover in the air, and then all three women burst into fits of laughter, at the end of which Dorinda felt a great deal better.

After all, when all was said and done, the prince was a man, and if he made a play for her she would just have to deal with him as she would any other gentleman and keep him on tenterhooks without insulting him.

As the hairdresser and Blanquette continued to hover and fuss it seemed to Dorinda that the best thing was to detach herself from the situation and try to remember what it was that, in a few hours' time, she should be doing, and how she should be doing it.

'Remember, with royalty, at all times the deepest curtsy, Dorinda darling, always. Despite its being a quite informal occasion, whatever happens, the back is never turned on royalty, unless you want to end up taking breakfast in the Tower!'

Some twenty minutes later Gervaise collected his Dorinda Blue from the hands of her maid and hairdresser and was obviously quite delighted with the result of all their efforts. Dorinda, as he informed her as he offered her his arm, was going to make every other woman present look dowdy and shop soiled, such was the shimmering quality of her youthful beauty, the silver grey of her gown showing off the blue of the Indian sapphires to perfection. Her hair was set about with small diamond stars, and the sapphire and pearl choker showed off the slenderness of her neck, so delicate that it seemed it must snap.

Exactly one hour later, Dorinda, her heart beating most dreadfully fast, found herself sinking into her best and deepest curtsy as she was presented to His Royal Highness the Prince of Wales.

From under her thick eyelashes Dorinda could

only marvel at his elegance, at the rubies on his fingers, and the exquisite cut of his evening coat with its decorations. Gervaise noted with some pride that the prince himself, always eagle-eyed when it came to details, appreciated the colour of the eyes that had been only momentarily turned up to him, and the way they matched the Indian sapphires in Dorinda's ears and at her throat.

'My dear Gervaise, you are to be congratulated. Mrs Montgomery is indeed *en plein beaute*!'

Dorinda blushed with pleasure.

'Yes, yes, you may rise, Mrs Montgomery, and come closer to me. I want to look into the famous Dorinda Blue eyes and tell my grandchildren about the experience.'

There was a great laugh at this, not just from the prince, but from the entourage surrounding him, and then he passed on, quite slowly, for he was already stout. Dorinda, realizing that his breathing was not as good as it should be, thought that he might not be quite as well as he would have liked. She was sorry for it, but also relieved because, after all, if he was not so well, he would not be so – *ardent*, surely?

Whatever the state of the royal health, seconds later Dorinda and Gervaise were joined by a tall, dark, older man who brought with him a feeling of impatience and danger, which Dorinda realized at once must mean that he was a sportsman at least, if not an explorer.

Gervaise obviously knew him very well, since as soon as he came across to them he said, 'My dear

Brancaster, I don't think I have introduced you to Mrs Montgomery, have I?'

John Brancaster shook his head, and looking down at Dorinda through the most appreciative of dark eyes said, 'I know I would have remembered had you done so, Lowther.'

Dorinda curtsied yet again, and he bowed, and after some small talk about racing and horses, which Dorinda could not follow, supper began.

It was an occasion that proved riotous, as full of good food and wine as pretty married women. Yet despite this Dorinda had the feeling that everyone there was performing a dance of which they had long ago tired. All, that is, except Mr Brancaster, who kept looking towards Dorinda with amused eyes, finally saying to Gervaise, in a voice quite loud enough for the object of his appreciation to hear, 'You are a lucky dog, Lowther. Where did you meet her?'

'Over lobsters, Brancaster, over lobsters. It is the best place to meet beautiful women, would you not say?'

The evening was shorter than expected, for HRH was unaccustomedly tired, and besides, as Gervaise remarked to Dorinda later, 'Little Mrs George' now held centre stage for him, and HRH was really rather more inclined to play bridge and chat over brandy and cigars than to disport himself after supper with some new pretty object of his manly desires.

'You did very well, darlingest,' Gervaise murmured, as Dorinda's carriage let him down outside the back entrance to his own house, round which he would shortly walk to let himself in, be put to bed by his Italian valet, breakfast with his wife, and generally behave himself as he should, for the benefit of his family and – most of all – Society. 'I will see you for luncheon tomorrow. Meanwhile I am most proud of you.'

Dorinda sat back in her leather-lined carriage, and surveyed her life as she realized it was now. She was part of the *demi-monde*, she had a loving and devoted patron, she had most of London at her feet, she had her own carriage, and she had her own house in St John's Wood. She just did not have love.

But love, as she well knew, was not for the likes of the kind of woman she had now become. When she had thankfully and daringly surrendered herself to Gervaise on the boat journey from the Channel Islands, she had also surrendered that particular emotional luxury. Love was for wives and daughters, *making* love was for women such as herself. To expect any more was just foolish.

She stared at her new sapphire and pearl ring. She must not, whatever happened, mistake what Gervaise felt towards her for *love*.

Besides, Gervaise was such a generous and kind man. To expect him to love her as a husband might would be heading for insanity. In fact she was quite sure that it would be asking too much of life as a whole, pushing her luck, inviting the wrath of the gods. She was not just lucky in Gervaise, she was blessed. She knew this from one particular event, and that was her meeting with the renowned ladies' man John Brancaster. If she had met him on the boat coming over to England, she would never, ever have felt tempted to join him in his private dining room, however many lobsters he had ordered for luncheon. John Brancaster spelt the one word that Dorinda was anxious to avoid – danger.

Part Two

In the Swim

Seven

It seemed that the rain would be incessant before Ascot that year. Indeed every time she had cause to put up her umbrella Lady Violet referred to it as 'Ascot weather'.

But happily, before that particular week opened, it stopped, as if on command, and all the ladies were able to breathe a sigh of relief, crossing their fingers and hoping against hope that the weather would prove to be less than typical of the first week in June, while the sigh that their dressmakers breathed was not unnaturally one of even greater relief.

As Madame Chloe had often observed to Mrs Dodd over the years, 'Whatever we make, and we make everything as beautifully as we can, there is no doubt that the weather makes a fool of us in two seconds. And the ladies, God bless them, of course they blame us if they feel the cold, whereas it is Almighty God they should blame, not their dressmakers.'

Naturally fashion too had changed that year, for fashion had to change each year, or persons such as Madame Chloe would not be able to survive. The acknowledged and excessively seductive hourglass silhouette of the fashionable lady, however, remained.

A woman was still expected to seduce the eye of the beholder from both in front and behind with her tiny, corseted waist, her sway of silk skirt, her ruffled lace-strewn shoulders, and her large head of shining hair, atop which would sit a small, enchanting hat trimmed with flowers, or feathers. Her forehead would be covered with curls, her earrings long and delicate, and her hands always gloved.

Shoes would not be seen. Dresses were to the floor, and this year those summer dresses, being made of the purest silk, floated, lace-trimmed, over the ground, held by one of those same gloved hands, while in the other was a parasol to match the dress, and keep the sun away from the pure rose and cream English complexions, for the sun was considered by all ladies, of whatever age, to be the enemy of good looks and health. Only servants or people who worked outside had the misfortune to have a brown skin.

Mercy was to be fitted for her Ascot dresses at home. Madame Chloe spent morning after morning at the Cordel house, for that was part of her special service, and one on which she prided herself.

And while some debutantes – and the lucky girl who had been proposed to at that early ball was one of them – had parents and godparents who were quite happy to let their young relatives dance through the Season in a few white dresses and some loaned jewellery, Lady Violet would have none of that penny pinching for Mercy.

'You need help.'

Mercy knew that by this her stepmother really meant that she needed to be made to look pretty, because her natural looks were not pretty at all.

'Help' had been forthcoming in the shape of expensive ball gowns, and walking dresses, and tailored riding habits from Busvines, all designed to show off what Mercy described jokingly to Madame Chloe as *my complete lack of looks*.

This particular morning Madame Chloe had, besides a large velvet pin cushion strapped to her wrist, a mouthful of yet more pins, but, as always, this did not stop her protesting.

'But this is simply not true, Miss Cordel. You have very pretty looks – despite your not yet being engaged. You just do not have confidence in them, my dear. That is what you need more than anything in the world if you are to be successful as a woman – *confidence* in your looks. Once you have it you will become twice the person you are at the minute, and in a matter of seconds. It is just a fact.'

From where she was standing, above the kneeling dressmaker, and facing the dressing mirror, Mercy gave the top of Madame Chloe's vast chignon a wry look.

'Oh, I think I have confidence all right, Madame Chloe. I have the confidence of knowing that I am no beauty, and to pretend to be as much would be as vain as it was foolish.'

Mercy and Madame Chloe had actually become

great friends over the past weeks, Madame Chloe having apologized for the trouble over the mannequin, and Mercy, in return, having promised her stepmother never again to step in where angels fear to tread, at least until the end of the Season.

'How rightly named you are – *Mercy*,' Lady Violet had teased her.

The loss of Lady Violet as a customer would have been more than a disaster to Madame Chloe, it would have been a catastrophe, except Madame Chloe called it a *cata-stroph*.

'So there we were in the middle of preparing the bride, and this if you please only halfway through the Season, when the *cata-stroph* struck. Lady Elizabeth was just about dressed, to all intents and purposes anyway, when I *saw* it, and upon my soul, I cannot tell a lie, I screamed. There was no other word for it. Yes, I admit I screamed. Happily it was a soundless scream – I expect you know the ones. For it was her little terrier dog, and the end of the twenty-five foot train bore the impression of his devoted attentions. Well, you can imagine?'

Madame Chloe was round the back of the dress now, so although there were fewer pins in her mouth it was still difficult to hear her. Mercy strained her head to keep listening.

'I have to be plain, Miss Cordel, I shall never know how we managed to get the tinkle out of the silk – *and* dry and iron it before the footman came up to ask her down to the reception rooms below to stand with her father for the photographs. Can you imagine? I have never been so close to fainting right out in my whole life, and no amount of burnt feathers under my nose would have brought me to again, I am sure.'

'And what about Lady Elizabeth? Was she near to fainting too?'

'Lady Elizabeth – near to fainting? Gracious heavens, she was far from fainting, dear Miss Cordel, she was *laughing*. The little *minx*! And I mean laughing fit to *bust*. And you know what she said to me? She said, "Madame Chloe, I am sure that this is going to be quite the only entertaining moment in my wedding, let alone my married life." And she about to embark on her *lune de miel* on a steam yacht in the south of France, and I don't know what.'

Madame Chloe had raised herself from her knees and was now standing in her black dress just behind Mercy, who turned her honest eyes towards her and frowned.

'She was perhaps not marrying for love?'

'No, dear.' The dressmaker nodded vigorously. 'She certainly could not have been marrying for love. Persons marrying for love do not allow dogs to romp on their wedding trains. Poor girl, though, she was to be dreadfully pitied, for her mother so hated her, was so cruel to her, that the poor child had to be taken away from her and brought up by a governess in London until she was seventeen. She never did forgive her for being a girl, you see.'

'Poor Lady Elizabeth. And what happened to her?'

'Well, dear Miss Cordel, seeing as you have such a bleeding heart, I will tell you. Her mother had nothing to do with the girl, all that time. Sometimes I thought I was the only person in the whole world who loved that child. Because the governess and the rest did not care a shred for her, except that on account of her they were paid. I dressed her, see? And when I dressed her, believe me, she caught every eye in the Park, and in the street too. But then, of course, one day, her mother came up – good excuse to escape from the country I thought it was – and Lady Elizabeth was hardly presented at Court when she was engaged to be married – to the man of her mother's choice, naturally.'

'And so that was that?'

'Good Lord, bless you, by no means. No, she was married all right, train or no train, dog or no dog, and gave birth to a son nine months later, thank God, for there was a title involved, after which, poor child, she died. Eighteen years is no age, is it? Not for becoming a mother and dying too.'

Mercy could not help herself asking, 'And her little dog?'

'I went up to Scotland for the funeral when I heard the sad news, and I fetched the poor little dog, and brought him back, and he is at home with my husband in Surrey. Lovely little dog he is too, but not allowed near weddings, you can be sure. Oh, but God rest her though, Miss Cordel, she did love him. And it was the least I could do for her, to do something for him.'

'The husband?'

'No, Lord bless you – the dog. I could not very well bring the *husband* back with me, dear, that would have been most awkward.'

'No, what I mean is did she love him, in the end, or did he love her, do you think? Her husband?'

'Oh, yes. Lord Chastleton? Oh, I should imagine that he loved her all right. Well, stands to reason he must have, I should have thought, or he would not have built her a monument in marble, and a really good likeness of Skipper – that's the little dog, her little dog, who is at home now with me – sitting at her feet.'

As her head re-emerged through the top of yet another sumptuous silk creation, Mercy went on, 'I am so very glad that he must have loved her. You see, I want to marry for no other reason, whatever anyone says. I think one must marry for love, or else there is truly no meaning to life, wouldn't you say, Madame Chloe? I know I must.'

Madame Chloe turned and stared at Mercy as if she had gone quite mad.

'You want to – you want to marry for *love*? Well, that is original anyhow, I will say, Miss Cordel. But if you take my advice you will do no such thing, really. That sort of thing, love and all that, well, I dare say it is all right in songs and such like, but if you want to be truly happy sometimes it is far better, in my opinion, to *learn* to love. We women do not have to be led up the garden path by love's young dream and foolish notions of roses around the cottage door. We can learn to love our husbands after marriage, and sometimes that is a better way, to my mind. More sensible too, if we are to be truthful, for ourselves, for Society. You don't want to expect too much from marriage, Miss Cordel, believe me you don't. That way lies a great deal of misery, and I say so what has seen it, I am sorry to tell you.'

Mercy pulled a little face as Madame Chloe tucked and pinned the upper half of the dress, and all this before the arrival of the hats, and the fitting of the gloves, and all the other endless details that would go to try to make Mercy look modish and attractive for the Ascot races.

As a matter of fact, as she stared at herself in the looking glass, Mercy had to hand it to Madame Chloe and the dressmaker's art. For once in her life, it seemed to her, in this particular dress, she could almost be taken for looking quite pretty.

Dorinda was not pretty, she was beautiful, but goodness she was bored. There she was, in her house, everything just as it should be, everything excepting Blanquette her maid whom not even Dorinda's mother, at her most perverse, could find beautiful.

It was all the fault of Ascot week, when the husbands and lovers of the ladies who were kept in chic luxury in St John's Wood had to be surrendered back to their families for this most important of occasions.

Still, it was no good pretending that she did not miss Gervaise. She missed him terribly. She was like an old maid, or a nun, just sitting and staring about her, sewing, or painting a water colour. She had even had to read a book, for heaven's sake! An awful, dreary confection by Marie Corelli, or some such, full of gloom she had found it, nothing amusing to it at all, and this despite the fact that Gervaise had given it to her, for it seemed it was much recommended in Court circles.

'There is a visitor, madame.'

Blanquette was at the drawing room door.

Dorinda, who was seated at the fireplace with some embroidery, looked up and smiled at the maid with something close to sweetness. She was thinking how dreadfully amusing it all was, for if anyone else was to stand where Blanquette was standing, and take a look at herself through the open door, what with the fire and the embroidery, they might even think she was virtuous.

'I am not expecting anyone, Blanquette. Please do not admit them. Tell them to leave a card in the approved manner.'

'I did, madame.' Blanquette shrugged her shoulders.

'And?'

'There is no point in 'im leaving madame a card, becos he is your 'usband.'

'My 'usband! My husband?'

'Yes, madame.'

'In that case you must admit him, Blanquette.'

Dorinda knew that to admit Harry to her drawing room, even though he was still her 'usband, was a great mistake, but she was looking

193

so particularly ravishing in a promenade dress of tiny white and blue check with a silk *ceinture*, and she was so awfully bored with no-one seeing her in it. That was how tedious her life had become during Ascot week – she had taken to trying on her promenade dresses *indoors*.

In contrast to the beauteous sight Dorinda was certain that she herself presented, Harry came into the room looking perfectly dreadful. Grey and gaunt, white and wispy – not at all the thing.

'Harry! What is the matter? You look terrible.'

'I am not at all right, Dorey.'

He spoke in such a pathetic voice that Dorinda was immediately alarmed, and of course his calling her *Dorey* in such a sweet unaffected way touched her heart. No-one had called her by her *petit nom* for so many months.

'Sit down, Harry, sit down.'

She could see immediately that he hardly had the strength to do even that, so she went to him quietly and lowered him into a seat. As soon as she had made him comfortable she rang for Blanquette and told her to bring some chicken broth up to the drawing room on a tray, while she herself sat down beside her husband and held his hand.

'Ever since you left me you have been haunting me, Dorey.'

He looked into her eyes and his own filled with tears.

'Everywhere I go I see your picture in the fashionable shop windows. They even sell it on the street corners in the cheaper districts. Boys are selling pictures of you for as much as sixpence or a shilling. I should have been able to forget you, but I can not. Try as I might, Dorey, you are haunting me.'

Dorinda felt terrible. She understood for the first time just what a punishment she had handed out to her hopeless husband when she left him for Gervaise Lowther. With gathering remorse she remembered how often her mother had warned her that Harry Montgomery would be bereft if she left him; and now that she looked at him she realized that her mother had been right. He had always been weak and a fool, but now he was stricken.

'Why do you not have some of our cook's good chicken broth? That will stop you feeling so out of sorts, Harry.'

She spoke to him as she would have done to a young relative who was in a bad way. Not that she had any young relatives, but she imagined that if she had that was how she would have spoken, in a maternal voice, while looking as kindly as she could.

As they waited for the soup to come up from the kitchen Dorinda asked him, in that same kindly voice, and hoping that conversation might help to take his mind off his condition, which was obviously very serious, 'How are your butterflies, Harry?'

'Oh, bugger butterflies,' he said, brokenly. 'I have not been able to look at one of the damn things since you left me. To tell you the truth they

195

might as well be moths now, I hate them so much. You see,' he said, looking into his wife's beautiful face as if he had seen heaven once more, 'you see, I really only loved butterflies, Dorey, because they reminded me of you. Loved the blasted things, darting and flying from plant to plant with their gorgeous colours, because they were so like my Dorinda, my Dorey. If you only knew how much I loved you . . . But now you have gone, just like the butterflies. With the summer, my beautiful summers with you have gone.'

'It is still summer, Harry. Look out of the window. The sun is shining a little after the rain of this week.'

'Not for me, Dorey. Anyway' – he turned his head away – 'who can blame you? You have money now, and a fine house, and your own maid, and a cook. You have a carriage and the smartest pair of thoroughbreds to pull them, and you look heavenly, so who can blame you?'

Blanquette placed the tray of soup and crisp rolls and cold butter on a small table and brought it to his side.

'Monsieur . . .'

Dorinda picked up the soup spoon for him, for he was making no effort, and said conversationally, 'Do you remember, Harry, when you won twenty pounds at cards and you came home and gave me ten? Do you remember that?'

'Twenty pounds.' He sipped at the spoon gratefully. 'Twenty pounds will not bring you what Lowther has given you. He has been able to give you everything. All the things you must have wanted so much.'

'Now, Harry, be a good fellow and take your broth. It is very nourishing, you know.'

He nodded, white faced, but just the effort of a few sips seemed to take it out of him terribly, and he rested back, his eyes closed, and gave a great sigh.

'It's no good. I've had it, Dorey. I've done myself in, and I know it. Been living it up for so long since you left me I'm more dead than alive.'

Dorinda leaped to her feet.

'Well, never mind that. You really can not stay here and be ill, since I truly do not own the house, although it is mine to live in.'

In not much more time than it would have taken Harry Montgomery in his present state to drink a bottle of wine, Dorinda had packed some of Gervaise's nightclothes and other items befitting a gentleman of a certain station into Harry's Gladstone bag, and it was not long before she had them both dressed for the street and seated in the back of her Dorinda Blue leather lined carriage, trotting off towards Sister Angela's Nursing Home.

'But madame!' Blanquette called after her mistress, suddenly remembering her other duties. 'Madame, what shall I tell Monsieur Lowther when he come back?'

Dorinda wound down the window of the carriage and stared down at her maid.

'Tell Mr Lowther I have gone to see a sick friend.'

Blanquette watched the carriage with its roguish coat of arms trotting off towards Sister Angela's nursing home. The horses' black, tightly knotted manes glistened in the light rain, and what with the wheels and the sides painted smartly black, it seemed to the maid that Harry Montgomery had just stepped up not into Mrs Montgomery's carriage, but into his hearse.

'*Le pauvre*, he is nearly dead, and *rien à faire*,' she murmured, crossing backwards and forwards between two languages as she sometimes did at moments of crisis.

Two hours later Gervaise Lowther called at his mistress's house, and on tenderly enquiring for her was told that she had gone out some time before.

Having placed his hat and cane on the hall table, Gervaise promptly took them up again, for he could not abide to be by himself, let alone left bored and waiting.

'Where has Mrs Montgomery gone, and with whom?'

The maid smiled coquettishly up at him. At least, looking down at her, or trying not to look down at her, Gervaise realized that this was what she was trying to do.

'She has told me to say to you that she has gone with Mr Montgomery, monsieur.'

Gervaise closed his eyes briefly against the sight of Blanquette's flirtatious expression. She was such a plain Jane after Dorinda's beauty that it was almost unbearable. He longed for Dorinda, not just her, but the sight of her. But since she was not there he might as well hurry on to some wretched family dinner, and listen to a lot of claptrap about hats and dresses at Ascot and how Princess Alexandra was looking, or not looking, and similar twaddle.

He scribbled a note and gave it to the maid before leaving. But Blanquette, having read it the moment she closed the door behind him, promptly, and with a great deal of satisfaction, threw it into the fire.

After all, she thought, as she watched it burning, if Madame Montgomery could be kept in great luxury, why not Blanquette herself? All she needed were the trappings of the rich, provided by a rich gentleman, and she too could turn herself into a beautiful, kept woman. She just needed the trappings.

Dorinda, arriving in a great hurry at Sister Angela's, had not considered any details. All she had thought of was that she must get Harry some medical help – quickly, quickly.

Once there, however, she wished that she had not acted in such haste, especially when she found herself confronting Lady Angela, who was stationed – there was no other word for it – behind her desk. Dorinda, although seated some way away, was made to feel very much 'on the other side' of Society.

Lady Angela Bentick was tall when standing, and such was her presence, even when seated, that she still gave the impression of looking down on whomsoever she was addressing. Facing her,

Dorinda was quite thrown. She simply could not understand why this beautiful, patrician woman with her blue eyes, her immaculate appearance, and her man's fob watch pinned to her dark Victorian dress would have wanted to take up nursing, let alone defy Society and run a home for the sick and the dying.

'I am sorry for your husband, but I have no beds,' she was saying to Dorinda, but Dorinda, being Dorinda, and among many other things half French, simply chose not to believe her.

'I too am sorry, Lady Angela,' she said, pretending a courage that she certainly did not feel and fixing her with her own violet blue eyes, 'but you will have to find my husband a room, or at least you will have to find room for him somewhere. He is, as you can see, at death's door. At the very least he must see one of your doctors immediately.'

'Dorey, please . . .' Harry implored quietly, only to sink back in the large leather chair in which he was seated and stare listlessly at the floor. 'We really must not impose on Lady Angela. Ascot week must be a busy time for a hospital, people enjoying themselves, bouts of indigestion and what not.'

'It is not an imposition, Mr Montgomery, it is, I am afraid, an impossibility. I am sorry, but we are at the moment in the middle of something of a crisis here, and there are simply no beds.'

At that moment the door behind Lady Angela's desk opened, and Dorinda immediately smelt not just a rat, but the strong scent of something familiar, which after a few seconds, such was its pungency, she recognized as eau de Portugal.

She had smelt that scent before, she was quite sure, and very recently, so recently that she could almost feel the silk of the dress that she had worn that night, and see the decorations of the gentleman. So sure was she that she stood up and leaned forward impulsively as she saw a hand, covered with rings, beckoning silently to the still seated Lady Angela.

'Sir!' Dorinda cried, not just impulsive but imploring, because of one thing she was sure, and that was that the future King of England and Emperor of India had a kind heart and would help her out of this terrible situation. 'Sir! Please put in a good word for me with Lady Angela. I know you will.'

The Prince of Wales paused by the now quite open door, frowning, as Lady Angela curtsied, and Harry Montgomery struggled breathlessly to his feet to bow, and Dorinda smiled winningly from the depth of her own, best and deepest Court curtsy. She knew that she had chanced everything on the kind of impertinence and cheek which will always carry the day with a man if you happen to have a nineteen inch waist and a pair of large violet coloured eyes, not to mention a tip-tilted nose, charming, white, even teeth and a wonderful smile.

The Prince of Wales immediately, and gallantly, stepped in. Knowing that only the most desperate plight would have compelled Mrs Montgomery to appeal to him so cheekily, he said to Lady Angela, 'Might I put in a good word for my little acquaintance? I can guarantee she plays the pianoforte most beautifully, and surely that alone would be of great benefit to your patients?'

Lady Angela looked round at Dorinda momentarily, and for a second it seemed that, looking at Dorinda and her charms, she was imagining that it was not just Dorinda's piano playing that had so delighted His Royal Highness.

'Sir, as you well know, I can refuse you nothing.'

'*Merci, ma belle dame*,' he murmured, and closed the door behind him as quickly as he had opened it.

There was a long silence. Dorinda had the good sense not to say anything and Harry had the equal good sense not to cough, for one coughing fit and Dorinda knew that he would have given Lady Angela Bentick all too good an excuse to refuse to give him a bed, such was the very real terror of the spread of tuberculosis among the upper classes.

'Very well.' Lady Angela nodded. 'I will take your husband, Mrs Montgomery, but you must understand, we can only nurse here.' Having taken in Harry's shaking hands, his high colour, and his general air of having slept in his clothes, she looked straight at Dorinda. 'We cannot cure.'

She quickly rang a small, ornate brass bell on her desk. So brief was the ring that Dorinda knew immediately that there must have been a nurse standing outside her door the whole time.

'Miss Lynch, please conduct Mr and Mrs Montgomery to the room overlooking the gardens at the back of the house.'

Dorinda followed Miss Lynch with Harry shuffling along beside her for all the world like some old down and out from the Nicol.

As they walked down the pale green corridors behind the elegant figure in its really rather appealing nurse's uniform, Dorinda wondered what it could be that would attract such young women to tend sick people, and indeed why someone so obviously patrician as Lady Angela Bentick would want to own a nursing home. She herself had never understood wanting to be around people who were ill. As a matter of fact she had no wish to be around Harry at that moment, but when all was said and done he was her husband, and she was grateful to him for marrying her, when possibly no-one else would have done, given the unholy nature of her mother.

For her part, looking at the young woman whose husband was so obviously at the very least an inebriate, and at worst a physical wreck, Leonie could not help wondering at the optimism of her sex. Why would a beautiful girl such as Mrs Montgomery give her hand and her heart to such a worthless individual?

Of course, she realized at once that he must be very rich, or Mrs Montgomery would surely not be dressed in the very latest fashion, a walking dress of such elegant cut, and a hat of such heart-stopping style. As Leonie stepped aside to allow the patient and his wife to pass into the large, elegantly furnished room where Mr Montgomery was going to be nursed, she could not help sighing inwardly at the perfection of Mrs Montgomery's hat, such was its beauty.

'Will you be looking after me?'

The husband was now staring up at Leonie as he collapsed thankfully on the bed.

'Yes, I and another two nurses.'

But seeing what Mrs Dodd had always called *that look* on the face staring up at her so helplessly, Leonie found her heart sinking.

And as Mr Montgomery said, his voice trembling a little, 'How reassuring to be in gentle nursing hands at last', Leonie could not help realizing that it was most unlikely that she would be looking after him for very long.

Meanwhile Lady Angela was dealing with her illustrious patient with her usual firmness.

'You must eat less at supper, Sir, and try to do without your lobster at tea, whatever the temptations of Mrs Keppel's cook. Lobster before sundown is not a good idea.'

'You are very censorious on an old body.'

'You are as young as you choose to feel, but Sir will undoubtedly feel younger if he is less eager at the table.'

Lady Angela smiled at her bearded patient and, taking one of his heavily ringed hands in hers, stared at his nails.

'I think Sister Nursey should give those a little trim, would you not agree?'

His Royal Highness sighed and nodded.

'You are very strict,' he said, happily.

'For your own good, Sir. Remember the nails tell us everything about the body, and Sir's are pink and perfect today, and we want them to stay like that, do we not?'

'If you say so.'

The Prince of Wales looked around Lady Angela's sitting room. It was always so cosy and so comforting with her, so unlike anything else he could currently enjoy. With his mother growing older by the day it seemed to him, for no reason that he could really understand, that his own feelings of mortality were increasing.

'Am I to have ...' He left his sentence unfinished.

'Eggies,' Lady Angela agreed. 'Cooked in a cup, with some softly toasted dippers, and a honey bun to follow.'

His Royal Highness stared up at her as she bustled about her sitting room, the look in his eyes almost pathetic with gratitude.

'And my nails are as pink as you would like?'

'Quite as pink,' came the reassuring reply. 'Now, shall I trim your beard a little for you?'

'No one does it with such gentleness,' he told her, using the German word. 'It is always so *gemütlich* here, alone with you. And it is marvellous to know that I am here without anyone knowing, which is very good, for I arrive in a hansom cab, a commoner and not a future king.'

'You like to play hide and seek with your equerries, do you not?'

The Prince of Wales would have nodded, but his eyes being closed, and a delicious feeling of being loved and wanted for himself alone having come over him, he said nothing. It was bliss for him to be seated, listening only to the sound of Lady Angela's little sharp scissors snipping at his *untidy bits* and waiting for his eggies in their cup to arrive. These simple joys in a life loaded with sophistication gave him the badly needed reassurance that he so craved.

It was true. Sister Nursey was right. He did love to play hide and seek. He always had. Hiding had always been his greatest joy as a boy. Hiding from his tutor, from his father, from his mother, from everyone, always dreaming that he would one day find himself alone with a warm and loving person who would be the companion without demand, the mother without censure, the nurse without strictures. Someone who would not want anything from him except that he just be a small boy again, and not a future king and emperor.

And after tea there might still be time for a more grown up form of love, but if there was not it would not really matter. Sufficient was his attachment to Lady Angela, sufficient was her attention to his inner fears, fears that he could not voice to anyone else in the whole world – not even to his wife who, poor creature, was deaf and a little silly. Certainly not to his mistress, Mrs George – with her he feared such behaviour would be seen as a weakness. Emphatically not to courtiers or socialites, or to his people – in front of them he must be strong and suave. No, it was only Sister Nursey to whom he could come and be a frightened little boy again, be made to 'eat up', told to be good, fussed over, comforted in every way.

And best of all, he had no need to tell her that he loved her. That was not their relationship. He was the centre of *her* universe, from her he received unquestioning devotion, and he knew it. Words were not necessary. That alone was a blessing beyond measure. Most of all with her he did not have to be handsome, witty, or charming. He did not have to be good at bridge, or a brilliant seducer. He just had to *be*. And blessing upon blessing there was no husband, no children, no-one whose feelings had to be sacrificed to his pleasure.

'You can open your eyes now, Sir.'

The Prince of Wales stared into the hand mirror that Lady Angela was holding in front of him, but the image he saw reflected was not that of an overweight man in late middle age, but a small boy, no longer so frightened by everything that the very act of waking was always a moment of terror, knowing what was waiting, or might not be waiting, for him.

'Ah. And now for . . .' He turned and smiled at her.

She too smiled, but she said in a firm voice, 'No, Sister Nursey knows what is best for Sir. Eggies first, and afters – after.'

'Sir' sighed happily. How he had ever gone through a day without Lady Angela he truly did not know. What he did know was that because of her he no longer awoke frightened, wondering what was to happen to him, worrying that before too long it would all be over, the parade gone by, and he only a jester at the pageant.

'Hold my hand, Dorey, please.'

Dorinda did so, but even as she pressed her fingers she could not help herself starting to worry about Gervaise and what he would be doing, and whether or not Blanquette would have given him the message.

'Don't leave me, Dorey, please.'

Dorinda looked down at Harry Montgomery. Her common sense was telling her to return home to Gervaise at once, but she could feel Harry's need for her, and she knew his need at that moment was far greater than anything that Gervaise might be wanting from her. She and Harry had shared something of a life together, after all. Not the kind of life to which she would have liked to return, but a life nevertheless. They had swum together from a secret cove, walked together in fields with spring flowers, and sometimes, she suddenly remembered, they had even found themselves enjoying many of the same books. These things were not, after all, nothing.

Of course she had not loved him as she loved Gervaise. Harry had only been a stepping stone towards something far more compelling, she realized now, but as such she bore him a duty, to be beside him in his hour of need, to help to nurse him, whatever the outcome.

She scribbled another quick note to Gervaise, *My friend grievously sick. Will return as soon as possible, Gervaise my darling. How I miss you!* and sent it back with her coachman and the empty carriage.

Of course Blanquette was the happy recipient of this tender communication, and of course, when Gervaise called again, late that evening, she was even happier to tell Monsieur Lowther that she had received no word from madame.

'Not one word?'

'I am so sorry, Monsieur Lowther, but not one.'

Already quite drunk, Gervaise turned on his heel and walked despairingly off into the night. It was obvious now that Dorinda had left him to go back to her husband. She had returned to the marital fold, and he would have to find someone else who could enchant him. Except – and here he paused and leaned his head against a lamp post – who else would love him in the way that Dorinda had loved him? With such imagination, with such elan, with such sweetness? She was unlike any other he had known.

From inside the house Blanquette watched with much satisfaction as Gervaise Lowther turned on his heel and went on to his late supper party without his Dorinda Blue. That she would undoubtedly lose her position if her deception was discovered was not a matter of the slightest concern to the young maid at that moment. Indeed any desire for security had quite fled in the face of the glorious possibility of causing her famous and beautiful mistress to lose her position in Society, and doubtless everything that went with it. The house, the carriage, the clothes, the jewels, the paintings, the furniture, the silk curtains, the porcelain, the silver, it would all go if Mr Lowther decided that it should.

And now that he was most likely thinking that Mrs Montgomery had gone back to her husband, that might indeed be the case.

Blanquette bit suddenly into her own clenched fist. The notion of Mrs Montgomery without anything except her street clothes, begging to be accepted back by an angry lover, was much more satisfying than anything she could previously have imagined, except of course seeing Madame Montgomery's head in a basket. But alas – this was England, and that was not, as yet, a possibility.

'Oh, Harry, we have had some fine times together, haven't we?' Dorinda stroked Harry Montgomery's forehead, and seeing the look of compassion in the young nurse's eyes as she sponged his forehead Dorinda knew, for certain, that she could not leave him until the worst, whatever that might be, was over.

As to her darling Gervaise, she knew that he would understand. After all, he was so tolerant, so kind, so understanding. He would just laugh and say, 'Come on, my Dorinda Blue, what are you going to wear tonight to please me?'

*   *   *

At the end of the private supper party later that night, so late it had in fact turned into the early hours of the following morning, Gervaise found himself leaving with a particularly appealing little blonde lady. She had been warmly recommended by Lord Faverdale, whose reputation and success with the ladies was something near to his own.

'She's a cracker, Lowther, an absolute cracker!'

In the face of the fact that his adored mistress would seem to have returned to her wretched husband, Gervaise did not care whether the blonde was a *cracker* or not. Indeed, in his state of extreme inebriation, it would not have made the least difference to him, given that his Dorinda had left him, because he was, as it happened, at that moment, completely immune to all the charms of every blonde lady within the vicinity. That he had been left by his mistress for her husband was not the kind of news that any man wanted to receive, not now, not ever, but particularly not, as was the case with Gervaise Lowther, if the man concerned happened – damn it – to have fallen passionately in love with that same mistress.

Before she opened her eyes the following morning Mercy said a prayer that what had happened the previous night at the ball would happen again, and again, and again. She wanted everything to happen all over again, up to and including the awful moment when her stepmother danced off into the mêlée on the ballroom floor in the arms of Sir Perry. It had all seemed suddenly to be so right, Sir Perry taking off the beautiful Lady Violet, when Mercy had ended up dancing with Mr Brancaster.

All the way home in the family coach she had stared out of the window into the summer night remembering how he had laughed at her remarks, and, despite his being such a sporting man, how well he had waltzed. Mercy had never realized just what an intensity of emotion one dance with someone who was not your dancing master could generate, let alone two. It was wonderfully exciting, and yet at the same time frightening, because John Brancaster was not a young man. He was quite old.

She thought for a minute. Yes, he was old. Indeed, he must be at least thirty-five years of age.

But now that she had not just seen him in the Park and at the cemetery, but had danced with him too, she realized that he must be a very fashionable figure, for all that he was so much older. She knew that he must be unmarried or he would not have been asked to a ball to meet and dance with debutantes such as herself, girls just out and still, to the disappointment of their families, ignominiously unengaged.

'At last, at long, long last, we were a success,' Lady Violet had told her brother, who was waiting up for them in the library of the London house when they returned from the ball. 'A great success.

In the end we danced many dances, and all was as it should be.'

'Splendid. So we will be taken into the conservatory before the end of the Season, and all will be well, I hope?'

Lady Violet, tall, beautiful, aristocratic and worldly, nodded at her brother behind Mercy's back. It was a nod that said 'Of course', as if there was now no question of Mercy's debut going in any other direction. Of course she would end up in the conservatory being proposed to, if her stepmother had anything to do with it. It was just a question of when, not if.

'Goodnight, my dear. And, in the event, how very satisfactory the evening turned out to be.'

Mercy climbed the stairs to her bedroom thinking of the disappointment she had felt in not being able to find Mr Brancaster to say goodbye to him, and worrying that she might forget him, as he had been. Most of all she worried that she would forget the sound of his voice, and the way he had of tilting his head back, away from her, when she spoke, as if – as if as she was speaking he wanted to see her better.

Her maid was waiting to undress her, and for once Mercy could not wait to climb into bed, not so that she could read her newest book, but in order to remember a certain gentleman and his beautiful eyes, his dark hair, his tall, slender figure. For all that he was so much older than herself, she thought he was most dreadfully handsome, possibly the most handsome man in the whole room, and he had danced with her, Mercy Cordel, not once, but twice. It was more than she could possibly have hoped, or would ever have dreamed, could happen to her.

Clarice handed Mercy a flower-decorated porcelain cup and saucer.

'I've made you some hot milk and 'oney, Miss Cordel.'

Mercy patted the end of the bed.

'Sit down there, Clarice, and just wait until I tell you what a wonderful time I had at the ball.'

'Oh, Miss Cordel, not a partner h'at last?'

'Oh but yes, Clarice, and such a handsome one.'

The two girls' eyes met, knowing just what this might mean.

'Who was it, Miss Cordel? Someone elegant and 'andsome?'

'Yes, Clarice. The man we saw at the cemetery, remember?'

The maid stared at her young mistress and a cloud came into her eyes, but seeing the innocence in Mercy's expression she turned away, and put aside the warning that she would have delivered if she had been a friend. Nice men, Clarice knew, did not attend the funerals of unknown mannequins – unless they had known them in some way that was not, perhaps, *convenable*. But what use to say anything? It was clear that Miss Cordel was already what they called in the kitchens *smitten*.

*   *   *

Downstairs in the library her stepmother and uncle were sharing something more than the hot milk and honey brought to Mercy by Clarice. But they too were talking, and Lord Marcus, his reddish lips a little wet, his eyes strangely shorn of eyelashes, his face somehow reminding even his loving sister of a tortoise, wanted to know, 'Well, Vile-lette' – he always called his sister that – 'did she fall for him?'

'My dear Marcus, fall for him? The moment Mr Brancaster came up to her, I think she would have married him then and there.'

Lady Violet laughed lightly, as she could and did quite often, and her beautiful eyes darkened with satisfaction.

'She had eyes for no other, Marcus dear, no other.'

'How perfectly splendid.'

'It is indeed perfectly splendid.'

Her brother nodded. 'You have made a very good choice, but then you always do, and always have done. Not for nothing are you nicknamed the Season's Godmother, my dear. No-one can touch you when it comes to matchmaking. But with good effect, for, as we all know, Brancaster needs someone younger, someone to give him children, and a settled home life. He has been a bachelor sportsman for far too long. If you stay a bachelor too long, people talk. I know. I have, and people have never stopped talking!'

They both laughed, but only briefly because it was an old joke, and every Season, year in and year out, Lord Marcus made the same remark. Lady

Violet did not really mind, because she had so enjoyed dancing with young Sir Perry that that was all she really wanted to think about at that moment. Dancing with Sir Perry she had felt quite seventeen again. She smiled at her brother, at her most benign and happy.

It was really very satisfactory. Not just the ball, but the added excitement of causing just a little scandal by dancing off with poor Sir Perry. But then, as it had transpired, she had no alternative if she was to induce Brancaster to dance with Mercy. Yes, it had all been most satisfactory, not least because she had quite forgotten what it was like to see that particular light of admiration in a young man's eyes, and she had indeed seen it in Sir Perry's mischievous blue ones. She thought she really must make a note of where he had his hunting box.

'Good night, Marcus, my love. Do not finish quite all my husband's port, for we still have a little bit of the Season left to us.'

Lord Marcus waved to her, once more seated at the eighteenth-century library table, most of the contents of the decanted bottle of crusty port already sitting comfortably in his ample stomach.

'La-di-da, Vile-lette darling, la-di-da!'

All in all Lady Violet thought she could not have put it better herself. It somehow summed up all the brilliance of the evening, as well as much else besides.

Of course an early engagement at the very start of the Season was never to be desired, unless, that

216

is, a girl had no dresses at all to speak of, but by the end of June, after Ascot, a girl's dresses were meant to have been seen, and any mother – or in Mercy's case, her stepmother – would want her to be safely engaged, and well on the way to the altar.

Later, as she woke up from her second sleep of the morning, Lady Violet lay listening to her maid filling the bath in front of the fire. It was always a most relaxing moment. She liked to lie and listen to the water being poured, the fire being heaped, in the certain knowledge that such day clothes as she would be needing for the next few hours would have already been laid out. Her eyes on the plaster-work of the ceiling above her, she thought quickly ahead to Mercy's wedding.

It would have to be a London wedding, of course. To hold it at Cordel Court would be ridiculous, especially seeing that it still took two days to reach Somerset.

No, it would have to be a London wedding, and not more than five hundred guests. More than that would really be rather unimaginable, if not vulgar.

Naturally she would be able to steal the show from the bride, since not only was Mercy not pretty, she was not really stylish either. As the stepmother of the bride, Lady Violet thought she would wear a dress of muted blues, blues that would set off her marvellous colouring and her beautifully dark, shining hair. She kicked the bedclothes down to the foot of the bed a second after thinking of this colour, and as soon as she had, she changed her mind. No, she would not dress in blue, but in the very latest of fashionable yellows. Yellow was so striking, and seeing that she would be so much the youngest of her generation at the family wedding breakfast it would be immensely appropriate, it seemed to her, to be dressed in spring-like clothes. After all, with yellow she could team the Cordel diamonds, although she might allow Mercy to wear the family tiara. Nothing thrilled Lady Violet more than the Cordel diamonds, so old and so brilliant, and gleaming as they always did with the particular dull glow that told the world they were over a hundred years old. She had worn them all Season, and even the Prince of Wales had commented on the Cordel stomacher.

It was a piece so cleverly re-made from other inferior items by Tarleton that it looked as old as the diamonds she had ordered him to take from other, duller, pieces that she never wore. This undoubtedly glorious centre to her long silken dresses and skirts was a decoration designed to draw all male eyes to the tiny waist and slender outline of Lady Violet Cordel, an outline whose beauty had never been thickened by childbirth, nor, thank goodness, was it now ever likely to be so.

'Your ladyship's bath is ready.'

Her maid stood by her bed, and Lady Violet turned and smiled at her. It was a beautiful smile, a smile such as the maid imagined an angel might give.

She stepped out of bed, past the maid, and trod

over the patterned carpet to the fire where the bath, full and steaming, lay waiting for her, the kettles and the towels beside it, the maid treading reverently behind her, knowing, as they both did, that she was so very inferior, in every way, to her mistress.

Lady Violet stepped out of her nightgown in such a way as to allow it to fall easily behind her into the maid's grateful hands. She knew it thrilled the girl to handle everything to do with her ladyship, and that when Lady Violet was not looking at her she cradled the clothes close to her face.

Not that she could be blamed. The nightgown was made of the finest of fine lawn and embroidered by hand by immigrants whose sole hope of scraping a living was to follow this line of work. Some stitched finely by hand, hour after hour, peering at their beautiful handiwork by the light of tallow candles, while others took it in turn to try to survive by dint of working in sweatshops where sewing machines turned from morning till night, and the sick and dying lay about in the same room as those who were stronger and more likely to survive to sew another day. The pay was terrible, the conditions worse, but the nightdresses that emerged from these traditions were very fine. Certainly Lady Violet could not have cared less how her nightdress had come to her, only that it had.

As her maid sponged her back, admiring her ladyship's white body and the thick dark hair that contrasted so beautifully with its soft texture, Lady

Violet thought a great deal about the delights that might be ahead of her. There was Ascot, very, very soon, and then there was just a little touch of Henley, but not too much since she only liked to see people in boaters and watch men rowing for a small length of time.

And now, after that, just as she would have been about to be bored and restless, there would doubtless be The Wedding. In July, she thought and then back to Cordel Court, and only a little bit of time until the hunting started and she would be off to her brother's hunting box in Leicestershire. Or visiting friends, or staying at home with the South West Wilts . . . and on and on the delights of the year unrolled themselves to Lady Violet, until it seemed to her that she must surely be the luckiest woman on earth.

But first and foremost it was imperative that John Brancaster proposed to Mercy Cordel. She, as the future stepmother-in-law, would see to it that he did so, very soon.

Mercy's father would be down for Ascot, not liking to miss seeing his old friends at least once a year. Just after Ascot, therefore, would surely be an ideal time for John Brancaster to propose to Mercy. He would first of all have to ask permission from Lord Duffane, naturally, and after that all would go as merrily as the proverbial wedding bell. Mercy was, after all, clearly head over heels in love with Brancaster after only one evening, so that was satisfactory in every way, for a bride in love would behave herself as her husband wished.

As a matter of fact Lady Violet had never seen Mercy's eyes shining so brightly as after last night's ball. She had observed that Mercy even hung about waiting for him afterwards, to thank him for rescuing her from her usual sojourn on the inevitable gilt chair.

Nor had Lady Violet seen John Brancaster, whom she had known for some long time, laugh so much in the company of a young girl. It was surprising, for everyone knew – it was common knowledge since every mama in the world had over the years thrown their daughters at him – that Mr Brancaster did not like very young girls. Nor did Mr Brancaster normally attend debutante balls. Indeed, in the normal course of things he would not have done so that night had not Lord Marcus prevailed upon him to go.

All in all Lady Violet was more than happy. She would bring about a wonderful match for her darling little plain stepdaughter, and at the same time endow a bachelor with a very young wife, who would in a very short space of time doubtless produce the two necessary boys – the heir and the spare. What could please someone of simple tastes such as herself so much? Brancaster would be happy. Mercy would be happy. Even her dear old husband would be happy, surely?

Here, however, Lady Violet had to admit to a fault in her character, and one about which she had been warned by her devoted maid. She lived too much for others. She lived only to make others happy. It had been the rule of her life, to improve the lives of others and to help everyone – even her poor little adoring maid – to appreciate the beauty that surrounded them in life's rich progress.

This, among many others, had been one of the reasons why she had married darling old Duffane, to make him happy, to make his children happy, to help them all. And it had to be admitted that in this, if in no other aspect of her life, she had succeeded, where many another might have been expected to fail.

She had been a mother to Mercy, and to her brothers. In her company it had to be admitted that her husband had quickly forgotten that he was a widower, and in the joy she had brought to him it had also to be said that he had quite forgotten his poor first wife, Mercy's mother. And what more could be asked for than that a man could be brought to forget his first spouse in favour of his second? What more could a woman do than to make sure that this same man be brought to love his children more than he had loved them before? What more could be expected of a chatelaine than that she and her servants, in the company of her husband and his children, attend their private chapel daily for family prayers? What more could she ask of God than to receive their thanks for these and all His other gifts, those gifts of money and property, of family history and titles, of coaches and carriages, of a London house, of a thousand shares in the American railways, in short all those things that God in His infinite mercy, had seen to shower upon Duffane and Lady Violet? It was inconceivable that she should not wish to thank God for those gifts, daily, sometimes twice daily. Without them she could not be herself, and He had always known this, guiding her through her life in the full recognition of what she wanted, what she needed.

And now most of all, for so many reasons, she needed John Brancaster to ask permission to ask for Mercy's hand in marriage. It had to be done, and soon. Her so-great devotion to Mercy demanded that she should not end the Season unengaged. Her so-great devotion to her step-daughter meant that she would walk on hot coals to get her married to John Brancaster, and thereby bring about a satisfactory situation for everyone.

The truth was that John Brancaster did not much like Mercy's father, Lord Duffane. He was just not his sort, not because Duffane was not a likeable old chap, but because they were so far apart in the way they lived their lives.

Brancaster was first and foremost a sportsman. He lived for his hunting and his shooting, and while he knew Duffane shot he also knew that he did not hunt, any more than his daughter hunted. Nor, as she had told him on a long walk in the Park, a walk carefully chaperoned by her maid, did she want to hunt.

She liked to ride, but since a childhood accident she had not jumped her horse.

'The most I have ever jumped since my accident

is a stream, and then not very wide. As a matter of fact I long for the day when women are allowed to ride astride. I think I could manage to jump better astride. I think I could put my fears behind me, if I was not consigned to the side-saddle.'

'The new pommel spring makes it much easier, surely?'

Mercy turned her large grey eyes up to the dark ones that were looking down at her.

'Oh, I know, the new side-saddle has made it easier for us ladies, but not so easy. If you think about it, we have to be twice as brave as you when we are out in the field.'

'This is true,' Brancaster agreed, but he did not seem all that interested so Mercy decided to press home the point.

'So many ladies are killed when their horses roll – because their skirts get caught and they are not thrown clear – that you would think someone would allow us to at least hunt astride?'

'The safety skirt has made hunting much safer for women, I should have thought?' Brancaster still did not sound very interested in what Mercy might have to say on the subject.

'There were two ladies killed hunting last year in our county alone, so it is still dangerous. I must say I worry about Lady Violet. I worry that she will be killed and break my poor papa's heart.'

'She has survived enough seasons now for you not to have to let it concern you, I should have thought.'

His tone was so avuncular and comforting that Mercy nodded.

'And now, to a rather more interesting subject, to me, at any rate.' Mr Brancaster turned towards Mercy, clearing his throat, and for a second she realized with surprise that this older man with his outwardly confident manner was actually nervous. 'Miss Cordel.'

At that moment Mercy's whole life stopped. She knew just from the way Mr Brancaster was saying 'Miss Cordel' that he was about to change her life for ever, that he was about to tell her that he had every intention of speaking to her father and asking his permission to make a proposal of marriage to her.

And, while the whole world appeared to be riding by on their hacks or driving by in their carriages, it seemed to Mercy that it was quite right that he should do so. After all, they had danced together at three balls now, he had walked with her, twice, and her stepmother was smiling so sweetly at her every morning when she presented herself at breakfast that Mercy knew, without a single word passing between them, that Lady Violet wholeheartedly approved of Mercy's having fallen in love with Mr Brancaster.

So why then had her whole life stopped, just before those words that every young woman always wanted to hear?

'May I say that I would very much like to ask your father's permission to marry you? But before

I do, I would like to know your feelings on the matter. In these modern times, at the start of the glorious twentieth century as we are, I think that a girl's own mind on a matter of such moment to her is of the gravest importance.'

Mercy stared ahead, while Clarice hovered tactfully some twenty paces behind them. Still the horses were trotting on, still the carriages and their immaculately groomed pairs and singles passed each other, and the nurses with their perambulators, and the ladies with their maids, walked on. Little girls with their hoops, little boys carrying their sailing boats under their arms back from the Serpentine, happy as she that the sun was shining and the air seeming suddenly to be filled with the singing of birds.

And so why did she find herself turning to Mr Brancaster and saying, 'Of course you have my permission to ask my father, Mr Brancaster, but I have to tell you, whatever his response, my own can not be guaranteed.'

As a sportsman *par excellence* John Brancaster's reaction was exactly that of the man who has just fired, and missed, a sitting duck. Yet he recovered magnificently.

'Naturally,' he agreed, stiffly.

They walked on in silence, and now, to Mercy's ears, even the sound of her maid's feet treading behind them was as loud as an army – tramp, tramp, tramp. Such was the awful look on Mr Brancaster's face she even imagined that she could hear muffled drums. Indeed, judging from the look on Mr Brancaster's face he was not, it seemed, used to being kept waiting for anything, nor was he used to a young woman – whatever he had previously said – having a mind of her own.

'Mercy.'

There was no trace of a possible question mark in the voice of Lady Violet. It was not 'Mercy?' as in 'May I have a word?' It was 'Mercy' as in *'Come here'*.

'Mr Brancaster is to speak to your father this afternoon, and then he will come to you, in the drawing room. Provided your father is satisfied with the arrangements, you might as well know now, my dear, that he intends to ask your hand in marriage.'

'Yes,' Mercy agreed. 'I know.'

'You know? Did you say you *know*?'

Lady Violet's mouth smiled, but her eyes did not.

'Yes, Mr Brancaster told me as much on our walk yesterday.'

'And?'

'And I said that I could not guarantee what my reply was going to be. As I can not.'

'You still can not?'

'No, I still can not.'

There was a long silence, and then Lady Violet said very sweetly, 'You have not been the Season's greatest success, have you, Mercy?'

'No, that is true.' Mercy smiled suddenly. 'But that would only be a disappointment if either of us had imagined that I was going to be, and as neither of us ever entertained such a notion we can not now be disappointed, can we?'

'What is it that makes you doubt Mr Brancaster?' asked Lady Violet, seeing herself well and truly defeated by Mercy's cheerful response.

'I do not doubt that *I* love him, not in the least. What I doubt is that he has the slightest feeling for *me*.'

'Oh, but my dear, if that is your worry, believe me I can honestly tell you that I have it on the greatest authority that he finds you quite enchanting. He has told Lord Marcus as much, and more. And he admires your sense of humour.'

'Maybe so. For my part I think that I am just the kind of girl that a man like him might find a convenience rather than anything else. I have the right blood lines, I am the right age – but, you see, I want to be loved too.'

'You will be! Of course you will be. He will *learn* to love you as much as you love him, be assured of that. That is the challenge of marriage, my dear. It is what makes it such a tremendous undertaking for our sex. If we can enchant the male of the species in every way, believe me, he becomes our captive for life!'

Her stepmother's words would have cheered Mercy had they not reminded her of the dressmaker's. They had used exactly the same words.

Could someone *learn* to love? Could Mr Brancaster *learn* to love her as she undoubtedly loved him? Was love just that, quite simply, a *lesson*?

Mercy smiled across at her stepmother, but more to reassure her than because she was feeling particularly cheerful, for in her heart she had yet to be convinced of love's being a lesson and Cupid some sort of teacher. Perhaps Mr Brancaster would be able to do the convincing? Or perhaps he had more feeling for her than his stiff announcement in the Park had allowed?

Later, waiting alone in the drawing room, it seemed to Mercy that it would take for ever, this strange ceremony of men talking over the future of a daughter. Discussing property, jewellery, income, and nowadays of course stocks and shares. Lord Duffane had arrived from Somerset the previous evening, and Mercy knew that he and Mr Brancaster would be negotiating the package mule of usual bribes that were so necessary to a successful union.

Mercy had no jewellery to speak of. The Cordel diamonds were for the use of the Lady Duffane of the day. She had no property. She had no looks. All she really had, when she came to think of it, was ancestry. She had clutches of the right ancestors, and she was young, and had caused no scandal.

Mercy stared at her feet as she waited for John Brancaster to come out of the library and into the drawing room. She still had no idea at all as to what her reply to his prospective proposal was going to be. She supposed that she was waiting for some sign from him, some hint that she could interpret as being a sign that he too just might love her? For one-sided love was no good, to her mind. If she loved but he did not, their union would quite surely be doomed?

For what the dressmaker and her stepmother had left out of the marital quandary was that whilst Society expected girls to marry men of whom their family could approve – men whom they would be in the natural course of events expected to *learn* to love – Society said nothing of the men's feelings. Were the men, too, expected to learn to love, or were they let off that particular nicety?

'Miss Cordel.'

Despite his being such a well-known sporting figure, famous for his courage, standing in the middle of the drawing room with its excess of flowered patterns and its crowded tables filled with ornaments of every kind, Mercy could not help noticing that Mr Brancaster was looking as if he would rather face a double oxer on a rainy, muddy morning with the wind driving towards him and the water dripping off his doeskin coat than a young unmarried spinster.

'Miss Cordel.'

'Yes, Mr Brancaster?'

Mercy, on the other hand, found that she herself, while experiencing all the usual emotions felt by a girl in love, was yet strangely calm, perhaps because she was determined that Mr Brancaster was not going to be the only person who would have something to say this particular afternoon.

There was a short silence during which Mr Brancaster breathed in and out.

There was a long pause.

Finally he said in a rush, 'Might we sit down, do you think?'

'I think we might.'

They sat down each to one side of a pair of pale yellow damask sofas, Mercy perching on hers, her blue and white pin-tucked blouse with its high collar and swept up skirt giving her a look of some bright but slender bird, while Mr Brancaster, darkly clothed in comparison, although also high collared, stared at her before swallowing hard once more, clearing his throat and beginning.

'Miss Cordel, as you doubtless realize, after our walk yesterday, I have spoken to your father, and he has graciously' – Brancaster cleared his throat again – 'he has, er, graciously agreed to my being allowed to see you alone, and, er . . .'

Mercy's eyes took on a set expression. Mr Brancaster might be old, he might be rich, and a famous sportsman, but really the reality now that he was facing her was that he was becoming tediously gauche, and minute by minute reminding her more of a shy and anxious schoolboy than a mature man.

'And er, Mr Brancaster?'

She saw that he had at once sensed her growing impatience and was both put down and encouraged by it.

'And er Miss Cordel' – he smiled briefly – 'and

er, Miss Cordel, I would therefore like to ask you, formally, for your hand in marriage.'

'I see.'

Another silence while Mercy glanced up at him before speaking.

'Why, Mr Brancaster?'

'Why?' He looked confused, almost affronted. 'Why, for the usual reasons, Miss Cordel! The usual reasons why a gentleman asks for a girl's hand in marriage, because he wishes to marry her, and set up house with her, and – and all that sort of thing. That is why' – he glanced around him – 'that is why a man proposes to the girl of his choice, surely? So that they may marry and set up house?'

'Mr Brancaster!' Mercy was now on her feet, and her hands were tightly clenched by her side to stop her from waving them about indignantly. 'How could you possibly ask me to set up house with you when all we have done is no more than dance six dances and go for two walks together. It is absurd. I am not some sort of thoroughbred to be sent off to Newmarket. I am a person. I have flesh and blood, and although you are a friend of my family and saved me from ignominy on the dance floor, I have to say I am not at all happy with your attitude to marriage.'

He had to stand up and face her now, since she was standing up. He was a great deal taller than Mercy, and yet, given the force of her emotion, an emotion that amazed and astonished him and would, he knew, appal her family, she seemed to be far taller than her actual height, staring up at him with quite apparent indignation.

'You are behaving in a most unconventional manner, Miss Cordel.'

'Well, precisely,' she agreed. 'I am behaving in an *unconventional* manner because I do not particularly like the convention of being pushed round a ballroom and then up an aisle. Marriage has never really held many attractions for me, Mr Brancaster, and now I can honestly say—'

The expression in his eyes was of amazement, but there was also something else, something dawning, perhaps respect, perhaps contempt. Whatever it was, in her indignation, Mercy found that she neither knew nor cared.

'What can you honestly say, Miss Cordel?'

His astonishment had now, she suspected, turned into a form of patronizing humour which, alas for him, only fuelled her indignation.

'I can honestly say,' she began again, 'that your stiff approach to courtship and the ties of marriage has by no means increased my regard for the institution. Of course I realize that if I do not say yes you may well go away and ask some other hapless and ignorant young girl for her hand in marriage – and I am sure you can find someone more beautiful, more rich, and more *conventional* – but if we are to be married, above all things, surely we should have a better understanding of each other than we now have? My father would be appalled to hear me speak in this way, but I am not a parcel to be left by the carter at any gentleman's door. I have more feelings than a parcel.'

Mercy found herself pacing up and down in front of the drawing room fireplace, her hands clenching and reclenching themselves in such a way that to an outsider she must have looked quite frantic, but as it was she found that she was caring less and less. She did not know why she had suddenly had cold feet about Mr Brancaster and his proposal of marriage, but what she did see was that he was now facing her with all the warmth of a piece of marble, and his attempt at humour had quite fled in the face of her spirited opposition.

It was not just that she felt as if she was a parcel, what with her father and him discussing her, handing her over, as it were, one to the other, but that he had made her feel as if *he* thought of her merely as a parcel, or a bag of washing, to be collected, or not, as the whim took him.

Perhaps too it was the memory of Mrs Dodd and the poor dead girl, whose only enjoyment in her marriage had come from her little dog's misbehaviour. Perhaps in the story of her all too short life Mercy had seen that marriage was not always the solution for women. Also, she had seen that there were other choices beyond becoming an old maid scuttling about the family home with pieces of lame stitching and an apologetic look. Perhaps she had seen, in Miss Lynch and again in Lady Angela and her nursing home, that there were more exciting ways to live your life than being pushed into marriage by your family and accepting the common lot of a wife and mother, and all too soon a matriarch and dowager.

She turned back to Mr Brancaster. Although she could see that he was very exciting as a person, that he was tall, impeccably dressed, a sportsman, fabulously rich with – Clarice had told her excitedly – three *'ouses*, not to mention a villa in Italy and heaven knew what else, he could hold no appeal for her if his heart was as cold as the marble chimneypiece in front of her.

The point was that he did not love her! Certainly not, as she had realized from the first, the way that she was prepared to love him. He did not feel the same excitement that she had felt when he first came into the room after seeing her father. In fact it had been all too obvious to her as he came into the drawing room that he had felt nothing but the kind of feeling a man might feel who has decided to go to church on a Sunday and after that intends to resume his life as usual.

He was determined on being married, probably because he was of an age to marry, but not because he was in love.

'I am afraid the answer is no, Mr Brancaster,' she said, her head a little on one side as she turned back to him, and her eyes suddenly feeling over-large with her determination to recognize some kind of truth in their situation. 'It has to be no because although you are undoubtedly a great catch and a famous sporting man, Mr Brancaster, I – I cannot marry someone who does not love *me*. Death in my opinion would be preferable.'

'I can learn to love you.'

'There it is again! Love as a lesson. And what a dreadful, cold notion that is. As if love was like Latin. Or history. Or French. *Time for your love lesson, my dear!* It sounds like the title of a classical painting.'

She smiled briefly.

'No, Mr Brancaster, love is not in my opinion a lesson to learn, it is a fire, a passion, something so great and so wonderful that beside it all else that life can offer – money or power, the finest gifts imaginable – is just a paler shade of grey. Without it life has no colour.'

He stared at her, openly astonished, his guard down.

'Have you – I mean, *you* have felt this feeling, for someone, for a man?'

Mercy was quiet for a second, but still feeling brave she finally nodded and turning away she admitted, 'Yes, yes, I have.'

'May I know the name of this lucky fellow?'

She walked off down the room, as far away from him as possible, quite surprised by the firmness of her own behaviour, but nevertheless determined to be honest, no matter what. She could not name the man who made her feel quite faint when he came into a room, whose voice made her pulse race, whose looks haunted her when she was not with him. But on the other hand it would be more than dishonest, when castigating Mr Brancaster for his lack of feeling towards her, not to admit her own towards him.

'I would rather not tell you the name, unless you insist.'

'Miss Cordel, am I not already humiliated enough? I have been put through my paces by your father, and now by you. You must at least let me know the name of the man who could inspire in you what you have just described. Surely you owe me that?'

Mercy turned, and finally said baldly, 'John Brancaster.'

She had spoken so flatly that for a second she saw that the words did not really sink in, and that he was about to say something, but stopped, quite suddenly, on assimilating the name of the 'lucky fellow'.

'John Brancaster? But . . . that is I.'

'Exactly. It is you.'

Mercy knew it was not the kind of thing that she should admit, but since she now had no intention of marrying the man what did it matter if he knew that she loved him, for heaven's sake?

'But if that is so, if *I* inspire in you those feelings that you have just described, then – forgive me, but why do you insist on humiliating me? Why will you not marry me?'

He was looking really very wretched and at the same time pleased, yet somehow appalled at his own lack of understanding, frowning, as if he was unused to being asked questions about his emotions – or indeed anyone else's.

As she saw all this passing across his face, Mercy

realized that Brancaster had never been brought to face his own feelings, let alone those belonging to anyone else. He might be *sans pareil* when it came to sport, but he was an ignoramus as far as the humanities were concerned.

'You do not understand, Mr Brancaster. You just do not understand. You inspire those feelings in me, but I do not inspire them in *you*. So do you not see that from the first the marriage would be hopelessly unequal? Awful for you, and terrible for me. Frankly there would be no point to it. I want to marry for love, not just someone whom I love, but someone who loves me in return. I realize that this is stubborn and awkward of me, that I am not conventional, and that I should be more than grateful to have the love knot tied about me, but I am not.' She turned her back on him. 'I am sorry, but that is how it is.'

Perhaps there was something about Mercy's long neck and her hair piled up that gave her a vulnerable air, or perhaps it came to him that this plain little daughter of Duffane's had more to her than he thought, but Brancaster walked across the room and touched her on the arm. Firmly he turned her back to face him, taking her hands in his. Hands that were tense with emotion, his own being the same.

'But don't you see, *Mercy*? I am already just that – at your *mercy*. I am already feeling more towards you than I would have thought possible a week or even a day ago. I am not learning to love you, I am being *inspired* to love you!'

238

'Can that be possible?'

She drew in a deep breath and as she did so Brancaster pulled her towards him.

'It is happening already. I love a woman with spirit and verve. I quite literally detest a doormat, and you have demonstrated so much honesty and determination in the last few minutes that you have more than convinced me that you are the perfect wife for me. Besides, I love a woman who makes me laugh, and you make me laugh a great deal. I am falling in love with you minute by minute, second by second. I promise you, you have inspired me to love you.'

Mercy stared up at him, but the expression in her eyes was still one of suspicion.

'I do not think that I can believe you, Mr Brancaster. You sound to me as if you have been inspired more by convention than emotion.'

He let go of her, and stood back.

'No, of course you can not believe me, I perfectly see that.' He thought for a moment. 'You are not able to believe me any more than I am able to prove to you how I feel.'

'No, love can not be proved. It is not a hat to be taken out of a box and admired.'

'Except, of course, perhaps with a kiss. You have never been kissed, but I can prove to you in my kiss that I am falling in love with you.'

He walked back to her and, looking down at her, suddenly and boldly put his hand under her small chin and kissed her on the lips.

Mercy stood back from him.

It was true. He could prove to her that he was falling in love, and maybe, perhaps, he just had.

'My nurse would tell you that now I have kissed you, you *have* to marry me! Now that you have been kissed.'

Mercy turned away. His nurse was right. She *would* have to marry him. Not because he had kissed her – she was not so provincial as to be convinced by that – but because one kiss had sent her into such a spin as to be utterly unimaginable. Just one touch of his lips on hers and it seemed to her that she understood everything that she had never known, and a great deal that she had hoped might be true became so. Shakespeare's sonnets, love songs, paintings, death, in one small clutch of seconds, had all become so simple.

'So?' He sounded impatient, and yet the look in his eyes told her that he was, at the same time, in an agony of uncertainty. 'So, will you marry me, or will you not?'

'I will marry you, but only on the sound understanding, Mr Brancaster, that you will continue to be inspired!'

The sun, fortuitously, had decided to come out, making one of those beams of light in which dust, or fairies, Mercy could never make up her mind which, are to be seen dancing. Brancaster took Mercy's hands in his and to her astonishment she saw that even in the last few minutes he had changed.

Could such a thing happen, she wondered? Could a man change in a matter of minutes? And yet, unbelievably, he did seem to have done so. It was as if he had seen a vision of something. It was as if, of a sudden, he had seen how things could be, not as he had come to accept them, but as he had perhaps, long ago, resigned himself to the fact that they never could be. That he and she might be able together to create a household filled with happiness, that they might love each other not in some false way that made women into goddesses, doomed to be forever failing their disappointed gods, but just as they were, loveable, and still loving.

'I think we will be fine together, do you know that, Mercy? As a matter of fact I thought so when you first told me that story about your birth, about how you came to be called Mercy! I thought, this young girl is so honest and so full of gaiety, I think I might like to spend my life with her.'

Mercy pulled her hands from his and laughed.

'Now *my* nurse would say "Master John is eating pickled peppers", which was her expression when she did not believe someone.'

He took hold of her small, white, long-fingered left hand and looking down at it asked, lightly, as if he knew exactly what the reply was going to be, 'Now, without more ado, would you like it if I ordered you a nice big engagement ring, surrounded by large diamonds, that will be the talk of the town?'

Mercy wrinkled her nose and looked up at him in astonishment.

'Oh, I don't think so, do you?'

He laughed and groaned at the same time.

'Yes, I do, as a matter of fact, or I should not have said so. I happen to quite fancy giving you a large ruby, perhaps, surrounded by diamonds.'

'I had really rather something less conventional. Something more Arts and Crafts perhaps? Large stones surrounded by diamonds are always seen on old hands at balls. I should prefer something more modern, with less of the flavour of the dowager to it. I have seen too many young women made old by jewellery. Besides, rich as you are, I had rather not spend your money on some sort of extravagant ring for me, but on something we can both enjoy – a pair of good thoroughbreds, or a motor car.'

'How original you are, and how lucky I am!'

When it arrived from Tarleton a week later, the ring was indeed, by common consent, one of the most original and beautiful rings that the famous jeweller had yet designed. The pattern was based on a love knot, set about with tiny diamonds and sapphires so small that they looked like stars, the rest of the ring being made of the oldest gold that the jeweller could find.

Only Lady Violet looked a little thoughtful every time the tiny perfect jewels on Mercy's left hand flashed in the light, and Mercy imagined that she must really rather disapprove of such an unconventional ring.

But the real reason for Lady Violet's strangely ambivalent expression was buried in the past, a past longing, as the past always does, to spring out of its dense darkness and confront the world with its venomous secrets.

Eight

Mercy had always imagined that honeymoons would be tiresome, full of long silences and a great deal of discomfort. Two people sitting about longing to be able to talk to each other, and yet still quite unable to hold a conversation of more than a few words.

Two people who did not yet know each other well enough to even take a holiday together, of a sudden thrown together for days at a time, very often in an uncomfortable and foreign situation, and making love before either of them had had the time to find out whether it was pleasing, or not, to the other.

She was to be agreeably surprised.

First, she had the good luck to marry not just an older man, but, more important and delightfully, an experienced lover, and so their time together was rapturous in every possible way. And secondly it was only on honeymoon that she came to realize how unimportant beauty was when it came to character, for, as John reassured her when she worried about her lack of looks, 'Time never speeds by just because you happen to be with someone with a perfectly straight nose, or a brilliant pair of eyes. Time is spent with a person, not their features.'

On the way back from the south of France where they had stayed both on Brancaster's yacht and in a borrowed château, Mercy said contentedly to her new husband, 'We have enjoyed ourselves, haven't we, John?'

He smiled across at her. 'More than that, my darling. We have been happy.'

There was yet more to come for which Mercy was to be grateful. For one of the pleasing side effects of marrying a sporting figure was that he was totally uninterested in the decoration of his houses, or indeed in anything that did not concern either the stables and the horses, or the direction of his sporting estates, his guns and his dogs.

'You can do as you wish, where you wish. As long as the food is hot and I have a warm bath and clean sheets I will be for ever in your debt, my darling. The house is yours and yours alone, just so long as you keep away from my stables, my motor stables, my horses and my dogs. Those are mine, and mine alone.'

Her first morning up, and looking around Brindells, the main part of which she gathered she was supposed to live in, Mercy had no trouble in believing that the house had been occupied by bachelors for more than twenty years.

John had inherited the property, a medieval hall set about with wings added in the 1850s, from his uncle, a bachelor and sporting man, who had made his nephew his heir from the moment his brother's child had made his appearance in this world. For, as he said, more and more often the older they both became, 'A woman can never take the place of a horse, and let us face it, you can not, even in England, alas, marry your horse.'

So, happily for Mercy, her husband's heart was in the stables with his horses and motor cars, or in Leicestershire in his hunting box, and she was left, at the ripe old age of eighteen, to bring Brindells into the newly arrived twentieth century.

At that time it was fashionable to look back not just to the eighteenth century, but still further. Indeed, as can so often happen at the start of a new century, everywhere in monied circles people's tastes were turning back to Tudor days, to the fifteenth and sixteenth centuries, to the idea of life in the old days of rush matting and pewter plates, to the simpler weaves and woven tapestries of olden times, to smoking fires, and the reading of Horace and Virgil.

'Just imagine,' she teased John, 'with rush matting and pewter plates, with minstrels playing in the gallery, you will be able to spring off your horse, bring the game in from outside and just throw it across the hall table for the servants to put onto a spit and cook.'

It seemed that John found Mercy's interest in turning Brindells into a comfortable home all too gratifying.

'A woman who is not interested in the home is not interested in the man.'

'Not your nurse again?' Mercy teased him.

'But of course. Every good Englishman is brought up by a nurse who makes old saws the bane of his life. It is what forms his character and makes it easy for him to understand, not just the rest of his life, but everyone else he should ever happen to meet for its duration. Without Nurse and her old saws we would grow up to think that we are the inheritors of the earth, instead of, if you are British, just one third of it!'

'Do you know, John?'

This morning Mercy looked up from her newspaper. He loved the way she said *Do you know?* every time she wanted to claim his attention.

'Do you know that, at this moment, as much is spent on hunting, racing and gambling in this country as is spent on the whole of the Empire's *navy*? Imagine!'

'I can perfectly believe it, and what is more' – he looked back at her, halfway to the dining room door, the outdoors already beckoning him – 'I find it perfectly understandable that it should be so. After all, there are more English gentlemen around today than ever there have been at any other time. And we are the richest nation on earth. Once they have money people have to be amused, and if there was no sport, no hunting and no shooting, no racing and no breeding, what would the rich do, Mercy, my dearest? Go to church?'

He was gone before his wife could reply, leaving Mercy to frown at where he had been. She knew that John was not religious, as she was, but he did believe in nature, which she thought was probably a very good substitute, for if you revered and respected nature you surely revered and respected God?

'I wonder where I can find an architect who can help me turn Brindells into something more than a house for taking your boots off?'

Because she was alone Mercy looked round at one of the footmen who attended them at breakfast, but he, his country tweed livery setting off his wide rustic shoulders, continued to stare wordlessly ahead. So Mercy smiled at him vaguely, and wandered off to her morning room to write letters before ordering the pony trap to be brought round to the front of the house.

She enjoyed driving herself about the countryside with Clarice bobbing about in the back. This morning she determined to drive herself into nearby Ruddwick, where there was, she knew, an antiquary selling oak furniture. For where there was oak, there would necessarily follow an interest in Tudor houses, and surely where there was an interest in Tudor houses there would follow an interest in Tudor architecture?

'I would like to buy your oak armoury chest for the hall at Brindells, if you will sell it to me?'

Gabriel Chantry, the antiquary, was yards younger than John, but not as young as Mercy.

He had not said anything more than the usual greetings when Mercy and Clarice came into the shop, but now he stepped forward, and as soon as he started to talk about the history of the chest Mercy knew that she had found her man.

He spoke with a passion and intensity that meant that the subject had absorbed him for so long that it was second nature to him to be able to communicate his enthusiasm.

'I love to hear people talking about what interests them,' Mercy confided to him, when he at length came to a stop and a small silence had necessarily followed, simply because Mercy had no idea of what to say next. For she was certain that intelligent questions had to be firmly based on previous knowledge, and she had none.

'It is a lovely, sturdy piece,' he ventured, finally.

'Would you mind coming out to Brindells and advising me on the redecoration of its rooms? My husband, Mr Brancaster, has given me *carte blanche*, but I am wholly ignorant, except of one thing, and that is that I need help.'

'I am very flattered, but I have to tell you I am not a trained decorator or architect, Mrs Brancaster.'

Mercy turned at the door and smiled sweetly, if mischievously.

'No, but if you help me with Brindells I am sure you soon will be!'

In actual fact the only thing about Brindells of which Mercy was indeed quite sure was its horrid discomfort. Not that she had not been used to some discomfort at Cordel Court, which too was a sporting household, but Brindells had the added misery of being a badly managed house. The draughts and the damp were less uncomfortable than the distances between the kitchens and the dining hall, or the kitchens and the morning room, so that even tea served at four o'clock was not just a headache but a *sick* headache for the servants.

And the servants that she had inherited, like the house, left everything to be desired. For if, Mercy had swiftly and shrewdly come to realize, there is one kind of employer more beloved than any other by his servants, it is a bachelor of long standing who lives to be out of doors.

Servants can take ruthless advantage of a man who is not only grateful for any food and wine that they care to throw at him, but can be counted upon to be happily absent for great stretches at a time. Absences due to hunting in the Shires or shooting in Scotland had left Brancaster's servants free to do as they pleased when they pleased. And of course, perhaps because he was all too aware of his neglect of them, Mercy quickly realized that John must always have been only too anxious to curry favour with them when he was around.

From the first, Mercy, who had always loved the servants at Cordel Court, was astonished at the slovenliness that had been allowed at Brindells, and would have none of their lazy ways and their impudence, whatever their age. She would have the place clean, and she would have it tidy, and she would have them wearing their tweed livery, as was the custom in the country.

'You are being a little hard on them, my darling, are you not? I mean cream custards and French pastry – they are not used to serving anything except the heartiest food, as you may imagine.'

Mercy looked at John. He might be older by almost twenty years, but he was completely ignorant of housekeeping in a way that she certainly was not.

'John. You must understand that if you do not get behind servants, they get behind you. It is up to us to keep them up to the mark, not for them to set the mark. Do you know—'

John waited, once more at the door, pausing only momentarily before he plunged off into the outside air and his beloved trees and fields, his gardens and his estate.

'Do I know what, my darling?'

'Do you know that Lady Dawsett has sixty-five indoor servants and because she is American they will not so much as serve her with a sandwich, or even a glass of water? That she sits at the top of the table in London, all alone, while downstairs the servants do just what they like, when they like? But what can she do, John? She is all alone, one against sixty-five, and if she dismissed them all, what then? Whom would she be sent, even if she should go to one of the best agencies? Quite possibly another set of sixty-five servants who would behave in just the same manner. And why, John?'

Brancaster frowned. It was quite obvious that he did not know, and was not prepared to even hazard a guess.

'Because, John, Lady Dawsett does not know how to run a house. They run her because she cannot, herself, do any of the tasks which she

251

demands of them. You understand, John, if you ask someone to make a *crème anglaise*, or a galantine of duck, or a confit, you must be able to do it yourself. How else will you judge their competence? Women like Lady Dawsett are quite able to be beautiful in ballrooms, but they should also, as our ancestors always were, be competent at running their houses, or they will never earn respect, and without respect you can not have the sound running of a house, John. It is just not possible.'

It was not a problem that John Brancaster had considered before, but now that he did he quite saw the reasoning.

'Gracious heavens, Mercy, the future could be black indeed.' He smiled suddenly. 'Except now that you are here at Brindells, everything is rosy, and thank heavens for a wife who knows how to make a *crème anglaise*, if that is what we were given last night at dinner. It was superb. To make men weep, my dearest, but weep.'

He kissed the tips of his fingers to her, and quickly shut the door before he had to hear more.

'Run away, Mr Brancaster,' Mercy called to the closed door, laughing. 'But by such things as *crème anglaise* are our lives ruled. And if you want me at any time this morning, you will have to drive a motor car, or ride a horse, for I am taking the fly into Ruddwick to meet Mr Chantry.'

The door opened again as quickly as it had shut.

'Who,' asked her husband, 'may I ask, is Mr Chantry?'

Mercy gave her husband a purposely innocent look.

'John. I told you that Mr Chantry was here to see me yesterday. Mr Chantry? The expert on Tudor times and oak furniture who is to help us restore Brindells to a great and former glory?'

'Oh yes, of course. The expert. But an expert with a keen eye to the costings, I hope, my dearest wife? For I have two other houses in England, and I can not afford to give up my hunting box for Mr Chantry, however correct his taste.'

'Mmm, but if we become hard up, we can always sell your guns, my darling, can we not? Or shoot poor Mr Chantry with them?'

Brancaster kissed his fingertips once more to his young wife. He knew that he could count on her to be careful how she spent his money. He shut the door behind him again, and sighed with the happiness of his life. Their characters were very different, and yet their sense of humour being so exactly the same he found that when they were together they were always laughing. He could hardly believe that he had already been married three months, and that he had even put off going to Leicestershire so that he could stay with her at Brindells. It was an unheard-of testimony for a hunting man that he should ignore the start of any season in order to be with his young wife.

As he had said, only that morning, when they finished making love, 'My dear, any more of this and our marriage will cause a scandal!'

Once again Mercy took the trap into Ruddwick with only Clarice to accompany her. She loved to drive the pony, and the sensation of the hedges flashing by, and the smell of the sea, which was never very far away at Brindells, was so refreshing that if the weather were fine she would not swap the experience of driving for the grandeur of her carriage for anything at all.

'Mr Chantry, now what have you for me today? Oh, and by the way, the medieval chest is such a success that Mrs Anderson has already decided that it must have been made for the house and has only now, at last, returned to its rightful resting place.'

Mr Chantry looked momentarily confused. He had, as yet, no real idea of who 'Mrs Anderson' might be, presuming only that she must be the housekeeper at Brindells. Indeed, although she did not know it, it was part of Mercy's charm that she always took everyone she met into her confidence. She was, in effect, totally artless, not suspecting anyone else of possessing different motivations from her own, which were to be as honest as possible, and to make the best of anything and everything that the day might bring.

Today it brought Mr Chantry back in the pony trap, or *fly* as Mrs Anderson called it, to Brindells.

'I want you to help me with Brindells. I love the place already, but it is so terribly uncomfy that I think even my husband's dogs are hard put to find a bed where they can lay their weary heads after a day out shooting. Will you fetch your outdoor coat and come back with me now? It would be such fun to show you round and watch your face falling to your boots. I am sure you will cover your face with your hands and weep your aesthetic eyes out when you see the horrors that have been flung at what was once a noble Tudor house built around a medieval hall. In fact there is so much gilt there it makes you understand the word *guilty*!'

As Gabriel Chantry climbed into the fly beside his patroness he looked at Mrs Brancaster and saw a really rather beautiful young girl. Not, to be sure, conventionally beautiful, but beautiful none the less, because the nature of her character was such that it shone – or in her case bounced – through her eyes and her way of being. And when they reached the house, even as she moved ahead of him, talking rapidly and enthusiastically, telling him what she knew of the house, and what she did not know about the house, and what she hoped to know about the house – even as she did so, it seemed to him that he might be going to fall in love with her.

Most likely this infatuation was based on the fact that he had never known a woman like her. Falling, as he had, into the antiquarian business more by luck than good judgement, since he had been left a small inheritance by his mother, he had also fallen into a world that was as full of ancient men as of ancient furniture. He never met young women, and seldom even young men of his own age. He met only the old, intent either on selling him something or on buying from him. Mrs

Brancaster was, therefore, a complete revelation to him.

And yet, watching her fluttering hands, her enthusiasm, as she moved from room to room and he followed her obediently, making notes in a parchment covered book while silently deploring the furniture, the taste, and above all the neglect of the house, he knew that had he not been an antiquarian, had he been in some other trade where there were men and women nearer his age, he would still have had to give his heart to Mrs Brancaster. She was enchanting.

'So.' She had her head to one side as she turned and addressed him. 'So, Mr Chantry, what is your opinion? You must be honest. Do you think that Brindells can be rescued, or shall we start again, setting fire to it, upsetting SPAB and bringing disgrace around our shoulders?'

'The Society for the Preservation of Ancient Buildings would indeed be our enemy if we were to set fire to Brindells, Mrs Brancaster, but – and this is very important – it might applaud us if we were, on the other hand, to remodel it in such a way as to make it easier and less costly to run, far less uncomfortable, more in keeping with its heritage, and above all beautiful.'

'This is what I wanted to hear, Mr Chantry. But' – she looked at him, her head still to one side, reminding Chantry of a small bird – 'd'you see, we will not be given an unlimited budget. My husband has other houses, Mr Chantry – his hunting box in Leicestershire, his house in London.

So you see, much as he loves Brindells he can not be over-generous to us, and I don't think we can expect him to be, do you? With so much to keep up, I must be prudent for him. Can you be prudent, Mr Chantry? I must say I find prudence when it comes to furnishings and beautiful things does not come naturally to me.' She laughed. 'In fact it has been a revelation to me in these first months of marriage to find that I can not wait to buy a dozen, if not a thousand, beautiful things that will look breath-taking in such a house as this.'

Her enthusiasm, modesty, kindness and light-ness of manner had left Mr Chantry breathless. She was someone, he sensed, who took herself as lightly as possible.

As he wrote swiftly in his parchment covered notebook he found himself deeply regretting that he was not rich and powerful, and able to sweep a woman like Mrs Brancaster off her feet. He imag-ined himself dressing her from head to toe in cloth of gold, worshipping her not day by day but hour by hour, minute by minute.

Yet, as he followed her from one dreary over-painted and over-gilded room to another, reality told him that for him there was only one way to satisfy his feelings for her, and that was to create a house of which she could be proud. It would be in the best possible taste, and at the same time it would be a personal tribute to his immediate adoration of her. A testimony not to Brancaster's wealth, but to Chantry's love.

Brindells would become hers, by way of him. It

would be his way of claiming her affections.

They sat down for tea in the drawing room and the footmen in their country tweed liveries waited on them before leaving to light all the lamps in the house, which were left ready and assembled in the same way, by tradition, that the candles used to be.

'We are not of course electrified, but we do have our own gas, and our own ice, so we are not completely behind the times. We are not in the dark ages, Mr Chantry.'

Gabriel Chantry ate his small teatime titbits with relish. In his shop he never ate tea, his maid of all work going off at two o'clock to work in the village butcher's.

'I think we must begin at the beginning, Mrs Brancaster. First and foremost, you must understand that I am not an architect. Secondly, I am not an expert. Thirdly, and most important, I hope – I think I can help you. And for a fraction of the normal cost. I am not a professional, but then professionals are not always what we would want in our homes, unless we were entirely at a loss for what was appropriate, would you not agree?'

Mercy smiled. 'You are a man after my own heart, Mr Chantry, particularly' – she looked across at him, immediately mischievous – 'particularly because you are hinting at being less *costly*. My husband will be very happy at anything or anyone who is less costly.'

'Very well. May I also, then, be frank?'

'Of course.'

258

'Brindells is a disaster. It has been ruined by over-decoration. It has no need of gold and plaster, of chandeliers and heavy drapes with fringes of gold and heavy brocades. It needs to be returned to its origins. To rushes and oak, to unwaxed candles and polished floors, to all that our ancestors knew and loved, and Brindells cries out to be – an *unadorned* masterpiece.'

Mercy nodded. Everything Mr Chantry said echoed her own feelings. Poor old Brindells was such a mess inside, the essence of the house was now hardly discernible amid the chaos of conflicting styles.

'I am afraid Brindells is only a reflection of our times. Why do we insist on trying to make our houses reflect our times, rather than their own? It is so awful for them. It is as if I was made to wear a dress belonging to someone else, wouldn't you say?'

She laughed lightly, and at that moment her husband came in. Instantly, Mr Chantry was afraid that his open adoration for Brancaster's wife would become rapidly clear to Brancaster, probably within a few seconds. He was afraid that he would take a dislike to the antiquarian for no other reason than that he was in his house and criticizing his furniture. He was afraid that the man would despise someone like Gabriel Chantry, who wore spectacles and was not a sporting man of any sort, and liked to stride out not with a gun, but with a sketchbook.

But he was wrong on all counts. Mr Brancaster,

having been introduced to Mr Chantry by his wife, smiled briefly, and turned back to Mrs Brancaster immediately, obviously needing to tell her something of some urgency.

'Your stepmother and father are to come here on a visit, passing through as it were, my darling. They have sent to say that they will be arriving on Friday.'

Mercy's heart sank. The very idea of her father and stepmother coming to Brindells was somehow too awful. 'Mr Chantry is just going,' she said, hastily, and she gave Gabriel Chantry a look as if to say *Later* before quickly turning back to her husband and saying, 'Of course, my darling. I will prepare everything as soon as possible.'

There was only one way to prepare things, Mercy knew, and that was to arrange everything to please one person, namely her stepmother, who she knew had rigorous standards when it came to the running and maintaining of country houses.

So it was that, by the time Lord and Lady Duffane stepped out of their brand new motor car on the following Friday, Mercy was able to greet them with composure, if not total confidence that Lady Violet would find nothing at which to cavil in her entertainment.

Once inside the house, white-moustached, and looking very like the Duke of Connaught, Lord Duffane looked around the drawing room, first at the old furniture and the country liveries of the footmen, and then at the floor coverings and the fireplace, and smiled suddenly.

'Do you know, Violet, my dear, this is very pleasant, coming to see our dear Mercy in her marital home. A home, I have to say, that reminds me very much of our own. Home from home indeed.' He smiled proudly across at Mercy. 'Well done, Mercy, my dearest, well done.'

Mercy blushed and smiled and looked about her with a sinking heart. She could not tell her father that it was all about to be changed, for ever, and irrevocably, just so that it would *not* remind anyone of Cordel Court.

'You are going to do what did you say, my dear?'

Mercy looked away at something, nothing and everything, before murmuring, 'Oh, you know how it is, Step-maman, change a few things. Make everything a little more authentic, more Arts and Crafts, if you will. Only in a few rooms.'

'You are to make it *Arts and Crafts* in style, did you say?'

'Only a little of it, enough of it, not completely, of course. But then the original parts of Brindells are Tudor, so a little Arts and Crafts influence will not come amiss I should have thought.'

'You are not, I hope, going to tamper with the gold and the brocade, the plasterwork and the ornamentation, the chandeliers and the velvet?'

'I could hardly say at this point, but there will be some remodelling, particularly of the kitchens which are so far from the dining room that it is impossible to keep anything warm that is not already on fire. Oh look, there is Papa!'

Mercy turned away, relieved to see her father at the end of the long corridor down which she and her stepmother had wandered. She had no intention of carrying on their conversation unless absolutely essential.

'But which architect are you to use for this? Not *Lutyens*, I hope. I do so hate Ned Lutyens, all that insistence on cosy-cosy, and Tudor motor-homes. And I particularly hate that dreadful Gertrude Jekyll's gardens. Surrey, Surrey, Surrey, and not a pack of hounds to be found worth their weight in breeding.'

Lady Violet always did become a little different once the hunting season was well on its way, and Mercy was quite used to this. When she had first come to Cordel Court even Mercy's brothers would make hounds in full cry noises the moment the hunting season began, and say to anyone who called *I am afraid Lady Duffane is gorn away!* which they always found immensely amusing, but which was not really.

'Oh, I don't think Mr Lutyens would be remotely interested in Brindells, Step-maman, really I do not. No.'

Mercy paused, because she knew that she was about to tell a lie, and before she started to tell her lie she needed not to ask for God's forgiveness for so doing but to demand it.

The point was that she felt sorry for the bearded

young Mr Chantry. He was, after all, such a nice young man. The second reason for her untruth was that she knew that if she told Lady Violet whom she had in mind for the alterations, her stepmother would throw up her hands in horror and demand that Lord Duffane tell John to tell Mercy that she was out of her senses, and that using a mere anti-quarian to carry out alterations at Brindells was madness, because, Lady Violet would surmise, he would know *nothing*.

Even as she heard herself say, 'We have not thought whom to use, yet,' Mercy was aware of her stepmother's voice telling her that she was far too young to take on Brindells and that she herself would be able to recommend someone much more suitable. She would also be sure to tell John this, and so all would be lost.

Yet Mercy had the feeling that Chantry knew a great deal more than any so-called trained archi-tect, or builder, about the Tudor period. And he knew it, she felt, in the only truly valuable way of knowing anything – he knew it not just through scholarship, but through instinct.

Alas, the subject was by no means exhausted, however.

At dinner that night Lady Violet turned and said sweetly to Brancaster, 'I hear Brindells is to be remodelled, John? And Mercy tells me that you have given her a completely free hand.'

'Yes, it is to be remodelled.'

'But with a concentrated effort on the kitchens, Mercy tells me?'

'Oh no, Lady Violet,' John told his beautiful guest with some relish, 'it is *all* going to be re-modelled. Mercy has the most tremendous plans. But I am to stay well away, for this is a woman's business, is it not? To talk to artistic men with sketchbooks and make the place a home for both of you. Would you not say this is a woman's preserve, Lady Violet?'

He looked at his stepmother-in-law with a serious, if mocking, expression.

'But will this mean a complete change of style at Brindells?'

'A complete change? Well, I dare say. But then I have been an old bachelor for far too long. The place needs to be given a good dose of salts, if you will forgive the vulgarity. It needs a young hand to make it a home.'

'And what kind of home would that be? Will the brocade go, and the gilding?'

'I have no idea, Lady Violet, but if Mercy so wishes, then, yes, it will go, and if she wants it to stay it will stay. As she said, I have given her a free hand. She is a sensible person, she will do what is right. I trust her.'

'I think you should put your foot down. I really think you should. Young gels have very little taste to speak of, you know. It takes a few years of marriage to acquire it. And as to doing away with the brocade and the gilding, I think I should have a word with her, really I do.' Lady Violet lowered her voice. 'I must insist. And if she talks of doing away with the Italian chandelier in the library—'

'I have told darling Mercy that she has a free hand. Besides, what is taste compared to the exuberance of youth? Youthful enthusiasm in a house is so touching, I find. She has already brought this place to life. Even my dogs have changed – they are gayer, more full of life, take themselves less seriously.'

John laughed as his stepmother-in-law frowned.

'I think it is very unwise to allow dear Mercy a free hand, very unwise.'

'And I think . . .' He paused. 'I think it is none of your business.'

The effect was as if he had thrown a glass of water over her, but Lady Violet was too well versed in the ways of the world to be upset by this put-down. She smiled with all her usual grace and, sensing defeat, immediately changed tack.

'Oh, you men,' she said, suddenly lightening her voice. 'You will never be told, will you, except of course by your grooms! Now tell me, when are you coming to Leicestershire? This must be the first time you have missed the opening meet of the season in ten years. Are we never to see you up there with the rest of us? Has marriage changed you so much, John Brancaster?'

Brancaster smiled at his beautiful stepmother-in-law.

'I shall be up soon, but to tell you the truth, for once in my life I have not missed my hunting.' He looked down the dining table at his young wife. 'I cannot remember ever being so happy. And do you know, Lady Violet, it is all the better

265

for being such an unlooked-for happiness.'

Lady Violet smiled. 'That is good. That makes us *all* happy, as it must. But nevertheless, once things have settled here, perhaps the sound of the horn and the cry of the hounds will bring you back to Leicestershire after all.'

Nowadays the Brancasters were so happy at home together, making plans, and talking about everything that they hoped to do, that it seemed that not even hunting held any of its old fascination for John.

'I had promised to go for a week or two to Leicestershire while you get on with the alterations here, but I find I can not leave you.'

'No, John, no. I insist you go to Leicestershire for your hunting. You love your hunting. You must go.'

'I find I have no wish to do anything without you. If I am out, I think only of coming back to you.'

Mercy felt the same, and indeed she did not want him to go to Leicestershire, but considering all the chaos and disruption to come, she thought it would be better for him really if he did go, leaving her and Gabriel Chantry to oversee the alterations.

'Show me the plans for the house again.'

They spread Gabriel Chantry's beautiful, delicate drawings out over the library table, holding them down at either end with ink wells and paperweights of silver foxes engraved with souvenirs of days out, *Ten miles clinking without a check*, and horse shoes from old mounts, the bases silvered.

Old horses, old memories of days with the Quorn or the Beaufort, or weeks spent with the Galway Blazers in Ireland, or some other pack. Mementoes of John Brancaster's great sporting past, albeit a past in which he seemed to have really rather lost interest since his marriage.

'So, here it is, or how it could be, we hope.'

Mercy leaned over and put out her hand with its love knot engagement ring on the plans to straighten them, and as she did so John Brancaster became overwhelmed with love for this young woman who had changed his life so completely.

He had never realized before what a tedious round of the same pointless pleasures he had been enjoying before he met Mercy. He regretted leaving her now, even for his hunting, but he knew that whatever his own feelings he must go to Leicestershire, if only for the sake of the groom who had been keeping his horses up and hunting fit for many a long day now. The man would be furious if he had spent so much time on keeping the string fit, only to have his master prefer to spend his time making love with his new wife, or shopping, or doing any of the other innumerable things with which husbands, John had come to realize with pleasurable surprise over the last months, occupied themselves.

'You have changed me completely,' he said suddenly to Mercy, and she, smiling, touched his cheek, before saying, 'Now, John, pay attention, like a good boy. We have to think back to when the house was first built, and how it would have been.'

'Mercy, I find I must ask you to come upstairs.'

'No, John, not now. Before dinner, when we are changing, perhaps!'

She laughed, and John obediently turned his mind from love-making to housekeeping, to kitchens and ovens, to drawing rooms and libraries, and to the realization that no matter what – and this was to his great amusement – the chandelier in the library was definitely going to be given its marching orders.

'I shall miss you so much.'

Mercy kissed John. He looked devastatingly handsome in his travelling clothes, so much the sporting aristocrat that of a sudden she said, 'I think it is very dangerous to let you out of my sight, John Brancaster. You are, after all, everything that every woman wants. Not just tall, dark and handsome, but long-legged, tall, dark and handsome.'

He smiled.

'You are in no danger, madam, I promise you. I have eyes for no-one but you, and will never have eyes for anyone but you. You are my sun, my moon and my stars. God bless you, Mercy.'

She watched him climbing into the coach below her bedroom window, and she wondered that she had ever held back from marrying him, that she had not suspected that beneath the reserve of the sporting man was a character of such generosity and gentleness.

She went to his dressing room and taking one of his handkerchiefs from his cupboard she put it into her pocket. Thank heavens there was so much to be done that she could not feel sorry for herself for too long, and the three weeks that he would be away would be spent pleasantly enough, choosing colours and materials with Mr Chantry, and overseeing what now seemed to be about a thousand men. Craftspeople of all kinds swarmed all over the house from breakfast till dinner, some of whom, even now, were being put up in cottages on the estate.

Chantry was the greatest fun at this time. He had overcome his inhibitions with Mercy and was now, she realized, taking the place of her younger brother in her day to day life. Like her brother he loved to tease and joke but not about the same things.

He teased her most particularly about her lack of architectural knowledge.

'If we take that down, Mrs Brancaster,' he would say, straight-faced, 'with the greatest respect, we will be taking the house down.'

He always said *with the greatest respect* because, as Mercy insisted, he actually meant *quite the opposite*.

'You have no more respect for me than my brothers have, Mr Chantry. And the more you profess it, the less I believe you.'

She pretended to look stern, but immediately after smiled.

'Do you know, I never realized that restoring a house could be so exciting? I feel ashamed to say it, but I was so ignorant. I can not think when I have enjoyed shopping with someone as much as I enjoy shopping with you, just because, I suppose, you are so knowledgeable. I learn something each time we are together.'

Gabriel Chantry looked modest, but appreciative of her praise, as Mercy continued, 'You may be surprised to know, Mr Chantry, that you more than anyone have taught me to appreciate the world I live in. Even the woods and the fields, which I thought I understood along with the rest of the world, take on a different aspect because of your ideas. What a wonderful thing it is to realize what the life of a single tree really means, and how many oaks went into the making of just this one table. It is truly amazing. And humbling too.'

She looked up from examining a large oak trestle table that had newly arrived in Chantry's shop.

'Just think how many trees went into the making of this, and how long they took to grow, and what it takes to grow them. Reverence for nature is reverence for life, would you not say, Mr Chantry?'

Gabriel looked across at Mercy, feeling almost dizzy with emotion, but remaining outwardly polite and detached while at the same time half wishing that this lovely young woman had never come into his life.

'You are entirely right, and that is what William Morris and the Arts and Crafts movement are all about. We must try to fight the emergence of machine manufacturing, to hold on to the hand crafts of our ancestors, or they will be lost to us for ever. One day we may not even have a single man who will know how to thatch a roof!'

Mercy nodded, straightening up from examining a large oak dresser with much ornate carving.

'I will take this piece, Mr Chantry. It is very well made, is it not?'

'It is not just very well made, it is the same date as Brindells,' he told her, and was delighted to see how gratified she was that she had shown the right instinct.

Once they had decided on the carved oak dresser Mercy drove him back to Brindells in the trap, and Gabriel was asked to stay for dinner, because 'the rector is coming and he is quite serious, not to mention his daughter of whom everyone in the village is terrified, our housekeeper tells me. Every time she pays a visit all the villagers hide under their beds, or leave a pig in the front garden to put her off. Alas, it seems that it does not always have the desired effect and she carries on into their cottages anyway, insisting on giving them her home-made preserves, which they all loathe and feed to those very pigs the moment she leaves.'

Gabriel Chantry had been brought up in London, in the environs of Putney, quite near but not near enough to fashionable stamping grounds, and so he realized at once just how unused he was, how unexposed he had been, to the preserved gentility which exuded from the rector and his daughter as they entered the library to take drinks before dinner with Mrs Brancaster.

Not so Mercy, who was well used to the Church coming to dinner at Cordel Court. Necessarily so, for the incumbent of her father's parish church was his cousin, and most welcome at the Court at any time of day, if only so that Lord Duffane could instruct him in the exact nature of the next sermon he expected him to preach. But Lord Duffane's cousin had enough of the irreverent hunting parson in him – irreverent towards humanity although not towards the deity – to make him excellent company.

The same could not be said of the rector and his daughter, Miss Tingles. Indeed, they entered the library with the air of two people who were well aware that at Brindells they were, in a spiritual sense, in darkest Africa, and that the incumbents of the house were as much in need of God as the African heathen. But unlike the heathen they were virtually living at the bottom of the rectory garden. The fact was, as they all knew, until his very recent marriage it was common knowledge in the village that Mr Brancaster had taken as much interest in the Church as the rector took in motor cars.

'This is Mr Chantry . . .'

As he was introduced to them and lightly shook their hands Gabriel Chantry saw the words *in trade* flashing up into the eyes of the rector and his daughter. This was swiftly followed, a few minutes later, when they realized that he was an anti-quarian, by the words *dangerously artistic young man*.

'Surely Brindells should be left as it is for future generations to marvel at, Mr Chancery?'

'Chantry.'

'Yes, quite so. As I was saying, if I were you,

which happily I am not, I must admit that I would feel considerable qualms at the idea that I was helping to destroy the past of this ancient house.'

The rector's tone was really quite accusing, so much so that even the footman who was holding out a dish of chicken from which Gabriel was expected to help himself glanced briefly at the parson and sighed.

As Gabriel interpreted it the sigh said, *Here goes the Church, at it again, poking their nose where they should be minding their own business.*

Heartened by the feeling that he was not alone if the footman was on his side, Gabriel retorted, 'With the greatest respect' – at which opening Mercy concealed a smile – 'all I am doing at Brindells – all we are all doing – is restoring the house to how it was before it was swamped by gilt and brocade.'

'Oh, come, come, Mr Chantry, surely you can not criticize the taste here? We have always found the taste in this house to be impeccable.'

The rector looked across at Mercy, and then back at the young antiquarian.

'Why, most of this house was redecorated under the firm guidance of Mrs Brancaster's own step-mother, Lady Violet Duffane.'

The next morning found Mercy lying staring at her bedroom ceiling. She remembered so much now. How often, when her stepmother had been away *helping a friend with his house, a bachelor you know,* she had come back to Cordel Court with stories of how the mud in the hall had taken a team of labourers to remove it, and how there had been pigs in what had once been the rose garden and hens in the conservatory, not to mention tramps and undesirables in the music room. Her stories had always amused Mercy, and now she found herself laughing again at the memory of all Lady Violet's tales, at the same time realizing how strange it sounded to be laughing out loud when she was all alone, by herself with the servants tucked away in another wing.

But it was also strangely cosy, like summer nights at Cordel Court sometimes spent in the old shepherd's hut when she and her brothers were small and Nurse allowed them to gather firewood and cook their own supper, and life seemed a whole lot more exciting than it did when you were in the house, and even the simplest things such as washing up your own plate in a stream, or sleeping just in a blanket without sheets, were somehow wondrous.

Despite being alone with only the servants Mercy was not lonely, any more than she was unhappy at the idea that Lady Violet had helped John, among other bachelors of his generation, at some time in the far distant past. Far from feeling threatened she found it most amusing, especially because, from the moment she had walked into Brindells as a very young bride, time and time again she had thought how much it reminded her, and in so many, many ways, of Cordel Court.

Now, of course, all was revealed, and she knew

precisely why. The same hand had guided the choosing of the fabrics, the placing of the furniture, that wretched chandelier in the library that spoke more of Italian palazzos than it did of Tudor houses and rush matting.

They had not, as yet, had a telephone installed, and so, missing John as she did, she decided to write to him. Not such a long letter as he would inevitably find tiresome, but just enough to make sure that he knew she was thinking of him.

Dearest John – how I miss you! she began, but before she could sink into pathos she went on, *I realize, however, that as a sporting man you will not be missing me, and as long as there are foxes that will continue to be the case. But what I do hope is that you will come back to your adoring wife very soon, and you can hold the writer of this as closely and as firmly in your arms as she is holding this pen. Always and ever, your Mercy. PS I am now sleeping in the maid's room, over the kitchen, but the builders are working so fast that Mr Chantry says they could build a Sphinx in half the time it took the Egyptian slaves! I do not think that you would recognize the kitchen. Perhaps you should not come home until it is ready to welcome you with a dinner fit for a king – or a huntsman! I am once more your ever loving Mercy.*

After she had given Mrs Anderson her letter to post Mercy settled back into a chair in front of the maid's fire. It was strange, and interesting too, to be living in the domestic quarters of the house, for it gave her a better idea of the lives that their servants lived. Of necessity it gave her a clearer understanding of the length of their day, the endless corridors they had to walk, the dozens of trays and wheeled trolleys that had to be taken to and from the old kitchens. It was going to be much better now that the kitchen would be near the dining room and she had the little bell under her chair that she could ring whenever she wished someone to come in. So much better than having footmen plastered all around the walls straightening their backs and clearing their throats.

Yet she could not help wondering what John would think when he came back from his weeks away hunting with all his old friends.

'Yes, but Mr Chantry, do you think that a *man* will like that kind of patterning?'

Mercy looked over to Gabriel, and he sighed inwardly, thinking that if he had been given sixpence for every time she asked him such a question he could open another shop.

'I think Mr Brancaster will understand everything we are doing here, Mrs Brancaster, I really do. After all, the only major alterations are happening in the area in which most men are least interested, namely the kitchens. And as to the rest of the house, we are merely stripping back the gilt and the brocade to make it not only more in keeping with the age of the building but more in keeping with our times. I know the Queen does not approve of motor cars or motoring, but let us face it, Mrs Brancaster, the motor car is here to stay, and the stables that we are converting to just such a use are being adapted everywhere in the bigger houses.'

'But – Mr Chantry?'

'Yes, Mrs Brancaster?' Gabriel turned from holding up a piece of crewel work to the light.

'Supposing we have use only for the motor cars, what will happen to the grooms, and the horses? What will they do?'

'Oh, they will doubtless do as we all do, Mrs Brancaster.'

Mercy looked at him questioningly.

'Adapt!'

But fast as the builders from the village, and the craftsmen from the Cotswolds, and everyone else worked, the alterations to the kitchens extended themselves from three weeks into four, and from four into five and from five into six, until it seemed to Mercy that they might as well be rebuilding the Sphinx as remodelling the kitchens.

And so, as each new week presented new problems, she wrote to her 'darling husband', often in great haste, to warn him against coming back until 'the worst is over'.

I never thought to say so, but I am tired of hunting, so much do I miss you, Mercy my little angel. John.

Mercy kept all of John's letters to her. Brief as they were, she found that they fitted very nicely into the top pocket of the cotton blouses that she changed sometimes three times daily, so pervasive was the dust and the dirt at Brindells.

Your letters are next to my heart, she wrote to him

at the start of his sixth week away. *Literally, just by where it beats.*

'There is still so much to do.'

Mercy looked around, suddenly despairing, and then at Gabriel.

'I can not put my poor husband through such discomfort.'

'Just a fortnight more, Mrs Brancaster, and we can hang out the bunting for him.'

Mercy smiled. Gabriel Chantry was always referring to villagey things like that. It was really very sweet. It was always a question of 'hanging out the bunting' or 'not the kind of thing that we could say in front of the rector' or 'looks like harvest supper without the supper'. Sometimes Mercy found herself envying him his cottage and his shop, his bicycle which he used to come up to Brindells, often twice a day. His life seemed to be lived on an easier scale than her own. His surroundings did not dwarf him, and not much was expected of him, except by himself. Most of all, and sometimes this made Mercy more envious than anything, he was not a woman. He did not have a duty to produce an heir.

John's next letter to Mercy was from a different address.

Dearest Mercy, I have come to Cordel Court because you force me to be homeless! I am sleeping in your bedroom, hunting a little with Lady Violet, and trying

not to find your step-uncle Lord Marcus tarsome!
Please, please have me back soon. Your John.

At last the alterations to the kitchens were finished, and although there was still a long way to go with the furnishings and the placing of the new furniture, Brindells was once more, after two long months, at least habitable.

'I know it seems a long time, Mrs Brancaster, but really, considering the amount of alteration necessary, it has been very, very speedy. The builders have had innumerable problems.'

'Oh, Mr Chantry, who cares? Speedy or not speedy, my husband is coming home!'

The look of longing on Mercy's face gave Gabriel such a jolt that it brought him into a new emotional enclosure. He had never seen such – love was too over-used a word – such adoration for a husband in any wife's eyes. It filled him with envy, and silent amazement. For what kind of man was Brancaster, that he could inspire such adoration in his young wife? To Gabriel, unused as he was to such people, he had seemed too much the sportsman to be a loving husband. He now realized he must have been wrong, for otherwise such a lovely young woman as Mrs Brancaster surely would not feel as she did?

John was proudly returned to her, finally, by one of his new motor cars, carefully preceding the second, following in case of breakdown, both of them driven by newly hired chauffeurs from London.

When Mercy saw him she could not believe her eyes. It seemed as if she had not seen him for a century, and she found herself running into his arms and being wrapped around by his motoring cape, which smelt strangely and strongly of dust and petrol.

'Oh, John, how I have missed you!'

But as she stepped back and looked up into his eyes she realized that her John was gone. For some reason that she simply could not understand, the dark haired rider with the grim expression whom she had glimpsed riding in the Park when she first came to London, before the start of her ill-starred Season, was back.

Nine

The weather was fine and warm for October and there was much outside that could be appreciated, Dorinda found, despite the views being from the window of a nursing home. She tried to think of cheerful things. She thought about how pretty her dress was, and how much she liked it, and she thought about how kind the nurse, Miss Lynch, had been. She thought about all these things to take her mind off the fact that Harry was dead, and she was, to her great astonishment, missing him.

Of course she had paid a terrible price for her dreadful treatment of him. She had run away from him because he had been weak and silly and gambled, or collected butterflies – she had really no idea which had been the more tedious in its way. But finally she had helped to nurse him in his last weeks, as a result of which she had lost her lovely house in St John's Wood, and even her carriage with her beautiful coat of arms painted upon it.

Gervaise had thrown her out. Not physically, of course – that would not have been his way. But he had terminated her lease, or whatever it was that the lawyer had said she had been given – she had not really cared – and as a result she had been homeless for weeks now. And of course, having paid for the funeral and the burial, and the headstone, by the sale of her Indian sapphire necklace, her stomacher and even, yes, her pocket watch, she was now in that most unhappy of positions – she had nothing more to sell.

Only a few months before she had been on top of the world. She had had a lover whom she adored, clothes, jewellery, a house, a maid, and a beautiful blue leather lined carriage. But now, because of her really rather worthless husband, not to mention her wretched maid, she had nothing but her clothes, and a very little money.

Still, being of a philosophical nature, which she undoubtedly was, she could never bring herself to regret having helped to nurse Harry. Whatever his faults, he had taken her away from her mother and her dreadful boarding house. To live with her mother, who had been so unkind and cruel, had been far worse than living with Harry, for all his gambling and his butterflies.

If only Harry had not been so hopeless, Dorinda would never have allowed herself to be seduced by Gervaise on the boat. But Harry had only to have money in his pockets for it to find its way through them in a matter, not of minutes, but of seconds. So, all in all, there was really very little point in crying over spilt milk, lost carriages and horses, or any other little detail of her short but glorious life with Gervaise.

Miss Lynch came into the room.

'Here it is, Mrs Montgomery, your husband's

watch.' Leonie leaned forward and placed the timepiece in its leather box reverentially in Dorinda's gloved hand. 'And – forgive me, but knowing how much you have need of the *wherewithal* upon which we all depend, I have to tell you that Lady Angela has just commented, as she took it out of the safe, that it is very rare, and she imagines really very very *valuable*.'

They both stared at it, and then at each other. They had become such friends over the last weeks, it seemed hardly possible that they had not always known each other.

Dorinda had come to respect Leonie Lynch in a way that she had never imagined being able to respect another young woman of her own age. She knew that all the time Leonie had nursed Harry she had made him feel as if he was in heaven. Because of her he had died truly at peace, even happy.

Now, as they stared at the watch, there was no need for either of them to say what they both knew, that if the timepiece really was valuable, it might be the end to Dorinda's problems. If she could sell it she could perhaps buy herself a lease on a small house, or at any rate a great deal more security than she had at present. The money obtained for her Indian sapphires and various other items was not so great that it would last her more than a few months, and they both knew it.

As soon as she knew of her predicament, Leonie would have liked to ask Dorinda to stay with Mrs Dodd, but it was impossible. Unfortunately Mrs Dodd already knew all too much about

Dorinda Blue. Along with the rest of the world she knew that her carriage, in happier times, had been painted with a coat of arms made up of cherubs and a heart, of the sapphires that matched her eyes, of her outstanding beauty that had ensnared a well-known aristocrat. Dorinda's allure had already been widely publicized, and it followed that it was quite out of the question for anyone from a respectable background to entertain this member of the *demi-monde*.

At present Dorinda was lodging round the corner from Leonie Lynch and Mrs Dodd, in a clean enough place with large rooms. It was poorly furnished, with factory made pieces and cheap paintings, but clean enough to satisfy her needs, if not to inspire her to improve it with anything but the bare necessities.

'To whom should I go to have it valued, do you think?'

'Not to Tarleton. He is not the kind of person to place it in the right hands.'

'I only know Tarleton. I do not know any other fellow who sells jewellery privately.'

Dorinda sighed, but Leonie was, as always, there to reassure her.

'Mrs Dodd will know. She knows everyone in that way. She will find someone of quality who will take it for a much better price than Tarleton will give you.'

There. It was out. The word had been said. Price. Money. They all depended on it, and just because it was so important, because everyone did depend upon it, it was never, ever, ever, mentioned in *good* society.

Although, Dorinda thought wryly, this rule did not really apply to her, for she no longer counted as 'good society'. She was neither a woman of good reputation, nor in a position to pretend to be. Gervaise had ruined the chances of all that for her for ever. And now, what was worse, she was not just a member of the *demi-monde*, she was also that worst of all possible worsts for a young woman, she was – and might always be from now on, for all she knew – a widow.

She sighed again, but this time only inwardly.

There was something about a widow that put off the whole world. To begin with, her own sex did not like to become friends with a widow, in case widowhood was in some way catching. Or they were afraid that their husbands might be attracted to the luckless woman. The men on the other hand had quite another reason for their dislike of the state of widowhood. They did not like the freedom of it. They abhorred the feeling that where love might be given, marriage might have to follow, a situation which would never come about if they conducted an affair with a wife.

'I think we need to snare someone like Sir Joseph or even the matchless Lawrence Leveen with a timepiece as beautiful as this is. Do you know that?' Mrs Dodd said as soon as she saw the watch. It was not just a gentleman's watch, it was perfectly, outrageously, beautiful. It was the timepiece of a tsar or a king, or someone who had thought of himself as such, and had been made by a great artist, judging by the delicacy of the mechanisms, and the enamel work. It was a Rembrandt of timepieces.

'Yes, there are two people who would pay any amount for this, I would say. I mean, dear, the enamelling alone is out of this world, is it not? Yes. It should be offered privately to someone like Leveen the art dealer,' Mrs Dodd went on in her briskest fashion, 'or Sir Joseph Porter, who is said to have done so much for Mrs Keppel's fortune that she has more stocks and shares than the Prince of Wales himself. Tell your poor dear widowed friend that I will find the right buyer for this. Lady Angela is right, it is quite outstanding. The workmanship so delicate, the movement so light . . .' She held the pocket watch to her ear for a few seconds. 'It is as if angels made it, so clear and light is its sound, and its little bells and chimes are exquisite. It is a delight. Invaluable, I should have thought, Leonie dear, quite invaluable. I have met Lawrence Leveen, my late husband knew him. He is a great collector, a great character. He will be more than interested. Like all widowers, he has time on his hands, time enough to appreciate a timepiece of this kind.'

For the interview with Mr Leveen it was necessary for Dorinda to look more than respectable. She must look inspiringly respectable. To this end she dressed in her most beautiful widow's weeds, all silk skirts and rustling petticoats, and a lace jabot at the throat. In fact so dramatically dark was she that she knew her eyes looked more blue than ever against the black.

Dorinda knew from Gervaise Lowther that, as far as the aristocracy was concerned, Lawrence Leveen was a character around whom people circled with circumspection. He had been married young, and his wife had been tragically killed. Generally, though, he was considered to be a man of great taste who nevertheless had earned himself a reputation, among some of the upper echelons, for being a little too sharp in business.

Dorinda remembered Gervaise's opinion. 'He pays too little for paintings and then sells them for too much to fools whom he has already seen fit to help in business. But there. The Prince of Wales loves him. Mrs Keppel loves him. He is fabulously rich, and very much part of the new order of things. People are moving their money away from land and the countryside, looking towards railways and roads, motor cars and flying machines. Away from horses and carriages and towards the combustion engine.'

Crossing the street, with her skirts held high in one gloved hand, it seemed to Dorinda that the combustion engine would be a godsend to cities. It was so much cleaner and less offensive than carriages and horses, whose muck and manure caused mayhem to pedestrians, and assailed visitors' nostrils a good half hour before they entered London.

Dorinda reached the safety of the pavement and rounded the corner to Leveen's town house. It had balconies and a magnificent front door, and its first floor drawing room had an uninterrupted view of the Park.

She had been shown up the wide and beautiful staircase and was enjoying watching the riders and the carriages far below when the door opened and Mr Leveen came in. Dorinda had not given any thought to what he would actually be like, only to whether he would give her enough money for her timepiece to enable her to remove herself from her dull, grey, rented rooms and set up once again in a small charming little house somewhere near to where she had lived before. She just wanted a nice little place with dear little curtains and chintzes and flounces and fringes, somewhere to call her own. Nothing too much, just a small, or even tiny, little London house.

'Good afternoon, Mrs Montgomery.'

His voice was rich with amusement, as if the very notion that this young widow was in his house was immensely diverting to him. Everywhere there were flunkeys, and marble, and gilt, and paintings, and objects of great value, but Lawrence Leveen did not seem part of the setting that he had given himself at all. He gave the impression of being quite other, more like the smugglers that Dorinda had occasionally glimpsed while she was growing up in the Channel Islands, more like the gamblers that Harry Montgomery was forever being lured by, more like herself, someone on the outside of Society.

Dorinda dropped a curtsy, Mr Leveen bowed, they sat down, and within seconds Dorinda knew that he wanted her.

'You have the most beautiful blue eyes, Mrs Montgomery. I had heard of them, I have read of them even, but now that I see them for myself they are quite as breathtakingly beautiful as any eyes I have ever seen. And your hair, that rich chestnut, rarely seen, always appreciated.'

His dark eyes were literally brilliant, and his aquiline nose and pointed chin quite as fine and noble as you would wish to see, reminiscent, Dorinda suddenly thought, of the kind of looks seen in Elizabethan portraiture.

She looked across at him, as if he was as much an object as the timepiece in her possession, assessing him, summing him up. She concluded that despite his lack of height, he was immensely attractive. He had a vitality at the centre of him which, again like the pocket watch, was intricate in the extreme. His inner mechanism however was balanced between intelligence and mockery.

'Mr Leveen, I am here because I was told that you like beautiful things, and therefore would be interested in my late husband's timepiece.'

'Certainly.' He looked around him. 'I hope that my love of beauty is obvious.'

'It is.' Dorinda too looked around her. There was too much of everything for her taste, but the everything that there was too much of was certainly magnificent.

'Would you like to continue, Mrs Montgomery?'

She knew that he would know exactly why she had requested to see him. She also knew that he would be on tenterhooks to see if the timepiece was as beautiful as he had heard, which of course it was.

'I was told that this timepiece came into my husband's hands by way of business, and that it would be interesting either to you, or to Sir Joseph Porter, or to one of the Rothschilds, so exquisite and rare is it.'

'May I see it, Mrs Montgomery?'

'Certainly, Mr Leveen.'

She did not move. He did not move, but looked across at one of the footmen. Without saying a word the footman trod across the carpet to where Dorinda was seated and, taking the leather box from her, trod back to his master and placed it in his hands.

Leveen opened the box, and because his face reflected no emotion when he took out the watch Dorinda knew at once that it was of the greatest interest to him. After a minute or two spent in examining it in reverential silence, during which Dorinda could hear the ticking of what now seemed to be a thousand clocks set about the great room, he looked up at her.

'Where exactly did you say your husband obtained this, Mrs Montgomery?'

Dorinda sighed inwardly, already toying with the idea of pretending that Harry had inherited it from an uncle, but sensing that Leveen was too shrewd a businessman to be fooled by some genteel lie she said, 'I am sorry to tell you, Mr Leveen, that my late husband won it at cards. But he was so foolish, and so profligate in a way, that he forgot all about it, and it only came to light in one of his pockets when the nurses were laying him out. He is dead, you see.'

'It is reasonable to presume that he would be dead, if he was being laid out.'

Leveen's face was so serious that Dorinda bit the inside of her cheek in an effort not to laugh. She was remembering how Miss Lynch had taken the watch as quickly as she could to the safe especially kept for such things.

'Never leave anything for the undertakers,' she had warned Dorinda. 'Undertakers are the biggest robbers you will ever come across. They would follow you underground if they could. Oh yes, it's not just ghouls that go to churchyards, you know, Mrs Montgomery, but undertakers too.'

It had surprised Dorinda that Leonie knew so much about such things. She had supposed it was because Miss Lynch was a nurse, and had been surprised to find out that it was actually because she had been brought up near enough to the East End of London to make her, Dorinda thought, a cockney born within the sound of Bow Bells.

'I will buy this timepiece from you, Mrs Montgomery, but on one condition only.'

'And what would that be, Mr Leveen?'

'That you have dinner with me, here, tonight.'

Dorinda smiled. 'I am afraid that is not possible, Mr Leveen.'

He looked momentarily taken aback, as if he was not used to not being able to buy anything and everything at the very moment that he had a mind to do so.

'Not possible, Mrs Montgomery? Have I to take second place to someone else? Is there, could there be, someone more important to you than the prospective buyer of your beautiful timepiece?'

Dorinda perfectly understood that he was using business methods to bribe her, but since she was a humble landlady's daughter, she was neither impressed nor shocked.

'No, certainly there is no-one to take the place of the buyer of this timepiece,' she returned briskly, because she never had much time for misunderstandings. 'Of course there could be no-one more important to me at this moment than you, Mr Leveen. I am not a rich woman and I want the best possible buyer for my timepiece. But that is not the reason why I cannot come to dine with you tonight.'

'What could be the reason then, *Mrs* Montgomery?'

He said her name, 'Mrs Montgomery', just a little mockingly, as if he did not truly believe that she could have been married. Or perhaps because he was longing to call her 'Dorinda', which she could never allow, not until the skies fell in, or something just as extraordinary.

'The reason, Mr Leveen, that I can not have

dinner with you tonight is quite simple.'

Dorinda looked around the room in which they were seated, and imagined that through the double doors to the next room, and doubtless in the next, and the next, and above them, and below them, all around them, in fact, was nothing but gold and more gold, very nearly a surfeit of gold, if that was possible.

'I cannot dine with you here,' she continued carefully, 'because while I can wear my newest Worth dress, which is exactly the colour of my eyes, I no longer have any *jewels*.'

Now the look in his eyes turned from shrewd appraisal to suppressed laughter, for he was with her at once, realizing that he had perhaps in her met a worthy adversary. And of course Dorinda herself could not keep from smiling, so that the look in her wonderful orbs was the same, although of course, she realized, her eyes were yards more beautiful than his. So there they sat, suppressed laughter in both their gazes, and for a second neither of them moved, knowing that to do so would mean that they would dissolve into laughter.

At last acknowledging Dorinda's gesture to the flagrant beauty and moneyed luxury which surrounded them, Mr Leveen walked across to her sofa, and taking her hand in his surprisingly elegant white fingers he bent low and just brushed the back with his lips, in what was the approved fashion for married women. Dorinda appreciated his meaning at once.

'Mrs Montgomery, I will have Tarleton send you round some suitable jewels. What colour is the gown, did you say?'

'Why, Dorinda Blue, of course. I can surely leave off mourning if we are to dine alone, would you not say?'

'Very well, I will have Tarleton send you round some sapphires to go with your gown. No, better than that.' He stared down into her famously blue eyes. 'Better than that, I will go to Bond Street and choose a necklace for you myself. A very good necklace. Not so good that it will make the Princess of Wales jealous, just good enough to make Mrs Keppel look up and stare when you enter a room.'

He did not choose just a necklace, he chose a set of three pieces, which he sent round by his carriage.

In fact his coachman delivered to Dorinda's landlady a gratifyingly large leather tooled jewellery box, attached to which was a small card with two words written on it.

For tonight.

Once opened, the box was found to be lined with black velvet. A necklace lay in the centre, while to each side were placed earrings, and beneath the main piece a bracelet. Each piece was studded with small, perfect diamonds, so that as Dorinda opened it up both she and her landlady gasped as the light from the cheap overhead lamp caught the diamonds that were clustered about the perfect sapphires.

'That necklace is so beautiful, Mrs Montgomery,

I think I will faint,' exclaimed Mrs Goodman. 'What a generous man Mr Leveen is, to be sure. Or do you think, Mrs Montgomery, that he has more money than sense?'

The two women stared at each other.

'Oh, he has money, all right, Mrs Goodman.' Dorinda looked at her landlady. 'He has money, and lots of it, so much that I think it would be better if neither you nor I ever know just how rich he is. The question is,' she hesitated as she looked at the older woman, 'do I have sense?'

Leveen had perfectly cut evening clothes. In fact they were so perfectly cut that it occurred to Dorinda that they were *too* perfect, and that Gervaise, whose evening clothes too had been most elegant, looked better simply because he *wore* his clothes, whereas Leveen looked as if the clothes were advertising his tailor, and not setting off the man.

'You really should not have sent me round quite such beautiful jewels, Mr Leveen.' Dorinda made a tut-tutting sound and looked at him, straight-faced. 'But I have to tell you that I am so glad you did. I could not possibly have dined with you here, in this Aladdin's Cave of beauty and art, bare-necked. It would have been insulting both to you and to your taste, you will agree. But you see, circumstances have forced the sale of so much in my life, due to my husband's death, and so on.'

'Of course you could have come here bare-necked, Mrs Montgomery, but I have to tell *you* I should straight away have sent round for something for you, no matter the hour. I could not have borne not to have decorated such an exquisite neck with jewels. By the way, we are dining downstairs. Quite alone. We can talk business there – quite frankly.'

'I always think if one must talk business it should be frankly. Not to do so would be to risk being taken for unworldly, don't you think?'

The room was beautifully set out as a second, very intimate dining room, which as Dorinda immediately appreciated, had been designed for just such a dinner as they were to enjoy. There were the latest in electric hot plates on the sideboards, so that they could serve themselves, and although candles were still used there was a delightful sense of sitting in a room that had the best of both possible worlds.

And of course Dorinda was already so well versed in the way of amusing a man with gossip and stories that once dinner was under way there were no awkward silences, only a great deal of laughter. As a result she forgot all her vows to be sensible, and enjoyed herself to such an extent that, as she said, ingenuously, to Mrs Goodman the following afternoon, *I am afraid I quite forgot to come home.*

That afternoon also saw Mrs Goodman sailing out of her rooms, in the second of Mr Leveen's carriages, leaving behind her lodging house, her cheap furniture and her maid of all work, in favour of becoming Mrs Montgomery's personal maid.

It is quite the best thing I have done, she told herself, as she saw just exactly where Mrs Montgomery had forgotten to come home from. *It is quite the best thing either of us have ever done.*

'Mrs Goodman is my personal maid. She must be given the best rooms possible,' Dorinda told Leveen's housekeeper.

'Naturally, madam.'

Dorinda turned. There was something in the woman's tone that she did not like. It reminded her of someone else. The resemblance nagged at her as she climbed the magnificent staircase to the upper rooms, past all the classic paintings with titles so long that the words underneath them had to be painted in two sections.

'Why do so many of your paintings have such tarsome titles, Mr Leveen?'

'It was the fashion fifty years ago in painting competitions, such as the one Ingres won at Rome, to impress the judges by using very long titles, sometimes as much as twenty-five words long, or longer.'

Leveen smiled at Dorinda and, as he did so, embarrassingly, she realized that she still had not called him by his first name. Last night, and again this afternoon, he was still 'Mr Leveen'.

She immediately decided to make a joke of it. It was always her way, when faced with some piece of her own ignorance that she could not get around, that she made a point of it. It was a feature too of her personality that she could not bear to be bored. If faced with even walking a few yards, if she could not think of anything else, she would as like as not pretend to be someone else, with the result that nowadays it often seemed to Dorinda that she could not remember what she herself was actually like. It was just how she was.

'Mr L.'

He did not turn immediately, but a few seconds later, and as he did so she saw at once that he liked her to tease him in this way.

'Mr L, am I to have my own suite of rooms?'

'But of course, Mrs Montgomery. Under my protection you are to have everything.' He bent suddenly and, for him, almost dramatically towards her, the expression on his face serious in its sincerity. 'You are to have everything that you have ever wanted, and more. And if I hear that more than two seconds have passed and your wishes, whatever they are, have not been granted, I will dismiss whoever kept you waiting for your desires.'

Of course it was romantic nonsense, and yet as the impeccable Leveen straightened up and looked at her with his deep set black eyes, Dorinda could not help but be impressed. She dearly liked to see a man at her feet, she suddenly decided, but only if he was impossibly rich like Leveen, not if he was merely moneyed and aristocratic like Gervaise. She liked it because it was a game, and not real, for Leveen's money made everything really quite fantastical. It was as if she was living in a fairy tale.

The impression was strengthened when the footmen flung open the double doors of her 'apartment'. Dorinda realized with a sharp sense of satisfaction that she could probably fit all her St John's Wood reception rooms in just this space.

It was as she thought back to St John's Wood that the realization came to her, and she knew at once of whom the housekeeper downstairs reminded her. It was the wretched Blanquette. The plain maid who had landed her in such trouble with Gervaise, by, it was obvious now, letting him think Dorinda had left him for her husband. But of course, as always with such situations, by the time she had tried to write to Gervaise his pride was irrevocably hurt. With rumours of his humiliation already circulating in all the top circles he had sold her carriage, and anything else that reminded him of his beloved Dorinda Blue, and turned his attentions to a quite delectable young blonde – which was at least flattering.

To Dorinda's way of thinking, she was, as of that moment, going to be far better off where she was. She was *not* passionately or dangerously in love with her really quite fascinating 'Mr L', but she knew that she could love him if only for his generosity.

Even so, whatever her present complacency, she realized that the housekeeper would have to be watched. In fact – and here she glanced sideways at Mrs Goodman who was busy gasping at the marble bathrooms and silk furnishings, at the Aubusson rugs and the crystal chandeliers, at the silver on the dressing table, at the beautiful hangings of silver and turquoise around the bed – now that she came to think of it, it might not be very long before Mrs Goodman rose from personal maid to a new position as housekeeper.

But that was for the future. Now Dorinda frowned at her image in the old silver-backed mirror in the dressing room where Mrs Goodman had already begun to unpack and hang up her best gowns.

She must never, she told her face, ever again find herself in such a position as she had found herself with Gervaise. She must never again be at the mercy of servants, or indeed anyone else.

And so it was that Dorinda immediately began to secretly plan to replace Leveen's servants with her own. It was quite simply a necessity. If she was not to lose everything again, to be once more out in the street having to sell jewellery to keep body and – to a certain extent – soul together, she had to surround herself with servants whom she could trust. She would begin with the housekeeper.

Dorinda looked round at Mrs Goodman.

'We are here to stay, Mrs Goodman, and you are going to be part of this with me, always.'

'If you say so, Mrs Montgomery.'

'I certainly do. Would you like that, do you think?'

Mrs Goodman smiled, and it was a smile of such warmth, such affection, such hope in the future that Dorinda knew at once that they had both made the right decision.

Mrs Dodd was seated comfortably in front of the fire when Leonie came into her first floor drawing room. She came in nice and quietly as Leonie, Mrs Dodd was happy to say, did everything, without fuss or calling attention to herself.

Tonight however, it seemed, was going to prove an exception. For Leonie, quiet as she was, and seating herself in front of the fire and taking a book on her knee as always, was quite unable to be still. Indeed she was very far from even pretending to read. She kept looking over the top of her book until Mrs Dodd knew there could be no holding her. She had something to tell her godmother, and she had to tell her now, or burst.

'Very well, my dear. My novel is excessively dull, on and on and on, and getting nowhere very slowly. What is it you must tell me, if you are not to explode with the effort of keeping silent?'

'It is – Mrs Montgomery.'

Mrs Dodd always pretended not to know who exactly Mrs Montgomery was. By feigning ignorance in this way, they both knew that she somehow preserved her own gentility.

'Ah yes, Mrs Montgomery. Was she not the lady whose timepiece you showed me?'

'That is exactly it. The young woman with the beautiful timepiece, or half-hunter or whatever it was.'

'Exquisite piece,' said Mrs Dodd, sighing with some satisfaction.

301

'She came to see me today, at the nursing home. We went out for a cup of tea together, since Lady Angela was perfectly agreeable.'

'Indeed. She is a very tolerant woman.'

'Mrs Montgomery has had a change of residence.'

'Indeed. How very salubrious for her.'

'She is living in Park Lane. She has moved there from Mrs Goodman's lodgings, taking Mrs Goodman with her. The house is as big as a palace, and Mr Leveen has bought the timepiece from her for a very tidy sum.'

Mrs Dodd paused before saying 'Indeed' for a third time.

'And all in twenty-four hours. She has changed her life completely, in twenty-four hours.'

Mrs Dodd tried to look surprised.

'Of course,' she said, diplomatically, 'Mr Leveen is always very philanthropical. He has hired her, doubtless, as a *companion*. Now that his sister is married, and he himself is a widower.'

'Precisely that. She is to run everything for him.'

Mrs Dodd smiled. 'Bring us each a glass of sherry wine, my dear Leonie, and let us drink to the good fortune of your acquaintance from the nursing home.' Mrs Dodd smiled again.

It was always the same with good business. It had been the same with Leonie when she was born, and now here it was again. Just a matter of being able to help the right people into the right situations. And afterwards, sitting back and watching the success was also part of the very real pleasure of good business.

Thanks to Mrs Dodd dear Leonie's friend and acquaintance Mrs Montgomery was now happily *placed* where her fortunes could only rise; and if they did not, well, it was not as if she had not been given a second chance. If she failed it would be her own fault and no-one else's.

'Leonie, my dear, I am delighted that your acquaintance from dear Sister Angela's Nursing Home has been able to find her feet once more, and that Society in the shape of the Prince of Wales and many others will be flocking to her dining table. As a matter of fact I understand that the Park Lane house has three different dining tables – but I must remind you, remembering that unfortunate incident with the mannequin earlier this year, that whatever the ties of gratitude between yourself and Mrs Montgomery you and she can only meet in the most private of circumstances. Should she ever invite you to Park Lane, you would have to refuse of course. You understand that, don't you, my dear?'

Leonie nodded, but in her heart of hearts she was disappointed. She would have loved to visit Mrs Montgomery in Park Lane. By all accounts the house was fabulously decorated. It had taken something like fourteen thousand books of gold leaf just to decorate the ballroom, or so one of the other nurses at Lady Angela's had told Leonie. Perhaps, even now, she imagined, Mrs Montgomery, her beautiful, large, violet blue eyes looking about her, would be planning to decorate a drawing room with another few thousand books of gold leaf?

The maid was standing at the sitting room door.

'A caller has come for Miss Lynch, Mrs Dodd. Two of the other nurses has been taken poorly and a gentleman brought in very bad needs attention all the way round the clock. A huntin' accident, or so the boy said, and can you come as soon as possible?'

As a matter of fact Leonie was really rather pleased to be called back to the nursing home. Much as she loved the fire, the sherry and the conversation, which was gossipy and mundane by turns, both moods always having a soothing effect on at least one of the two parties present, she was always flattered to be called back to the nursing home in an emergency. It meant that Lady Angela trusted her. Better than that, it meant that she had come to rely upon her.

'That is that, then,' said Mrs Dodd flatly. 'I will be having a lonely drover's dinner all by myself. But no, you must go, of course you must. Patients must come first.'

Leonie kissed Mrs Dodd's round, soft, dimpled face and went off to fetch her cloak. Patients must come first. Yet as she hurried back into the hall and from there into the street outside, there were such delicious smells coming from the basement that she was rather sorry, this particular night, that Mrs Dodd was having to enjoy what she always described as a 'lonely drover's dinner' without her.

'Very well, you are here.'

Lady Angela was just crossing the hall when she

heard Leonie's quick footsteps echoing along the stone floors of the old house that made up her nursing home.

Having curtsied to her Leonie walked alongside her listening intently as she told her as rapidly as she could what had happened to the new admittance.

'Miss Broderick could not come back as she is poorly with the influenza and Miss Llewelyn has measles, or else I should never have sent for you.' She paused suddenly, thinking, and then started again. 'It's Lord Freddie Melsetter. He has broken his back out hunting, do you know. The doctors who have examined him fear he will never walk again, or indeed ever lead a normal life. But we must not let him know this until such time as he is able to take the news.' Again Lady Angela paused. 'Put it this way, Miss Lynch. Lord Freddie will not lead the field again for many a long year, but we do not say this to him when he comes round.'

Leonie had no idea what was necessary for anyone suffering from a broken back. She knew only that her patient would be helpless, and, as Lady Angela had said, there would be little hope of his recovering at all, except to stay as he was now, unmoving and bedridden.

Much of the more intimate nursing of the male patients was carried out by young men trained by Lady Angela to lift and help where necessary, but the day to day care was undertaken only by women, and then only from a certain kind of background. 'Respectable' is what Mrs Dodd would call it but Leonie knew better. Lady Angela had an 'eye' for the kind of person that she wanted in her nursing home, what she looked for in a nurse. And even Miss Scott, who would be on duty with Leonie that night, was a great deal more sensible than anyone would have guessed from a passing acquaintance.

Leonie hurried on down the corridors, the gas lights flickering over her starched white head-dress, and her floor length starched white apron. Part of her was very much looking forward to being up all night, seeing herself, as she did, as a guardian angel to the sick.

'He must be very handsome,' said Miss Scott, speaking in a normal voice, shortly after Leonie joined her.

Leonie looked over to where their patient lay. Surely the girl could have no possible idea as to whether Lord Freddie was handsome or not. He was so much bandaged and so much cut about. She glanced back at her colleague, briefly and questioningly, but carried on rolling the bandages that were part and endless parcel of their day to day working life.

'You can always tell a handsome man by his feet,' pretty young Miss Scott continued. 'He has the most beautiful feet. Long and slender, and toes to match. I caught sight of them just before Lady Angela arrived,' she explained. 'Still, it's curtains for him now, by all accounts, poor devil, and nothing more to be said or done.'

To her surprise Leonie felt quite angry that a young girl with so little experience of either life or nursing, should be standing about dismissing a patient's chances of recovery in this ruthless manner. She stared at the bed where the man lay. The light was set low above his head, for Lady Angela firmly believed that a light close to the face helped to bring a patient back to consciousness, and yet, of a sudden, even to Leonie's eyes the light seemed to be sinking.

'I heard that Lord Freddie Melsetter is, or was, a real ladies' man.' Miss Scott raised her voice, seeming to be, if anything, more confident now, perhaps because their patient was, if anything, more feeble. 'I heard too that his poor mother, and then his poor wife, could not keep a maid in the place, or a housekeeper, and that there was no-one in the neighbourhood who did not succumb to his charms.'

'Hush, Miss Scott, really, we must shush! You know what Lady Angela says. Patients, even when they are unconscious, can always hear what is being said. Ask any of the older nurses. They have been told, afterwards, every word that has been said by them. It can prove most awkward, if you are indiscreet, and you will regret it, I promise you; particularly with someone as well connected as Lord Freddie Melsetter.'

Miss Scott looked sulky at first, obviously a great deal put out that she had been discouraged from going on with her tittle-tattle. She loved to gossip, and was known to be more than a little forward, if not *fast*, when it came to the male patients, but when all was said and done she was completely dedicated.

'I think you are prudish beyond belief, Miss Lynch. Why, even if Lord Freddie sprang off his bed and waltzed round the room, which he quite definitely never will again, he would admit that he was a *ladies' man*. It is just a fact, like your turquoise eyes, or my big feet!'

'Of course I am a ladies' man,' came a shaky voice from the bed, 'and will always be so, if allowed.'

The two nurses stared at each other. A minute before Leonie could have sworn his breathing had been growing a great deal more shallow, but now here he was speaking.

They both hurried over to his bedside.

'God have mercy on me, you were right. He is only awake and hearing us.'

Leonie leaned over the bed, the light from the lamp falling on her beautiful face.

'How are you?' she asked the mass of wounds beneath the bandages.

The swollen lips moved slowly, and the voice came, whistling slightly, through broken teeth, but he was speaking none the less.

'Still – very – much – a – ladies' – man, just sorry I can not see you.'

Leonie looked across at Miss Scott before addressing their patient once again.

'Are you feeling any pain?' she asked, gently.

'Yes. Damn. A great deal.'

'I will give you something for it, but don't move, whatever you do.'

Even as she said it Leonie recognized how unnecessary that last injunction was. But Lady Angela was right – no-one, but no-one should be told they were paralysed until they were strong enough to take the news.

'Nature allows for the first moments of over-confidence, then comes despair, then gradual realization, and after that acceptance.'

Nothing that Leonie had seen during those first few months while she was being taught so much by Lady Angela led her to argue with the principal's assessment of patients' mental adjustment to their situation.

'We are not God, although some of us think we are,' Lady Angela said, often and often, as she moved briskly from room to room, followed obediently by a covey of junior nurses. 'We are not God, Nurse Lynch, and since God does not choose to tell us when we are to die, then God forbid – and I truly think He does – that we ever try to step into His shoes and tell anyone else what He would not.'

Leonie had tremendous respect for Lady Angela. The other nurses might be afraid of her, or mock her sometimes because she was so authoritarian, but as far as Leonie was concerned there was no-one she had ever met whom she respected more. *Lady* Angela might 'entertain' the future king. She might be, as Leonie had heard rumoured, both his mistress and his nurse. That was her affair. So far as Leonie was concerned, *Lady* Angela was everything that Leonie herself would like to be.

Ten

Never, ever try to hit a man about the head with your version of the truth.

Mercy knew this statement by heart, as indeed she should because she had heard her stepmother say it time and time and time again while Mercy was growing up at Cordel Court. She knew it, and she believed it, because her stepmother had run her own life in such an exemplary fashion, balancing her hunting and riding pursuits between the London Season and her country house, being adored and worshipped by Mercy's father, always looking beautiful and sounding charming.

Not only must you never accost a man with the truth, you must not scare the opposite sex with so-called truths. Much better to coax them into a good humour, and find out the truth later, at your leisure.

Mercy had been told all this, and she knew it to be perfect advice, and yet here she was doing all three things at one and the same time.

She was standing in the middle of her so recently and beautifully decorated bedroom, sobbing tearfully and asking him what it was that could possibly have changed his attitude towards her so much.

'But I kept all news of the *petit quelque chose* as a surprise for you! I only wrote to my stepmother. Otherwise I kept it to myself, so I could tell you myself as a surprise. It was meant to be such a surprise,' she heard herself repeating, while she attempted to stop the tears from coming so fast by stabbing at them with a small lace-edged handkerchief. 'I thought you would be so pleased to return to find your house beautified and your wife expectant. Also – Mrs Blessington our neighbour said – it's not so nice for husbands when their wives are being unwell at first. Better for the husbands to be hunting, she said.'

'Mrs Blessington is quite right, my dear. Of course it is better for husbands to be away, but I have been away so long, for so many weeks, I had almost forgotten that I *was* a husband. And I am sure, young as you are, that you could be forgiven for forgetting that you are my wife.'

The look in John's eyes was implacable, as if he no longer saw Mercy at all as she had been, or as she was, whatever that might be.

'You are in a certain condition and that changes a woman's outlook. There is really no more to be said. Except I would remind you that it was you who had such a passion to change the house.'

Mercy stared at him, appalled, not understanding.

'It was *you* who sent me away to hunt. I had no desire at that time to take up my old pursuits; and after that it was you who kept putting me off from returning. I finally had to take refuge with your parents since there was no-one in town to dust down my house except the scullery maid and the hall boy, and I had rather not just continue in my hunting box leading the life of an unmarried bachelor. Had you told me as you should have done before I left that you were *enceinte*, I should never have gone. But you did not. You sent me away, and when I return, hey presto, suddenly, my house is transformed and you are having a baby.'

'But, John, it was for *you*. I wanted to make everything beautiful at Brindells for you.'

Mercy could hear herself, her broken voice, see and feel her own tears, and all the time she knew it was all so wrong. She should not be indulging herself in this way. She should be trying to stay composed.

'And you – and your friend, the *antiquarian* Mr Chantry – have made everything beautiful at Brindells, Mercy. Really, you must be congratulated. Now, if you will excuse me, dearest, I must go and see Forster – the stables call.'

He looked embarrassed, and at the same time somehow bored by her behaviour, by their situation, by his life at that moment. It was as if he was not there by choice but because he had to be, because it was his duty, rather than his pleasure.

'Oh, but John, this house would be – is – so empty without you, that is, without me and you, together. Could it not be as it was before you went away? We were so – well, I thought we were so in love.'

'That was then, dearest, now is now, and you – you have your confinement ahead of you. And I must, for many reasons, return to Leicestershire after Christmas.'

'Oh, please, don't go and leave me again, alone here. Please don't, please, John. I feel so alone, here. I have no friends, no-one to whom I can talk. And when the wind howls and the rain falls – it is just – so lonely.'

She saw at once, through her own despair, that he was appalled not just by her outburst, but worst of all, by the tears, which just would fall, no matter what. It was as if all the pain she had felt since his return and his seeming indifference to the news that she was to have a *petit quelque chose* was pouring out of her. As if inside her was a great well of unhappiness that had suddenly decided to spring out of the centre of her being. It was shocking, and she knew it. But the truth was, seeing John again had broken down all her defences.

'I am so sorry, John.' She straightened up. 'I have lost control. It is very wrong of me.'

His eyes, which in the early days of their marriage, before he left for Leicestershire, had always looked so full of fun and delight when he was around her, softened momentarily, and it seemed to Mercy that despite her shameful weakness he might still feel for her as he had done before he left, that they might again be as they had been.

'I think you had better ring for your maid,' he said, gently. 'It is the baby. Doubtless your *petit quelque chose* has brought on a fit of the *laudanums,* as my nurse used to call it.'

He kissed the top of her head, but left the room, and then the house, driving off in one of his new motor cars with the chauffeur seated beside him instructing him as they went. He did not come back until late that evening, and by that time Mercy had made up her mind never to tell him how she felt ever again. She must be proud. She must be resolute. He must never, ever again see her in such a state of tears and confusion. She had, it was quite plain, disgusted him.

But first she must apologize to him. She knew that the male pride would expect this, and that unless she did so there might be what her step-mother always called *a dreadful pall of silence* over the house for weeks, if not months.

Dear John, I am truly sorry for making such a sorry scene. You are right. It is probably my condition. I hope it is a boy condition! Your ever loving Mercy.

She was right to write to him, and to leave flowers in his dressing room along with the note, because he came to her the next morning, and of a sudden he seemed to Mercy to be very much the old John. Laughing with her, and teasing her, and altogether behaving as he had done before he left, fatefully, or so it seemed to her now, for his hunting box in Leicestershire.

'Madam is quite her old self again,' he said, matter-of-factly. 'And that is good, for now it is Christmas and we have more to do than you would believe possible.'

315

It was true. There was the tenants' and building workers' carol service in the Great Hall, the decoration of all the rooms, the supervision of all the meals – the family waiting on the servants, by tradition, on Christmas Eve night.

And all this time, it seemed to Mercy that her old John might have come back to her. Solicitous and kind, even presenting her, on Christmas morning, with a gift of a musical box for her dressing table. It was a beautiful gold box inlaid with enamel, and when you opened the lid it displayed figures that circled to the same waltz that John had first danced with her, on the night of what Mercy liked to refer to fondly as 'my great rescue from the permanent gilt chair'. But then, of a sudden, it was all over, the ivy, the mistletoe, the jollity, and he was off once more to Leicestershire, and Mercy was left all alone at Brindells.

The moment something happens you will let me know, my dearest, won't you? I want you to know that I will always stand by you.

Mercy stared at that particular line in John's last letter to her until the words stopped making sense. How would she let him know in time? How would she send for him? She might not be capable, after all – she might die, and he would be in Leicestershire. And why did he find it necessary to tell her he would *stand by* her? It was such a funny way of putting things. But then he was so much older than her that much of how he phrased things was quite different from the way she would express herself – something which, in the

past, had been a subject for joking between them –
but not now.

'My dear, I tell you, you do not want your husband
near you when you are having a baby,' her neighbour Mrs Blessington comforted her once more
when she heard of Mercy's worries. 'Good
gracious, far from it, my dear. Believe me. Men are
useless, except with calves and foals and such like,
when they have the strength to pull where we
women can only pluck!'

Mercy had made fast friends with old, jovial
Mrs Blessington over the pre-Christmas festivities
when her till then unknown neighbour had
suddenly called on her, and left her card,
prompting Mercy to return the favour prior to
inviting the lonely old widow to join them all at the
carol service in the Great Hall. They had liked each
other at once, despite, or perhaps because of, their
great age gap.

She now went on, 'Husbands are always fainting
or drinking brandy when babies arrive. Much
better just to let him settle into his hunting in
Leicestershire, and leave you in peace. Besides, his
going away is not proof of his indifference, far from
it. It is his way of showing anxiety. Believe me, men
are strange in this way. There has only to be a baby
on the way for them to start behaving as if they are
having the infant and not you.

'When my first was on the way, my husband was
on the point of leaving the army to take up farming
his father's estates. And what did he do? Decided

317

to fight a duel, imagine? I think they were illegal, even then, but no, that did not deter him. He still went ahead and was duly shot in the leg.

'I always think he was trying to draw attention to himself, silly fellow. Or put himself into pain at the same time as I was. At least nowadays, thanks to the dear old Queen, your generation do have the wonderful consolation of chloroform, and it *is* wonderful, I hear.'

Mercy looked up from her sewing. She was making a beautiful coat for the baby with embroidered sleeves and a silk dress to go under. Her tiny, delicate, silk stitches, as beautiful as the material, were a constant source of admiration to Mrs Blessington.

'So, would you think it would be better if I say nothing to John until the baby is safely arrived? That I write to him as if it is the most natural thing in the world for him to be off hunting while I wait, would you think that would be better?'

'Much better, my dear. The person to inform when your new arrival is on the way is the doctor, not the husband. All those things that we understand about babies are understood by women, not men. Men only understand hunting and shooting – everything else is alien to them. Of course that does not mean they do not feel fondly for us, or their babies, when they arrive. But you see, my dear, they do not understand them. It is not given to them. It is just a fact, like the sun coming up in the morning.'

'I only hope I can give John the boy he wants.

Nothing else will do, I know. I keep pleading with my *petit quelque chose, be a boy, be a boy, be a boy!'*

'Well, and I am sure he will be, but in my experience men become just as proud of their daughters as they do of their sons. Believe me, once a girl is presented to them, no other man will do for her but her father!'

Mrs Blessington's ample form shook with laughter and her hat, large, veiled and old fashioned, tilted forward a little so that the firelight caught the diamonds around the mourning brooch she wore to one side of it.

'I must admit, I am afraid, despite the idea of the chloroform.'

They were standing up now, because the light was fading and it was time for Mrs Blessington to leave. Mercy had put aside her sewing, and Mrs Blessington took her hand in one of her gloved ones and looked into her eyes, holding her gaze with her own calm, humorous one.

'I have had six children, my dear, and I was always afraid. The way each child arrives is always, always, so different. There are no two births the same, whether they are the first or the last.'

They both knew that this was really very forthright talk for the drawing room, but since Mercy had dismissed the servants for the afternoon, leaving only a maid to serve them tea and then go back down to the kitchen fire, they were quite secure with each other.

'I will remember everything you have said, Mrs Blessington,' Mercy remarked thoughtfully, as she rang for the maid to call her carriage round to the front steps. 'And I am so very grateful to you for coming to see me, and for being so truthful with me.'

'My dear, when it comes to it, and afterwards, you will hardly remember a thing for the joy you will experience. I sometimes think that these are the best moments of our lives, for our sex, the arrival of babies, the joy that they bring.'

Mercy stood waving to her as the carriage set off. The Blessington estate, comprising a large manor house and farm set about with its own church, adjoined the Brancasters', but even so, given the size of all of both their estates, the house was a good quarter of an hour's drive away.

She turned to go up the steps to the house. The servants would be back from their afternoon off at about six, and then she would at least have the sensation of feeling that there were other people about the place, but until then there was only the maid, and Twissy.

As soon as she saw the poor quivering puppy, Mercy had insisted on bringing her inside, bathing her, feeding her, and keeping her. So now Twissy lived with Mercy, even to the point of coming up to her chintz bedroom with its four-poster bed, which John's dogs were never allowed to do when he was home. Being an optimist, Mercy told herself that John would be sure to love Twissy as much as she did, within a very few hours of arriving home.

*   *   *

There was nothing that Mrs Dodd looked forward to more than the moment when she heard Leonie's light tread coming down from her bedroom, and to see her coming into the drawing room with her hair freshly brushed and put up, her Chinese gown, of which she was so proud, drawn about her, and the small, gold slippers on her feet catching the light of the drawing room lamps as she moved easily between the many pieces of furniture that were set about Mrs Dodd's through reception room with its dark wallpaper and brocade curtains, and its brass lamps placed low at some points and high at others so that Mrs Dodd could embroider by them when she so wished.

'So how did he do today?'

Leonie knew that her nursing of such a famous roué as Lord Freddie Melsetter was fast coming to resemble a serial in a periodical for her warm-hearted patroness. It was not just that Lord Freddie was not making quite the progress that had been hoped, so that Mrs Dodd was genuinely concerned for his well-being, but also that, by chance, Leonie had become particularly close to him.

'I don't want you, I want my own special little nightingale,' he would demand from behind his bandages, between bouts of unconsciousness, thereby giving offence to the other nurses, and causing Leonie to feel both flattered and embarrassed.

This particular evening Leonie had to admit that Lord Freddie had done no better as far as his physical state was concerned. There had been no improvement, alas, from the day before.

'But when he was conscious he was more talk-ative than usual. And he told me such stories! All to do with hunting and that sort of thing, but such funny stories. About when he was a boy and laid a trail of aniseed across his father's lawn so that the pack flew off in a different direction and he could save the cubs from being eaten by hounds. And how he rode his best hunter up the steps of the house and tied it to the dining room doors when the Queen was having dinner with his parents, and he was exiled from England for his pains until the scandal blew over. But you have to hear him for yourself, it is the way he tells you. He has obviously been so naughty, and yet although his family, it seems, gave up on him years ago, everyone at the nursing home loves him.'

'Everyone loves a charming rogue, dear, it is just a fact. The charm always outweighs the roguery, if there is such a word. Besides, I dare say you have all given him your heart, and nothing to be done.'

Leonie blushed. It was true they all had, even Miss Scott. But Leonie sensed that she was special to him, and in consequence hardly liked to leave him to attend to anyone else, so much did she feel that she was needed by him.

'Your interest in him will bring him back from the brink, I am sure of it, dear,' Mrs Dodd said, suddenly sounding over-firm, because she felt for Leonie, seeing how much she had put into nursing Lord Freddie.

'I hope you are right.' Leonie smiled. 'I am going

back to the nursing home after dinner, if you don't mind. I feel I must be there at the moment. He needs me a lot at this time. Just being with someone can give our patients strength. I believe some of our healthy strength really does pass into them.'

'Don't tire yourself too much though, even on his account, dear. Remember you do have other patients.'

But she had barely finished her sentence when the realization came to Mrs Dodd that just at that moment, for Leonie, there really was only one patient who truly mattered.

The following morning Leonie was summoned to Lady Angela's office. Quickly splashing her face with water to give herself a less tired look, she hurried to see her and found the principal standing staring at something outside the window. Leonie was not sure what it was, but she knew that it must be something very interesting for Lady Angela went on staring at it long after Leonie had entered the room in answer to her 'Come in'. So much so that Leonie finally started to feel uneasy.

'Miss Lynch.' Lady Angela turned finally towards her junior nurse. 'You have been here some months.'

Leonie felt her unease turning to fully fledged fear as she suddenly became quite sure that she was going to be dismissed, summarily, without a chance to speak for herself.

Her mind raced through the possible mis-demeanours she could have committed during her time at the nursing home. Would it be that she had not rolled enough bandages? Had her hygiene around the patients been at fault? Had she been seen talking too long to another nurse? The starched surface of her apron under her hands began to feel limp as her hands grew warm with anxiety and the heat from Lady Angela's office fire.

'Yes, Lady Angela, I have been here for some few months.'

Leonie decided to speak in a strong, firm voice, and to look her employer firmly in the eyes as she replied. She must look unafraid, as she had often had to do growing up in Eastgate Street, when old men tried to accost her when she went to the shop that sold much prized and very precious tea for Sundays. Or boys threw stones when she and her schoolmates walked in a crocodile to Church from the little convent.

'And during all these months, Miss Lynch, I have to say, I can not criticize your work in the least way. Your nursing, your attitude, your whole demeanour can not be faulted. Our profession has changed indeed. Gone are the days when nurses were considered to be the lowest of the low. Thanks to Florence Nightingale those days are over.'

The relief that came to Leonie on hearing those words was extreme, but she was careful not to show it. She knew, she was too wise for her years not to know, that there was still something to be said, or why would she be there?

'So, Miss Lynch, I am sure you will understand

very well what I am about to say.' She paused. 'You are a good nurse, and hard working. Your conduct has been exemplary – until now. Recently I have realized that your devotion to Lord Freddie Melsetter has become excessive, and I must ask you not to continue to nurse him.'

Lady Angela raised her hand as if to fend off any emotional rejoinders with which Leonie might be preparing to defend herself. At the same time she smiled at her with a sudden warmth and understanding, as if she knew just how she felt, but was still not going to allow her to speak up for herself.

'You see, Miss Lynch, as nurses we can, and often do, get trapped by our patients' charm and personalities. You have, I am afraid, by all accounts, been trapped by the engaging Lord Freddie.'

Of a sudden Leonie was short of the usual words that would normally have sprung to her mind, and for a good reason. It was true. She had been 'trapped', as Lady Angela put it, by Lord Freddie's charm. And also by his courage. He had suffered so much.

'Lord Freddie is a great character, Miss Lynch. It is perfectly understandable to be trapped by his charm, I do assure you. But I must ask you, whatever happens, whether God wills that he is gathered or not, to allow the other nurses to attend to him at night. I am afraid you may have allowed emotion to come between you and your patient, and, as you know, that will never make for good nursing. We cannot allow ourselves to feel as we imagine our patients might be feeling. We can only allow ourselves to feel *with* them. You have become, as Florence Nightingale would put it, not just the bandage but also the wound. You feel what he feels, and that is not only bad for him, it is bad for *you*. And the other patients, of course, for they should have just as much of a claim on your nursing skills as Lord Freddie, despite the fact that they do not, alas, have his golden charm.'

Leonie nodded. She could see the reason, the truth and the logic in everything Lady Angela had said, and as a result there really was nothing for her to say. Much as it broke her heart not to try to alleviate Lord Freddie's loneliness and pain, and much as it struck her as being hard, she could see, from every point of view, that she might indeed have become too close to him.

Lady Angela must have guessed, or sensed, her conflict of feelings, understanding perhaps just how much Leonie's heart had become involved with Lord Freddie's recovery, despite the fact that he was really a very old man. She laughed suddenly.

'My dear, can I tell you something that I have learned here? Men, and women, never lose their appeal, no matter what their age. I have nursed one man who was even a centenarian, yet every nurse with whom he came into contact would have cheerfully run off with him, such was his attraction. You see, they wanted to be with him because of his personality. He made life exciting and gay for them. Shocking though it is, it is also true.'

The sudden kindness of the woman, the sweetness of the expression in her eyes, made Leonie feel dreadfully sentimental. If good old Eastgate Street had not made her a great deal tougher than most of the people who worked at the nursing home, even the men, she might have cried if only from relief. The truth was that Leonie knew what it was to go without, not just of a Monday, but of a Tuesday too. She had seen her foster mother weeping into her apron from the anxiety of losing a sixpence in the street. It had not made her hard, it had made her *used* to life. After all, there was no point in *not* being used to life, not if it had to be lived. She felt strangely bereft at the thought of not nursing Lord Freddie, but it had to be accepted.

'It has always been a fault in my character to become too involved with patients, I do realize that.' She paused, remembering the young mannequin, and Harry Montgomery too. 'And I *have* become too involved with Lord Freddie, more than a nurse should, I can see that. I will remember from now on never to become the wound, only the bandage.'

She dropped a curtsy to Lady Angela, who smiled and nodded not patronizingly but because they had, the two of them, reached a rich understanding. The kind of understanding that few can reach who do not share the same commitment.

Or, Lady Angela thought with sudden irony, as she watched the slender young figure hurrying off, the same ancestry, for if Lady Angela returned to what her aunts always called the *begat book* and looked at their mutual ancestral lines she thought that Leonie Lynch would most likely prove to be a third cousin once removed, or some such nonsense, not that it really mattered.

The older woman turned back to the window. Her view, of the buildings of London, of the bustle of city life, gave her the greatest satisfaction, because buildings meant people, and people, she knew, would always need to be mended in the best possible way. She had been brought up in the country, but it was to London that she had always aspired, knowing that her deep desire to heal could only be satisfied by a city, or – and God forbid that it should happen – a war. She had needed to found a nursing home because she had a vocation to heal, and because she herself had needed to be healed.

By touching sick and wounded people, finding people who needed her, in turn she had found her self-respect. That respect which had been removed from her by her parents in childhood had, bit by bit, returned to her once she had set up her nursing home. She had become a person, a figure, someone to whom others could turn. She hoped very much that this was happening to her poor dead friend's daughter, that she too would find her self-confidence replaced by something more important than family pride – fulfilment.

Outside the door Leonie drew herself up, smoothing her hands down the sides of her crisply starched apron. She had been through a horrible ordeal, and it was useless to pretend otherwise. She had known, somehow, as Lady Angela spoke to her, that the principal must be aware of Leonie's origins, and that she understood that she was neither fish, nor flesh, nor good red herring. She was one person sometimes, and another at others. She did not now belong in Eastgate Street, but she was only, when all was said and done, a lodger, however welcome, in Mrs Dodd's house. Realistically she knew that no-one from a distinguished family could ever marry her, yet she could not see herself marrying a man from the same background as herself. So, truly, her vocation was everything to her. It had to be. She resolved to think of nothing else from now on. And although her zeal to heal could not now include Lord Freddie Melsetter, nevertheless she knew that she was needed, and that, when all was said and done, was as much as anyone should ask of life.

Mercy stared out of the window at the black of the night. Sometimes it seemed to her that the darkening sky outside was reaching forward and enveloping her, and never more than at that moment. She did not want to think about John and why he was not coming back to her, and so she thought about her brothers, and how jolly they were, and how much she longed to see them.

Their childhood had been a happy one, despite the loss of their mother. Perhaps it was due to the kindness of their nurse, who was not the normal run of strict nanny, and was married to a husband who worked on the Cordel estate. Or perhaps it was just because if you give children a pony, or a bicycle, a hoop or a bat and ball, and fields in which to run about, and streams in which they can jump, they are as happy as the livelong day.

And of course she had always felt safe at Cordel Court. Never mind that her father had been taciturn and shy of his children, at no time while she was growing up did she feel that unhappiness was just around the corner, that because her mother had died nothing was ever going to go right for them. On the contrary, if, as sometimes happened, she stayed out too late riding and saw the lamps of Cordel far off in the distance, she would ride towards them as fast as she could, fearing all the time that perhaps they might go out, and she would never find home again. Now, all alone as she was with only her little dog Twissy and the servants, she was coming to feel the same about Brindells. Whatever happened, it was there for her now, it was home.

Not wanting to give in to her feelings, she stood up and decided to start to rearrange her bedroom and dressing room. It would take her mind off her loneliness, and tomorrow she would drive herself and Twissy into Ruddwick and call on dear Gabriel Chantry to ask him to come and advise her about the hangings in one of the bedrooms. They were falling into ribbons and she did not know whether it was worthwhile to restore them or to have them copied, but what she did know was that if she folded them up and took them in to Gabriel Chantry he would tell her straight away.

Besides, nowadays she rather longed to see him again. He was so cheerful, such a delight to be with. She had missed him, and since the house had been all but finished there had been no excuse of which she could think to call him back, until now.

There was a great deal of commotion in the high street as Mercy drove the fly into Ruddwick the following day, with Twissy, not Josephine, sitting up behind her. She pulled the pony to a halt and watched with some amusement as two chauffeurs, irate to the point of comedy, shouted and pointed to their privately owned cars while the owners sat, unmoving, in the front passenger seats.

'How much better,' she said smugly to Twissy, 'to bump, bump, bump into Ruddwick with the pony.'

When the shop bell rang out and Gabriel Chantry appeared out of the darkness of the back room, he looked astonished to see Mercy. Since the house had been finished they had not so much as caught sight of each other in the village.

'Mrs Brancaster, how perfectly delightful to see you. Come in, come in.'

He escorted her into his shop, and at the same time twisted the card on the door to read 'Shut'.

'Mr Chantry—'

Mercy stopped, and stared. The shop had been transformed. Whereas before she had to creep about poking and peering between any amount of chaos, now everything was in its place, and there was a place for everything.

Gabriel looked suddenly concerned. 'There is nothing wrong, is there? I mean, your husband's bed has not collapsed, or the ceiling in the kitchen fallen in? You seem to have arrived in such a flurry.'

'No, bless you, heavens, no. Why would you imagine such a thing?'

'Probably because you have not brought your maid with you, I think.'

'Josephine, my maid, is sick with a feverish cold. You haven't met Twissy, have you, Mr Chantry? She is acting as my maid today.'

'Good morning, Twissy.' Gabriel Chantry patted the dog courteously, but straightening up once more he looked at Mercy anxiously.

'I do not wish to be presumptuous, Mrs Brancaster, but it appears to be about to snow. The sky is quite blue and heavy in its greyness out there. I am sure it is a snow sky. And that being so, was it quite wise to drive yourself in – in this way?'

He did not say *in your condition*, but they both knew perfectly well what he meant.

'Oh, I know, probably not – why, Mr Chantry, you clever person, what a perfectly delightful bed!' Mercy exclaimed, trying to change the subject.

'Don't you think I should drive you back, before the road becomes impassable? If Mr Brancaster knew, what would he say? I mean, he would be quite upset, I should have thought.'

'Mr Brancaster is in Leicestershire. Or is it

Yorkshire, or has he gone to Somerset, to Blackmore Vale country? At any rate he is hunting foxes, while I am hunting a beautiful oak bed, which you just happen to have here in your shop.' She stopped, smiling at him, her head on one side. 'As a matter of fact, Mrs Blessington told me of your bed, and to tell you the truth, since I have seen no-one *but* Mrs Blessington for months and months, or so it seems – actually it's weeks and weeks – I was determined to bring myself here, willy, nilly. So here I am.'

'Nevertheless, I will drive you home. If I may say so, it seems a little foolhardy to have come all this way in the fly.'

Mercy turned away. She could not confide in him, much as she would like to. She could not tell him how lonely she felt, and how much she wished that she had not married in such a hurry, for she suspected now, as she had thought at the time, that she had been far more in love with John Brancaster than he had been with her. For if not, surely he would not have left her to return to Leicestershire, or Yorkshire, or wherever it was? And if he did love her why was it he wrote so seldom, always 'in haste' and then only a scrawl between convivial dinners and entertainments, not to mention the hunting.

'I must confess, I just had to get out, I just had to do something. It is always better to do something, is it not, Mr Chantry, than to do nothing, wouldn't you say?'

She spoke with such simple charm, and for all

her added girth had such a forlorn dignity about her, that Gabriel Chantry found himself suddenly moved. If she was his wife and in such a state, he could not prevent himself from thinking, he could not leave her to go *hunting*.

'You are all alone, aren't you?'

'Yes, quite alone, except for the servants, and I am afraid, since I have inherited all of them from my husband's bachelor days, they do not like me very much. Servants much prefer to work for bachelors than for a married woman. It is just a fact.'

Gabriel Chantry's maid of all work, Mrs Dewsbury, appeared from the back room of the shop at that moment. Gabriel at once waved a warning hand at Mercy, who, equally promptly, sat down on the antique bed behind her and started to bounce up and down on the mattress.

'This is surprisingly comfortable for a bed which dates back to Tudor times, or so you are about to convince me, are you not, Mr Chantry?' she said, laughing. 'It is most bounciful and beautiful, and – and – and – oh, oh, dear!'

Leonie knew. She did not know how, she just knew that Lord Freddie was no longer on this earth. The feeling came upon her perhaps because it seemed she had suddenly awoken in the middle of the night, so sharply that it had been as if she had been shaken awake by someone who had come into her room and put a hand on her shoulder.

She lit the candle beside her bed, sat up, and stared around her. It was still the same room, and she was still the same person who had gone to bed that night in her thick cotton nightdress and, with the aid of her Bible, read herself to sleep.

But now it was quite different. She was sharply awake, and the light from her bedside candle flickered around the room, creating pockets of darkness where she was sure someone was standing watching her, silent and unmoving.

She trod across the carpet and turned on the newly installed electric light by the door. There was the heavy old mahogany chest, and there the red upholstered easy chair, and there the embroidered *prie-dieu*. Opposite her on the wall above the chest was a print of one of the Queen's favourite pictures, a stag at bay, and on the chest a pair of Staffordshire pottery figures of Chelsea pensioners.

In other words, everything was in its place, just as it had been when she had finally fallen asleep.

'Who is it?'

She felt absurd asking a room with no-one else in it such a question, for although she believed in an afterlife in heaven if you were good, and in hell if you were bad, she had no belief in spirits or ghosts. Up until now reality had been quite enough for Leonie Lynch.

And so it was with a great many misgivings that she now gave in to this urgent feeling that there was someone watching her, someone whom she had known who had come to see her in spirit, for some reason that she could not guess.

'Who are you, and why have you come here?'

She knew, and her blood became chilled at the realization, that there was someone there. Someone whom she knew. She crossed herself, feeling a deep unease because the person, whoever it was, was not happy. They were disconsolate, their soul unrested. They were waiting for someone or something. She now knew the meaning of the phrase 'frozen to the spot'. She could not have moved even had she wished to, not if there had been someone screaming for help outside her door. She could move neither forwards to where she felt the presence, nor backwards to where she might free herself from the feeling.

My life has been spent in drunkenness and fornication. You must redeem me with your prayers, free me from my wretchedness, or I will be condemned to roam the spirit world with no resting place.

There followed a terrible sound, a sound that Leonie had heard described as a witness to the torment of the human spirit, a groaning of such a sonorous nature that it could have no earthly connection, and yet a sound which she had heard sometimes in the night when she, in company with some other nurse, lantern in hand, would hurry to check on a patient thinking to find them in their death agony, only to find them sleeping.

I will pray for you, she silently told the tortured presence.

Seconds later Leonie again felt a hand on her

shoulder, but it was no more than Mrs Dodd shushing her, saying, 'That was a terrible dream you were having, dear. Such groaning as you were making. I came in thinking you were ill, really I did.'

To Leonie it was as if her room was heaven, after the hell of her dream, despite the dream being so real. But now it was truly real and there were the curtains being drawn, heavenly curtains, and there from outside the large old window came the sounds of the first carriages of morning going past below in the street. And there was a London sparrow on the sill outside her window and Mrs Dodd wearing an old-fashioned deep maroon top with the wide balloon sleeves of some ten years before, and a skirt with velvet bandings.

Leonie jumped out of bed. She was so pleased to see daylight that she found it hard not to point to the light beyond the window, as if she had been blind and could now see again.

And it was hard not to hug Mrs Dodd, and dance around the very room where the spirit had silently begged for her prayers. And hard not to run round to the nursing home, which was so near to Mrs Dodd's house, and jump up the steps, and find that Lord Freddie was just as he had been the day before. Not dead as she had dreamed, but terribly, beautifully alive.

'Oh, oh, yes, yes. It is a most handsome bed. Oh, yes.'

Gabriel held out his hand to Mercy, for what with one thing and another she was finding it a little bit of a struggle to get to her feet.

'And I will buy this handsome bed from you, Mr Chantry.'

'Thank you!'

Mercy felt literally warmed by just the feel of Gabriel's hand, just the rich sound of his voice, which was, she realized suddenly, a most mellow voice, rounded and full of the same warmth as his hand. He had brown eyes which were large and kind, and dark brown hair which seemed to match his beard most exactly. He had always been, she realized, a good friend to her, such a good friend, such fun, that she suddenly found herself longing to stay with him in the shop for ever.

'What else have you here, Mr Chantry? Oh, look—'

'You must go home, Mrs Brancaster,' Gabriel interrupted, perhaps already sensing her real reluctance to leave the cosy ambiance of the shop. 'You should never have come, all alone without your maid, with only your dog. Look, outside, it is just as I said. It is beginning to snow.'

He hurried to the back of his shop to put on his caped coat and hurried back again, carrying his hat.

'I will drive you home in the gig. Really, you should not be here, you should be at home. The trap might overturn, or you might become snow-bound on the road. The consequences could be terrible.'

338

Mercy, feeling extraordinarily light of head and heart at the very idea that Gabriel Chantry was going to be coming back to Brindells with her, that she would not be all alone for yet another day with just the servants, went ahead of him to the pony and trap, Twissy following at her heels. Taking Gabriel's proffered hand she climbed up into the fly.

'If you insist on driving me, you will stay for luncheon, of course.'

But the wind had already got up and his head was bent, one hand holding on to his hat and his coat collar well up around his ears, and he did not hear.

The drive back to Brindells was conducted in double quick time, perhaps because the wind twisting and turning about them as the trap bowled along drove the scurrying snow into the pony's ears and behind his tail, with the result that his spanking trot became faster and faster until even Gabriel, who was a good driver, feared he would lose control.

Mrs Tomkins, the housekeeper, looked astonished when she opened the door to Mrs Brancaster returning to the house without her maid, only her dog and Mr Chantry following along behind.

'Mr Chantry is staying for luncheon.'

'Yes, madam.'

Mercy watched her walking off in the direction of the kitchens with a feeling of resignation as she realized how deep was the old housekeeper's disapproval of the new chatelaine of Brindells.

Indeed, even after so many months it sometimes seemed to Mercy that she would never be able to settle the servants around her the way her step-mother had somehow managed to do at Cordel Court.

When all was said and done, they were still John's servants, not hers. Clarice had been long ago reclaimed by her stepmother, and Josephine, who had taken up the position in her stead, seemed unaffectionate and wary, as country girls often did.

Mercy shrugged her shoulders and rang for one of the footmen to replenish the fire in the drawing room, which was looking sadly low, and at the same time smiled ruefully at Gabriel Chantry.

'They know they should do all this, that they should keep the fire banked up, but, as you see, they still do not listen to me. I often think that servants despise women, and do not really like to take orders from anyone but men. Still, my husband is due back soon, so he will doubtless have them scurrying about like the mice in the eaves.'

Yet as she chatted on Mercy realized that, like the servants, Gabriel Chantry was not really listening to her. He was looking around the drawing room, in whose transformation he had such a hand, making sure that all was looking as it should be.

Indeed, as Mercy watched him, it seemed to her that he was filled with the kind of quiet pride that an artist might feel when seeing his picture hung in the right place. For herself, as she watched him moving about the room, his height and warm presence lending immediate vibrancy to the place, she could almost imagine that he was the master of Brindells himself.

In London Leonie had discovered that her dream had, alas, been a premonition. She had breakfasted as usual with Mrs Dodd – porridge, cream, honey, bacon, kidneys, mushrooms, kedgeree for Mrs Dodd, rolls and butter for both – and then walked briskly round to the nursing home as usual, only to find that Lord Freddie had indeed, despite all her dearest hopes and fervent prayers, died in the night.

Leonie was immediately sad, and she was not alone. The other nurses too had become devoted to Lord Freddie. Despite his terrible injuries, in between his bouts of unconsciousness he had always seemed determined to charm whenever he could. But following on the normal feelings of sorrow naturally came others of practical reasonableness. Lord Freddie had been blinded and paralysed by the terrible hunting accident. He had been old. He had not accepted the way he was, though he had, thank God, never known the full extent of his injuries. All these factors made the nurses sad but resigned to his death

As Leonie helped to lay Lord Freddie out she found herself thinking back to the night, and the terrible pleading of the spirit in her dream, and she shivered inwardly. It was dreadful to think that all that gaiety and humour might now be condemned to everlasting darkness. But she had been brought up to believe whole-heartedly in hell fire, and much as she wanted everlasting happiness for Lord Freddie she found it impossible to believe that a man who had thought only of his own pleasure would be gathered straight away to some heavenly mansion. He must, she found herself realizing, be helped on his way by the prayers of those who loved him, and so, silently, in the hours that followed his laying out, Leonie prayed for Lord Freddie to an all merciful God who would, she imagined, love him for what he was, as everyone at the nursing home had, and in His forgiveness would lie Lord Freddie's redemption.

Much later in the day Lady Angela called Leonie into her office.

'We are all feeling sad that Lord Freddie has been gathered, Miss Lynch, but we are all of us assured that it was indeed a happy release.'

'May I have your permission to attend Lord Freddie's funeral?'

There was a small silence before Lady Angela shook her head.

'No, Miss Lynch, I am afraid not. I do not, for many reasons, think that would be wise, really I don't. We do not make a practice here, as you know, of attending the funerals of every patient who dies, although I shall be going on this occasion. It would be a bad precedent, I am afraid, if I allowed you to come with me, although I know that Lord Freddie seemed to have become rather dependent on you in his last weeks. But you do see,

342

if I let you in this case – well.' She stopped and then went on, seeming to want to change the subject. 'You know he called you his "little nightingale"?'

'In that case it is just as well perhaps that he never heard me sing.'

Lady Angela smiled. She always liked people who counteracted a rebuff with humour.

'It was your speaking voice. He said you had such a pleasing voice that just hearing you say "good morning" made him feel better.'

'I shall miss him.'

'We all shall. It is always the same with patients such as Lord Freddie Melsetter, you will find, Miss Lynch. Although sometimes we are, in many ways, glad that they have been released for their sakes, they do tend to leave a big gap in our lives.'

Perhaps that might have been that, as is the way of things, had not Lord Freddie been such a very special kind of character, as generous, it seemed, as he had been dissolute, for a few days after his funeral Leonie was called again into Lady Angela's office.

Lady Angela's expression was so solemn that Leonie found her heart beating faster, yet again.

'I shall not waste time, Miss Lynch, but get straight to the point. Lord Freddie Melsetter . . .' Lady Angela stopped, clearing her throat. 'Lord Freddie Melsetter has left you a great deal of money. I can tell you, on the authority of relatives encountered at the funeral, that it is in the region of five hundred pounds, in other words a sizeable bequest.'

Leonie stared across the desk at Lady Angela. Money, left to her? It did not seem possible.

'Why me?'

'I suppose because, in some way, you became special to him.' Lady Angela looked at Leonie quite calmly. 'Remember how, in those first days when he was brought in here, you made it your duty never to leave his bedside? And I had, eventually, to reprimand you, as you remember, fearing that you were becoming too involved in this case? Well, you may have become too involved but for his part you were, I think, never very much out of his mind.

'And then, of course, having been told that you had gone away for a few days, and fearing, I think, that he would not last until you returned, he made his last will and testament and being Lord Freddie he included you in his bequests. It often happens with the older patients and their nurses. I happen to find it, as I am sure you do, most touching.'

Leonie could not describe her own feelings. She had never thought about money as she was nursing Lord Freddie Melsetter, or indeed of anything except that she wanted him to get better, to be free of pain.

'But – it does not seem possible that he should single me out in this way. To suddenly leave a person he hardly knew such a large sum of money. What can he have been thinking?'

'Oh, that is Lord Freddie Melsetter all over, believe me. He was always famous for being as generous as he was foolhardy and impetuous. Oh dear, no-one ever knew what to expect of him next. Believe me, Lord Freddie was what my old nurse would call *something other*. If he wasn't in a jam he really and truly thought life had come to a stop. No amount of exile ever straightened him, and in the end he was accepted by everyone for what he was – something other.'

Leonie was surprised at the older woman's sudden change of tone. It had become fond and amused, and yet it was as if her words had been spoken on a sigh, and behind them, of a sudden, it seemed to Leonie that she could hear an orchestra playing, a little too slowly, at some country ball in the early eighties of the nineteenth century.

It seemed that Lady Angela was in the mood to be reminiscent, because she went on, 'You have no idea what a fellow he was when he was young. By the time his reputation had recovered from locking royalty and his parents into the dining room with his horse, we were all in love with him. Every woman in his neighbourhood, or anyone else's for that matter! It was not just that he was handsome, but that he was so – so debonair, and so witty. He could ride all day, dance all night, and then if you bumped into him a few hours later walking down St James's you would find him quoting Horace. He knew the Georgics by heart, and Shakespeare's sonnets, all of them; he quoted them as if they were nursery rhymes. He could play tennis and swim like a champion and lost his best horse on the turn of a card. We will indeed never look on his kind again. It is said of many, but never so truly as of Lord Freddie Melsetter.'

Leonie stared at Lady Angela, entranced by her description of the old man when young but somehow feeling that there was something more she was leaving unsaid.

'I always felt, when I was nursing him,' Leonie ventured at last, fearing that she had glimpsed tears in Lady Angela's eyes, 'that Lord Freddie Melsetter was just the kind of man every girl would dream of having for a father, Lady Angela. Do you not think, dashing, and handsome as he must have been, and charming too? And now he is gone, and alas I can not thank him in person for being so kind and generous to me.'

'Quite so, quite so.'

Lady Angela walked over to 'her view' of London and stared out, not really seeing very much, except perhaps the past.

'Well, well, this is good fortune for you, Miss Lynch. Always remember that good can come out of bad. Always. It is a lesson for life. That will be all.'

After the young nurse had left her office, Lady Angela turned and looked at the closing door and gave a great sigh of relief. She raised her eyes to heaven and imagined Freddie Melsetter smiling his impish smile, his turquoise eyes lighting up at perhaps the sight of a pretty girl sitting on a cloud next to him and playing a harp.

'Oh, Freddie, Freddie, I could wring your neck. Twenty years on and we are all still sweeping up after you, you attractive wretch!'

Eleven

The time was exactly four thirty in the afternoon
when the heir to Brindells in Sussex, a town house
in London and a hunting box in Leicestershire
made his first appearance in the world. The snow
outside his future inheritance seemed to its present
occupants to be six feet deep. And indeed it might
as well have been twice that, for all the roads were
quite impassable when they finally realized that
there was no longer any point in hoping that the
doctor could get through to help with the birth of
young John Edward.

Upstairs on the first floor, in a back room next
to one of the new bathrooms, Mercy had long ago
surrendered her soul to the Almighty, so sure was
she that she was going to die.

The old housekeeper, as she ran in and out with
hot water kettles, was also satisfied, seeing how her
mistress was suffering, that she was going to die.
She had mentally laid out Mercy in her best dress
and pearls before the baby's head at last started to
make its appearance.

Only Josephine, Mercy's personal maid, and one
of a long line of children, was quite certain otherwise. She, who had been quite used to helping to

deliver her mother's babies from an early age, and in far more cramped conditions, was quite sure that Mrs Brancaster was not going to expire.

'Baby came out head first, no cord round his neck, and here you are both alive, now what more could a body want, Mrs Brancaster, ma'am?'

The girl, younger than Mercy by about a year, looked down at her, smiling, while at the same time mopping her mistress's brow with a cold flannel.

'And don't you worry, 'bout nothin'. As soon as the snow's cleared Mrs Tomkins has promised to get the news through to Mr Brancaster. Although, judging from the wine drinking and the celebrations downstairs, there might be no need – Mr Brancaster will hear the cheers for hisself in Leicestershire!'

'Mr Brancaster said he would be coming today. Nothing to do with the baby, but he was coming! He did say.'

Josephine nodded, smiling, efficient, and full of her own importance at being able to safely deliver the son and heir to Brindells.

'Like our mother's always saying to us when we was growin' – *You don't want gennelmen at the births, theys only goin' to get under our feet, Josie. Theys a bloomin' nuisance to be truthful, and same can be said for doctor*. Last doctor that attended our mother, and that were by mistake, he passed right out on the floor and our Gran and I we had to put burnt goose feathers under his nose. Such a nuisance, men is. Still, this one is going to be that different, isn't he, Mrs Brancaster? Now let him suck, if you would, Mrs Brancaster, and then you'll feel your belly all tight an' nice in a trice.'

Mercy took hold of her son, already feeling the power of his personality, and seeing to her astonishment that he looked the spit of her eldest brother – in other words, all Cordel and not a hint of Brancaster. She stared from his pink and crumpled face to Josephine's beaming round one and smiled. It was no good denying that she was pleased. She was really more happy at that moment than she had ever been.

In Park Lane, as the snow fell, despite the weather, the dreadful dirty look to town snow, and the strange silence of the few trade horses and carts passing below her window – so quiet were their feet and the wheels of their trade carts, it was as if they were ghosts – Dorinda was feeling not just on top of the world, but on top of her world. She had now been living under her dear Mr L's protection for a whole month, and to be truthful she was adoring every minute of it.

To begin with, and indeed to go on with, she had quickly made it her business to become used to being not so much rich as wealthy beyond the dreams of woman. That, happily, had not proved as difficult as she might first have thought. Mr L was more than generous as far as she was concerned, he was overwhelming in his generosity, so much so that she found herself actually holding back from admiring anything, in case he felt compelled to buy it for her.

'You know you should not buy me all these things, Mr L,' she reproached him, twice daily. 'It is very bad for a person to have everything they want, really it is.'

'I have more than most men to give, my dearest, that is the only difference between me and anyone else. If I was a street trader I should give you a shiny silk garter once a year, but since I am not I buy you, like the street trader, what I can afford, and I can afford a great deal.'

'Yes, but Mr L, there is a question of restraint. If you buy me jewellery every day what will you then give me for my birthday?'

Dorinda was ever practical and she could see that this amused him no end.

'For your birthday? Well now, let me see. Hampton Court. Or a country house. Or a string of racehorses. Or a painting by Sargent. Or a golden coach. Or a skating rink. Or a swimming pool so that you can swim up and down with your lovely hair streaming behind you. That is what I shall give you for your birthday. After all, anyone can give jewels.'

'Except the street trader.'

'Well, quite.'

'But Mr L – should you . . . that is, I mean . . .' Dorinda held up a diamond that he had hidden in the napkin on her breakfast tray. 'Diamonds for breakfast. That is a little too extravagant, surely?'

'This is an extravagant age, I must treat you

extravagantly. You know very well how I feel about you. You are my jewel. That is why I give you so many.'

There was a short pause while Dorinda, lying against her sumptuously dressed and pillowed gilt bed in her great boudoir with its vast silk curtains, looked genuinely modest.

'As a matter of fact I do not actually know how you feel, Mr L. After all, you could have any woman you wanted. The thought has to occur, why would you want Dorinda Montgomery?'

Leveen was standing by the bedroom door, about to hurry off to his offices, to conduct his empire along its usual profitable lines.

He was not prepared to show his hand so early in the game, so he waited for a few seconds before he framed his reply.

'I wanted you from the first moment that you came here, and you know it. I wanted you because you have the most beautiful sapphire coloured eyes, because you are impudent, because you have a brilliant smile, and because I was lonely for someone just like you and had quite given up on finding anyone who would be half as beautiful, or kind.'

Dorinda sat up, suddenly indignant.

'I am not kind! How can I be? I left my poor husband and ran off with—'

She stopped suddenly, instinctively knowing that it would be a mistake to mention the name of her former lover in front of the present incumbent.

Unfortunately Lawrence Leveen mistook the

hesitation, and the look of what was actually caution in her eyes, for some remaining hidden emotion, some perhaps still deep rooted affection for her former lover, and such was the possessiveness he felt towards her, it cut into him so sharply that had he been asked to describe the sudden pain he would have said crisply, *Lemon juice in an open wound*.

'My dearest,' he told her smoothly, after only a fraction of a pause, having taken in her sudden hesitation, the look in her eyes, the way the name *Gervaise* had been avoided, 'we will meet for luncheon, and you will doubtless be ready to amuse me with your chatter then, I hope.'

He closed the door of her boudoir behind him, but did not move away from it until he had composed his thoughts. He knew Gervaise Lowther, Dorinda's former lover, really quite well. They were both members of the Prince of Wales's set. Lowther was likeable and handsome, and perhaps, as far as women were concerned, even mesmerizing, but he did not have Leveen's money, which was at least something. Dorinda might not be in love with her 'Mr L', but she was at least here with him. He did, for the time being, possess her.

He walked down to the great marble hall of his Park Lane house, nevertheless, feeling oddly restless, even ill at ease with himself. He had not wanted, or sought, to fall in love. In fact, as he had explained to Dorinda, it had not been among his priorities even to search for another woman to occupy his house, or play hostess to his friends. He had loved his wife, and only her, and she had filled his every living moment until she had been killed when her coach had overturned returning from the races. And he had thought never to replace the irreplaceable.

But then Dorinda had happened to him.

Perhaps if she had not walked into his drawing room that day looking quite so beautiful, and somehow, for a member of the *demi-monde*, so utterly ingenuous, perhaps if she had not offered him her late husband's watch with all the guile of a young girl quite unused to talking about money, and in fact looking for all the world as if she could not have cared less about it, he might not have fallen in love with her. But since she had, and he had been on the receiving end of all this enchantment, he had fallen hopelessly and passionately in love with her at that moment, and perhaps for ever.

But while he recognized that he could afford most things in this world, he also knew, from seeing the look in her eyes when she nearly mentioned Gervaise, that he could not afford to tell Dorinda how he felt about her. He must keep her in suspense, until, perhaps, one day, she discovered how she felt about her 'Mr L'.

Upstairs in her beautiful, vast, gorgeously decorated bedroom with its Louis Quinze and Louis Seize furniture, her new silver backed hairbrushes and hand mirrors, and her endless tea gowns, all sent round from Mr Worth in London, with her new jewellery box that was already overflowing with the kind of jewels of which sensible women never dream, Dorinda became seized with guilt. She had been brought up from babyhood to believe in sin, and now she was living in sin, and she was far too aware of sin not to feel that she should not be receiving diamonds in her napkin at breakfast when outside the window there were people who did not have a bread roll in theirs.

'Mrs Goodman,' she asked her former landlady, suddenly very worried. 'What shall I do about Mr L?'

'In what way, Mrs Montgomery?'

'His generosity, Mrs Goodman.'

Like Leonie's Mrs Dodd, Mrs Goodman was a shrewd woman.

'If I were you, my dear,' she said, lowering her voice for no reason that Dorinda could imagine, 'I would just take what is your due, while the going is good, and worry about Mr Leveen's generosity later.'

Dorinda could see the barefaced sense of this. It was true. After all, she would not always be beautiful, so it followed, surely, that she would not always be rich?

'Do you believe in sin, Mrs Goodman?'

'Oh yes, Mrs Montgomery, but only other people's!'

They both laughed.

'Should I come out of mourning soon, do you think? Could we give a soirée, so that I would be officially out of mourning?'

'If I were you, seeing that your late husband left you little to remember him by, and cared less, I should consider myself out of mourning as of this morning.'

Mrs Goodman's expression was sage to the point of banality. 'Besides, apart from ourselves and Miss Lynch at the nursing home, who would remember that you are a widow, Mrs Montgomery? As few people as there are rings on my fingers. Most people in Society, and the public too, only remember you as Dorinda Blue, not as the wife of Mr Montgomery.'

'In that case, I shall tackle Mr L with the idea at luncheon.'

'But only, my dear, after the entrée.'

Dorinda snorted lightly.

'Mrs Goodman,' she admonished her companion-maid, 'are you implying that I would be so naive as to approach a member of the opposite sex with any new subject before the dessert, or the angels on horseback? I might be a poor widow, but I do know my men.'

They both laughed at this.

It was, after all, not only funny, but the truth.

For luncheon that day Dorinda wore her first gown bought from Lucile, Lady Duff-Gordon. It was an elaborate silk two piece with a wide waistband which emphasized the brilliance of the cut of the full skirt beneath, a skirt made to match the yellow of the yellow and white pin-tucked, high-necked, lightly boned, long-sleeved, lace-edged blouse.

Lady Duff-Gordon believed in extravagant underclothes. She did not consider that petticoats should be skimped. As a result of her almost messianic belief Dorinda was feeling and looking simply superb, and she knew it.

Happily she was not alone. Her own admiration for herself, she was pleased to see, was reflected in the eyes of her dearest Mr L.

'Mr L,' she said after the entrée had been cleared, and the various dishes following, and a flunkey was offering him the cheese on a cut glass and silver dish. 'I think that we might give a soirée, do you not? A small soirée, an intimate rout, here in Park Lane. Some friends, mutual acquaintances, perhaps Lady Finborough, and the Earl of Dorchester? Lady Londonderry, and Lady Elcho, perhaps? Music could be a feature, I thought, given that you are such a great patron of the musical world. It would be an occasion for me to show you what a good hostess I can be.'

Lawrence Leveen paused as he took some cheese, and then, having replaced the cheese knife, he looked across at Dorinda.

'I think we should discuss this later, dearest, really I do.'

Dorinda pouted, but only lightly.

'Oh, very well, if you think that is best.'

'I do.'

Later, after Dorinda had changed from her luncheon clothes to her afternoon walking dress, and from her walking dress, in which she went out in her new carriage, to her tea gown, in which she lay on her chaise longue and pretended to read a book with her long chestnut hair loosened,

Mr L called on her, as he was meant to do.

Later again he too changed, into an elaborate silk-collared quilted gentleman's robe, before he took it upon himself to explain why it was quite impossible for Dorinda to give a soirée at the house, or expect anyone to call upon her, let alone exchange visiting cards, or any of the normal practices common to the aristocracy, new or old.

'We are not married, my darling Dorinda. And that being so, you must understand, it would not be possible for people like Lady Elcho or Lady Londonderry to leave their cards.'

Dorinda pouted again, but this time with more intent.

'But you are so rich, Mr L. And Lady Cardigan entertained when she was not married to—'

'Money is not an entrée to Society in London, dearest Dorinda. Besides, Lady Cardigan is that rare creature, the brilliant exception to the inevitable rule. And besides . . .'

'Besides?'

'She hunts.'

Lawrence Leveen smiled across at his blue-eyed goddess with her red gold hair, and her red Chinese patterned tea gown. Dorinda did not just look beautiful, she looked stunning.

'You are a stunner, Dorinda, did you know that?'

Dorinda smiled dreamily at him. Mr L was really very, very . . . *delightful*.

'And you are delightful, Mr L. Do you know, I like being with you more than anyone I have ever known? I was thinking this morning that when I am with you I simply do not know the time.'

He looked at her, amazed. This was the nearest to being openly affectionate that Dorinda had ever been with him, and while he realized that only so much could be asked of a man's mistress, particularly one as beautiful as Dorinda, it was still wondrous to him that she had said what she had to him.

For her part Dorinda too was amazed by what she had said. Her astonishment stemmed from the fact that it was only after she had spoken that she had suddenly realized the utter truth of her words.

She *did* like being with Mr L more than anyone she had ever known, even Gervaise Lowther, who, when she thought about it, could be quite dull when he was talking endlessly about horse racing and gambling, which Mr L, thank the Lord, never did.

'And so how should things go, do you think? I mean, how do you think they should go?'

'These *things* are most difficult, Mrs Montgomery,' he said, deliberately making fun of her slack language. 'You know the rules of Society rarely, if ever, bend. Yet we have to have rules in order to know just how to go on. If we did not, Society would become muddled, and I for one would not want that. We have to have yardsticks, if only to know when we have all departed from them, or all is lost.'

Dorinda looked thoughtful, and then resigned.

'So no-one would come here, even if we put on the most splendid display in the whole world?'

'No-one whatsoever. The women rule Society. They have made the rules by which the men must abide – or be exiled. It is just a fact. The day the women stop making the rules will see the collapse of Society, the collapse of standards. Women should govern Society the way that men govern politics. Each understands their own world far better than the other.'

'I know some of the rules, but not all of them, and certainly not by heart.'

Dorinda knew them all and only too well, of course, but she always liked to hear them repeated. She was like a child in that way, wanting to hear the same story told to her over and over again.

'Married women do not call on ladies living under the protection of gentlemen to whom they are not married. It is not *convenable*, however rich the gentleman concerned. However well connected.'

Lawrence took a cigar from a nearby thermidor, most unusual for him at that hour, but it meant that he was thinking hard, and they both knew it. He was a good card player and often partnered Mrs Keppel. Of a sudden he had seen that his emotional hand might have more than one ace. It might even have a trio of aces.

'You do not mind my cigar in your sitting-room, dearest?'

'No, of course not. You know how I love to smell your cigar smoke. It is delicious.'

She struck a match for him.

'Of course,' Lawrence said, looking carefully at

the tip of his cigar before replacing it in his mouth and looking across at his beautiful mistress, 'there is a solution to your difficulty. An easy and most effective solution, and that is – I can marry you.'

Dorinda leaned forward.

'What did you say, dearest?'

'I said, dearest Dorinda, I can marry you. Or, if you like, you can marry me.'

'And then what would happen?'

Dorinda did not know how to keep a straight face. She was suddenly so delighted with the idea of marrying her Mr L that she realized she was not smiling, but laughing.

'What would happen is that we would be married, possibly at my estate in Sussex, but out of town anyway – could be Scotland. And then we would return and you could have as large a soirée as you wish. Daily if you wanted, but as Mrs Lawrence Leveen, not as Mrs Montgomery.'

Dorinda stood up and walked over to Lawrence and sat down beside him, putting her hands up to his face. His brilliant eyes, which she found so fascinating, stared into her own beautiful blue ones.

'What if I say no?' she teased him.

Lawrence shrugged his shoulders, his face poker straight, while his heart raced with the disappointment of the very idea of her refusing him the honour.

'You say no and I will ask you again tomorrow. And whenever the subject of a soirée or a formal dinner party, or a box at Ascot, or anything else, comes up, I will remind you of the rewards of marriage to me.'

'You are so suave, Mr L. That is what I love about you, that and the fact that you know things that I do not. You know so much, it makes me love being with you. Then there is the fact that we like the same things. And the fact that you are so awfully rich. And the fact that you put diamonds in my breakfast napkin. I like all those things. In fact, I like them so much that I think, I think – I would love to marry you.'

Lawrence looked at her and smiled.

'Good. I think that you will, eventually, find that is a good decision. We are so alike, Dorinda, you and I. You like to keep your cards close to your chest, and so do I. And we are both adventurers. You as much as myself, my dearest. Now, tell me, what sort of ring would you like for your engagement?'

'Oh, Mr L, not *another* ring!'

'Oh, very well. If jewels have grown so boring I will have Tarleton make up this morning's diamond into a showpiece setting as an engagement ring for you. Is that what you would wish?'

Dorinda smiled mischievously.

'If you like, but you choose the setting with him. You have far better taste than I.'

She sighed, and her eyes grew suddenly dreamy.

'Oh, Mr L, just think of all those women who will now have to call on me, right down to – or up to – Lady Londonderry.'

'Do not put that particular cart before the horse Dorinda my dearest. Lady Londonderry will be the hardest nut you have to crack, as far as true Society is concerned.'

'She will call. You wait. I will wager you anything that she does.'

'Lady Londonderry is – Lady Londonderry, Dorinda.'

'Yes, but you have something of which she is envious.'

'Which is?'

'Even more money than she has!'

She had not said that she loved him. Lawrence realized that. He even appreciated it. On the other hand, she had not said that she did not love him. She had been honest, and he loved that in her more than anything. Indeed, Lawrence Leveen knew that honesty was the rarest of all qualities in the opposite sex. Like the pearl in the oyster, he had thought it was something you only ever heard about.

The Queen had died by the time Lord Freddie Melsetter's bequest came to Leonie. The nation was in mourning and the state funeral that followed was going to be one that no-one would forget. The Empire must be represented by all its members, every little South Sea island, every state within a state. Everyone had to walk behind the small white coffin, dressed in state regalia, or their uniforms, or, simply, in deepest black.

And so to one small island known as Britain came every kind of representative from all over the world, and as the capital bent double under the burden of putting up so many hundreds of foreign dignitaries and their massive entourages, it seemed as if the influx might become too much.

Lady Angela was now summoned to the palace a great deal, for it seemed that the King needed her even more than ever. Alas, it was no longer possible for him to take a hansom cab or the wobbly mahogany lift to Lady Angela's private rooms for tea at the nursing home. She must go to him, for the intolerable honour of kingship was already taking its toll of a man in his very late middle age.

'Such is your dedication to duty, such your serious outlook, that I feel you are quite able to take my place in those hours when I expect to be ever more absent, Miss Lynch. And of course, as always, I must count on your discretion in this matter.'

Being taken into Lady Angela's confidence in this way was immensely worrying to Leonie. She had not expected to be singled out for such a great responsibility so soon in her life, but, as Lady Angela went on to tell her, she had chosen Leonie most particularly for this purpose since she would not seek to exploit, or even enjoy the power of her position.

'Anyone else here given a position of power, albeit for only a few hours, would take some sort of advantage from the situation. I feel I can trust you to be both efficient and discreet.'

As the days went by, Leonie found it easier and easier to make herself busier and busier. It was as if she felt doubly responsible for the nursing home in Lady Angela's frequent if short absences.

'He is becoming so caught up with the coronation arrangements I fear for his health,' Lady Angela confided more than once to the young woman upon whom she now seemed to lean more and more. 'I fear as with all excess that these arrangements will end in tears.'

When the King contracted appendicitis and the world prayed for his life, Lady Angela's absence was necessarily prolonged, and it was many weeks before the administration of the nursing home returned to normal and Leonie could finally think of taking a day off to see her longed for family.

'You away tomorrow?' one of the younger nurses asked, seeing Leonie suddenly turning away to hide her face.

Leonie nodded, suppressing a yawn. Although Sister Angela's Nursing Home had become a second home to her, and she prided herself that she put duty before everything, the fact was that at that moment she could not wait to go home to Eastgate Street and be spoiled by her foster mother and father, whom she had not seen for months.

Naturally enough, Leonie had said nothing to Aisleen Lynch about Lord Freddie Melsetter's generous bequest. It seemed quite wrong to mention such a thing, and most certainly before it became a fact. But once a bank account had been opened for her by Mrs Dodd, and the money lodged, it also seemed more than delightful to surprise them all.

Of course Leonie knew that her first duty to such a sizeable bequest was to be sensible. She would never, she thought, be left money again, and that being so she had to think of the future. She had no idea of property values, but every now and then, when she was on night duty, she found herself dreaming of the possibility of buying herself a little cottage in the country.

But first she delighted in picturing the faces of her foster parents and brothers and sisters when she showered them with the presents she was intent on buying for all eleven of them.

Once Leonie had written a list of the names of those to whom she wished to give presents, Mrs Dodd took it upon herself to shop for her. She shopped wisely, and was able to do so at trade, for she had been more than happy to help out many of the traders in her area when their daughters or nieces, cousins or wives landed themselves in the kind of trouble that Leonie's mother had so regrettably found herself in some nineteen years before. Everything she bought was in the best taste, and the two of them wrapped the gifts together in the finest of tissue papers, tied with fine gold string which glittered in the gaslight as they worked, both of them feeling that particular kind of excited interest that goes with generosity.

The last of Leonie's real extravagances was to take a hackney out to Eastgate Street. Snuggling in the back of the carriage, hearing the clip clop of the pony's hooves, putting her new pretty muff up to her cheek and feeling the matching hat on her head, watching the buildings and the houses and their occupants becoming poorer and poorer, brought back the reality of Leonie's present position ever more forcibly to her.

She had been given a chance to become a nurse in a place where all the aristocracy came, where the King himself had used to come, and yet here she was revisiting those back streets from which she actually sprang.

This was her home, this was where she had grown up, among these narrow streets with their shabby brick fronts. And she had grown up with the men and women who hurried through them, men and women so different from the *raffinés* patients whom she had already become so used to nursing at the nursing home with their *doncher knows* and their *rahly how too too*s – people so different from the Lynches that they might as well be not only from a different world, but from a different planet. Yet somehow, now that she was back among them, these streets and these people meant more to her now that she was free of them than they had ever done when she was living amongst them.

And when she pushed open the front door and saw the small rounded figure of her foster mother, she realized that she meant more to her than Mrs Dodd or Lady Angela or anyone else who had come into her life over the last long months.

Of course the moment Mrs Lynch saw her youngest foster child she started to cry, using the corner of her best, lace-bordered apron as a handkerchief to dab at the corners of her eyes.

'I thought we would never see you again! I said as much to Ned. *We've seen the last of her*, I said, when you followed Mrs Dodd into the carriage. *That's it*, I said, *we'll never see our darling pretty Leonie again.*'

Leonie looked over to Ned Lynch, standing in the background. The top of his head seemed, to his foster daughter, to have flattened even more, what with the weight of the wide heavy trays that he had spent most of his life carrying on its top. He had grown more stout and with the added girth looked older, but even so she would have known him anywhere, and ran to embrace him for all that he was looking at her so shyly that you would have thought he did not know his own foster daughter.

'How well you look!'

'More food now you lot's gone, and that's for certain,' he said, gruffly, but he kissed the top of her head and closed his eyes as he did so, as if Leonie was a rose that he was smelling.

Mrs Lynch had at last found her handkerchief and was wiping her eyes with it, and having removed her pinny was now standing in glorious array in her best skirt. Among all the numerous children at number fifty-three, that skirt had always been called *Mother's Sunday Skirt*. Looking at it now, Leonie realized, brought back such memories, it was like bumping into an old friend.

As a child she had always revered its embroidery, and even knew its history.

It had been given to Mrs Lynch by the grateful daughter of a woman whom Aisleen had nursed when she was dying. All the flowers and fruit on the border were raised and heavy, so that when she was little Leonie had found herself imagining that one day they might take it into their head to imitate real flowers and fruit and shed their petals or fall to the ground.

'I brought you a fruit cake, Mother.'

'A fruit cake. My, Ned. Look, a fruit cake.'

'And Father, I brought you some tobacco.'

'Tobacco, Ned. Look, tobacco.'

Ned took the tobacco. 'Never tried that, but won't stop me, will it, Mother?'

'No, Ned. It won't stop you.'

'Silk for Mary.'

'My, Ned, silk for Mary.'

'Teacup and saucer for Susannah.'

'My, Ned, teacup and saucer for Susannah.'

And on the gifts went until the small living room of Eastgate Street was beginning to resemble a shop of great quality with numerous fine wares.

Finally Ned, pulling happily on the new tobacco, asked, 'Have you married and not told us, young Lee?'

She was always Lee to her foster father.

'No, Father, I have not married, but I have had the best fortune. I was left – now don't faint, Mother – a patient left me *five hundred pounds*. Imagine. A man who never saw me.'

369

Her foster parents stared at her, horrified, and there was a long and terrible silence following her happy announcement.

Finally Mrs Lynch said, 'If you never knew him, dear, why would he leave you money like that?'

Leonie stared at the two faces looking at her so grimly, and gradually the penny dropped and she realized what they were thinking.

'He never saw me because he was blinded, and paralysed, in a hunting accident,' she told them gently. 'You must not think wrong of him, or me. It seems that he was like that, apparently, a ne'er do well in his youth, but suddenly foolishly generous, if he took a shine to someone.'

'Fool*hardy*, more like.'

Ned stood up and knocked the still smoking tobacco out of his pipe. There was a look to him now as if he no longer wanted to smoke tobacco that might have been bought with ill-gotten gains. The Lynches were churchgoing folk and proud of it. Now Ned rocked to and fro on the balls of his big feet, the collar line of his collarless shirt showing white against the deep tan of his neck, the shine on his best shoes catching the light that came through the small window.

'Should our Lee have accepted this, Mother?' he asked Mrs Lynch, finally. 'Should she have accepted money from a man she hardly knew, would you say?'

Mrs Lynch's eyes searched the floor as if she was convinced that she would find the words necessary to her sense of fair play and good judgement somewhere on its pristine surface.

'I dare say,' she said, eventually. 'Leonie was left the money as a *nurse*, Ned dear. Same as when, if you remember, Mrs Zwyvoski gave me this skirt handed down through her family. Nurses are often left money and china and so on by grateful patients in nursing homes and hospitals and such like. Nurses are different now, Ned dear. People appreciate them now, love, not like when we were young and they were – well not considered very nice.'

'Very well, Mother. If you say so.'

Satisfied, Ned began to top up his Sunday pipe once more. He would not want to smoke tobacco that was tainted by sin, but once he was assured it was 'nursing money' that had bought it he could not wait to draw on its rounded flavours once again.

Finally he beamed at his foster daughter.

'If you're so rich I dare say you could buy our house!'

Leonie jumped to her feet, at once abandoning any idea of buying herself a cottage in the country in some dim and distant future, for it came to her immediately that this was what she *would* do. She would buy her beloved foster parents their house in Eastgate Street. After all, once the house was theirs, there could be no more dread of bad times to come.

Never again would Mr Elliott, the rent man, come round banging on the door. Never again would Ned Lynch have to pawn his only suit, as he had done once when they were young, to buy them a Sunday joint. Leonie could pay them back for everything they had done for her, above all for the toughness they had given her, the ability to survive. With one single stroke of good fortune they would never again have to be afraid.

'I will buy your house for you, Ned. It will be my way of thanking you for loving me and taking care of me. For seeing that I have landed on my feet, and have my feet under the table now. I can give you your own roof over your heads, for the rest of your lives. And never again will the poorhouse beckon. Not ever.'

Mrs Lynch promptly fainted into her husband's arms. Of course it was only a pretend sort of faint, and they all pretended to sigh with relief as she 'came round' laughing and crying by turns.

As for Leonie, she thought this must be the happiest day of her life, or anyone else's for that matter, and no exceptions; but, as it turned out, she was to be proved wrong.

Part Three

Crossing Paths

Twelve

The snow in Ruddwick's main street had long ago melted, and John Brancaster was still away. Sensing Mercy's loneliness and confusion, Gabriel Chantry had made it his business to continue to call in at Brindells on every conceivable occasion. As her decorator it was not difficult to find some excuse – a piece of material that needed matching, some embroidery work he had found that would be just what was wanted to go with the new crewel work curtains in the informal sitting room. It was easy for him to call at the house without causing suspicion.

This particular afternoon he had a chair to take back after rewebbing, and a pair of wall fittings to try in that same informal sitting room which, he had noted during past days, Mrs Brancaster had really rather made her own.

He was about to fetch his caped coat and wide-brimmed hat when the street door opened. Hearing the light-sounding tinkle of the Austrian cow bells that his new maid of all work had insisted on hanging on its back, he turned.

The young woman was wearing a ravishing blue coat, close fitting to her silhouette, a lace jabot at her throat, and a brilliantly tailored matching skirt with tightly laced buttoned boots. Through the thick veil of her motoring hat Gabriel could see that she had burnished red gold hair and a pair of the most mischievous sparkling eyes, so blue in colour that they outshone even the sapphire cloth of her coat.

Gabriel stared at her. She was the most extraordinarily lovely sight, particularly in Ruddwick of an afternoon, where normally all that could be viewed would be elderly folk taking their constitutionals or stout ladies emerging from the haberdasher's with mysterious packages. As soon as the visitor addressed him, however, Gabriel realized that she could not be quite English. There was something about the way she spoke, quickly, almost nervously, as if she was anxious not to bore the listener, and at the same time aware that he must be amused, that told him she was just a little foreign.

'I am so sorry to trouble you, but I have lost my way. My friend Miss Lynch and I are here to visit an acquaintance who lives close by, we think. A, er, Mrs Brancaster.'

She said 'Mrs Brancaster' as if it were some sort of pseudonym, or as if she might long for it to be such, just in order to make life more interesting and exciting.

'Mrs Brancaster?' Gabriel was astonished. 'But I am about to visit Mrs John Brancaster at Brindells. It must be the same one?'

His visitor – for by the look she gave his oak

furniture she was certainly not going to be a customer – opened those large violet blue eyes and looked as amazed as Gabriel himself.

'But how fortuitous!'

'I shall be taking my pony and trap. Will you wait until I am round the front and come after me, Mrs . . . ?'

'Mrs Lawrence Leveen.'

A slight hesitation before they shook hands, for Gabriel had heard of Lawrence Leveen. It was common knowledge, and often discussed in the papers, that King Edward liked to surround himself not just with racing men but with men of business like Leveen, shrewd men who knew how to manage his affairs to his – and their – greatest advantage.

Nothing could have been more revealing of the visitors' different stations in life than their progress to Brindells, with Gabriel, head down, keeping his hat on with difficulty against the still cold spring wind, the pony clip-clopping its way through the narrow Sussex lanes, and Mrs Leveen and her friend in their sumptuous new chauffeur driven motor car, followed by another in case the first broke down.

Mrs Tomkins, the housekeeper, was expecting Gabriel Chantry, but she was quite obviously not expecting Mrs Leveen and her friend. She coloured and then looked bad tempered as if, it occurred to Gabriel, he had brought these unwelcome visitors unannounced to Brindells principally to annoy her, and put out her tedious little afternoon routine.

'Mrs Brancaster is in her sitting room. She is feeling a little better today.'

The housekeeper in her really rather stained gown nodded towards the small sitting room which Gabriel knew that Mercy liked to occupy, and sighed, but before she had finished sighing Mrs Leveen had taken stock of Mrs Tomkins and was lifting her motoring veil.

'Mrs . . . mm?'

'Tomkins, ma'am.'

'Ah, *Tomkins*, yes. My husband had a Tomkins, a footman – alas, dismissed only last month, for *all* the usual reasons – gone to be a stoker. No relation I am sure. Mrs *Tomkins*. Should you not send for the footman, or the maid. The cold in this hall is too terrible, and so bad for Mrs Brancaster, if she should pass through here. And please do not let us stop you from announcing us to Mrs Brancaster. I know you will wish to do so.'

Gabriel's eyes could not but register the amusement he was feeling at the sight of Mrs Tomkins being made to do her job. He knew all too well from Mrs Brancaster that the older woman made her life miserable, whenever and wherever possible, but it was impossible to dismiss her since she was employed by Mr Brancaster, and had been with him for over fifteen years.

As soon as they were announced Mercy sprang out of the chair in which she had been seated pretending to sew, and the expression on her face changed from funereal solemnity to something near to youthful gaiety.

'My dear Miss Lynch! And Mrs Leveen! I have heard so much about you from Miss Lynch. And you live within driving distance! I now feel I have friends just around the corner, truly I do.'

Mercy might have felt twice the thing as soon as she saw her guests, but Leonie was horrified by the change in her former friend's appearance. She thought that had she not already met her, she would not have even known her.

It did not seem possible that a young, vibrant girl had been reduced to such a pitiful state in such a short time – hardly more than a year, surely? Admittedly she had given birth only recently, but compared to Leonie and Mrs Leveen she looked as if she was about to expire, so pale and thin had she become, and so sad. That was the worst thing. The expression in her eyes was strangely defeated, as if she was lost in a place where she had never been before.

If this is what marriage and having a son and heir does to you, I shall never, ever marry.

As they all talked about nothing in particular the words kept stealing through Leonie's mind. She had met Dorinda again some few months after her marriage to Lawrence Leveen. Since by marrying Dorinda had become once more respectable, the two young women had been able to renew their friendship. Following a gregarious tea together in London, Dorinda had invited Leonie down to Leveen's country mansion – no-one could call it a *house* – while he himself was abroad on business for the King.

Leonie had been given a Friday-to-Monday off by Lady Angela, on account of the King's having gone to Sandringham for a week, and she had travelled to Sussex by private coach to be confronted and indeed amazed by the grandeur of Dorinda's country home.

It was a large and magnificent eighteenth-century house, which Dorinda's Mr L had been able to stuff full of antiquities bought in from other less fortunate establishments. Indeed, it had been so filled with gates and columns, classical statues, marble fountains, and ancestral paintings from other sources, that Dorinda told Leonie that when she had first been shown around she had turned to Leveen and remarked, 'You know, Mr L, this place is like nothing less than a pawnbroker's palace where no-one's come to claim anything back!'

Happily Mr L found this remark most amusing, and after that Mr and Mrs Lawrence Leveen, when alone at home, always jokingly referred to their country seat as *Pawnbroker's Palace*.

The house was actually called Shepworth Place, and beautifully set in Sussex parkland with distant views of the sea, albeit quite liberally stuffed with ancestors who were not Leveens and furniture that had not been handed down from father to son.

'Still, give Mr L his due,' Dorinda told Leonie on their first evening together, when Leonie was finding it hard not to let her jaw drop at the sight of the gold plate at dinner, and the very idea of twenty indoor servants, 'he did rescue Shepworth

380

when it was falling into disrepair.'

They were on the second of their eight courses, and Leonie had only nodded, her overriding concern being not to hold up the procession of dishes being brought so painstakingly from miles away in the kitchens, so she had opted for listening and eating, rather than talking.

'I mean it was really not of interest to anyone but Mr L, because it was so big, do you see?' Dorinda continued. 'And too much land, which no-one wants nowadays. And of course, no-one else could afford it, except perhaps the King!'

Dorinda's large, sapphire blue eyes, so beautifully matched to her silk evening gown, had widened at this before she started to laugh.

It had been such a gay, light moment that Leonie thought she would always remember it, what with the footmen with their backs flat against the wall, and the candlelight playing on the gold of Dorinda's hair.

'I would call this place a bit of an albatross myself, but there – Mr L has to entertain the King. Mind you, every time I pass the lodge gates, I have to tell you, I find myself looking in and envying the inmates their cosy fires and being able to put a log on them without having to wait for some flunkey to do it for them. Such a bother sometimes, it seems to me, having to depend on so many for so little, but Mr L likes it, and nowadays I dare say he would not know how to light a fire himself, let alone find the log store, or the ice house, or indeed anything practical. Wealth does seem to have that effect, does it not? It makes men as helpless as babies.'

But all that was yesterday and now Leonie was at Brindells, trying to feel cheerful, despite the sad look to their young hostess, and despite Dorinda's turning aside every now and then and asking, 'What *can* be the matter with your poor friend Mrs Brancaster?'

Of course it did not take very long for the new Mrs Leveen to make it her business to find out.

'May we see around the grounds, or would it be *importunate* to ask you such a favour, Mrs Brancaster?'

'But of course. Let us go before the light fades.'

Even this most ordinary of remarks seemed to Leonie to be full of some kind of regret, as if Mercy was all too used to the light fading. And once outside she seemed fearful of the servants, always glancing round as they walked as if she thought they were being spied upon, which they well might be by the bad tempered housekeeper or one of the two large tweed-costumed footmen who seemed to be determined not to show their faces and had to be continually rung for to deal with the smoking fires, or to call one of the maids.

After only twenty-four hours with Dorinda, Leonie was only too aware of the difference between Shepworth and Brindells. The one so rich, so smoothly run, that it might be a remote fairytale palace, and the other so seemingly cosy, but full of recalcitrant servants and a hostess who looked as if one breath would blow her away.

'I'll go ahead and talk with Mrs Brancaster,' Dorinda told Leonie, dropping her voice. 'I think she needs my help. And seeing that we are practically neighbours I think it would be just as well if we furthered our acquaintance with each other.'

She moved quickly ahead of Leonie, leaving her with Mr Chantry.

At first there was a long pause, because although the gardens at Brindells were undoubtedly delightful, the spring colours at their best and many varieties of shrubs and trees in flower, Leonie, coming from Eastgate Street as she did, was as knowledgeable about gardens as she was about riding and horses. She could only murmur 'Quite delightful' until, at last, she finally had to confess her ignorance to Mr Chantry.

'I am so glad that you have no knowledge of gardens, Miss Lynch,' Gabriel told her, smiling broadly.

'Why would you be glad, Mr Chantry?'

'Because I live in a village, Miss Lynch, and no-one, ever, speaks to me of anything else! You see,' he confided, dropping even further behind their hostess and Dorinda, 'everyone in Ruddwick, and certainly everyone who comes to see me in the shop, is a gardener. So although I have no garden myself I have had to learn as much about gardening as if I had a large estate, or they would never have become the loyal customers they are!'

Leonie smiled. 'What about Mrs Brancaster? I presume she is very knowledgeable?'

'Mrs Brancaster,' said Gabriel, with far too much reverence in his voice to be allowable, Leonie realized wryly, 'is perfection in the garden. She has brought this place back to life in such a short space of time, she is to be congratulated.'

'She has a young son, I believe?' Leonie could not help remarking, as if to remind both of them that Mercy, besides being a wife, was also a mother.

'Yes, she has a baby son – John Edward. He was born here in a snowstorm, and is now, I am happy to say, a big bonny baby of some weeks, albeit that his father has still not arrived to see him.'

Gabriel Chantry stared ahead with what Leonie saw was an almost ferocious longing at Mercy's thin form, which even he must have recognized was in pitifully sharp contrast to Dorinda's slender, but rounded, silhouette.

'Is Mr Brancaster abroad, then?' Leonie asked in some surprise.

The look in the kind, deep, dark eyes that were turned on her said everything.

'No, Mr Brancaster is not *abroad*, Miss Lynch. Mr Brancaster is still hunting.'

For all that Brindells was so cosy, and so charmingly decorated, and Mercy so sweet and kind, Leonie could not wait to follow Dorinda into the motor car and return to Shepworth Place.

Dorinda was speakingly silent, most unusually for her, on the drive back. Knowing people just a little in her short lifetime, Leonie made sure that she asked no questions, realizing that her young hostess must have learned more from Mercy Brancaster on their walk than perhaps even she would have wished to know.

So, when they arrived back at Shepworth, there was nothing for them both to do except part company in the hall, to meet again in the library before dinner.

'I am so glad that there is just the two of us,' Dorinda confided as they sat in front of the fire in evening dress sipping warming cordials, because Shepworth was so large that even the newly installed heating was insufficient when the weather, spring or no, was still so cold. 'It means,' she went on, 'that we can talk at length, with no regard to anyone else, about this terrible question of Mrs Brancaster.'

Leonie could not help feeling a kind of pent up excitement as soon as Dorinda said 'terrible', for she knew at once that it must mean that Mercy Brancaster was now in need of just such compassion as she herself had shown towards the poor starving mannequin.

It was not that Leonie wanted Mercy in any way to be some sort of suffering heroine from a tragic tale, it was just that seeing that she looked so terribly thin, and that even her voice had sounded lacklustre, and hearing from Mr Chantry (who was clearly passionately in love with her) that Mr Brancaster had not yet even bothered to visit his son and heir – well, it was all too terrible not to be fascinating.

'You know that sometimes it is very much easier for people, if they are unhappy, to confide in a complete stranger than to talk to a friend?'

Leonie nodded, and then said 'Yes' as an added encouragement.

'Well, my dear, she did confide in me, and I almost wish that she had not. This is the sort of tale that would make a penny dreadful, if not a twopenny or threepenny dreadful. A housemaid's read of a tale, believe me.'

Dorinda paused as one of the footmen came in and fed the library fire with coal. She waited to hear the door close behind him before beginning again.

'I shall begin at the beginning. First and foremost, it seems that your poor friend Mrs Brancaster made the mistake of her life, a young girl's mistake.' She paused, breathing in and out quite rapidly to add drama to what she was about to say. 'My dear – she only went and married for love!'

Leonie stared at Dorinda, not quite comprehending the significance of this, nor indeed why there was such a look of amazed shock in Dorinda's eyes.

'But – do not most people nowadays marry for love?'

Dorinda shook her head. 'Whoever gave you such strange ideas, Leonie? No, no, *no*. You must *never* marry for love. It is the most shocking, and perhaps the most stupid, thing that a woman can do. A woman must always marry to *better* herself.'

'And a man?'

'He must marry to better her too!'

Leonie laughed, but Dorinda only managed a smile, probably because she was still so shocked by what Mrs Brancaster had told her earlier.

'You see,' she went on, 'your poor friend married for love, and being young and inexperienced in the ways of the world she imagined that her husband, despite being so much older, was marrying her for the same reason.'

She paused again, trying to think logically.

'Which, it seems, he very nearly *was*, until the hunting season was upon them and she, thinking to be kind (such a weakness in women, I find), sent him off to his hunting box while she set about redecorating and furnishing Brindells in the appropriate manner – which we have to agree she has achieved magnificently with the help of that charming antiquarian. But since then, despite the birth of the baby, Mr Brancaster has not returned to her side, except over Christmas.'

'Yes, Mr Chantry told me that Mr Brancaster has never seen his baby son. It seems heartless to a degree.'

'It is tales such as hers that make me thankful that I did not marry my Mr L for anything except respectability and enormous wealth. If you marry a man for his money you both know exactly where you are. But then of course not everyone is as kind and generous as Mr L. Very few, as I know to my cost.'

'But your first husband, Mr Montgomery, whom you helped to nurse so devotedly when we met at Sister Angela's – were you not in love with him?'

This time Dorinda did laugh, and quite heartily.

'Oh, Leonie, my dear! If only you could see the expression on your face. No, no, no, my dear, no woman could really *love* Mr Montgomery – he was far too selfish. Until it was too late, of course, and then he was very tearful and sorry and destroyed himself with drink. You can't love a man like that. I took pity on him, the way he had taken pity on me.

'He rescued me, you see, from my mother's boarding house and a life of penury, scrubbing floors and sewing cheap clothes and so on, and in return I nursed him until – as you would say – he was *gathered*. It was the least I could do. But *love* him? No-one could love Mr Montgomery, for he loved himself far too much. Loving yourself is like feeling sorry for yourself – there is nothing left for anyone else to do! But to return to Mrs Brancaster—'

'Which we must, if we are to help her at all.'

Dorinda stood up, a magnificent sight in her close fitting deep plum evening dress, her white throat encircled with pearls, and her hair decorated with a little lace cap of them too. She wore her clothes, and her brilliant jewels, as if she was oblivious of them, which was why, Leonie decided, they looked so perfect on her. Had she been aware, as all too many women were, of her finery and her riches, they would have instantly become cheapened and looked tawdry.

'Mr Brancaster has obviously a great interest in hunting, but of course as we both know that is usually not the only interest that takes a gentleman up to his hunting box in the middle of winter.' Dorinda poured them both another glass of cordial and returned to her seat by the fire.

'Lady Cardigan and Skittles have quite set the tone for activities in Leicestershire, and elsewhere. Not that I approve of such ladies, but on the other hand, my dear Leonie, for me of all people to *disapprove* of them would be hypocritical, to say the least. It seems to me that very often women such as Lady Cardigan and her like can help many another woman safeguard her marriage, if not save her life, given that wives so often become worn out with child bearing, and so on. Well, you are a nurse, my dear Leonie, you will understand, and all too well, exactly what I mean. Men do need women who *don't* have babies, *n'est ce pas?'*

Leonie nodded. There was much that she was still not too sure about in life, but she had always known quite enough to keep herself from falling into the kinds of errors that she had all too often seen other girls make. Above all, Leonie did not want to be like her mother. She still went to sleep at night praying that God would make sure that, whatever happened, she did not make her mother's mistake and fall in love with some man who would promise her everything and leave her *dead in childbirth*, as she had so often heard Mrs Lynch say dramatically of some poor girl.

'It is very hard for women, is it not?' Leonie said,

deciding to bring about a slight change in the subject under discussion. 'It is very hard for them to marry without love, and yet, from what you are saying, it is equally hard for them to marry *for* love.'

Dorinda held up her large diamond ring – the same that her darling Mr L had commissioned Tarleton to make from what she still called her 'napkin diamond' – and moved it slightly to and fro so that the newly installed electric lighting caught at its many facets.

'Of the two, the first – to marry without love – is by far the preferable. After all, if you marry for – let us say *practical* reasons, there can be no disappointment. There is boredom, and sometimes there is no security, but there is no real *disappointment*. No, of the two, my dear, I should always plump for the first. Alas, it is now far too late for poor Mrs Brancaster to turn back, and so I would say that the best we can do is to help her extricate herself from the situation in which she has found herself. She knows all, and it just cannot be allowed to continue.'

'What cannot be allowed to continue?'

'Why, her husband's liaison.'

'What can she do to help herself? What can anyone do in such a situation? Divorce for a woman in her circumstances is, after all, unthinkable.'

'Naturally, you are quite right. Divorce would put her in the wrong – women are always put in the wrong by divorce. The next choice open to her is to be frank with Mr Brancaster, but that – in my experience, which is slender – never does any good. It is usually quite fatal to face a man with his infidelities, unless you are an heiress, or he is an American. Englishmen are too used to having their own way. No, I have advised her most strongly to face this woman down. As it happens, she is in a unique position. Unlike most wives, she can black-mail the lady.'

Leonie was shocked, too shocked at first to remember to ask the name of the lady.

'Blackmail?'

Growing up in God-fearing Eastgate Street she had never even heard anyone mention the word. Dorinda saw the shock on her face, and continued, 'Oh yes, my dear Leonie, I know it is not a nice word, but then there are boundaries and there are boundaries, and this lady has gone too far. It is an unwritten rule in Society. When a man marries for the first time his mistress gives up her affair with him. That is the rule. One backs down, one bows out, it is just how it is.'

By now Leonie was feeling less shocked and more curious. Who was this lady? Who could possibly have so fascinated Mr Brancaster that he had continued to have an affair with her after marriage, and during his young wife's pregnancy? Dorinda must have felt the weight of her friend's curiosity because she turned her magnificent blue orbs on Leonie, and sighed.

'Do you know I have never been more shocked since my mother informed me of the exact nature of the marriage act on the eve of my wedding to Mr Montgomery? But, as I say, Mrs Brancaster can at least blackmail the wretched lady. She can threaten to go and tell her father, and that will certainly put a stop to the whole horrid business and bring the wretched man back to her side.'

'But why would Mrs Brancaster's *father* be interested in hearing about Mr Brancaster's *petite amour*? I mean to say? As I understand it fathers are never interested in daughters once they marry, just thankful that they are no longer a burden on their incomes. Why would Lord Duffane be interested?'

'Why? For the very good reason that it is Lord Duffane's wife who is having an affair with Mr Brancaster!'

Leonie opened her mouth to say something, and then closed it again. She had not been so intimate with Mercy Brancaster before her marriage that she had any idea of how or why such a situation should come about. Her mind raced as she tried to remember what kind of woman the stepmother was meant to have been.

And then she did remember that, as they sat together keeping watch over the poor dying young mannequin, Mercy had spoken now and then about her *beautiful stepmother*, in tones of such reverence and admiration that it did not now seem possible that the same woman could be carrying on, as she seemingly was, with her stepdaughter's husband.

'Forgive me, but is Mrs Brancaster quite sure of all this?'

The expression in Dorinda's large, sapphire blue eyes was suddenly and unusually sombre.

'Oh yes, alas, she is more than sure. She has been told on the best authority of the liaison between the two wretches. It has been, as it were, verified.'

'By whom?'

'Lord Marcus Stanton, the brother of the lady in question.'

Mercy had not been looking forward to a visit from Lord Marcus. She did not feel that he would approve of the work that had been carried out at Brindells, and that he would not see the point of oak and rush matting and pewter in the kitchens and her informal sitting room, albeit that it was actually perfectly fitting in a house of such age. She felt that he would be looking for gilt and chandeliers, for everything that he liked and was used to living with, as older people seemed so often to do.

And then, too, she realized, she did not like her step-uncle anymore. She did not like his ruby red lips that seemed to be set in his whitened, bloodless face in such a way as to startle the onlooker into watching only his mouth when he spoke. She did not like his habit of settling himself into her father's London house at the start of the Season and staying there for its duration. But since she was alone with the baby at Brindells, and there was no prospect of other visitors, least of all her husband, it was quite impossible for her to refuse to entertain him, and he knew it.

'My dear little Mercy!'

He arrived not by motor car but in a hired trap from the station, much wearied and covered in dust and smuts from the journey. This was a happy circumstance, since it meant that he could be shown to his room and not expected to reappear until drinks before dinner, which nowadays Mercy held in the hall in front of a roaring log fire.

'There are so many changes at Brindells that quite honestly, my dear, I am convinced there will be little or nothing I will recognize from before John's marriage to you, when, as you know, I used to come here a great deal.'

Mercy nodded and smiled, and one of her two footmen in their country tweed offered Lord Marcus a tray with the usual array of drinks. With a look first at the tray and then at the footman, and then back to the tray, he started to laugh.

'I am afraid, my dear, these are what we call at the club *ladies' drinks*,' he said, laughing heartily at his own joke – if that was what it was meant to be.

Then he took one drink and poured it into another, and poured a third into the same glass, making Mercy blush with embarrassment at his lack of manners.

'That is better.'

He ignored the settles in front of the fire and instead sat himself in a large chair so far away from the fireplace that Mercy had to draw up a footstool in order to hear him speak.

For a good few minutes there was nothing to which she could respond, since all Lord Marcus did was to sip at his drink, loudly, and breathe out, equally loudly, which Mercy was quite happy to allow him to do while she herself wondered for perhaps the thousandth time what it was exactly that had brought him in almost unseemly haste to Brindells to see her.

It had to be something of great importance or he would not have bothered to travel so far from his usual stamping grounds in London, particularly at the end of a long, cold winter.

'Mercy my dear, after dinner we must have a talk. It is vital that we reach some sort of understanding.' He stopped, having obviously rehearsed what he had to say to a certain point, but not beyond. 'But let us have dinner first.'

Mercy did not want to eat the dinner, but she had to. She had to cut it up and swallow it, and pretend to appreciate it, both for the cook's sake and for her own. It was vital, and she knew it, that she did not show her fear of whatever Lord Marcus was to say to her.

So she cut and swallowed, and drank her wine, and nodded and laughed at the same old anecdotes (he did not seem to change those any more frequently than he changed his collars) until at last she could withdraw and leave him to his port, and eventually he joined her in the drawing room where she sat in front of the fire pretending to be absorbed in her tapestry.

'Well, my dear,' he said at last, obviously having had time to think out his approach in the dining room. 'How very splendid it is that you have given birth to a son and heir, and how thrilled John is with you, as I am sure he has told you.'

'He has written to congratulate me, yes, and Garrards sent John Edward a silver rattle from his father.'

Mercy threaded her needle through her tapestry, determined not to show her step-uncle the depths of her feelings.

'A fine strapping young fellow he is too, I hear.'

'Yes, he is very well, thank God. And doing all that he should.'

Mercy's protective feelings towards John Edward were also well concealed, for she had already worked out that should she show the slightest vulnerability in her attitude towards her baby, he might well be taken from her by his still absent father.

She was not so young and stupid that she had not heard of vengeful husbands taking their offspring from their wives and then declaring those same wives insane. Mercy well remembered that it had happened to a young woman living near to her father's Cordel estate, and of course the poor young wife subsequently did actually lose her reason, from the shock of being consigned to an asylum, where she eventually committed suicide. Within months her poor baby, too, had died in the charge of a drunken slut of a nurse who was quite unfit to look after other people's babies.

With this to the front of her mind Mercy smiled briefly across at Lord Marcus, outwardly all serenity.

'That is good, that is good.' Her calm, together with the port, seemed to have induced great enthusiasm in Lord Marcus, and having licked his lips, a most unattractive habit, he continued, 'So all is well, as they say.'

'Yes, of course. Except I *would* like to see my husband sometime!'

Mercy laughed, mocking herself, knowing it would lead her step-uncle into gossip, and knowing also that it took very little to induce him to talk.

'Now, Mercy, my dear,' he began again. 'I want you to understand that I think, we all think, that you are a very good person indeed.'

Mercy felt herself stiffening, but continued sewing.

'And that being so I have come to explain a little of your present situation to you, in a way that I know you will understand.'

'You are here to discuss my marriage?'

'In a way, yes. You see, you were very young and innocent before you were married, and it just would not have been possible, or indeed suitable, to explain to you certain mature attitudes which pertain to marriage. But now that you are older, a married woman and the mother of a son, and perhaps even beginning to be a woman of the world, I know you will perfectly understand what I have to say.'

'I hope I shall.' Mercy's head remained bent over her tapestry.

'My sister, Lady Violet, as you know, is a very beautiful woman, and when she married your father we were all delighted for her, of course. But your father, as you have no doubt noticed, is very much a countryman, and while Lady Violet enjoys her hunting she does not enjoy being in the country twelve months a year. No woman of spirit does, after all. So she and your father have over the years evolved a *modus vivendi* – a way of going on that is congenial to both of them.

'Lady Violet performs all her marital duties as required, but during the months when she is away in town, or at the family hunting box, she has, shall we say, certain freedoms, freedoms which are consistent with her position in Society and with her status as a married woman. Over the years she has come to realize that her long association with a certain gentleman is a mainstay of her life. It is not something which either of them is, or ever was, willing to surrender – and so, my dear, as I am sure you have guessed, that is why your husband will not be returning until the last day of the hunting season. They have what you would call a *hunting marriage* and it would be as well, as I am sure you will agree, to accept this, and their hold on each other, while understanding that it will not in any way affect your marriage to John.'

At that Mercy had looked up from her sewing. 'Too late, Uncle Marcus. It already has!'

Leonie breathed in and out, slowly and regularly as Dorinda finished relating the story as told to her that afternoon.

'I was hoping that you would say she had thrown a glass of wine at the wretch.'

'Would that she had,' Dorinda agreed. 'At any rate, she did tell him that her stepmother was not to come to Brindells ever again, and that while she was not able to do anything about her husband she could not be expected, any more than any other wife, to receive her husband's mistress, even if she did happen to be her father's second wife!'

'How contemptible it all is! I simply can not believe that they expected her to go on entertaining her stepmother.'

'I must agree, although my own life has been far from straightforward, as you know. But when I was living' – Dorinda lowered her voice – 'when I was living under the protection of Mr Lowther I would never have expected to be received by his wife, or any of her friends. Nor would he have wished it. Lord Marcus seems to have implied that Mr Brancaster was expecting to be able to bring Lady Violet to the house in the normal way, precisely because she is the poor young woman's stepmother. But now it seems that Mercy

Brancaster has put her foot down, and I, for my part, think that she was right.'

Leonie shivered with a mixture of fear and a strange sort of excitement.

When she had heard from Mrs Dodd that, shortly after the end of the London Season, Mercy had married John Brancaster, it had all seemed so very nice. Indeed all the best wishes of Society had gone to what other people always see as that most perfect of unions – a marriage between a rich older man and a young innocent bride.

'I have absolutely no wish to be married,' Leonie confessed, suddenly, and rather formally. 'In fact the more I have seen of marriage the more it has seemed to me to be not so much a knot as a *noose* for women. What can possibly come of it that is good for them? Except this kind of unhappiness – when a man can put his wife aside on a whim, or take up with his mistress again on another, just as if nothing much has happened – just a wedding and a baby? While the burden of marriage is upon women, surely Society should insist that married men be made to behave as they ought?'

Dorinda smiled. 'You are right, marriage *can* be a noose for a woman, I agree, but it can also be the most pleasurable of, let us say, love knots! Sometimes one is tied to someone not from convention, or the rules of Society, or from religion or any other tie, but simply and solely of one's own volition, because one loves.'

She sighed suddenly, thinking of her darling Mr L. She did not love him, of course, that would be quite wrong and inappropriate, but she could not help missing him dreadfully and hoping that he would be back with her very soon.

'But earlier you yourself indicated that it was not wise for a woman to go into marriage in a state of loving expectancy.'

'Nor is it. What one should do is to go into it with one's eyes wide open, and then afterwards be pleasurably surprised. Afterwards, one can suddenly realize that – one does perhaps love, after all.'

Dorinda frowned as if she had suddenly puzzled herself, as well as Leonie.

'Well, there we are. It is a conundrum, marriage. A bouquet of great differences that brings at once wonders and horrors, sometimes, it seems to me, all on the same day.'

Since Leonie was not married there really was very little she could add to this, so she changed the subject.

'I noticed that Mrs Brancaster has a ring in the shape of a love knot, a very beautiful ring.'

'Exactly. Is it not ironical? You see, whatever she says, and whichever way she turns, the truth is that she *loves* John Brancaster. I could not, you could not, I know, but she *does*. And it is quite clear that despite everything that has happened, she *still* loves him. And when a woman loves a man there is nothing she will not do to win him back. But even if she succeeds in parting him from her stepmother, I am not sure that he will return to her.'

Dorinda was pacing up and down now.

'I do not have such a very great experience of men, but I sense that men like John Brancaster are never won back, believe me. Those hard hunting men simply do not understand the winning, or the losing, of a woman. They take each day, or each woman, or the events of each moment, and they react to them. You cannot win back that kind of man.'

'So what would you do?'

Dorinda looked down at Leonie, thinking that she was almost too beautiful, her turquoise eyes quite round with expectation, her perfectly blonde hair set off by an eau de Nil evening gown lent to her by Dorinda. The gown, although admittedly a little loose at certain points, because their measurements were not identical, nevertheless showed off Leonie's girlish figure and matched complexion in the most charming way possible.

'I would do nothing. It is always best when in doubt, particularly with the opposite sex, to do absolutely nothing.'

Leonie looked up in admiration at her friend.

'Of course. Do nothing. You are very clever, Dorinda.'

'It seems to me that if you do nothing in such situations you find that someone else somewhere is somehow forced to do something, and that being so they will be more likely to make a mistake than you.'

402

'Do you think that Mrs Brancaster will do nothing?'

'No, my dear.' Dorinda looked sorrowful. 'I am dreadfully afraid that she will do something, and very soon.'

Thirteen

As Mercy alighted from the old fashioned carriage in which she had elected to make the journey from Sussex to Somerset, it occurred to her that her old family home was exactly the same as it had always been and that it was holding out its arms in welcome to her. Yet as she stared up at its old edifice she realized that she had absolutely no desire to be embraced by it because, quite simply, although the house might not have changed, she had.

Torn between continuing to feed John Edward and settling the matter which now confronted her, Mercy had travelled not only with the baby but with Josephine to act as both nursemaid and lady's maid.

'We will not be gone long, but I cannot leave the baby,' she told the ever patient Josephine, who far from minding the upheaval was in a state of excitement for some few days before they travelled.

Realizing that of late she had not been looking her best, Mercy had gone to a great deal of trouble over her appearance. She could not of course become fatter in a matter of weeks, but she had packed the best of her new clothes, which would at least be as fashionable, although perhaps not as elegantly shown off, as those that would be worn by Lady Violet.

The whole incongruity of the situation struck her forcibly as, closely followed by Josephine, she walked up the steps to the front doors to be greeted warmly by the housekeeper, the old servants and her father's old dog – in short, by everyone and everything except the person she had actually come to see.

'Papa.'

At last she had tracked her father down, in the library as usual, reading and making notes, before doubtless riding his old bay hack round the estate, inspecting fences and talking to tenants, and performing all the other duties which he so enjoyed.

Lord Duffane frowned at Mercy, as if he was not quite sure, this early in the day, who she might be exactly.

'You have not brought a baby with you, have you?' he asked, suddenly looking alarmed as the sound of John Edward's crying came filtering through from the hall.

'It is all right, Papa. I have brought his nurse and the servants are not at all put out – in fact they are spoiling him. And besides, you know how it is, one must take one's babies with one or else they—'

She was about to make a joke of still feeding John Edward herself and say *starve*, but remembering how horrified her father was by any natural process in humans – although, strangely, not in horses or dogs – she stopped, and started again.

'They need their mothers so very much in the first few months, you know.'

'Foal at foot, eh?' Lord Duffane laughed suddenly. 'Foal at foot. Well, well, and you hardly look old enough to have a horse of your own, let alone a child. Well, well, my dear, Step-maman is waiting for you in the drawing room. She tells me that you are only to stay the night, and then you are off to pastures new.' He was unable to keep the look of relief from his face.

'Yes, I am off again tomorrow morning, to see friends in Buckinghamshire, and then home after that.'

Lord Duffane nodded briefly before his eyes began to stray back towards the library table.

'So, there we are,' he added, lamely.

'Yes, Papa. Or rather,' Mercy went on, over brightly, 'here I am, and here you are.'

There was a long silence, broken only by the sound of her father clearing his throat. He so obviously had nothing more to say to his only daughter that Mercy was forced to say, blushing with the realization of how little they knew each other, 'Well, I'll leave you to your work, Papa, and go . . . in search of Lady Violet.'

'Yes, Step-maman will want to see you straight away, I am sure,' he said, the look of relief now so speaking that had she not known her father as she did, Mercy felt she might well have been insulted.

Looking around her old home, Mercy saw at once that Cordel Court was just like Brindells when she had first seen it. Had not this fact been such a threat, she would have laughed out loud as she turned each corner and observed yet another little artifice, yet another Venetian chandelier, yet another use of the same dark red set off by green. The same eye for colour, the same feeling for grandeur rather than simplicity, had been brought to bear on both houses. Both had been touched by the same hand, the same woman had commanded the gilt and the red, the tiger skins and the plush.

As she pushed open the drawing room door, disdaining to be announced by anyone since she had, after all, been born and brought up in the house, Mercy thought back with grateful relief to the simple, elegant lines that could now be seen at Brindells. It was so important to allow the house to show off its graces uncluttered and unfussed. She thought with sudden pleasure too of the oak in her own little sitting room, the delicacy of the colours in the main rooms, the gravity of the dining hall now adorned only with oak settles and a long table, Brancaster ancestors and rush matting. She thought of all this to take her mind off how much she hated her stepmother now that she was in the same room as her.

'My dear.' Lady Violet's dressed petticoats rustled silkily as she walked towards Mercy. 'My dear, dear Mercy.' Her voice suddenly sounded to Mercy as silky as her petticoats.

As she looked up into her stepmother's beautiful face Mercy thought of her own mother lying in the graveyard. She had not been beautiful as this

407

woman was beautiful, but she had been good, and that, it seemed to Mercy, was to be better and more lovely than this woman with her perfect profile and her haughty demeanour, her worldliness and her false smile.

For of course once belief in a personality crumbles, so much else disappears. And so it seemed now to her stepdaughter that Lady Violet was false in everything she did or said.

Lady Violet's smile, Mercy realized with shock, did not light up her eyes, and her laugh now seemed inappropriate, coming as it so often did after she had said something really rather unamusing. Her hair that had once seemed so lustrous and dark now looked *too* dark, her mouth *too* full and red. Her eyes were hard and her voice the same. Everything that had once seemed so lovely in both her appearance and her personality had gone. Worse than that, it seemed to Mercy now that all the beauty she had once thought to be her stepmother's had never really been there.

'May God forgive you,' she said quietly.

'I beg your pardon, Mercy. *What* did you say?'

'I said, *May God forgive you*, because at this moment, Lady Violet, I can not.'

'This is no way to greet your stepmother, madam.'

'I am no longer your stepdaughter. As of today we are nothing to each other. Worse than nothing – we are each other's enemies, as must always happen when a woman comes between a man and his wife.'

'I am your stepmother, your father's second wife, and there is nothing, my dear, I am afraid, that you can do about *that*.' Lady Violet laughed humourlessly.

'As far as I am concerned, Lady Violet, you are my husband's mistress, and the ever present cause of my unhappiness. Do you think I can any longer love or respect you?'

Lady Violet sat down, but not suddenly. She sat down most graciously, placing herself carefully in her favourite chair, taking time to rearrange her skirts, as if she was entertaining some cleric's wife and they were about to discuss the arrangements for the carol service, or the harvest festival.

'Do sit down, my dear. Oh, very well, stand if you must. You are not going to tell me that you have travelled, with your baby son and his nurse, all the way to Somerset to tell me all this? Why did you not write to me, if this is what you felt?'

Looking at her with barely concealed dislike, Mercy replied, 'Because, Lady Violet, I wanted to hear your reply in person. After all, if I wrote to you, and you wrote back, it would give you time to think about how you should reply, instead of which I hoped to have surprised you.'

Lady Violet laughed, and for once there was a great deal of amusement reflected in the sound.

'Oh, Mercy, you have always been so *stupid*! It has been something that I have always loved about you, that your father has always loved about you, and possibly your mother too. Didn't you think that I would be *expecting* you? After all, John has been everywhere with me the whole hunting season, including staying here! *I* sent Lord Marcus to tell you. He did not ask himself to stay of his own accord. I thought it better to break the news to you through a third party. And you did not write because you wanted to surprise me. So amusing of you, my dear. Particularly since you chose to write to me and not your husband that you were *enceinte*! That was stupid of you, my dear.'

'Please don't keep calling me *my dear*. It sounds so – false and awkward. I wrote to you as a daughter might, confiding in you in my excitement, because I trusted you, and because – you are right, I am stupid. Only someone really extraordinarily stupid would trust a woman like you to keep a confidence. However, that is all in the past. I realize now what a mistake that was, laying me open as it did to who knows what innuendo, since I was at the same time urging my husband to stay away. I will not try to imagine what reason you gave to my husband for my not wanting him to return to Brindells at that time. It does not really matter now. One thing I must ask you – does my father know of your *arrangement* with John?'

'Your father does not know anything that he does not want to know. He knows that I am happy, and he is happy. He is too intelligent to wish to know anything that might come between us. We are perfectly happy, and we always have been, and he knows that I intend that we shall remain so. That is your father's way. Unlike you, dear Mercy, he is

410

clever. He chooses not to fight the world and its ways, and I am quite sure that he will never do anything to hurt or upset me.'

Mercy sat down, suddenly defeated. She had meant to stand up to this woman who had taken not just her husband from her, but his love, and yet here she was, her knees giving way, feeling faint and sick instead.

Her mind had become a blank. The shock of being told that her own father accepted the situation in which his only daughter found herself, that she would not be able to turn to him, was more terrible than the shock of finding out that John had resumed his long standing love affair with Lady Violet.

Mercy tried to marshal her thoughts, but for a minute found that she could not. It seemed that the complication of her situation had indeed rendered her momentarily mindless. At last, as the silence around her seemed to grow, and she felt her stepmother watching her with a mixture of amusement and contempt, thoughts began to form themselves again, and she took herself back to the beginning, to her step-uncle's visit, and his revelation. While Lord Marcus had been under her roof she had felt so brave, so determined to right matters, to stand up to her stepmother, to bring John back to Brindells where he would become once more the old John, her darling friend and lover, the man who had been her whole universe.

She had thought endlessly about how John seemed to have changed so completely when he returned to her at Christmas. And it seemed to Mercy that the change had come about through associating once more with the hard drinking, hard riding hunting set. That once back in Leicestershire he had become trapped once more in the same hardened personality from which the happiness of his marriage had seemed, just for a while anyway, to have rescued him.

'The worst of it is – it's all my fault,' Mercy murmured suddenly out loud, staring into the fire. 'If I had not wanted to transform Brindells, if I had not been so concerned with restoring the house, he would not have gone back to you. He did not want to go, but I made him. He wanted to stay with me, the new John wanted to stay with me at Brindells. And he was so *happy*! We both were so happy.'

For a second it seemed that Lady Violet winced.

'Yes, well, my dear Mercy, people are, at first, and then the bloom wears off, the young wife becomes *enceinte* and life returns to normal. The husband goes back to his mistress, who is usually most understanding, and the wife has another baby, or perhaps two, and after that, in time, she too takes a lover. That is the way of the world. Your father accepts it and you would be wise to do so too, and the sooner the better. Besides, John and I share a secret that you and he could never share.'

At first Mercy seemed hardly to have heard her and perhaps because she felt suddenly uneasy at her stepdaughter's extreme pallor Lady Violet rose up from where she was sitting and went to her, as she would have done in former, happier times.

'My dear—'

But on hearing the rustle of Lady Violet's silken petticoats Mercy sprang up immediately, walked to the other side of the fire, and re-seated herself, removing herself from any possible contact with her stepmother. She might feel sick and ill, she might feel as if just forming a thought was too much effort, but she had enough emotion left not to want to be anywhere near her husband's mistress.

She gathered her thoughts as she heard her step-mother murmur, 'Oh, very well, have it how you will. But that is the way of the world, my dear – love is not, alas, confined to marriage, and since it never will be, the rules of Society can be most beguiling.'

'So that is the way of the world, is it? To have one's cake and eat it while breaking *God's* rules? Is this why members of Society are at pains to be so very correct in public, in the hunting field, in the dining room or ball room? So that you can all behave quite incorrectly whenever you wish in the bedroom? Is that why we are married off so young? So that we will not dare to question how things are, but have to accept the way of the world and be done with it? Snatching at happiness in a shabby, illicit way, whenever we can, turning a blind eye to everything that is going on around us? How disillusioning it all is!'

'Only because you are young, my dear. Once you grow up a little, and become, let us say, more *versed*, you will see how truly sensible Society is!

413

How much better to be discreet and not wash our dirty linen in public. How much better to be correct, accept our own *weak* natures, if you will, but put a polish on the top of it all for the sake of the servants and the children. Much better to keep things elegant and polished, and exercise discretion for the sake of generations to come.'

But even Lady Violet could tell that her stepdaughter seemed hardly to have heard her, only staring almost blindly at something her stepmother could not see. For a second she thought that Mercy might be going to faint, but now, happily, the older woman realized that she had effectively silenced her, or perhaps even convinced her?

She was wrong. Mercy's silence, her momentary inability to respond to Lady Violet, was not because she was convinced by her stepmother's arguments but because she was remembering the thousands of punishments she had meekly endured as a child, and the many thousand prayers said before the little altar in the private chapel upstairs, in front of which she had asked that God would make her as *good* as Lady Violet and her father.

The truth was that all the time she had been growing up Mercy had worshipped the older people in her life, believing as she had that they were living up to their own strict values. Her brothers had been beaten, herself punished, in the sure and certain hope that if they took their punishments as rewards, one day, when they grew up, they too would be as good and as virtuous as their parents.

But the truth was that the people that had punished them had been no better than they. They had not even been trying to be virtuous, but had been busy gratifying themselves.

Mercy stood up, realizing with horror that if she did not hurry John would be late for his feed, and knowing that to mention it to the childless Lady Violet would bring a look of marked disgust to her ladyship's face, as such things always did.

'You are leaving, my dear?'

'Yes.' Mercy hesitated, and then said with slow deliberation, 'Yes, I am leaving. I am going to feed my son, Lady Violet, and after that we will return home.'

'But you have only just arrived. Your room has been prepared. The horses will be tired. You can not suddenly decide to leave again. It is unreasonable.'

'I am leaving because, like many another young bride before me, I find it impossible to stay under the same roof as my husband's mistress. I do not think that is *unreasonable*, Lady Violet. From my standpoint it is entirely understandable.'

'You will break your papa's heart if you leave now.'

Mercy smiled bitterly. 'Oh, I doubt that!'

'You will show yourself to be without feeling. I will say you have taken a sudden and ridiculous *umbrage* and that your post *petit quelque chose* state has made you over-sensitive and intolerant.'

415

'If you wish, then you must,' Mercy agreed, sounding almost reasonable. 'If my father knows everything, as you say he does, he will believe or not believe what he likes about me. There is nothing I can do about it. Nothing except hope that my son will grow up into a world that does not allow women like you to behave as they wish, and men like my husband to do the same. The natural and best state that a woman and a man can live in is one of love and trust. You are both living in a state of lust and deceit. *As you sow you will reap*. Goodbye, Lady Violet, I hope never to see you again. I hope I shall stop hating you. I know I will never understand you.'

'No, Mercy, don't go. Your papa will ask me where you have gone, and why. He will not understand.'

For a second Lady Violet's voice sounded almost pitifully pleading, and although she did not pause as she walked from the room Mercy could not help remembering how often she had acted as a companion and friend to the older woman. How she had taken her on rides and walks whenever she was bored, showing her things that children find interesting and adults at first find dull but then become enchanted by. Mercy remembered how she would point out secret badger setts, and fox cubs playing around the old oaks, and skylarks singing above them while trout lazed in the streams and lakes. She remembered how she had helped to nurse her stepmother whenever she was sick, and read to her of an evening as she sewed her beautiful tapestries.

Well, that was all in the past. Now she would have to find someone else.

And so a greatly disappointed Josephine was told to once more pack up their luggage and the baby, while Mercy said a dutiful goodbye to her seemingly indifferent father.

'Off already?' he asked in mild surprise, once more in the library after his outdoor exertions, only this time with a pre-luncheon drink rather than a book for company.

'It's the baby, Papa. I think it was a mistake to bring him,' Mercy told him, and seeing the familiar look of relief on her father's face she smiled.

'Before you go, my dear, I want you to take this. It's a letter,' he said, possibly unnecessarily since they could both see what it was. 'It's addressed to you, but I would rather you did not open it until you have left the estate. You will see why.'

He nodded, dismissing her, and Mercy curtsied and left.

Lady Violet, wisely, absented herself from Mercy's moment of departure, and as her step daughter settled herself back against the worn dark blue leather of the old carriage she imagined she could hear, above the sound of the horses' hooves and Josephine talking to the baby, her step-mother saying to her father, 'Well, you know, Mercy was always a very difficult girl. I was always having to punish her, but not enough, it seems. She lets her emotions come between her and correct behaviour and that is a grave fault in her character, I am afraid.'

And she could see her father nodding his head in agreement, and then shaking it in sorrow, before going in to luncheon with his beloved second wife, and thankfully forgetting all about Mercy. But that was before she opened the envelope containing his letter to her.

Dorinda had enjoyed her Friday-to-Monday in the country with Leonie Lynch, but it had been quite enough. She never liked to stay in the country too long, for while she appreciated that the country was green, and the country was brown, and the sky was sometimes grey and sometimes blue, and at other times a mixture of both, and that once the summer came there were definitely flowers blooming and leaves on the trees, to her way of thinking the country actually lacked the one thing that was needed to really brighten it up – people.

Nor was Dorinda the kind of woman who was content to stay for a week at a time at one house after another, spending the morning writing letters, the middle of the day hovering around shooting lunches, and the remainder of the day changing from morning to afternoon clothes, or from walking clothes to ball gowns. And so she discouraged her darling husband from having her invited to stay at the houses of his shooting friends. It was a kind of tacit understanding between them that Mr L went off shooting to Sandringham or Scotland quite alone while Dorinda enjoyed a life of her own, well away from such rural pursuits.

Because Dorinda was the possessor of an easy-going nature, she never minded being alone. She never had any wish to be with someone who did not accept her for what she was. She was not socially aspirant. She was however socially mischievous, and although country society was, as far as she was concerned, happily out of bounds, she had started to really rather enjoy the thought that now that she was rich, and because Mr L was a friend of the reigning monarch, Society would eventually have to come to call on her.

Some did come to call on her and left their cards, after which it was possible for the Leveens to ask them to their house. Once there, even the aristocracy were beguiled because the Leveens were too rich not to be able to offer the kinds of entertainments in which such people revel – the best wines, the most elaborate menus, and more servants to cook and serve them than any other household, including that of the King. But others did not call, and still others did *not* leave their cards.

The dowagers and the leaders of Society still remembered Dorinda Blue, not the newly respectable Mrs Leveen, and they therefore resisted, knowing that they could give their husbands a respectable reason for so doing.

On this particular day Mr L was once more away shooting, and Dorinda sat down at her George III mahogany writing table with its rosewood banded top to make out a list for a projected grand dinner and ball to be held sometime in the coming season. Mrs Goodman, her newly created secretary-companion, was seated to the side of her as she sat staring at the list which she had so carefully started to pen.

'None of those who should have called on me, Mrs Goodman, have deigned to do so,' she told her companion. 'Not one, least of all Lady Londonderry, the queen of London. As a matter of fact, now we come to mention it, don't you think that the poor Queen must be quite put out, knowing that Lady Londonderry is meant to be the queen of London, and poor Queen Alexandra merely an appendage?'

Mrs Goodman did not smile. She loved Queen Alexandra and did not approve of the King and his mistresses, or indeed of Lady Londonderry, despite or perhaps because of the fact that she was known to make or break reputations, and thereby had caused a lot of mischief to innocent men and women whose careers had been gaily ruined by her, usually on the strength of nothing more than a spoilt whim.

'Queen Alexandra, God bless her, is queen of our country and our Empire. That is more important I would think than the capital, Mrs Leveen. Far more important to be loved and respected by the real people rather than a handful of Society jackanapes.'

'Oh, I forgot, Mrs Goodman. You are not an admirer of the King, are you? I love the King, although I only met him a few times when he was

420

still the Prince of Wales, but he procured a bed at Sister Angela's Nursing Home for my Harry when he was dying, and you know how it is – one always sees so much good in a person once they have helped you, I find!'

'In that case perhaps you can bring the King's attention to your own awkward position. Although I doubt that even the King can force Lady Londonderry to call on you, Mrs Leveen.'

Dorinda pouted. 'I did think that once I was rich everyone would call on me, but it does not seem to matter to the aristocracy how rich you are if they decide against you. The only person who might be able to help me is the King, but although Mr L sees him sometimes twice a day he will never ask a favour of him. He says to do so would be to destroy in three seconds their long and happy friendship. Mr L helps the King. He is one of the few people whom the King can trust. To ask him a favour would be to make the King feel uneasy, and Mr L would never make the King feel uneasy. Everyone asks favours of the King. Only Mr L never asks favours.'

Dorinda paused. She could well imagine how dull and upsetting it must be to be a monarch, always being *asked* things and then expected not to *mind*. It would make you very uneasy thinking that people only liked you for your crown, or what you could do for them, and such was not the case with Mr L. Her Mr L had made such wise investments for the King, he had doubled or quadrupled the value of his stocks and shares – or anyway made him a great deal richer. The King had been able to ask favours of Mr L and that had made him feel happy and secure, and if the King was happy and secure – well, the people probably were too.

'There is another person I could ask to help me with my quandary, Mrs Goodman.' Dorinda turned to stare into Mrs Goodman's small, shrewd grey eyes, and then back to the list in front of her. 'This person is a relation of Lady Londonderry—'

'Everyone is a relative of Lady Londonderry, I believe.'

Dorinda nodded, not really hearing. It was a risk to get back in touch with Gervaise, although she had written to him when his wife had died.

'I could call on—' She nearly said 'him' but quickly changed it to 'them'. After the way that Blanquette had behaved she had never quite trusted a servant again. Not that Mrs Goodman was a servant, exactly, in fact she was very far from being so – but she was nevertheless paid to be where she was, so she was not exactly a friend either.

'If you are going to call on *them*,' Mrs Goodman said, the expression on her face purposefully blank, 'I wonder if I should accompany you? It is sometimes better when calling on Lady Londonderry's relatives to have a witness to proceedings, I believe.'

Dorinda then made what might prove to be the mistake of her life.

'Oh no, no need, I do assure you. I know and trust this person to be discreet.'

It was only vanity really, just sheer vanity. She wanted to call on Gervaise, but not as she should, at his family house in Grosvenor Square, but at the little house from which she had been so summarily ejected, to see for herself how fortunate she was that he had rejected her as he had. She wanted to sit down in that little drawing room again, her Lady Duff-Gordon petticoats rustling sensuously, and flash the large diamond ring on her left hand, and smile up at Gervaise and thank him for not trusting her. She just could not resist that particular temptation. And, of course, there was one other thing. To call in at St John's Wood would be dangerous, and it had to be admitted, on a dull, grey day when summer was not yet upon them, that danger was suddenly very appealing. She picked up her pen to write to her former lover.

Following her flying visit to her old family home in Somerset, Mercy had stayed overnight at an inn and then journeyed, long and slowly, first to London, for a night and day, and after that back to Sussex with Josephine and the baby.

Arriving home she had been greeted neither by the wretched housekeeper, Mrs Tomkins, nor by the footmen. She had found that the footmen were drunk and the housekeeper gone to visit her sister without Mercy's authority, while a fall of soot in the drawing room meant that Twissy had walked black footmarks all over the house, particularly, of course, on the new pale furnishings in the drawing room, because no-one had seemed to have given much of an eye to her, except to feed her.

Of course Josephine was shocked and at once set about helping to tidy and wash down. But Mercy was not shocked, most unusually for her – she was furious.

Perhaps some of her anger with her 'husband's mistress', as she now thought of Lady Violet, had spilled over into her daily life. Mercy determined that she too would now become a mistress – but of a rather different kind. She would at long, long last become mistress of her own house.

'Mrs Tomkins,' she told the housekeeper, who was busy chewing a peppermint to cover the smell of her recent drinking, 'I have put up with your insolence, I have put up with you making fun of me when I came to this house and wanted to make things nice for my husband, I have put up with your tittle tattle behind my back – and believe you me, everyone knows if someone is talking behind their backs. They might not hear it, Mrs Tomkins, but they can certainly sense it. I have put up with all these things, but what I will put up with no longer, I find, is you. You may have been here for nearly twenty years, as you are endlessly pointing out to me, but if you keep my house in this way while I am away then I am afraid I am going to have to ask you to leave.'

'No-one has ever spoken to me like this before, Mrs Brancaster, not ever.'

The sound of the peppermint being sucked was

too much for Mercy, and she very nearly started laughing.

'In that case, perhaps someone *should* have spoken to you like this. This place is not being looked after as it should, either by you or by the other servants. Either you decide to do something about it, or I shall decide to do something about *you*.'

'I have been with *Mr* Brancaster, as I say, for twenty years. He has never had a complaint, nor indeed has anyone who has come to the house, Mrs Brancaster, not even Lady Violet, and she has standards if anyone has, I should have thought.'

And so at long, long last the impertinence of the servants, their lack of proper attention to what she wanted, became clear to Mercy. All the time they had, all of them, been laughing at her because they knew what she had not known, that before her marriage, her own stepmother had been lying upstairs with her husband.

'Yes,' Mercy said, at her most Cordel, and she stared icily into the housekeeper's eyes. 'I must agree, when it comes to housekeeping Lady Violet does have standards. What a great pity that she does not have the morals to match. Now, you had better pack your things and I will ask Josephine to take over your duties, with me, until such time as you can be replaced. Goodbye, Mrs Tomkins.'

'But my reference, Mrs Brancaster?'

'For your reference I should apply to Lady Violet and my husband if I were you, Mrs Tomkins.'

In some strange way Mercy knew that she would

pay for dismissing the housekeeper, but she felt so much better at that moment, she really did not care. And far better again when she saw the wretched woman climbing into the trap that came to collect her to take her to the station.

But it was a temporary triumph, for following Mrs Tomkins's dismissal, one by one the other servants left too, until Mercy found herself calling the London agencies and practically begging them to send her down more servants.

Domestic servants do not like the country, nor can they be expected to take to it, unless they've been brought up there, madam, the owner of one agency wrote to her.

Mercy was still in the middle of her crisis when Gabriel Chantry arrived one fine spring afternoon with a pair of splendid oak chairs for the hall. And Gabriel brought with him, besides his warm presence, his gaiety and his self-deprecation, the solution to Mercy's servant problem.

'What you need are the Shaughnessys. They have been in the village for years, and they have seven children. Three strapping sons, two good girls of their own and two adopted cousins who lost their mother. I would think they would spare you at least three or four of their family to come and dress up in country tweed and stand around putting logs on the fire, or whatever your requirements are. And being that the sons are so tall, they will look more than handsome.'

'Oh, Mr Chantry, do you think? Not a servant to

426

be had at the moment, not for the country, not that anyone would wish to have in their house, anyway. Or so the agency says, but then people at agencies are so snobbish they have the practice of making everyone else feel inadequate down to a truly fine art.'

Gabriel laughed, and Mercy saw herself from his point of view – a rich young woman, with a house in perfect modernized taste, a husband and a son, and no cares. But what he said next rather disproved this.

'I am so glad to see you – *better*, Mrs Brancaster. If you will forgive the impertinence, I have been worried about you, knowing that – for whatever reason – you have been suffering.'

Mercy stared at him. 'Was it so obvious?' she asked sadly.

He looked down at the hand he was about to shake, reluctant to let her see the emotion in his eyes.

'I am afraid so.'

As always Gabriel Chantry's taste proved to be impeccable, as much in potential servants as in furniture or curtaining. Two of the Shaughnessy boys were hired as footmen and two Shaughnessy sisters and cousins for maids, and the London agency, perhaps sensing they were about to lose out on their fees, finally sent a tall, middle-aged man who arrived from London with impeccable credentials and a loathing for cities, which immediately prompted Mercy to hire him as a butler.

It was he who finally opened the door to John Brancaster when he returned home.

Brancaster stared at the tall impeccable butler at the door. 'Who the devil are you, man?'

'Jessop, sir.'

'Where is my – where is Mrs—'

'Mrs Brancaster is in the library, sir.'

'That is my wife, Jessop. I meant my house-keeper.'

'As I said, sir, Mrs Brancaster is in the library. No doubt she will be able to bring you abreast of events for herself. I am only newly hired.'

'Well, that is as maybe.'

Jessop stared after Mr Brancaster. He was not such a fool as to attempt to announce a man to his wife in his own house. Nor was he such a fool as to tell that man that he had long ago lost the reins of this particular steed, and forfeited for ever the right to hire or fire the butler. Gossip was such, in the village, and in the pub, not to mention the servants' hall, that everyone knew that Mrs Brancaster was at last determined on getting her own way in her own house. Josephine had told Mrs Shaughnessy in the village, and of course Mrs Shaughnessy had told Mr Shaughnessy, who had of course to go to the pub to refill his pot of beer, and he had fallen into talking, as men will, and the upshot of it all was that everyone, except Mr Brancaster, knew that Mrs Brancaster had changed.

'John.'

John Brancaster knew as soon as he pushed open the library door. It was not just the new grown-up look to her hair, the cottage loaf style that so many women still favoured, nor the flattering tucked linen blouse worn with a straight skirt of darkest green and a *ceinture* with a silver buckle. It was not the small watch set to one side of the blouse, or the tightly buttoned boots of soft kid to match her skirt – it was the look in her eyes.

John saw at once that at Christmas he had left a girl, and he had returned to find a woman.

Mercy was no longer the girl he had married, and John saw it in one awful moment. It was such a frightening moment that he forgot that he was angry at finding a new butler instead of Mrs Tomkins, and that he was standing in dusty travelling clothes, and that he was carrying, for some reason that he could not now remember, a whip.

'How are you, John?'

He removed his motoring gloves one by one, staring at her. 'I am, madam, as you see me. And you?'

'Quite so.'

He moved towards her. 'May I greet you?'

'But of course.'

He did not dare use the word 'kiss', but nevertheless Mercy leaned forward and proffered her cheek. For a second John found his eyes closing as an unknown fragrance filled his senses and he remembered how soft and young Mercy's skin was in comparison to that of Lady Violet, and how youthful her figure, how attractive her voice and how gentle her ways compared to her stepmother. And as if waking from an illness he remembered how badly he had treated her in continuing with his hunting when he should have been by her side when the baby had arrived.

Lady Violet had said, before they parted in London, 'Do not be surprised if there are dreadful reproaches. I hear my poor stepdaughter has gone mad. She certainly showed every evidence of it when she visited us at Cordel Court. A great many women go quite mad after childbirth.'

But it seemed that Lady Violet was wrong, because far from looking insane Mercy was smiling in a calmly affectionate manner, and a new footman, resplendent in new tweeds, was offering 'sir' his favourite pre-dinner drink, and the flowers everywhere were beautifully arranged in great cascades of early leaves and blooms, and the library fire was crackling in the way a fire always does when it is burning young wood.

'How beautiful everything looks, Mercy.' He sighed, suddenly unafraid to be appreciative. 'I have really been away far too long. I have missed – seeing you.' He watched her as she sat, perfectly composed, opposite the fire by which he now stood. 'I have even missed hearing your voice, do you know that?'

His tone was that of a man waking up from a dream, a man who had been away on a long voyage and known many excitements, most of which, to his own puzzlement, he could not now quite remember.

He stared down at Mercy and for a second she had the feeling that he might be going to ask her where he was. That she might be going to have to say to him, as to a man waking up from an unconscious state, *You're here in the library at Brindells, John,* so much did he suddenly seem to be coming back to an old but familiar – even, it occurred to her suddenly, *loved* – reality.

'Would you like to come up and see your son, John? Would you like to see John Edward?'

'John Edward? Yes, of course I should like to see the baby.'

He looked suddenly so nervous that Mercy put out a hand to him and squeezed his arm, remembering how much her father had feared babies, only wanting to wave at them from afar and then get back, as quickly as possible, to his own life.

'It's all right, he is all bathed and beautiful. Josephine has him as brushed and bouncing as if he was going in for a baby competition at the village fair!'

She laughed suddenly, and again she had the sensation that John was waking up from a bad dream, that he had been in some kind of hell and was only now coming back, if not to heaven, at least to an earth that he could recognize.

If John Brancaster was nervous, no-one could have been more nervous than John Edward's nanny.

She bobbed a curtsy to Mr Brancaster while keeping one arm around the baby, propped up against some temporary cushions in his cot and blissfully unaware of the emotions that surrounded him at that moment.

Josephine did not really like men. She never had, not really. Perhaps it was something to do with the fact that she had seen what her mother had suffered, and now she had seen how Mrs Brancaster had suffered these last months nothing much had happened to change her opinion of the opposite sex. She did not care to think about how long Mr Brancaster had been away, or of the unhappiness that had been her young mistress's lot, and so it was really against her principles to smile at this tall, dark middle-aged man standing in her nursery. Indeed, on hearing that Mr Brancaster was expected that day she had fantasized that she would not acknowledge him, so badly did she think of him. But, on the other hand, given that her monthly wage of five pounds was badly needed at home, when all was said and done it would have been foolish not to look at least pleasant in some sort of a way.

John Edward, bless him, smiled at his father too, and it seemed to both the women that there was no need to state the obvious, which was that he looked almost exactly like the man bending over his cot. The same dark hair, the same eyes, the same long, elegant fingers. As babies sometimes do, John Edward had obligingly changed from looking like his mother in the first few weeks of his life to looking like a mirror image of his papa.

Mercy broke the long silence that had followed John's entrance into the nursery. 'We are changing for dinner, John. Your clothes should be laid out by now in the old suite of rooms which are now yours.' And then she said, 'I expect you would like to hold John Edward first though, wouldn't you?'

Josephine, most reluctantly, picked up her charge and placed him in his father's arms, and a look that was quite untranslatable crossed John Brancaster's face as he stared down into a miniature of himself.

Later, at dinner, John's eyes, ever appreciative of women and all their devices, every nuance of costume and hairstyle, every touch of style, stared down the dining table at Mercy in approval.

'You look *en plein beauté*, Mercy dear, really you do. Wonderfully pretty, prettier than I have seen you look in many months.'

Mercy forbore to comment that he had not actually seen her for many months, and instead smiled her thanks for the compliment.

She was wearing a low cut evening dress of delicate chiffon. It was actually over two years old, but she had thought that most probably John, being a hunting man, would not remember it. The skirt was cut in three layers with a lace-edged train, while the bodice was of a dark blue and had its own train which fell slightly shorter than that of the skirt, both in width and length.

John raised his wine glass to her as she raised hers to him.

'To John Edward.'

'To John Edward.'

They both drank.

'He looks so like his papa, don't you think?' Mercy asked.

'Let us drink to him again, my dear.'

Mercy stared down the table at her husband, realizing of a sudden that his deep desire to toast his son had more to do with his equally deep desire to become inebriated than with celebrating the safe arrival of an heir to Brindells.

There were no servants in the room, which was probably why he was suddenly prompted to ask after her life since Christmas.

'Oh, I have been doing very well, thank you, John. I have quite finished the decorating, and Mr Chantry is as pleased as I am, and I hope you are too.'

'Ah yes, Mr Chantry. He of the beard and the deep knowledge of antiques.'

John drank again, once more too fast, and this time alone.

A silence fell, a silence which Mercy had no intention of filling, for she had vowed that she would not return to that particular form of conversational anxiety.

Perhaps this unnerved her husband because he was the first to break their silence.

'You have changed, Mercy,' he said, blinking slightly in the candlelight. 'I truly would not know you as the girl I left.'

Mercy smiled. 'But that is good, surely?'

'It is not the same, certainly, but – I have to tell you, I would like to see the other Mercy coming back, some time soon. Perhaps it is not possible immediately, but perhaps soon? I liked the other Mercy. She was not so . . . serious, was she? She was more innocent, I suppose is what I am trying to say.'

Feeling that she might be about to say something she would quite definitely regret, Mercy stood up suddenly and left him, but she was not alone for long. Only a few minutes later John joined her in the drawing room, bringing with him a large glass of port.

He sat down opposite her, the fireplace between them, obviously determined to speak in as frank a way as possible, and equally obviously more than a little worse for wear.

'I understand that Lady Violet has sustained a visit from you, Mercy, that you went to see her at Cordel Court,' he said, clearly having found the determination that he needed in the vintage port.

'Yes, that is quite right.' Mercy remained as still as a statue, and only the gentle tapping of her fan against the palm of her hand gave any indication of her inner nerves. 'Yes, I went to Cordel Court.'

'You went to Cordel Court, but you left shortly afterwards?'

'Of course.'

'Of course?'

'Yes, of course. As a married woman I could not be expected to stay under the same roof as my husband's mistress, after all, John, could I?'

'But she is not – but she is your stepmother. You hurt her feelings, by acting as you did. She told me so. She was most hurt.'

'I hate to contradict you, John, but Lady Violet has few feelings, and those that she has she does not keep in her heart, but in quite another part of her body.'

He was in the act of finishing his port, but at this last statement he started to cough. Mercy waited, in silence, for him to stop coughing, where once, only a few months before, she would have rushed to his side, all concern, to pat him on the back.

'That is not a very pretty thing to say about Lady Violet, Mercy,' he said, eventually.

'Pretty or not, it is the truth as I see it, John. You may see it quite differently, I suppose.'

'Please don't be like this. It is almost as if you have become – hard, overnight.'

He looked at her and his voice was sad, almost pleading, echoing almost precisely how her step-mother's had sounded just before Mercy left her what seemed like weeks before. It was as if they were both saying, *But you're not like this, you're soft and pliant and you see everything from everyone else's point of view. If we are as we are, you must remain as you are.*

Mercy looked across at him, and knowing that she had the advantage of not having drunk more than one glass of wine she put her head on one side, and smiled.

'No, John, I have not grown hard, I have grown used. I have grown used to the idea of my husband lying with another woman. I have grown used to the idea of life not being about love, but about love *making*. I have grown used to the way that nothing is as we wish it to be, and most of all I have come to understand that I was right. I should never have married you. You did not, and never could, love me as I loved you. You did not and would not, and have not. It is a fact. There is nothing to be done about it. There is no blame. I understand. I wish I did not, but I do. You and Lady Violet have not just a passion but a *secret* between you, something that I can never share, she told me.'

John frowned, suddenly looking genuinely puzzled and about to say something, but Mercy carried on determinedly.

'Most of all I understand that what my step-mother said was true. I *am* stupid. I *was* stupid. But at least now I have actually grasped that, and so I have a small chance of becoming less stupid. I realize of course that I will never be hopeful again. Nor will I ever try to turn people into saints simply because that is how I want to see them. I accept that to be a foolish vision of the world. What you see as being hard is, believe me, merely acceptance of my own stupidity and a determination to change, and to go on – with truth.'

'You exaggerate your stupidity, believe me. It is because you are still hurt. All you have ever been, surely, is just young?'

Mercy shook her head sadly, feeling for him suddenly, feeling for his sudden longing to undo the hurt, as if he were her child, and not her husband.

'No, John, I have changed. I am only too aware that you thought of me as a poor sort of creature, a plain little girl to be rescued from a gilt chair and roped into marriage for want of something else to do, as my stepmother did, and I can understand that.'

'I never thought of you as anything but fine and lovely, I promise you. Of course you were innocent, but – I mean to say, we were so happy together – until – I went away. Until *you* sent me away.'

Mercy flung open her fan and moved it impatiently up and down against her face.

'Oh, never mind who sent you, me or you, or both of us, what does it matter? And never mind who went and hunted or who stayed behind with Mr Chantry and decorated – love should be stronger than that, surely? It should be stronger than everything – there should be no changing because someone has to *go away*. The truth is that your love for me, whatever it may have been, was not strong enough to resist returning to your old ways once you *went* hunting! I grew up in the country, I know there is more to hunting than flying the hedges and ditches, believe me. Hunting is a secret society. It is a way for gentlemen to meet fast ladies and enjoy hard drinking as well as hard riding. Lady Violet has a passion for you. It will never go. Just as you have a passion for her.'

'Not any more, truly, not any more.'

He stood up and started to pace about the room.

'I did have a passion – of course I did, she is a very beautiful woman, and we liked the same things, shared the same things – but not, believe

438

me, any kind of secret, at least not one that is at all interesting. I am not the kind of man to have secrets, and God knows I tried to act honourably as far as all this was concerned. It was only that you would keep putting me off from coming home, so that I became convinced that you were in love with that fellow Chantry, and then of course – Violet and I, well, we fell into our old ways, but they were boring old ways after what we had, here, we two.'

Mercy looked at him, her head on one side, knowing that he was speaking the truth but finding that it made little difference to her now.

'Everything a little too fast, or a little too slow, all the stories so old, the laughter a little too sharp. I longed for you. And then when it turned out at Christmas that you were having a baby – God forgive me, I was convinced that . . . much as I loved you, I was convinced that it had all happened in my absence, let us say. That Violet was right, and the baby could not be mine. And yet I still wanted to stand by you. That was how much I loved you.'

Mercy sighed, somehow strangely unsurprised by what John had just said. She knew of course that she could, if she wished, spring to her feet and become quite indignant, but she had no real desire to shout about her honour being impugned and berate him for believing her to be 'that kind of woman'. If he had been able to make love to Lady Violet it was only too likely that he would be quite able to believe that Mercy was the same kind of

439

person as her stepmother. No, it was far too late for histrionics and anger, too late for anything except the dull grey of a certain kind of truth that can only come out of misunderstandings, explanations delayed, and misplaced love.

'I am sorry you thought the baby was not yours, John. You must have suffered. And I am sorry that you fell into love again with Lady Violet, and that now, perhaps, you might be coming out of it. But, you see, all that – everything you have said – does not change anything, because the last few months have changed *me* so entirely, so utterly, that I can not see life in the same way as I once did, before I found out about you and Lady Violet.

'Nowadays I see only deception in everyone. As people are talking to me I see only that they are lying – to me, to themselves. And when I look in the mirror I see only a stupid girl, who once believed everything that Society and the Church told her, but found it all to be just lies, and as a result is now – quite dead.'

Fourteen

Dorinda was certain that she must have lost her reason when she found herself seated in her carriage outside the door of her old residence in St John's Wood waiting for an unknown maid to answer the door to her coachman's knock. What was she doing there? And why? Why would she, Mrs Lawrence Leveen, be going to such trouble to see her former lover, when she knew very well it would matter not a whit to her dear Mr L if Lady Londonderry called on them or not. What did it matter?

But the truth was that it did matter. It mattered a great deal to the daughter of a seaside landlady that her husband and herself be received by everyone. Besides, Dorinda refused to be denied the pleasure of standing at the top of *her* stairs, in *her* town house, and seeing the ghastly set expressions of that bunch of old aristocratic tigresses known as 'Society' *having* to come to her ball.

And she did not just want it for herself, she wanted it for Mr L, for she knew only too well from living with Gervaise that the true aristocracy looked down their noses at men like Lawrence Leveen. However close they might be to the monarch, however dear to his heart, they were not *one of them*.

And so she had determined that she would make him *one of them* in one great and fantastical evening. She would ensure that they all came tripping up his marble stairs. His rooms would echo to the sound of their slang, their asides, and their precious attitudes, and after that they could be done with it.

Of course her dear little friend and confidante, Leonie, had advised against it, and most strongly. Dorinda was not quite sure from where Leonie culled her wisdom but she thought it might be from having to see so much of death, and illness, and all those maturing experiences that being all day, and sometimes all night, at a nursing home must inevitably provide.

Or it might be that she knew it instinctively, for, without any doubt, it seemed to Dorinda anyway, Leonie was not the run of the mill personality to be attracted to the nursing profession, any more than Lady Angela herself. Dorinda knew, because Gervaise Lowther had taught her, that to comment on a person's background or compare their looks to those of another person of your acquaintance was just not done. No-one in Society ever said, *Oh, but you look so-o like Lord Clanmaurice*, it was just not something that anyone said. Dorinda was glad that Gervaise had taught her this, and much else besides, of course.

'Mr Lowther is in and will receive you, Mrs Leveen,' her coachman told her, opening the

442

carriage door and staring up at her from under his hat.

Dorinda nodded, quite curtly for her, for she at once judged from the coachman's expression that he did not approve of bringing a woman such as herself to a house in St John's Wood of all places, and that as far as he was concerned they might as well have been in *Tulse Hill*, so renowned was the area as being a place where the nobility kept their mistresses, and the rich their girlfriends. But since she knew that Gervaise had divested himself of her successor – the famously endowed blonde lady with the flashing brown eyes – she felt quite able to call, albeit not in her own carriage with its proclamation of *Vincit Quae Amat* but in the family barouche, all done up in sombre dark brown paint – very respectable.

The door was reopened by a very ugly maid. Dorinda could not help being entertained by this, for she remembered that she herself had, after all, kept on Blanquette not because she was particularly adept, but purely and simply because Dorinda had judged her to be no temptation to Gervaise. And yet, give the young Breton maid her due, she had finally defeated Dorinda and Dorinda had been, momentarily, the loser and Blanquette the winner. The famous blonde had doubtless chosen this one for the same reason. Gentlemen were ever susceptible when it came to maids. Dorinda had heard it was something to do with their uniforms, although why a healthy man would prefer fustian and serge to silks and satins she had no idea at all. Happily her Mr L was not like that. He liked only the best, and then only when it was dressed up, or down, to the nines, if not the tens.

'Mrs Leveen, sir,' the maid announced.

Dorinda rustled forward, as ever thankful to Lady Duff-Gordon for her impeccable taste in styling Dorinda's beautiful undergarments.

'Dorinda!'

Gervaise was by the chimneypiece, handsome, beautifully dressed, and as drunk as a footman on his day off.

'Gervaise.'

Dorinda kissed the air beside his head, and then backed away hastily. She hated the smell of drink on men in the morning. She did not mind it in the least after luncheon. Then it could be quite attractive, particularly if the gentleman was 'calling' on you in the library or your upstairs rooms and you were in your tea gown on your chaise longue, but before that it was really very much not at all the thing. She noticed too that Gervaise had broken veins around his nose where he had never used to have them, and that his hands shook a little.

'This is such a pleasure,' he kept saying, 'you have no idea. Since you married I have longed to see you again, to talk over old times, and to be a friend to you. And of course, I have been reminded of you as often as I have seen Leveen, and that is very, very often, seeing that the King does so dote on his company, and I am always around the King.'

Gervaise was still the same charming person, but now he was old in a way that was sad, because he had matured himself in wine and not achievement, and the way he spoke, his whole conversation, was that of a man who had said the same words over and over again, time and time again, until really it was quite obvious that he knew no others.

'I do not blame you in the least for returning to your husband when he was dying, and now that you have a new one I must congratulate you – for you have never, ever looked better. And besides, I have to say, having taken a part in your social education, I take a pride in your social elevation.'

'Oh, Gervaise!' Dorinda laughed her purposely pretty laugh and smiled at the same time. 'How funny you are. We have not been elevated, by any means. Mr L is still a Mr and I am still a Mrs even when not travelling, as today, quite incognito.'

'Dorinda, I fear, no matter how rich and powerful your husband, he will have a hard time of it refusing a title from the King. The King, I know, may wish it.'

Dorinda rearranged her skirts, also in a purposely pretty way.

'Well, quite so, Gervaise, but we must understand, must we not, that whatever the King may wish for Mr L, he wishes more than anything to make the right investments, and that Mr L will do, and does, for him, *n'est ce pas?* The King will not force Mr L to do anything he does not wish, he is too much the gentleman. He is a gentleman king, and that is why the populace likes him. That and

445

the fact that the King enjoys himself, now he is over the Coronation and his appendicitis.'

'Yes, it was a pity about the Coronation, so few countries able to attend the second innings.'

'Gervaise, I am not here to discuss the King. The King is my husband's business, and indeed your business, but I am here to ask you a favour.'

Gervaise leaned across to the woman whom he had loved so thoroughly, and thought sadly of how he would never do so again.

'For you, for all the happy memories that you have given me, which I still treasure, I would do anything. Oh, by the way, do you know that my poor wife died? I did so love her.'

'Yes, Gervaise, I knew. Remember, I wrote you a letter of condolence? I always knew that you loved your wife, first and foremost, and she was what mattered. That she could not make love with you, that was the pity, but you both loved each other. I was a mere diversion.'

'Yes, you are right, she was what mattered, but now my children are married I have no-one. Which is a hell of a pity, to be alone, with only one's mistress or someone for company of an evening.'

Dorinda laughed gaily. 'Touché, Gervaise, touché. Was I such dull company?'

'No, no, not you – just in general, you know? At any rate, here we are, and I must do my best for you, for you were the best of my mistresses, and I always said so.'

'This is not the easiest of undertakings, believe me, Gervaise, and I will appreciate it in a great many ways if you can bring it about. And if you do, Gervaise, I think that it is within Mr L's power to help you – help you with some sound *advice*.'

Gervaise knew exactly what Dorinda meant. He was in need of sound advice. The cost of keeping up his houses, let alone a mistress, was beginning to be a strain, even for him.

'Railroads, and such like, is that the way to go, Dorinda? I heard as much in the whisper at Whites.'

Dorinda made a tut-tut noise. She knew that money was never discussed in Society, for the very good reason that no-one ever thought about anything else so really it was quite dull to talk about it.

'We shall not speak between *us* again of business, Gervaise, but suffice it to say that I will advise Mr L to advise you. More than that I can not say. I do not understand business. I understand running a house, and making love, and ensuring that no-one steals your cook, that is all.'

'I should be grateful for advice, Dorinda. Really I should.'

Inwardly Dorinda sighed and putting her head on one side she smiled, because of a sudden she too remembered the old days when they had spent such pleasurable times together.

'Well, Gervaise, this is how it is.'

'Tell me how it is – God, it is so good to see you, Dorinda. Really it is.'

'This is how it is, Gervaise. Lady Londonderry – well, all the famous three – we have no need to name them, have we?'

'I should say not. They terrify the boots off me, I can tell you.'

'I know, I know, Gervaise, and I do understand, but they are so important, you know, and none of them, not one of them has called on me, d'you see? And I cannot give a ball and have the King come, and so on and so on, unless they do. They have been known to hold out even against the King, you know, and the King to hold out against them too, and really it is for Mr L that I want it so much. I want everything to be as perfect as possible and all Society present at our first ball, not just the King and people like you, but everyone.'

'Well, but Dorinda, I am nothing much, you know. I can not force the old battleaxes to call. They do as they wish, and that is all there is to it.'

'Surely you must be related to someone who will, let us say, be *persuaded*, I mean in exchange for the kind of advice that Mr L is disposed to give you?'

'Completely see what you mean, Dorinda, but to tell you the truth whom I'm related to and why has really always rather bored me, and, not to put too fine a point on it, I am now really too mummified by midday to remember anyway.'

Having expected just such a reply, Dorinda nodded. Opening a little silk case she had brought with her as an *aide memoire*, she settled back against the brocade fabric that she herself had chosen, and smiled.

'Oh, I know, Gervaise. Men hate ancestors and everything like that, not nearly as interesting as a hot tip from Newmarket, so before I called this morning I wrote it all out from the book of books to which my secretary is devoted, I have to tell you – and there we are.'

She pushed a piece of clearly written paper towards Gervaise who peered at it in a bleary way, and then gave it back to her really rather too quickly.

'No, no, just tell me, Dorinda, because really I have trouble with that kind of who married whom stuff and nonsense. So common to know anything about one's ancestors, unless it is something amusing, I always think. You know, unless they have called a cavalry charge at the wrong time, or split their hose in front of Elizabeth I, something of that nature.'

'Well, the exciting thing is that Mrs Goodman – she's my secretary – found that you are related to all three of the big three, Gervaise. Imagine? Lady Londonderry is just the beginning, and you are quite definitely related to *her*.'

Gervaise groaned. 'But they're such blown roses, Dorinda. You can't think that I can make love to them can you?'

Dorinda glanced at the ormolu clock that she remembered all too well, and then across at Gervaise.

'My, my, my, Gervaise, look at me. I have outstayed my twenty minutes.'

'Don't matter, Dorinda. So lovely to see you. Besides, when you've been in a man's bed, does it matter how long you call on him? I should think that is taking etiquette too far, isn't it?'

Having said this Gervaise tried to take her in his arms, but Dorinda stepped neatly backwards to avoid him, saying, 'Now, Gervaise, it was you who taught me never to stay for more than twenty minutes on a call, and preferably fifteen!'

'Just tell me, you don't expect me to make love to one of those old trouts, do you? I mean have you seen any of them? They could crack ice at a glance.'

Dorinda paused by the door. 'I don't *expect* you to do anything.'

Gervaise sighed with relief.

'I know you will make *sure* that one or all of them call on me, Gervaise, that is all. And don't worry about ringing for the maid – I think I know my own way out!'

Dorinda gave a laugh rich with the humour of the situation and skipped back down the steps of the house to her waiting carriage, and to her coachman, whose expression, Dorinda realized, as he shut the carriage door, was one of speaking relief that they were about to be leaving an area of London to which he remained stubbornly, and snobbishly, unaccustomed.

Dorinda settled back against the rich, faded, ruby red velvety interior of the coach, and thought suddenly how much she now hated blue. Dorinda Blue, like the house at which she had just called, was part of a past that she was more than willing to forget. Not because she thought of herself as having been particularly immoral, but because she was ashamed that she had ever thought that she loved Gervaise Lowther. He was really very uninteresting compared to her Mr L.

But of course, Gervaise did, in common with so many of his kind, have a tendency to overspend. She happened to know from Mrs Goodman who knew from a man at a certain royal bank who had, it was rumoured, imbibed too much at a party given by a cousin of that excellent secretary, that Mr Gervaise Lowther was in Carey Street (rather a frequent address for the aristocracy) and badly in need of some sound advice which would lead to fortunate investments, the kind of investments that would pay off his steadily accumulating debts and make his bank very happy indeed.

Gervaise would find a way to make Lady Londonderry, or Lady Elcho, or whoever, call on Mrs Lawrence Leveen, and in calling they would have had to capitulate to the fact that Dorinda Blue was now just as good as them – or just as bad!

After Leonie had bought the house in Eastgate Street for her beloved foster parents, the heart had seemed to have gone out of them. Admittedly, Leonie noticed this only gradually. At first she had thought it to be her imagination, but then little by little she realized that the Lynches quite definitely no longer had the same feeling of energy about them. It was as if now that they knew they were quite safe from such day to day terrors as being thrown into the street, as if now the poor-house no longer threatened, they felt uneasy. As if, inexplicably, now that they knew they did not need to dread the rentman's knock at the door, or face the idea of the pawnbroker's shop, their reason for living had quite gone, and with it all their old energy and boisterousness.

'But you've never owed money, never, not all the time I was growing up here. You never owed a penny piece.'

'No, Leonie dear, that is true, but there was always the threat of it, and that was what gave us the energy to go on with things. Now we don't have to go on with anything, and so we don't. It's quite taken Ned into a different world. He keeps talking to himself, and standing in the street. I wouldn't know him for the man I used to live with. He was always so cheerful, always out and about and making the best of everything. Now he seems to have lost it all, all his old zest has quite gone.'

'But all you have to do now you own your own house is to enjoy the freedom and put your feet up in front of the fire.'

'There is a definite limit as to how many feet can be put up in front of fires, Leonie dear, really there is. And now we can afford to have coal any day of the week, the fire's stopped being the treat that it was, don't you see? And now my Ned owns his own house he has no friends, because no-one else in the street owns their own house, and no-one else in the street has no worries, so it has put them on the outs with him. No, I am afraid it is a quite definite unhappiness to us, owning the house. We were better off before, when we were not so well off, and had the fear on us. There is nothing quite like thinking that you might owe someone sixpence to lend the necessary tara-boom-deay to life, dear, really there isn't.'

'So what do you want me to do?'

Leonie looked miserably round the little, clean, freshly painted room and wondered at this new and strange kind of misfortune that she had brought upon her family. It seemed so strange, so out of the blue unhappy, to think that good fortune did not bring happiness.

'We did talk of selling the place to someone else and using the money to go travelling, but my Ned hates sea travel, and foreigners, and nothing to be done to make him like it either, I am afraid, dear.'

There was a long silence, and as they supped at their tea and the canary in the cage beside the window sang, Leonie searched and searched in her mind for a solution to this unexpected turn of events, this soggy, grey sort of misery that she had unwittingly brought upon her beloved foster parents.

'There is a place to which you could go. It does not involve sea travel, although it does involve change.'

'And where would that be, dear?'

Aisleen Lynch's gaze reflected a kind of bored hopelessness as Leonie leaned forward of a sudden, and showing a degree of cheerful encouragement that she did not feel squeezed her foster mother's hands.

'The place that could be a change but does not involve a sea journey is – the country.'

'The country?'

'Yes, the country.'

'You mean where there are fields and trees, and that?'

'Yes, and that. After all, Ned comes from the country, that is where he was born before his father had to come to town to find work, and that is where he used to talk of returning, when we were little.

'Why, bless you, dear, he did, didn't he? But I mean to say, the country?'

'I have a friend, I went to stay with her at her country house if you remember – in Sussex, near to Ruddwick it is, and I know that she has great need of a lodge keeper and his wife, because she told me so at the time. The present people are not at all to her liking, being uppity and too good for the job and always wanting to close the gates if they don't approve of the style of coach, and not approving of motor cars. More suited to the style of the old Queen. They are not the kind of lodge keepers she wants.

'Lodge keeping?'

The way Aisleen said it made it sound like 'lion keeping'.

'She is Mrs Lawrence Leveen, and you will like her. Mrs Dodd's friend Mrs Goodman is a friend of hers, and Mrs Dodd's a friend of yours, so that is the best kind of person you could lodge keep for, the friend of your friend's friend, wouldn't you say?'

Aisleen Lynch's cheeks became quite pink with

454

a sudden excitement. She had been feeling out of sorts for weeks now. What with Ned not having to work any more, and everything the same, day after blooming day, gone were the excitements of wondering if he would stay at the pub too long and ruin his dinner, or how his day at the market had been. Without the need for paying rent, there really was no need for any of the usual excitements. Nowadays they had to look for something to do to fill their day. Before there had always been too much to do.

But it could be different if they moved to the country. There would be a job to do, and no-one to point the finger and whisper that they owned their own house, and were different from the rest of them.

And besides, a lodge keeper was a position of responsibility. It would keep Ned looking out of the window and herself busy doing the same, and they would not be house owners any more, they would have to mind their ways to keep in with this Mrs Leveen because she would own the lodge. The excitement would come back again, the feeling of racing against life in case you lost the roof over your head – all that would come back, and make her feel quite herself again, and Ned too.

'Very well, dear, you ask your friend, and I'll tell Ned to be ready to sell the house. That will cheer him up. Everyone in the pub will talk to him again. He will be able to hold his head up high and know that no-one can say that he is different from the rest of the street.'

At which Aisleen gave a happy sigh of relief and smiled for the first time that month.

Following her visit to the little house in St John's Wood Dorinda had found that the days seemed to drag drearily by. Mr L had paused only briefly between shooting weeks before he was off again to the Continent on business for the King.

And although they had made love and enjoyed themselves – perhaps because they had made love and enjoyed themselves – Dorinda now found herself in the awkward position of missing her husband, quite passionately, and with all her heart and soul, which was really not her. Her heart actually ached for him, and she could not eat. Not only that, she could not sleep, and had been forced, night after night, to take to reading books and such like, which again was really not her.

'If only we could get on with the invitation list for the ball,' she moaned every morning to Mrs Goodman. 'That would take my mind off missing Mr L. But as it is, we have not been called upon by anyone of any consequence, just the kind of people who wish to entertain *us*, and those are never the people one wants to ask to a ball.'

'Quite so, Mrs Leveen, but let us face it, there is hope, because Mrs Dodd heard from Madame Chloe who heard from that uppity Poiret, or was it Lucile, at any rate she heard that Lady Londonderry was speaking in praise of your beauty only the other day at one of her mornings, and that several people heard her too.'

'She was speaking of me?'

Dorinda leaned forward excitedly, because they both knew that being spoken of was the first step to public approval. But seconds later her eyes narrowed as she saw that there could be a catch to this rumour.

'Yes, but how did she speak of me, Mrs Goodman?'

'Well, that is the best part, Mrs Leveen. She spoke of you as Mrs Lawrence Leveen. No doubt of it at all, that is how she spoke of you, not as – not in the *other* way at all.'

Dorinda sighed with relief. She could not count how often she had cursed the soubriquet that had made her so famous overnight. Dorinda Blue had been known by the whole world. She had been truly famous. Yet here she was now, hoping against hope that somehow everyone would forget her fame, that no-one would remember the very reason why she came to the attention of everyone, including the King, namely her stunning blue eyes.

'Oh, I doubt that I care any more, really, anyway.'

She gave Mrs Goodman a sudden rueful look.

'After all, if one has blue eyes, and a pretty name, who minds that everyone knows you for them? Or anything else for that matter?'

Mrs Goodman nodded, but she did not believe her. In truth they both knew that her name had been linked to scandal and that without it she would not have been famous.

'I think you do very well, whatever anyone calls you.'

Mrs Goodman's affectionate look almost made up to Dorinda for the fact that they both knew that yet another morning had gone by without one of the big three hostesses making what was always known as a *morning call* even though it was often made in the afternoon.

And not only that, but Mr L was still not home.

Mrs Blessington was able to call on Mercy that particular morning, because John had left in his motor car to go to a meeting with his family lawyer in East Grinstead. The days following Mercy's outburst had been grim indeed, with breakfast taken in silence, luncheon the same, and dinner – with the sole exception of when Mercy played the piano afterwards – in the same deathly vein.

The toll on Mercy might have been terrible had she not felt so determined. Indeed she had never felt *more* determined. She would not and could not be put down ever again, not by her husband, not by her stepmother, not by her father. She was and would be true to her new self.

'You are not a suffragette, but you are, I think, as I am now, an advocate of the True Woman.'

Mercy was in agreement with this. She knew all about the True Woman movement that had come from America, although it had not touched the lives of any of her contemporaries – or if it had she had not noticed it – surrounded as they were by nurses and servants, and encouraged by Society to abandon their real vocation in life, that of mother-hood and nurturing, education and home-making, in preference to the worthless social round.

'The True Woman knows that the power of the earth, the power of the world is, in reality, all hers. She knows that her real vocation in life is the nourishment and continuity of life, that being a mother is the greatest vocation that a woman can aspire to. Being a mother is being a teacher, it is being an artist in the kitchen and the drawing room and – dare I say it' – Mrs Blessington gave a rich laugh – 'elsewhere too!'

Mercy loved to be with Mrs Blessington, and this despite the fact – or nowadays perhaps because of the fact – that she knew that John would not really approve of the friendship, seeing that Mrs Blessington was not a member of the County. Mercy, on the other hand, appreciated Mrs Blessington's direct understanding of life and her kindness. Above all she treasured her sound common sense.

'You must never ask Mr Brancaster to give up his hunting, because to do so will mean that you will find yourself married to a man who is not the man you married. You married Mr Brancaster for love, and you loved the man for what he was, and still is – it is now up to him not to give *up* anything, but to see what he can *give* to you. The ball is in his court. And if he chooses to leave it there, well, my dear, there is nothing much either of us can do, except pray for him, for you will certainly never change now that you have come to this new understanding of yourself. Once he has accepted this he will, I know, come to you. That is all there is to it, I am afraid. Mr Brancaster must learn to give – not give *up*.'

Mrs Blessington gave Mercy much-needed heart. Having lost her own mother when she was young she thought she knew what sorrow and making the best was about, and she was quite prepared to face such things again. Not that she *could* be eternally sorrowful any more. She had to think of John Edward, and of his future. He would not want a drippy kind of woman for a mother. He would want her to be strong, so that he could learn to be strong, not so that he could fight wars, but so that he could face up to the realities of emotions, and how they affected people. That was where true strength was needed – in facing up to life.

After Mrs Blessington left her Mercy went in search of her son, and picking him up from his pram she held him against her, and his warmth and his need for her gave her comfort. After all, when all was said and done, in the true scheme of things, he was more important now than either John or herself. He was the future. It was for him, more than anyone, that his mother had to be strong.

And she was strong, until she saw the grim expression on John Brancaster's face the following day, and realized that he was going to 'summon' her to the library, much as in the old days her brothers were 'summoned' to be beaten, or she was 'summoned' to be put in a back board or have the palms of her hands beaten with a riding whip. Immediately her stomach went up and down, and she felt that particular feeling which was so un-grown-up, but so real none the less, of her insides turning to water, and her mouth going dry. Yet she *would* be strong. After all, she have given birth to a son, she had a baby now. He needed her to be strong. She put a pin in her hand, and walking to the library, in answer to the summons, she stuck it resolutely into her thumb. Then, nodding to the footman to open the door for her, she swept into the library.

'Mercy.'

John was not alone, and this was awful, because she had thought she would only have to face him. He was with someone who, from the fusty look to him, and the frowsty look to his face, Mercy knew at once must be the family lawyer.

'Yes, John.'

'I have been a little worried, to say the least, about the events of the past months, so one way and another I thought it best, given that we now have a son and heir – I have a son and heir – that I call in Gibbon and perhaps formalize matters between us. Nothing more, you understand, just a formality, to talk things through with our lawyer, so that we can reach some kind of understanding.'

The lawyer stepped forward at this.

'Mrs Brancaster, I am Gibbon, from the family firm of Gibbon, Gibbon and – er – Gibbon. We have looked after the Brancaster affairs for many a long year, and before that too.'

'Mr Gibbon.'

Mercy did not shake his hand. She did not want to shake his hand. And more than that, she could not shake his hand because she was busy sticking her pin into her thumb to give her the necessary courage not to show the fear that she was feeling inside. She had pinched her cheeks hard, too, knowing that the pallor of her face too often betrayed how she was feeling.

Gibbon must have been somewhat put out by her silent refusal to clasp his own outstretched, stubby-fingered hand.

'As I say, we must reach an understanding before things go too far, and one or either of us makes a decision we might regret.'

Mercy nodded, but no more, for really there was very little she could say at this point to a man who thought fit to call in a family lawyer rather than speak directly to his own wife.

Gibbon here thought it was right for him to make plain his position.

'Mrs Brancaster, my family have been privileged to look after the Brancaster family for over eighty years now, and I have, today, been asked—'

'Mr Gibbon,' Mercy interrupted, after turning momentarily to look at her husband, 'you were very mistaken in coming here. Indeed, I am afraid you have very much wasted your morning.

Knowing what I do about my husband, and having been warned by my father, by letter, that he might well try to turn the events of the past months against me, I took the opportunity of visiting my own family lawyer in London.'

Gibbon glanced momentarily at his employer and then, because he too, like the lawyer, seemed momentarily stunned, finally said, 'And what might you know about your husband Mrs Brancaster?'

My father gave me a letter in which he has made quite plain his own knowledge of his second wife's adultery with Mr Brancaster. He knew of it for some years before our marriage, but had imagined that upon my marrying Mr Brancaster he would give up his mistress. Such was not the case, and because of this my father in fact sent a message to my husband. *The worm has turned.*'

There was a stunned silence.

'So you see, John,' Mercy said, at last removing the pin from her thumb, 'had you talked to me, instead of calling in this – man, things might have been made easier for you, or at the very least less embarrassing. This might have been a matter, as it should be, between husband and wife, not for a lawyer.'

'You should have spoken about this earlier, Mercy.'

'Had you not called in this man I might have done, or had you, John, not – what is it called? – *sent me to Coventry*. I tried to explain to you that I had changed, remember, at dinner?' She laughed suddenly. 'Really, when I think of it, the message should be *Two worms have turned*, should it not?'

Gibbon cleared his throat, and then, at a nod from John Brancaster, he picked up his papers and seemed to shuffle them endlessly until at last he left the room, and John turned to look at Mercy.

'You will regret this, Mercy. You will regret humiliating me in front of Gibbon.'

'Oh, I don't think so, John. I think it is *us*, not me, who will regret what has happened.'

She stared at him for a few seconds, realizing that the expression on his face was once again that of the man in the Park, and of the man who had stood at the graveside of the young mannequin in Mortlake what seemed like years ago.

'Do you know, John, when I first saw you, you looked just as you do now.'

'How very uninteresting.'

'Did you seduce that young mannequin who died? Is that why you were at her funeral? Is that *why* she died? Was she having your baby?' she suddenly added, thinking out loud.

'No, as a matter of fact I did not. I have never been interested in girls of no consequence. She was merely the daughter of a tenant here, always determined to go to the bad from the start, and of course she did go to the bad. She went to London and fell in with the wrong sort of women. I attended her funeral merely to represent her family who had no further interest in her. They were ashamed of her.'

Mercy nodded, believing him, and yet suddenly not interested.

'I wish you would not use that expression, *a girl of no consequence*. Surely everyone in this world, one way or another, has value?'

'She went to the bad at an early age, there was nothing to be done. She was a weak and silly girl, bound to go wrong.'

'Why do you say that? And how do you *know* that? Only because you have been brought up to view life as offering you only two sorts of women, the good or the bad. But there are more than two sorts, just as there are more than two sorts of men.'

'It's this kind of conversation which makes me long for the hunting field. Do you know that, Mercy?'

Mercy sighed. 'Yes, and I can perfectly understand it too, John. But what I would like you to *also* understand is that until we can both see each other as human beings – colourful, weak, strong, generous, kind, unkind, pompous, engaging, but above all as realities, in the same way that trees and flowers, all of nature, are realities – we will only be a disappointment to each other. It is the fact that we have to pretend to be what we are *not* when we are together, that makes our life so impossible. I can not return to being the helpless young girl you married, and you can not be the fascinating older man, but we could be ourselves, and find out that we still love each other. There is *that*. We could even find that we love those people, those two real people, more than those two others who did not really exist.'

John sighed impatiently, and after a second or

two of silence he said, 'Yes, I see what you are saying. You were too young. I should never have married you.'

'That is *not* what I am saying, John.'

'I should never have married you,' he insisted. 'You were far too young, and I hoped that you wouldn't be, which was foolish of me.'

This time it was Mercy who sighed, and said quietly, 'I was not too young. I just did not have a chance with you so long as you still felt that you loved – or were attracted to – someone else in your past.'

Her husband was silent, obviously not wanting to reply to this, but standing by the window, his back to her, so that Mercy half turned too, preparing to go, because addressing someone's back was really so dispiriting.

'I cannot feel sorry for you, the way I might feel sorry for myself. I mean – if we were not ourselves but friends of ours, I should feel sorry for the young woman, because I would know that for all her innocent foolishness she really loved you, John, whereas I would feel that the man did not love her as much in return. But now, well, I feel it would be weak and silly to go on as we were, not because of your going away, and – and making love with Lady Violet – although it still hurts me very much to think of it – but because I am so disappointed in you. I thought, when you came back, if I was strong with you, and truthful, that my so-great love for you would be enough, but it wasn't was it, John? You had to call in your lawyer. I saw you for what

466

you were, and myself for what I was, and both of us as we are now. But despite that, *I* found that I still loved you, whereas it seems that you only loved the idea of a young girl, all foolish compliance and love's young dream. And when I became real and pregnant, a real woman, you stayed away, willingly lapsing into your old ways with your hunting friends and your old mistress.'

'That's not true! You told me to stay away! And I believed Lady Violet when she said that you did not want me with you, that you were perhaps disgusted – as she said young girls could be – by the other side of marriage, that you were in love with that young man with whom you spent so much time – that antiquarian fellow.'

Mercy shook her head at this, determined to continue. She was halfway to the door now, and in some strange way she knew that the further she drew away from him the safer she felt to finish what she had to say.

'You know how much I always loved you to make love to me. It simply is not true that you were suspicious of poor Mr Chantry. You were inconstant because you wanted to be. That is the truth. Even should you have supposed that I had fallen for a younger man you would not have left me after Christmas as you did. You left me to give birth on my own because you chose to believe some tittle tattle from your mistress. You never really believed that your child was not yours, not really, John. It was just easier for you, at that moment, to convince yourself of it, that is all.' She stopped as she turned the handle of the library door, sighing suddenly with such sadness that it sounded even to her like the saddest sigh she had ever heard. 'We will never recover from this, I don't suppose. We are both now in mourning for those few lovely months that we spent together, months when we were really happy. Remember you said that our marriage was so happy that you feared we would cause a scandal? I will always remember that. And how we laughed together, how much we seemed to be one person. But all that is gone now, and so too will I be within the hour.'

John looked at the closed library door, stunned. And slowly and dreadfully the thought came to him, that until that moment it was true, he *had* never known love. He had known everything but love. He had known lust, and adventure, he had known the thrill of the chase, and its assuagement, but he had never known love, until it left him, and closed the door. For he realized at once – he was too intelligent not to – that everything that Mercy had said was true. His young wife had been a fantasy in his life, just an enchanting young girl, not a person at all, and now that she was real, and strong, she was actually a great deal more appealing to him than the innocent young sprite he had married. But looking into her eyes and seeing that terrible sadness as he just had, he knew that he must no longer hold any appeal for her. He should never have believed Violet's calumnies. She had some sort of obsession about their affair, as older women sometimes did. Nor should he have taken her advice and called in Gibbon. Mercy was right in realizing that he *had* meant to frighten her. But as it had transpired, she had merely succeeded in frightening him, for if Duffane was on the warpath, there would be a scandal, and such a scandal.

He sat down and put his head in his hands, understanding at last that one way and another he had in a matter of minutes lost everything that he truly cared for. So long did he sit, and so immersed was he in his own thoughts, that he did not even hear the carriage drawing up in the drive, nor see his son and his nurse, and his young wife, leaving him.

Fifteen

There is nothing like rumour of an impending Society ball to bring about an escalating sense of drama in a tight circle of friends. Certainly, the mere mention of a ball to be given by Mrs Lawrence Leveen brought out a sense of excitement in all her friends, and none more than Leonie Lynch. She had never been to a grand ball before. She had never worn a ball dress, or been loaned jewellery, or had proper dancing lessons, and now all three excitements were to be hers, thanks entirely to Dorinda Leveen.

Naturally Mrs Dodd was in seventh heaven. She had come to regard Leonie as being as close to her as a daughter might have been. Nowadays the day-to-day interests of her own life were as nothing compared to the comings and goings of Leonie. Above all she knew that Lady Angela was still as close as ever to the King, and since Leonie was now second in command to Lady Angela that was as close as you could get to your monarch, surely?

'He is a good king, our king, because he always seems to be enjoying being a king, and a king who enjoys himself is good for the country. That is why he is so very popular, that is why people shout

"Good old Teddy" when he drives by. People don't want to be sad when they look at their king, they want to think that he's going about being happy.'

Leonie seemed to listen to one or other version of this short speech of her godmother's every other morning, and usually just before she herself left for the nursing home and her patients, looking forward as she always did to seeing to their many and varied needs, to everything and anything that a nursing home might bring. But lately she could not deny that there had been a rival claim on her thoughts, a frivolous claim, but a claim none the less – the ball to be given by the Leveens, to which all of London Society, including the King, was now destined to be coming.

'My goddaughter, Miss Lynch, was one of the first to be invited, do you see? Mrs Leveen quite depends on her!' Mrs Dodd boasted, quite frequently, for now that she had sold her 'little business' and retired from medicine she had fully enough time on her hands to be able to impress her friends.

With great patience, and some fascination, Leonie had been among many to share the day-to-day agonies of who had called on Dorinda and who had not called on Dorinda.

She had also lived through the crisis over her foster parents' being about to change their mind about leaving Eastgate Street and taking up their position as lodge keepers on the Leveen estate in Sussex, and many more excitements. But now it seemed that everything had suddenly become oddly quiet, and all there was left for Leonie to occupy herself with was to be dressed for the great evening, with the help of a new French maid, and the knowledge that Gervaise Lowther's large debt to Coutts the bankers had finally induced – as is the undoubted way of things – Lady Londonderry to call on Mrs Leveen. At least, she did not call exactly, but her coachman did graciously leave her card on the vast marble table of the hall of Lawrence House.

Not to be outdone, of course, once Lady Londonderry had called so too did all the other hostesses of the day, not to mention other lesser luminaries who were really of little interest to Dorinda, but to whom she felt vaguely indebted as she found she always did to people who bored her. It was a rather dreadful form of social pity. As if the lesser folk who hung around the fringes of Society, needing, as they did, rather more of a push than the top of it, obliged Dorinda to consider them.

'I am at pains to be kind to a great many people who would not otherwise be asked to this event,' she had told Mrs Goodman more than once, 'for our ball is going to be the most talked about since the Coronation. It will be talked about for months if not years afterwards. It will be our way of making a quite brilliant mark on these first years of the twentieth century.'

The 'ess' shape was still in fashion despite the press of the newer couturiers to change the shape of women, to bring in the newer softer look, to allow women to abandon their tight corseting and move into a softer more fluid line, with higher busts and softer draping, with flowers pinned at the corsage and hair that curled about their heads at the front rather than being piled on the top. Fashion at that time was for the mature woman, not for young girls, perhaps because young girls could only wait for life to come to them in the shape of marriage, whereas marriage brought freedom and with it, very often, a love life that was quite definitely worth waiting for, once they had survived childbirth.

Daringly therefore Dorinda had chosen for Leonie, who was still an unmarried woman, the newer, softer, more Empire or Grecian look. For herself she had pursued the line that would, she knew, give her darling Mr L the greatest pleasure, namely the figure tightly corseted, the sway of the back of her dress and train lending emphasis to this part of her body, the front being pushed to the fore, the cut of the bodice low, and the shoulders shown to be soft and rounded.

When they were trying on their dresses in front of the endless mirrors at the couture house, Dorinda had laughed and said to Leonie, 'See how we look, Leonie, my dear. I am dressed as "England Past" whereas you are "England Future", wouldn't you say?'

Which was in a sense true, but also in another sense not true, for young unmarried girls had never been of much consequence in English Society unless they were crazed like Lady Caroline

473

Lamb or made scandals like Emma, Lady Hamilton. Society had always been run and ruled by the older women, and doubtless would always be, since they were meant to have more sense than either young girls or men.

As Leonie lay resting on her bed in her vast bedroom some few rooms away from Dorinda's palatial suite, she thought of all the other women who were lying resting on their beds, and tried to imagine their thoughts, or their plans, for the evening ahead.

Her own sex had never ceased to fascinate Leonie, knowing as she did, from the gossip of Eastgate Street as a child, and now from listening to Dorinda and Mrs Goodman, that women had to leave party politics to men simply and solely because they had their hands full with their own personal politics.

Leonie knew now, but only from her recent observations, that there were not enough hours in the day to embrace the personal politics of women. There were no summer recesses for her sex as there were for the politicians, and no holidays. Being a woman, and most especially a successful hostess, was a year-round occupation.

'Once they are married, women are not just the power behind the throne, they are the builders of it, they adorn it with gilt, or strip it to the wood, they place flowers on it or peacock feathers, they choose the attendants to it, and the families that will stand nearest to it. They are, and always will be, those who matter most. But that, of course, must remain their secret!'

Lawrence Leveen had made this little speech to Leonie one evening the previous week when they had been dining quite quietly together, just the three of them, all of them purposely conserving their energy for the following week.

And now the day was upon them, and everyone was experiencing the kind of butterflies that will always be associated with an event that will, within the opening few minutes, prove to be such a great success, or such a hopeless failure, that before long all of the fashionable world will know of it, and either praise or make fun of its hosts.

Everyone would be wondering, as Leonie was wondering as she stared up at the intricately plastered ceiling above her bed, who was going to be singled out to be presented to the King? Who chosen to take to the floor first? Surely at this ball, more than any other, no-one would be reprimanded by the King for wearing a dress he had seen before? Lady Angela had told her that the King had been known to reprimand many people, sometimes for a medal wrongly placed, sometimes for an unsolicited comment, or worse. *He* must always be put at his ease, and kept amused. Suddenly, the possibility of a royal reprimand seemed all too real, and a great part of Leonie now wished, most heartily, that she was not going to the ball, and that she had never met Dorinda Montgomery, that she was back at dear old Eastgate Street pouring the tea for her foster mother of a Sunday.

And yet if she had not met Dorinda at Sister Angela's Nursing Home, her beloved foster parents would not now be happily ensconced at the lodge in Sussex, and Leonie would not be staring at the beautiful ball dress hanging opposite her bed. And the little French maid whom Dorinda had hired for Leonie only the week before would not be about to help Monsieur Claude weave flowers into her hair, or pull up silk stockings of the sheerest kind over Leonie's legs as she lay on a great, gilded bed listening to the orchestra two floors below them briskly rehearsing the first of that evening's music.

'It is time to dress, mademoiselle.'

The little French maid peeped through the curtains of the bed and stared almost benignly down at Leonie, as doubtless she would into a crib with a baby in it.

'Mademoiselle will be visited any minute by Monsieur Claude, the coiffeur of madame. For this – mademoiselle must be *en chemise et baignée, n'est ce pas?*'

As she arose from the beautifully draped bed Leonie's thoughts once more turned to the rest of Society. It was not just the other women waiting to be bathed and dressed, as she was, nor the other maids waiting to do the bathing and dressing, it was everyone waiting, down below, and in all the other houses where dinners would be given before the start of the ball.

The florists, the cooks, the flunkeys, the hall boys, the assistant chefs, the pastry chefs, the husbands, the valets, the housekeepers, the butlers, the coachmen, the grooms, the carriage men, even the street cleaners, hired especially for the occasion and standing by outside. The flares would soon be lit in the garden, the fantastic spun sugar desserts given their final flourish, the sculptures in the hall draped suitably, the paintings placed appropriately, the great fireplaces, in all the houses, lit. The uniforms of the long-legged footmen would have been polished; the gentlemen's frogging and the medals buffed until they would catch the light as surely as the diamonds on the ladies' heads, or at their throats, or dangling from their ears. The long evening gloves would have been cleaned or, in the case of this great ball, freshly purchased (lest the smell of the cleaning fluid be detectable in the ballroom). And everywhere, all the ladies would have practised walking in their new gowns, for to hold your train, just so, your fan just so, and dance, just so, was an art of the most intricate and the most delicate, and that was even before it came to the all-important grand curtsy.

Dorinda had taught Leonie most assiduously both to dance and to curtsy whenever she could find them both a spare hour, but what she could not teach her was elegance. As they both new, elegance came from the heart.

'*You* have such elegance, Leonie, my dearest,' Dorinda told her once or twice, her eyes full of admiration, 'it makes me think that you surely must have the blood of kings running through your veins!'

Of course this made them both laugh, for such a thing was not at all possible for Leonie Lynch of Eastgate Street, any more than it was for Dorinda Lawrence. They both knew themselves to be outsiders, invited into Society for one reason or another, and what was more they enjoyed the notion.

Dorinda knew that Leonie, by reason of her illegitimacy, could never find a noble or even a wellborn husband, but what she hoped very much for her friend was that she just might find someone who was outside the aristocracy while being inside Society. Dorinda had her eye on just the person, someone of great warmth and kindness, someone who was affluent but not rich – someone whom she had, nevertheless, invited to her ball.

Speaking of these matters and others the day before with Dorinda, Leonie had laughingly admitted that had she had blue blood she might well have fallen passionately in love with the first duke who proposed to her, but since she had not, she confided to Dorinda, she would be quite happy to stay as she was, nursing at Sister Angela's while living with the devoted Mrs Dodd.

'You can't stay a spinster!' Dorinda, who had stayed a spinster about long enough for her hair to be put up into a chignon, had been genuinely shocked.

'Why not? Lady Angela is a spinster, and she is the happiest person I know.'

'She is not happier than myself,' Dorinda had

gently reminded Leonie. '*I* am the happiest woman I know.'

Leonie recognized the truth in this. Dorinda *was* the happiest woman that either of them knew.

'And,' Dorinda had continued, just a little severely, 'I have been married not once but twice. That is how it is with the opposite sex, you will find. It is always necessary to be married, in order to be married again. Very few men can trust their own judgement when it comes to marriage, whereas if a woman has *already* been married they find themselves quite able to trust some other member of their sex to have had good taste! If you remain unmarried the male of the species will always assume that you must be flawed in some way.'

'But Lady Angela is unmarried and has never, as I understand it, wanted to be anything else.'

'Lady Angela is wedded to the King, and you can not have a greater wedding than that, my dear.'

'No, no, of course, I understand that. So. Now we can see things as they really are.'

Dorinda had looked round from her dressing mirror at Leonie's suddenly impatient tone, her attention drawn away from her beautiful face to Leonie's own stunning looks, her eyes so turquoise that Dorinda could never look into them without thinking of the sea.

'The rules of Society are such that you must be married in order to be a man's mistress, and you must be married in order to be married *again*. But what if you are like poor Mrs Brancaster? What if you have loved and been faithful to your husband but been humiliated by him? Must you stay, as she was meant to do, and remain miserable under his roof, or do you invite scandal and bring unhappiness on your family by running away?'

'Mrs Brancaster has not behaved wisely. You do not leave your house because your husband behaves badly.'

'What would you advise? I saw her only yesterday and she is like a dying person, a wraith, and Mr Chantry, who has always been so devoted, is in despair.'

'You cannot advise a woman who is determined on loving her husband, except to try to stop loving him, anyway for a little while. And if she is too weak to do that, well, then there is only one course open to her, and that is to take a house in St John's Wood and find herself a different way of going on. That is how Society is, Leonie, my dear, and always will be, I would think.'

'In other words, what we are really saying is that Society rewards women only if they are unloving, and shrewd. It does not reward the loving woman who cares for her babies and is innocent and kind?'

Dorinda, who had known only unkindness when she was small but had managed to bravely accept her lot, had nodded, but the look in her eyes was of such surprise that Leonie had to laugh.

'Why are you laughing?'

'Because – because all this is not at all new to you while being very novel to me, I am afraid!'

'My dear, if we expect life to be truly wonderful

480

for women we are wishing for the moon. What we must accept is that we have to be stronger than men. If women are to survive they have to have hearts of oak.'

But all that was yesterday, and of a sudden there was a pounding, and it was not just Leonie's heart as she stared at herself and Monsieur Claude in the dressing mirror in front of them both. Pitou, the little french maid, went finally, if reluctantly, to the door, for she was much more interested in placing the flowers in Mademoiselle Lynch's hair than in finding out who might be the perpetrator of the sudden, hard knocking on the outer door.

Opening it cautiously, she was immediately swept aside by Mrs Dodd, who did not push but *flung* herself into the large, beautifully dressed and chintzed room, her outdoor clothes looking drab and odd beside her goddaughter's Japanese *kimono* – a gift from Dorinda to Leonie, and the latest thing to wear while being dressed and coiffed.

'Leonie, my dear, disaster is about to strike! There is about to be a terrible, terrible scandal, just like that of last season, only far worse.'

Leonie indicated for the hairdresser to stand back as she stood up.

'I was not living with you last Season, God-mother dearest,' she told her, taking her hands, and drawing her further down the room, in an effort to try to hold the subsequent conversation in private.

'You must go at once to Mrs Leveen and tell her. The most terrible, the most ghastly, the worst news! That wretched Monsieur P! He is so enraged with Monsieur Worth for not adopting his Grecian ideas of dress – I am sure it is he whom we must all blame! I am sure of it! At any rate I had the news just now from Madame Chloe who sent her maid round to my house with a letter to tell me, and she did, she told me in her own writing, that she was sure that it was Monsieur P who is at the bottom of all this . . .'

'At the bottom of what, Godmother dear? What is Monsieur P meant to be responsible *for*?'

'Why, for telling Lady C's maid which dress Mrs Leveen had chosen to wear for her ball. The ivy leaf motif on the train, everything, she has copied everything with the single exception of the colour. She is to be in a ghastly pink.'

'Is that so terrible?'

'Is that so – is that so *terrible*? It is a *disaster*. My dear Leonie, your friend Mrs Leveen is about to stand at the top of the ballroom steps receiving her guests in the same ball gown as that madwoman Lady Castlemount! Everyone knows that the wretched woman has some sort of nervous hysteria which means that she needs must draw attention to herself on any and every occasion. She will stop at nothing to bring down Mrs Leveen, who has been so kind to her, but of whom, I am now sure, she is violently, but violently, jealous, having herself married a penniless person.'

Leonie began to understand the whole awful drama that was about to come about. Dorinda in her own house being humiliated by the triumphant

Lady Castlemount whom, Leonie knew, Dorinda had only asked to the ball because she was on the fringes of Society and needed some kind of a leg up if she was to be asked to anything at all by the all-important three hostesses.

'Oh, madame, madame, Mrs Leveen to be in the same gown! What will she do? The King will leave!' Monsieur Claude, having made no pretence at not straining to overhear the whole conversation, now started to wring his hands. 'I will be disgraced! People will think it is I! Going as I do from 'ouse to 'ouse. I am sure they will think it is I! I am dead!'

'Monsieur Claude,' Leonie turned to the hairdresser, briefly, 'now is not the time to wring our hands, now is the time to gird our loins.'

'But I am not a girder, mademoiselle, I am an 'airdresser, and we are always to blame for everything. It is a fact. I shall kill myself, it is the only way!'

'*Mais non, Monsieur Claude, non!*' Pitou begged him.

'You will not kill yourself, Monsieur Claude, you will follow me, and we will go to Madame Leveen and tell her everything. The situation is not too late to be remedied, I am sure.'

None of them pretended to be trying not to run as, scrambling any old how out of Leonie's room, they fled down the corridor to Dorinda's suite.

'Come in, come in,' Dorinda called, all prettiness and relaxation as she surveyed herself in the dressing mirrors that surrounded her, ready at last to descend downstairs for her great evening.

She turned as they trooped in, but on seeing the white faces before her she knew at once that something quite terrible must have happened.

'Mrs Dodd, you here? And Monsieur Claude? What is the matter? Has there been an accident?'

'Not yet, Dorinda, not yet.'

Leonie's heart sank to the bottom of her slippers as she clutched the Japanese gown around her and told Dorinda of the terrible news.

And really it could not have been more terrible, for Dorinda had never looked more beautiful, in her tiara and her new ball gown with its wondrously decorated train, but of course she saw at once, as soon as Leonie had finished speaking, just what a social disgrace awaited her.

'I am afraid there is nothing to be done.' She glanced briefly at the clock on the chimneypiece. 'I mean I can not, I regret, send someone to kill my lady Castlemount because she will be on her way to dine by now.' She thought for a moment. 'I will have to change, of course. But . . .' and here she paused and closed her eyes for a few seconds. 'Due to my busy life I have not one ball gown left that I can be quite, quite sure that the King, or indeed anyone else, has not seen somewhere, some time. Oh, why did I not listen to Mr L when he advised me to order at least two for tonight in case of an accident of some kind? He is always right about everything, but I thought it was just too extravagant, seeing the cost of Monsieur Worth's gowns, and having ordered so many at the start of the year.'

Leonie thought for a second. It was true that Dorinda had what seemed like a hundred ball gowns, but it was also true that there was not one suitably grand gown that she could be quite sure had not been seen by the King, whose memory for such details was prodigious.

'There is one gown,' Leonie said suddenly, breaking the ghastly silence that had fallen. 'One gown that you can be sure has not been seen by anyone at all, anywhere, at any time.'

They all turned from staring up into the wardrobes that contained Dorinda's gowns and stared instead at Leonie.

'And that is, my dear?'

Dorinda was outwardly calm, but so white that everyone present knew that her insides must have turned to water.

'Mine. You can be quite, quite sure that my gown has not been seen by anyone.'

Of a sudden the whole possibility swam towards both young women. The gown that Leonie had been about to wear was not the 'ess' shape and it was not to be worn with a tiara, but with her hair dressed loose, and flowers – flowers which Leonie had already begun to take out of her own hair while the hairdresser, unable to bear the destruction of his so-recently executed art, sobbed hopelessly on Pitou's shoulder.

'No, my dear, I must wear my tiara for the King. He loves tiaras, and the more intricate the better.'

'Well then, wear your tiara, to the back, in the Roman way, and decorate it with flowers. But don't you see, with your chestnut coloured hair, and your wonderful beauty, the King will not mind. Besides, it is your house, and you may do as you wish in your house. Even the King understands that. He is coming to you, you are not coming to him.'

Dorinda suddenly looked decisive.

'You're right, Leonie. It is my house, and besides, I know that the King is always so bored, he may well be amused by my looking different from everyone else, may he not? I know for a fact that he has a kind heart. And more than that, it will give them all something to talk about! But what about you?'

'Me? Why, I will wear your dress, and so where will be the victory for Lady Castlemount? She will have been hoping to destroy your glorious night, planning to walk towards you, in front of the King, of the whole Court, wearing the same dress – she must have spent weeks planning it – but now all that will happen is that she will pass by the receiving party into the ballroom only to find that she has merely worn the same dress as myself, a nobody. It will be her disaster, not yours. As to me, it could not matter less, for in the event I am only one of hundreds invited, and no-one will remember me. What does it matter what Miss Leonie Lynch wears, when all is said and done? My patients will not get to hear of it, and if they did they would only laugh.'

Dorinda drew Leonie to her, and kissed her heartily on both cheeks.

'You are a wonderful young woman, and I will never forget your generosity and ingenuity. The dress on me will be the talk of the town!'

Lawrence Leveen turned as he heard the servants gasp at the sight of their mistress, with no heavy jewellery and only flowers decorating her tiara, set now in a classical way at the back of her rich chestnut hair. She looked more beautiful than they had ever seen her as she descended the great staircase dressed only in the simplest of silk dresses, decorated only by all that was natural, and wearing only the simplest of slippers on her feet.

After the barest of pauses as he took in her new look, Mr L said, 'My darling, I had no idea that you would decide to become a goddess for me tonight. You look younger and more beautiful than the flowers you are wearing. How brilliant you are to decide to look unlike anyone else! You remind me of a portrait of the Empress Josephine. I can not commend you more.'

'I am so glad you approve, darling Mr L,' Dorinda told him, at the same time smiling and inclining her head to the amazed servants. 'You see, this is to be the newest fashion, quite soon – and I do think we should always make sure to be in advance, don't you?'

'Such a graceful line – turn for me – and the tiara worn to the back in a classical mode, and the flowers – all so refreshing. You will make everyone else look like dowagers. I am in awe of your taste,

Dorinda, do you know that, in awe, as always?'

Dorinda smiled gratefully. She had always known that Mr L was head and shoulders above every man she had ever met, but never more than at that moment when he must have surely guessed from her late arrival and her changed look that there had actually been a near disaster, but he was much too much the gentleman to remark on it.

'I love you, Lawrence, and I always will.'

For a second, because she had never before called him by his Christian name, it looked to Dorinda as if her husband's eyes were filled with something more than admiration as he took her hand and kissed it.

London would always remember the Leveen Ball at Lawrence House. Not just because Mrs Leveen was the first hostess of the new century to adopt the Grecian or Empire style of dress, and to abandon the 'ess' shape – however temporarily – but because the King chose the unknown Miss Lynch to lead off the ball.

Her dress being a little too big for her, His Majesty was able to view a little more of Miss Lynch than would normally be altogether conventional, but, as with so many middle-aged monarchs, he did not mind in the least, for appreciating beautiful young women was one of his many interests, most particularly young women who danced as beautifully as Miss Lynch.

Lady Castlemount on the other hand was seen to leave the ball a great deal earlier than most, and without so much as a single name to her dance card, the all-powerful Lady Londonderry having remarked loudly and sarcastically on the similarity of her dress to that of Miss Lynch, and having within everyone's hearing condemned her for her conceit in choosing the same style of dress as such a young gel as Miss Lynch. As it turned out Lady Castlemount was quizzed and laughed at so many times that even her husband, who was very old, noticed.

The next day several of the less kind Society columns writing up the Ball at Lawrence House remarked on a certain Lady C——'s having had the misfortune to wear the exact same style of dress as a certain beautiful Miss L—— who, in the event, had been chosen by His Majesty the King to lead off the ball.

A rose and a cabbage can bear the same leaf but we will always look at the rose, and so it proved at the great I—— ball where a certain Lady C tried to emulate the beautiful Miss L and came off worse. How much better to be Mrs L, the hostess, whose incomparable beauty was set off by the newer simpler style, wrote one scribe.

And so the wretched Lady C was forced to go to Baden Baden to take the waters for a little while, and on her return to find herself exactly back where she had first begun, on the outskirts of Society.

In her prolonged absence it was left to Dorinda to sum it all up.

Lying on her chaise longue of a late afternoon

with her eternally adoring husband leafing through the many letters of admiration sent to them after the ball, she remarked, 'You know, they always do say, Lawrence, if you want to make an enemy, help someone.'

Sixteen

Mercy had only been able to read of the ball. Of course Dorinda had invited her, but both knew that it would be impossible for Mercy to accept, her position in Society being, to say the least, uncertain. She had contented herself with moving into a small house overlooking the Thames at Chelsea, a house so far removed from the fashionable stamping grounds of Mayfair that there was no risk whatsoever of her encountering either her husband, Lady Violet, or any other family acquaintance who might be disposed to cut her.

Naturally Mercy's little boy had become his mother's whole life, his growth and weight a matter of her daily concern and her whole day centred around him and his loving ways. And once the small house and garden with its river view and its ancient wistaria had been adapted to the needs of the little household, and some furniture purchased, not to mention curtains and lights, and a maid hired to help Josephine, Mercy found, to her amazement, that she felt more at ease with herself and the world than she had ever felt before. It was as if in the role of mother she had at last been able to find confidence. A mother could not be rejected as a wife could be. Motherhood was a simple, natural role and no-one, not even Lady Violet, could usurp her, or take her position from her.

Sometimes she thought of her father with surprise. He had always seemed so indifferent to her as she was growing up that his actions over her husband's infidelity had been astonishing to his daughter. Perhaps it had been the shock of his discovering his wife's continuing infidelity with his son-in-law that had prompted him to come to Mercy's defence so rapidly, and with such ruthlessness, that it was almost breathtaking. He had protected her from his adored Lady Violet, and remembering how much he had once loved his wife it seemed to Mercy that Lord Duffane had been more than kind.

But of course she could only guess at so much. What she could not witness was the scene in the library at Cordel Court when the sound of Lord Duffane's icy, dismissive tones fell about his astounded second wife's ears.

If only he would be angry, if only he would shout, Lady Violet thought half-heartedly, herself white with the shock and anger of her return from London and the discovery, only minutes before, that the stables at Cordel Court were quite empty of her beloved hunters.

'You ask where are your hunters – your hunters are sold.'

Lady Violet clutched at the back of the library

chair behind which she was standing.

'Pease Blossom, and Misty, and – not my Joey?'

'You are to hunt no more, Violet.'

'Please, tell me this is not true.'

'I can only tell you the truth. Your hunters are sold, on my orders. You are not to hunt again. If you wish to stay here as my wife you are to occupy yourself with the Church, with the Women's Guilds, with the Society for the Preservation of Ancient Buildings, with anything or anyone, but there is to be no more hunting. The horses will not miss you, they are too sensible, and besides, they have all been sold to your friends, who doubtless will greatly appreciate them – not to mention the reason why you are forbidden to hunt any more.'

'Please, please tell me this is not true. If I don't hunt, I shall die. I live for my hunting – you know that.'

Her husband looked at her but where once he would have listened to her now his eyes were hard with the humiliation that the discovery of her behaviour with his son-in-law had caused him. Her self-indulgence could have caused a scandal that would have made the world laugh at him. Infidelity was one thing, a scandal quite another.

'I have always known that I was not enough for you, Violet, but I did not know, until now, that you were prepared to cross those lines which no-one should cross just for the sake of your own self-gratification and conceit. I am afraid there is no more to be said on the matter. Good morning.'

Lady Violet began to go, dismissed like a

servant, but then rallied, for she would have one last word, whatever her husband said.

'What you don't understand – and why should you – is that I loved him. I really loved John Brancaster. We were twin souls.'

'When a person marries, Lady Violet, his mistress surrenders all claims and finds another lover, or in your case returns to her husband and changes her life, or leaves.'

For a few seconds Lady Violet contemplated leaving Cordel Court, the house in London, the carriages, the new motor car, her clothes from Monsieur Worth, the balls and the trips to Baden Baden for health cures. She contemplated love in a cottage with no servants, love with a bored John Brancaster, herself ageing daily. Finally and without much of a struggle she realized that not even her love for hunting or her obsession with Brancaster was worth such a sacrifice, and she turned, tears in her eyes, and left the library.

Her husband watched her go with a cold smile. He had always known that she would come to heel, and this time it was his heel, not someone else's, which, when all was said and done, was after all, satisfying, at least to him.

Meanwhile John Brancaster had determined to try to find Mercy, and demand that she return to Brindells. Knowing as he did, from the servants, that she had made friends with Mrs Lawrence Leveen, he took it upon himself to go to London and call on Mercy's new friend himself, realizing that by doing so he risked further humiliation, but judging that there was little other choice open to him.

Of course Dorinda was expecting him. She had actually been expecting him for some weeks now, but perhaps Brancaster's visit had been delayed by his knowledge of the Leveen ball, which, since it had been such a resounding success, she could now put out of her mind; at least until such time as Mrs Goodman brought her velvet-bound Commonplace Book in to her, in a few weeks' time, when they would both pore over the menus carefully stuck in, the photographs taken by Bassano of Dorinda in her original dress. It was an excitement to which to look forward, just as Brancaster calling on her was another, quite different excitement to which she was looking forward.

Although Dorinda fully sympathized with his wife for loving Brancaster, she herself could not like him. She did not mind a weak man, she did not mind a man who was on the outside of Society, nor did she mind a man who found it difficult to manage – as say Gervaise Lowther and Harry Montgomery had done – but she could not stand a hard man, and Brancaster, in Dorinda's eyes, was a hard, seemingly heartless man.

Whatever her judgement, the man himself was shown into her upstairs drawing room that afternoon looking every inch the gentleman, which of course he was not. He was impeccably dressed, and having placed his walking cane and hat on the floor he bowed over Dorinda's hand in a way that hinted at having been to Court enough to know not to hold a hand too long or too hard.

'Well, now, Mr Brancaster, how may I help you?'

'You may help me, Mrs Leveen, by being kind enough to tell me where you think' – he glanced round at the footmen, and lowered his voice – 'where you think I might find my wife, and my son.'

Dorinda paused for a moment.

'Where you might find your wife and son? But Mr Brancaster, if you do not know where your wife and son might be I certainly can not be expected to help you! I have to tell you that people of my acquaintance are not in the habit of losing their wives and sons.'

She was playing with him and he knew it, but it was ever Dorinda's weakness to tease a man of whom she could not approve. And she could not approve of a husband who carried on an affair with his wife's stepmother – whatever the temptation – nor of a father who had taken about as much interest in the birth of his son as a farmer might of a lamb born in one of his fields. She knew for a fact that Gabriel Chantry had taken more interest in the birth of John Edward than had John Brancaster, and more interest in his wife too, his feelings of chivalry dreadfully aroused by her bravery in the face of insensitivity. But all that was about to change, if Dorinda had her way.

'Mrs Leveen . . .'

Dorinda looked awe-inspiring that afternoon, as she had indeed meant to do, for she knew, from having been poor, that even the most sophisticated persons could have their arrogance tempered by a beautiful woman fantastically dressed, so that the sunlight caught at the jewels in her ears, and at the scintillating silk of her dress, and showed up the rows and rows of tiny stitching on her bodice, not to mention the insets of handmade Florentine lace. Not even the Queen of England could have looked more beautiful than Dorinda that afternoon, and she could see from the way Brancaster was hesitating that the diamond ring on her finger, and the marvellous arrangement of her chestnut hair, were distractions even to such a man of the world as he must pride himself on being.

'Mrs Leveen – I must find my wife, and my son, for without them, frankly, I am lost.'

Dorinda would have liked to have looked at him with pity, but she could not. She looked at him instead with cool appraisal, and just a little wonderingly, for he must have taken her, as so many men took beautiful women, to be an awful fool, to think that she would blurt out where her friend was now living. That she would betray Mercy in such a way – that she might, with all that she knew of him, be so stupid as to let him inveigle his way back into his poor, heartbroken wife's life.

'I wish I could help you, Mr Brancaster, but I can not. I have no idea where your wife is living, no idea at all.'

Dorinda looked at John Brancaster so sadly, and with such real regret in her voice, that, being an impatient person, he was at once prompted, as he was meant to be, to take his leave.

As he did so he passed the large marble table in the great hall downstairs, and while waiting for the hall boy to bring him his coat he glanced momentarily down at a letter that was obviously waiting to be taken to the post. By a strange coincidence it was addressed to his wife, and by yet another coincidence it was written in Mrs Leveen's hand. He could not believe the luck of it, and quickly memorizing the address on the envelope finally left Lawrence House triumphant.

Upstairs, standing at her first floor drawing room window, and looking down at the street with great interest, Dorinda watched John Brancaster climb into a hackney before letting out a peal of laughter as Mrs Goodman came in to join her.

'Oh, I do hope it has worked,' she told her secretary. 'I hope it so much. So naughty of me, really, but goodness, you must admit – so funny!'

Gervaise Lowther was woken from his afternoon sleep by a considerable knocking at the door. It was such a knocking that for one horrible second he had the feeling that it must be someone dunning him, but then, remembering that Lawrence Leveen's kindly financial advice had removed any fear of debtors, he relapsed back into his normal state of post-prandial drowsiness, hoping that Blanquette or one of her minions would take care of whatever it was in the hall, and leave him to carry on sleeping, as was his wont of an afternoon.

But, it seemed, afternoon peace was not to be, for minutes later the maid announced John Brancaster, and Gervaise found himself scrambling to his feet and frowningly allowing him to be admitted.

'Did we – do we – have some sort of an arrangement, my dear fellow?' he asked Brancaster.

Brancaster looked momentarily taken aback.

'Well, yes, Lowther, as a matter of fact, I think we do. I understand that my wife and my son are residing here?'

Gervaise's expression could not have been more astonished.

'Your wife and son, Brancaster? Have you taken leave of your senses, or are you as footled as me? Your wife and son in St John's Wood with me. You go too far!'

He knew John Brancaster from Leicestershire, but had never really liked him. A hard hunting man, he had been too much the huntsman and too little the courtier for Gervaise.

'I was – given this address by Mrs Lawrence Leveen.'

'Mrs Lawrence Leveen? Dorinda?' Gervaise started to laugh. 'She was just having you on – teasing you, Brancaster. She does that you know. Dorinda has always been a tease. I know, she teased me enough.'

'Are you sure she would do such a thing?'

Gervaise sighed. 'I am as sure as can be. Good heavens, man, do I look like a man who would take in another man's babies and wives, and whatnot?'

He went to the drawing room door and called down the stairs. 'Blanquette?'

Blanquette, newly attired in a brilliant orange afternoon dress of such a hue that even Gervaise was forced to blink, appeared at the drawing room door.

'Blanquette, Mr Brancaster here thinks we're hiding his wife and children. Are we?'

Blanquette shook her head. 'We 'ave no wife or *bébés* 'ere, Mr Blanchester.'

With another nod Gervaise dismissed his newest mistress, for apart from anything else he really could not stand to look at that orange dress for too long. On the other hand, he realized, Brancaster was left staring after her, his mouth wide open.

'I know – dreadful colour, isn't it? But the dear woman loves orange and yellow, and what can you do, my dear fellow? No-one else to take care of me now all my children are married. The servants at my town house laugh at me. Served me a chicken with all the feathers on the other day. So I am here now. Blanquette makes an omelette which would send you to heaven.'

As Gervaise was confiding his reasons for keeping Blanquette, Dorinda, having been careful to take a hackney cab, and not her magnificent coach, to see her friend Mercy Brancaster in Chelsea, alighted outside her friend's house followed only by her new French maid.

Mercy watched her arrival from her pretty, flowered first floor drawing room with its few pieces of eighteenth-century furniture sent to her by her father from Cordel Court. It amused Mercy to watch Dorinda trying to arrive at her house incognito, for albeit that she had arrived in a hackney cab, she had not bothered to change her afternoon clothes to a costume more appropriate to the dinginess of the cab. If anyone had been about at that teatime hour they would have gasped, for Dorinda presented such a beautiful picture of fashion, she suited her hackney cab as much as a brilliant butterfly suits the dry interior of a museum case.

The two young women kissed either side of each other's heads, more in sympathetic greeting than in cheerful acknowledgement. They both knew that Dorinda had sustained a visit from Brancaster. Dorinda did not of course tell Mercy of her little ruse, of her effective redirection of Mercy's husband to St John's Wood, a place so thankfully far away from bohemic Chelsea that it might be in another country.

She did not tell her for many reasons, but most of all because she knew her own sex, and she shrewdly recognized that Mercy would not find such a humiliation of Brancaster as amusing as Dorinda herself. And, too, she feared that thinking of her husband chasing all over London after her on wild goose errands might make Mercy start to pity the scoundrel, and that would never do.

'Mrs Blessington is also here,' Mercy told Dorinda. 'She is upstairs with Josephine in the nursery playing with the baby, but will be down shortly. She is staying with me for a number of weeks. It is somehow such a comfort to have her here, making it seem home from home in a way I can't explain.'

Dorinda liked Mrs Blessington the moment she appeared. She liked her affable round face, her still sparkling eyes, the rich laugh that shook her body when she found something amusing, which she seemed to do all the time. Dorinda also saw that, as with so many older and more ample people, she was independent-minded, and not to be fooled. It was as if in their whole-hearted enjoyment of life the rounder the person the more positive the personality that emerged.

They none of them touched on the reasons why they were visiting Mercy in a small Chelsea house, in a bohemian neighbourhood more suited to the artistic personalities of the day than to a nicely brought up daughter of a peer of the realm.

'Fortuitously,' Mrs Blessington told Dorinda, as one ringed hand stroked the top of Twissy's head, while the other was busy accepting a cup of tea in an aquamarine, flower painted cup, 'I have been able to buy a small business. It has been run, as a tight ship, by the godmother of Miss Lynch, your friend.'

'Ah, the worthy Mrs Dodd. Yes, I remember Miss Lynch did say that Mrs Dodd had retired, and was even thinking of leaving London.'

'It is something in which I have always been interested, helping poor distressed young women, and since farming and the land have fallen into such disrepair, and it seems to me that I am farming for no-one but my children, I have handed over my properties to my eldest son and settled myself in a rented property near to London, in Richmond Park, not more than an hour or so from here. Meanwhile I am looking for someone to run the business for me, for of course, at my age, such a thing is not possible.'

Mrs Blessington was all innocence and all satisfaction as she nibbled on a piece of cake and sipped at her tea, before setting the remains of both into the saucer and putting it on the floor for Twissy to enjoy, finally finishing by licking the old saucer, now bare of its tea, half way around the old wooden floor, until Mercy picked it up, and absentmindedly put it back on the tea tray.

If Mrs Blessington was all innocence Dorinda was all admiration for the blessed woman – rightly named, she suddenly thought – seeing at once from her seemingly artless conversation, just how she was thinking, and perhaps hoped to plan. For Dorinda was well aware that Mrs Dodd's 'business' had everything to do with the taking in and looking after unfortunate girls who were expecting 'mistakes'. It was good work, and finally not unpleasant, primarily because most of the families who could afford to send the girls up to stay under her care were immensely wealthy. She also knew that Leonie was the result of just such a case, but that the poor wretched young mother had died, and that she had been fostered thereafter by her now entirely excellent lodge keepers, Ned Lynch and his wife.

'Well, well, imagine,' said Dorinda, now also all innocence, her diamond earrings flashing in the firelight as she gave a delicate sigh. 'What a thing it would be indeed, if you could only find someone suitable to run your business. Someone who felt compassion for these poor wretched girls, abandoned by their families, and sometimes even by their husbands.'

'All too often by their husbands, Mrs Leveen, all too often, as I have come to realize in the last weeks.' She looked at Dorinda and shook her head. 'When all is said and done men take an awful lot of running, my dear, but then women taken an awful lot of satisfying!'

She gave her rich laugh, and finished her tea with the same satisfaction that she would doubtless show in her own home.

Dorinda replaced her own cup, delicately, on its saucer, and began again.

'Since I have never been a mother, I can not imagine how much in need of loving attention these poor young girls must be, how much they must long for someone to take an interest in them. I would have thought that you must be looking for someone who perhaps might understand their situation, let us say, from the heart?'

'Quite so. I am searching for someone loving and kind, someone who will understand their situation. It is a business, of course, but first and foremost it is about loving attention, about lack of censure, about kindness. If you hear of anyone, Mrs Leveen, you will let me know, will you not? Now, if you don't mind, Mercy my dear, I will just take Twissy into the garden for a little trit for I am badly in need of some country air, and Chelsea is after all still country, isn't it?'

Mercy seemed hardly to hear a word of what her old friend and neighbour had said but was staring out of the window towards the river and the great barges going up and down, staring into a possible future, and at the same time remembering the past.

'I know what it is like, Dorinda, you know that, don't you?' she said, after Mrs Blessington had eased herself out of the door.

'What what is like, Mercy dear?'

Mercy turned and her eyes were grave and sad as she stared across the short space between them. For a second there was only the sound of the fire crackling as some damp wood protested, and a spark flew out onto the hearth as Mercy turned back to watch Mrs Blessington with Twissy on a smart new London leash walking slowly up and down the little garden below.

'I know what it is like to give birth all alone, knowing that your husband has taken little interest in your condition, that he is off with someone else while you think you are going to perhaps die. I know what that is like.'

Dorinda made sure to look as compassionate as she could while hoping against hope that Mercy would take the bait being left out for her. It would be so much better, now that she had taken the extraordinary step of leaving Sussex and set about thinking how best to divorce Brancaster, if she could find herself some kind of employment whereby she could be seen to be both taking the reins into her own hands and following a profession which would, to all but the most narrow minded, be seen as virtuous and charitable.

After all, seeing that Mercy herself now had a baby, it would be quite impossible for her to take herself off to a convent. On the other hand Mrs Dodd's home would be a perfect place for the expression of Mercy's gentle talents, and at the same time no-one would be able to raise a word in criticism. A divorced woman would never be able to live a normal life like other married women, or even widows, but she could turn to good works.

'I wonder, do you think that Mrs Blessington would consider me forward if I offered myself to her for the position of running her business? I was always useful at home, before I married, and seeing that my situation is so changed it would benefit both myself and John Edward if I found some such situation, surely? I would not be forced to live abroad as so many divorcees are, and I would not be in the way of the fashionable, or my own family. No-one would know my situation, unless of course they had some poor daughter who fell into trouble. It could be the solution, wouldn't you say?'

Dorinda looked serious, her head on one side.

'My dear, how perfectly perfect, how perfectly,

perfectly perfect! You are the very answer. I mean, as you say, you know how it feels to be abandoned in childbirth, you know how it is to feel miserably alone in just such a situation, and although you are married, and your circumstances are not precisely the same, nevertheless you would understand. You would *know* how those poor young gels felt.'

Dorinda stood up. She had stayed beyond the required twenty minutes, and more than that, she had seen from a quick look to the window that Mrs Blessington was coming in from the garden.

'Why not ask Mrs Blessington now? Why not suggest this to her?'

'I was hoping that you might do it for me. It would lessen the embarrassment for her if she had it in mind to refuse me.'

And so Dorinda stayed far longer than the statutory twenty minutes, so long in fact that she was in time to see John Edward brought down from his bath and quite able to kiss him good night too.

As to Mrs Blessington, she proved to be a very fine actress indeed, and her reaction of surprise and joy at the news that Mercy would take on her 'little business' could not have been better. Indeed, so good was her acting that watching her Dorinda, who was no mean actress herself, felt almost envious. At the very least she hoped that, if needs be, she could carry off just such a moment as well as the warm-hearted Mrs Blessington.

'And now I really must and shall go. Come on, Pitou, away with us. Like the fairies we should be home by dusk, before someone who should

507

not sees us and we are caught in a big net.'

Once back in the hackney carriage, Dorinda sat back quite tired out, although certainly not dispirited. She stared out of the window at the small, narrow streets that led from Chelsea into Sloane Square and then on to those other, chic-er reaches, where she was so privileged to live. For a few seconds it seemed to her that Mercy's plight might well have been hers, had it not been for Mrs Dodd and her advice about the watch. She too could have been living in a narrow little house in Chelsea instead of with her darling Lawrence in a mansion with everything and anything she wanted.

Not that it would have been the same if she was in the mansion without Mr L. Then everything would just seem to be over-gilded and false. But since she had been lucky enough to find love too, she was that luckiest of all lucky people, a happily married rich woman.

Putting aside this complacent thought Dorinda began to think ahead, for there was still much to be done about so much, most of all her dear friend Leonie who was so plucky as not to mind about wearing the same dress as the wretched Lady C at the ball. She needed to repay her for that kindness. Thinking of this she realized that it would be sensible to ask Gabriel Chantry to luncheon. While in Sussex, a few weeks back, she had taken the opportunity to purchase some furniture from him. She could write to him and command him to come and place it where he thought it would look most suitable, and, having done that, stay to luncheon. And after that, Dorinda could, delicately, and with the utmost tact, find out if Leonie had, as Dorinda hoped, caught his eye at the ball. She knew that he had not danced with her, but had she caught his eye? She was longing to find out, and she could not wait for the days to pass until he came up to London to see her, and she could put the final part of her 'tidying up' plan into action.

Gabriel Chantry was one of those men, Dorinda realized as he walked towards her, who is so kind, so warm-hearted, so at ease with himself and life, that with the single exception of those unfortunate women who only like hard, unfeeling men – such as John Brancaster – no sensible woman could surely pass up the temptation of falling in love with him

It was for this reason that he had come to luncheon with her, because Dorinda knew that, Gabriel having fallen wildly in love with Mercy on account of her humiliations at the hands of John Brancaster, and Mercy having hardly noticed him in any other way than to treat him, always gratefully, but only as a sort of antiquarian brother, he would now be in the mood to do as Dorinda devoutly wished, and fall in love with Leonie.

Even as she smiled and drinks were brought and placed before them both, Dorinda sighed inwardly with impatience, as she always did when she was waiting to get her own way. She sighed because she saw all too clearly, and more than ever

509

now that he was in her drawing room, that Mercy could never have loved Gabriel, simply because poor Mercy was finally incapable of appreciating kindness in a man, her own father having been so very indifferent to her until it seemed it was almost too late.

Leonie, on the other hand, had known only kindness when she was growing up. Not only that, but Dorinda had guessed from what Leonie had simply *not* said about Gabriel Chantry that Miss Lynch had not remained unaffected by Mr Chantry, and had been disappointed that for all the dances booked into her card at Dorinda's ball, not one had been his, and that although they had talked for a few moments he had made no move to write his name, but seemed only too happy, most unhappily, to let every other man dance attendance on her in his stead.

'Mr Chantry still loves Mercy,' she had told Dorinda in a sombre voice the following day when they had met to gossip when Leonie had some hours free.

'Oh, I don't think so,' Dorinda had replied. 'He is too sensible to love someone who will never love him, surely?'

So she had asked him to luncheon to make quite sure that he was too sensible, for, if Dorinda had little time for women who loved unkind men, she had even less time for men who loved unkind women, seeing them as no more than pathetic pastiches of what a man should be.

*　　　*　　　*

The flower-filled drawing room was therefore all too ready for Dorinda and her guest long before his arrival. The arrangements were most especially designed to assail his senses, make him giddy if needs be, with their exquisite scents, not to mention Dorinda looking unaffectedly beautiful in a morning dress of exquisite tailoring, her old 'ess' shape having returned (with the aid of the all important health corset) to show off the fine, light cloth of which the skirt was made, albeit in a more modified and less exaggerated way than hitherto. Her hair was simply dressed in a great velvet bow at the nape of her neck, small, kid button boots were on her feet, and a beautiful sapphire brooch graced the neck of her lace-trimmed lawn blouse. She had chosen all her clothes with the greatest care, as she always did, but this time, in contrast to her receiving of John Brancaster, her clothes were designed to bring confidence and encouragement to the onlooker, not to impress.

From the shop in Ruddwick she had bought what she could, and having no need of oak, except in the servants' quarters perhaps, she had finally selected a 1787 inlaid Italian escritoire, and an English military chest, for the library, of the same date. Seconds after Mr Chantry had arrived, the servants and the removal men followed him into Lawrence House, and having mounted the magnificent marble staircase placed the pieces just so, and with the greatest care, in the great rooms for which they had been destined.

As it happened Dorinda really could not have

cared less how they looked, but not so poor Gabriel Chantry, who walked up and down and around them, looking pale and stiff with anxiety. Dorinda, who had only bought the pieces in order to bring him to town, felt suddenly really rather ashamed of her politicking, knowing as she did that it was quite likely that Mr L would sweep in and announce that he did not like either and order them to be taken away, to be put anywhere but where they had been placed.

Even after the removal men and the servants had left them, Dorinda found it impossible to put Gabriel Chantry at his ease. He stood, six foot and wonderfully handsome with his big brown eyes and beautifully trimmed dark beard, but as tongue-tied and nervous as a schoolboy, his eyes fixed on the escritoire in such a mesmerized and distracted way that eventually, having not been able to draw him into any kind of conversation, Dorinda suggested that they should proceed straight away to luncheon.

And it was there, in Dorinda's dining room, that the disaster that was to change Gabriel's life for ever occurred.

Leonie stared out of the window, her eyes distracted not by anything particularly startling outside it, but by her own thoughts. She had returned to the nursing home, after the excitements of the ball, a great deal more thoughtful than she had been before. She could not expect to be the same after such a momentous evening. It would be absurd to believe that leading off a ball with the King of England would leave her unmarked. Of course it had changed her, not for the worse she hoped, but certainly she was not the same as she had been.

She was proud that she had held her own that evening, that she had not given way to nerves, or giggling or gaucherie, that she had danced every dance, and sipped at her lemonade and earned approving glances from everyone – except, it seemed, the one person whose approval she truly desired, namely Gabriel Chantry.

He had seemed to be standing quite apart from the evening, as if he was a Society painter come to record the scene, and not a young man asked for his handsome looks and charming ways. She saw that he had been watching as she danced with the King, she knew that he had seen that of all the women there it was Leonie Lynch who had been singled out and approached by the equerry to be partnered by the King, and yet he obviously did not share the King's taste in young women.

As she rolled bandages with Miss Scott, it seemed to Leonie that very little had occurred at the nursing home, of late, that had involved her as it had once done. It was perfectly understandable. After all, there were times when more people were sick or had broken bones than at others. And of course the King being quite well, as he had been of late, Lady Angela was now in residence. It was inevitable, therefore, that Leonie felt a great deal less needed than she had done in previous months.

Certainly Miss Scott, who was to be married next month, had about as much interest in the rolling of bandages as Lady Angela would have had in the fashions at last year's Ascot. Dutifully Leonie listened to Miss Scott's description of her wedding dress, for perhaps the fiftieth time. It seemed it was being hand embroidered, but to judge from the time taken up for the fittings Leonie had started to imagine that Miss Scott was going to be crowned, not married.

'It is to be of the finest silk, and I shall wear orange blossom, very old fashioned, as Queen Victoria's daughter did years ago, to please my grandmother, you know. And I am to wear her veil – my grandmother's, not Queen Victoria's. It is of Brussels lace, and a more beautiful piece of embroidery I do not think I have ever seen, except of course on the royal christening robes. I think I told you that my grandmother once saw the royal christening robes, due to a lady in waiting allowing her in to see the last of the Queen's babies dressed and ready for his christening, a rare privilege indeed as you can imagine, and a moment that she has never forgotten. But then the lady in waiting had every reason to be grateful to her, I believe, although what for precisely we never did discover.'

Leonie had noticed that ever since the news had spread through the nursing home that the King had danced with her, every nurse with whom she had ever had a conversation was now at pains to point out their own royal connections, however tenuous. It was a great trial, but one that had to be borne, like rolling bandages, and listening to Miss Scott's endless descriptions of her dress and veil, not to mention her wretched grandmother's opinions of her train, and how many attendants would be fashionable, and whether or not the entrance music would be appropriate.

'So what do you think, Miss Lynch?'

Leonie came to and stared at Miss Scott.

'I – er – I couldn't have an opinion, not really.'

'But it was you who said yesterday that I should have my own choice, and not that of my grandmother or mother. It was you who made me go home and say that I thought the train would be too long.'

Leonie allowed her eyes to boss momentarily at Miss Scott, who, good hearted as she was, immediately started to laugh.

'You have not heard a word I have said, and what is more you could not care less. I swear, if I did not know that your dying wish is to remain unmarried like Lady Angela, you have been so dreamy lately that I would say that you are, at last, in love, Miss Lynch.'

Leonie turned away, colouring a little. Miss Scott, on the other hand, always so very obliging and talkative, began again. She had reached exactly the same point in her conversation and was busy describing, in long and very precise detail, her train, the embroidery on it, and the underneath of it, when the door of the room in which they had been standing for some good time now was opened, noisily and in haste, and a most relieved nurse announced gaily, 'A patient at last!'

They all hurried out into the corridor, each of them only too willing to be busy with a patient rather than to be rolling endless bandages, or sorting towels and washing down walls, which had, all too often, been their lot of late.

'What is the case?' Leonie asked as they hurried towards the entrance hall.

'Food poisoning. Some poor young man ate an oyster and it did for him. Except I believe it was not exactly an oyster, but oyster juice, I think Lady Angela said, and at any rate he has been dreadfully ill and will need immediate attention if he is to be saved.'

Leonie looked at the young man being carried in on a stretcher and saw at once that he was by no means just a case, or just any young man. He was Gabriel Chantry.

Seventeen

Once, when she was growing up in Eastgate Street, Leonie had seen one of Aisleen's caged birds fall suddenly from his perch and watched his little mate trying to revive him. The little bird had stood beside him at the bottom of the cage, calling and calling to him, singing frantically to him, until eventually, realizing that he would not be coming back to her, she too, quite as suddenly, dropped dead.

For some reason Leonie could not stop thinking of this as she watched by Gabriel Chantry's bedside.

It seemed that there was nothing to be done for food poisoning except to introduce liquids and hope for the best, the doctor, on a brief and uninterested visit, had said, but Leonie could not agree. She thought there was everything to be done, and between his groans and his sickness she put cold flannels on Gabriel's head and prayed.

Every now and then Lady Angela put her head round the door, and Dorinda, who had come in with her luncheon guest, but had had to leave to go to a levée with her Mr L, had left messages to send for her the moment there was any change in his condition.

'My dear, I cannot believe the bad luck of it. It was only oyster juice in the salmon entrée, but it struck him down within minutes. He just doubled over. I feel as though I have murdered him, just taken a gun and shot him, really I do.'

Dorinda, having hovered about unable to do anything to help, had eventually hurried off, her eyes filled with tears, leaving behind her a marvellous scent of her perfume – one that Leonie happened to know was made up for her, and only her, in France.

'What a beautiful scent Mrs Leveen wears,' Gabriel murmured in a hoarse voice from the bed. 'It is like something from *heaven*.'

'Knowing Mrs Leveen,' Leonie agreed as she rinsed a flannel in some cold water, 'it probably *was* made in heaven, Mr Chantry. Most likely she went there to have it mixed for her from the heads of divine flowers!'

'She is an angel. Such an angel. I worship her beauty.'

Leonie stopped in the act of squeezing out yet another cold flannel, for suddenly the flannel seemed to be her heart.

She had known that Gabriel was passionately devoted to poor Mercy Brancaster, but judging from his adoring tones it seemed to her suddenly that he might well have transferred his affections from Mrs Brancaster to Mrs Leveen. Perhaps he was one of those unfortunate young men who could only love other people's wives? Perhaps it was for that reason he had not danced with her at the ball.

'I feel so terribly ill, Miss Lynch, oh, so ill.'

Leonie frowned, and noticing suddenly that he kept clutching at one side of himself, and remembering that Lady Angela had described the onset of the King's illness as having started in just this way, she stopped squeezing out her flannel and put it down, because of one thing she was suddenly sure, and that was that cold flannels could do nothing for appendicitis.

'Mr Chantry, please forgive me, but I think I will call Lady Angela.'

There was always something so comforting in Lady Angela's demeanour when she examined a patient herself. Her eyes were always so calm, her touch so gentle, that it seemed to Leonie anyway that however ill the person they immediately felt, if not better, at least as if they were *going* to be better.

Gabriel's eyes looked from the older woman's face to Leonie.

'What is it?'

'I would say that you have what we here now all call *regal appendicitis*, Mr Chantry. I shall send for Mr Finlay. He assisted at the King's operation and a more dependable surgeon you will not find. Always so calm, always so patient.'

Lady Angela hurried off as her patient suddenly put out a hand to hold that of his young nurse.

'I might be going to die, mightn't I, Miss Lynch?'

'No,' Leonie told him, firmly. 'You are not going to die.'

'How do you know? How can you be sure?'

'For the very good reason that I am not going to let you, Mr Chantry.'

And again she remembered her foster mother's little birds, and held tight to her patient's hand.

It was not an easy operation, and he was so terribly ill after it that every now and then Leonie had cause to remember her words, and to wonder at her own confidence. In the event Gabriel Chantry had very nearly died, but with careful nursing and twenty-four hour attention he finally seemed to be pulling through.

Dorinda visited him so much that Gabriel finally confided to Leonie that she was tiring him out with her chatter, and Leonie had to pretend not to look relieved when Dorinda at last announced that she had to go to her house in Sussex. She commanded that they both came to stay with her just as soon as Gabriel was allowed to travel.

Of course the fact that Gabriel had found Dorinda's chatter 'tiring' gave Leonie tremendous hope that he was not perhaps as infatuated with her famously beautiful friend as she had feared. Not that it was any of her business, she told Mrs Dodd, for she had long ago decided to dedicate herself to nursing, a notion that made Mrs Dodd's eyes roll, once Leonie had her back safely turned to her.

'Shall we take a train together, down to Ruddwick?'

The voice was Gabriel's, but he was not in the nursing home, but at Mrs Dodd's London house, where Leonie's godmother had insisted that he spent his convalescence.

'Do you think you would enjoy that?'

'With you,' Gabriel told her, 'yes.'

Leonie smiled up at her dominoes opponent. Gabriel was now so much her friend that it was strange to think of a time when he had not been. She had even accepted his explanation for not dancing with her at Dorinda's ball, having, it seemed, been too *overcome by the previous incumbent*, by which he meant that he felt that he could not compete with the King.

'We can't play dominoes on the train, the pieces would fly everywhere.'

'No, but we can go on talking, and that is as good, I think. I don't think we have stopped talking since I came round from my operation.'

'That is an exaggeration.'

'You are a wonderful nurse.'

'Don't try to distract me because I am winning! That will not fool me, Mr Gabriel Chantry.'

'Perhaps not. Or, perhaps!'

Listening outside the drawing room door, Mrs Dodd smiled. Mr Chantry was so suitable. From the moment he had come to stay with her she had singled him out as being just about the most suitable choice for Leonie. Not so aristocratic as to mind her illegitimacy, and not so wealthy as to think that he could do better.

More than that he was kind. He was handsome. He was funny. All day long when Leonie was not at the nursing home Mrs Dodd was happy to observe that she heard nothing but laughter coming from the garden, or the drawing room, as they played dominoes, or spillikins. Naturally they were more like brother and sister to each other now, but given some fresh country air, and good food, she hoped they could be encouraged to be rather more than that.

Mrs Dodd sighed every evening when she thought about it and her palpitations sometimes increased at the very idea that *it might not happen*. But it would be such a feather in her cap if she could see her beloved goddaughter married and settled before the end of the year. Madame Chloe she knew would be interested in making the dress – at trade, naturally, and they could have attendants to match, and – her thoughts hurtled on, her excitement growing at the prospect. Mrs Leveen, having taken such an interest in Leonie, would doubtless lend her house for the wedding breakfast – as a matter of fact either house would do. Well, more than 'do' – either of Mrs Leveen's houses for the wedding breakfast would be out of this world.

But, Mrs Dodd knew only too well, no amount of machinations, alas, can ever make a man propose, however great his passion, at least not until such time as he feels that he will not be refused. When that would be, she really had no idea. All she could do was to hope, and pray.

Dorinda had felt so full of remorse, following Mr Gabriel Chantry as he was removed from her house on a stretcher, that she had quite driven darling Mr L and Mrs Goodman demented with her lamentations.

She feared at first that it had been the entrée, and then the strain of bringing the furniture up, and so on, and so on. Such was her guilt that she had been unable to drag herself from the poor young man's bedside, even managing to privately convince herself that it had been something in the entrée that had actually brought on the wretched appendicitis.

However, with the news that Mr Chantry was now out of the woods and being nursed at Mrs Dodd's house, Dorinda at once saw that she had a wonderful chance to make it up to him for his having been taken ill at her London house. At least she imagined that she had. Her plan was to ask him, and Leonie, naturally, down to Sussex for a period of convalescence. She had of course observed that Leonie was more than devoted to the antiquarian, and while she had always listened with great patience, and a serious expression, to Leonie's protestations of devotion to her profession, left to herself Dorinda thought that a girl as beautiful as Miss Lynch had about as much chance of remaining single as – well, as she herself would have had.

And so it was really delightful to Dorinda that she could go ahead to her country house in Sussex determined on making everything quite, quite beautiful for Gabriel and Leonie's stay. But shortly after she was assured that there were flowers of every kind in every room, that there were plans for picnics in the bothy, boating trips on the lake, and so on, Leonie arrived alone.

'I thought you were coming together?' Dorinda asked her, looking at her singleness astonished. 'I thought you were both coming by train? It sounded so – so adventurous, just the two of you on a train with only Mrs Dodd's maid!'

'Mr Chantry wanted to go to his house first, and to visit the shop. He will be here later, towards teatime, he said.'

'I expect he is collecting – something.'

In Dorinda's imaginative eyes she could see Gabriel Chantry perhaps choosing Leonie a beautiful antique ring from some cabinet in the back of his shop, and pocketing it before coming on to her house. That had to be the reason why he had suddenly decided to go first to his house and his shop, surely?

'It is a miracle he is here at all, isn't it?' she asked Leonie. 'And do you know I still feel, because he was taken ill in our house, that it was in some way our fault.'

'That is always the case. Someone has only to slip on one's front doorstep for one to blame oneself for having a door,' Leonie agreed.

'I have to say that we were all convinced that he would die. Thank God he did not.'

The expression on Dorinda's face remained serious as she remembered Gabriel Chantry doubled up and moaning, and to take her mind off the frightening image she put her arm through Leonie's and squeezed it.

'Is he not an angel though, our Mr Chantry?' she asked Leonie, and tried not to notice the way her friend's eyes looked away at something that was definitely not happening on the edge of the ha-ha.

'He is a very nice man,' Leonie agreed, blushing, and she thought of Gabriel standing among all his precious items in his shop, or looking through his books perhaps. He had told her that he loved everything that he bought, and so found it difficult to sell anything.

'I dare say once Mr Chantry gets amongst his furniture and his paintings, his silver and his antiques, we will be lucky if he returns.'

They prepared themselves for tea, and waited in the library. Tick, tock, the beautiful, large, serious faced Victorian clock's gold hands moved, it seemed to them both, now too slowly, now too fast.

'I think he must have had to meet someone at his shop,' Dorinda reassured her friend as the servants cleared away the large tea, left uneaten by both the ladies.

'I hope he is feeling quite well.'

Leonie stared out of the window. Perhaps he did not want to come? Perhaps he did not want to stay with Dorinda, with only Leonie for company? Perhaps that was the kind of invitation that a young man, once he was quite better, could find dull and unexciting, and that was why he had decided to travel alone?

Six o'clock came and went and the hands of the clock now seemed to be moving faster and faster as they both glanced at it every few minutes in a fatigue of anxiety, as in both their minds Gabriel Chantry became ever more handsome, ever more charming, ever more irreplaceable than he had ever been before.

A knocking at the great hall door brought immediate relief, and Dorinda, forgetting all the proprieties, immediately ran out into the hall, hardly able to bear the relief that she was feeling at the idea that he had at last arrived. Inevitably she was followed closely by Leonie.

As it transpired it was not Mr Chantry but someone quite other calling from the village to ask for funds for the local orphanage. Dorinda was so exasperated and disappointed that she immediately donated what looked to Leonie, and doubtless to the lady concerned, to be enough money to support not one but two orphanages.

The hall door closed behind the fund-raiser, and as her housekeeper stared in astonishment Dorinda stamped her foot and exclaimed, 'Do you know, having nearly killed Mr Chantry, I could now murder him!'

The two young women trailed desultorily back to the drawing room door where a footman was waiting, but as he opened for them a voice from across the hall called, 'Shoot, Mrs Leveen, shoot, right to the heart!' and a tall figure which now proved itself to be Gabriel Chantry appeared between the great doors at the opposite end of the hall, removing his hat and bowing.

'Oh, you wretch, we had quite given you up,'

Dorinda cried and she darted across the hall to drag her guest back to the library, making sure to take his great coat herself, noticing with some satisfaction that before she was allowed to hand it to one of the servants Gabriel took from one of its pockets an old leather box in which could only be housed the all-important ring.

Well satisfied that he had the look of a man about to propose – half sick with fright and at the same time really rather thrilled with himself – Dorinda shut the library doors behind the lovers, and went to order champagne to be brought in to them some ten minutes later.

As to herself, fainting with the relief of his arrival, she took herself off for a hot bath and a nice lie down before being dressed for dinner by her maid. Really she thought she should appear in the guise of Cupid himself, so satisfied was she that she must have brought about the engagement of Gabriel Chantry and Leonie Lynch.

*   *   *

Dorinda's encounter with Mercy in Chelsea having entailed helping Josephine to put John Edward to bed, not to mention kissing him goodnight, had the all too inevitable result on his visitor – in the event, a most happy result. The following year a little girl was born to her and Mr L. Since the birth took place, by special permission, in Mrs Blessington's nursing home, and since Mercy and Dorinda were now so close, it was natural to the two young women to immediately decide that their children should, when the time came, marry.

Leonie on the other hand, having herself married Gabriel Chantry and being happily ensconced with him in a small town house at Ruddwick, had to wait to view Dorinda's baby until her friend at last brought the two month old Oriana to enjoy the fresh air at her Sussex estate. As soon as she was installed, Leonie, leaving Gabriel with a promise to return by teatime, went to visit and admire what she realised had to be a beautiful baby, born as she had been to such a beautiful woman. Oriana was indeed beautiful, but Leonie, having admired her inordinately, was, after an hour of exclamation, a delicious tea, and a yard or two of gossip, sent smartly on her way. For, as Dorinda remarked, bearing in mind Gabriel's handsome looks and charming ways, 'My dear, an attractive man cannot be left for more time than it takes to boil an egg . . .'

As to Mrs Dodd, she visited her goddaughter and her husband several times a year, but when in London there was nothing that her friend Madame Chloe and she liked better than to remember Leonie's wedding to Gabriel Chantry.

Their teatime sessions together would always begin with the taking out of the photograph albums, and the placing of the newspaper cuttings upon the white lace tablecloth, the cuttings now so yellow that they looked like Chinese wallpaper.

Mrs Dodd, having had a generous amount of tea, would sit back while Madame Chloe purred over the compliments heaped by the fashion writers on the cutting and excellence of Miss Lynch's wedding dress, on the numbers of exquisitely turned out page boys (eight in all), on the list of presents – a rose bowl graciously sent by the King and Queen, a set of gold vases from the Maharajah of Raipur, a bracelet set with love knots from Mrs Lawrence Leveen, *whom our readers may better remember as Dorinda Blue.*

And so on down to the list of guests who enjoyed the wedding breakfast at Lawrence House, *the Princess Polignac, the Duke and Duchess of Claremore, Lord and Lady Londonderry, Lord and Lady Hervey Davidson, the Lady Balniel of that Ilk, the Hon. Mrs Hugh Morrison . . .*

Each and every detail of the wedding was delicious to Mrs Dodd and Madame Chloe – the length of the embroidered train, the satin breeches on the page boys, the ten flower girls, each of whose dresses took ten yards of organza and the same of taffeta, not to mention thirty rosebuds each for their headdresses.

The two women never tired of the details or their teas together, both appreciating that it had been a long way from Eastgate Street to Mayfair, but in the event, not so long after all. And as to Leonie, she never enquired of either Mrs Dodd or her heroine, Lady Angela, as to who her real parents might have been, taking the sensible view that it was their secret, not hers.

Epilogue

Standing under the street lamp's kindly light the woman looked up at the outside of her little Chelsea house, reassuring herself that while her nanny's light was still burning her little boy's nursery light was not. The man standing beside her also looked up, as if to reassure himself too, and then taking off his immaculate top hat he bowed to her, and kissed her hand.

Tomorrow morning they both knew that she would be up and gone before the lamp under which they were standing was put out by the early morning lamplighter, but just at that moment less serious matters occupied both their thoughts, as they must do, when a man and a woman, greatly attracted to each other, have had a rare but mutually enjoyable evening dining and visiting the opera.

Bending over her small, ringed, white hand he kissed it lightly, his dark hair, greying at the sides, covered seconds later by the shiny opera hat. As his arms retreated back into his opera cloak the lining showed beautifully and magnificently red.

The woman was not such a puritan that she could not appreciate her companion's elegance and style, and not least his exquisite and elegant manners.

'Thank you. It was a lovely evening.'

'May I call again? Please say I may.'

She hesitated for what seemed to him to be a thousand hours.

'Yes, you may, but – you know – nowadays my evenings off are rare. Perhaps in two weeks?'

'Whenever you say. Send me a message and I will be waiting, always.'

The woman smiled back at him from her front doorstep before fitting her key into the lock of her front door.

'We enjoyed ourselves, didn't we?'

'I am only ever happy when I'm with you, you know that now.'

The woman nodded, seemingly unmoved by the intensity behind the man's words, but nevertheless she kissed the tips of her fingers to him, and closing the front door behind her she leant against it for a few seconds, listening to the sound of the hackney horse trit-trotting its way into the distance of the London street.

The nanny leant over the banisters and smiled down at her.

'Nice evenin', Mrs Brancaster?'

Mercy nodded and smiled.

'You look lovely in your opera clothes. I love you in that yellow.' Josephine nodded with satisfaction. 'And Mr Brancaster?'

Mercy paused, her large eyes thoughtful. 'He is – well, Josephine, quite well, if not quite – better.'

'Well, that is good, then. John Edward has been fast asleep all the time you was out, I'm here to tell you.'

Mercy followed the nanny upstairs as she chattered away about her charge. Soon it would be morning, and other matters would be upon her, but just at that moment Mercy was more than content; it seemed to her at that moment that she might actually be happy.

THE END

THE KISSING GARDEN
by Charlotte Bingham

'A perfect escapist cocktail for summertime romantics'
Mail on Sunday

As children, George Dashwood and Amelia Dennison loved to roam the Sussex Downs and, just as their two very different families were friends, so too were they, until they are caught in a thunderstorm. Sheltering from the elements, the now mature George realizes that the way he feels about Amelia has changed. But it is 1914 and the declaration of war cuts across any romantic plans that the two might have.

George is away at the front for four years, but when the miracle happens and he returns home safely Amelia realizes that the boy she loved has gone. Although they marry it seems that George does so from a sense of duty. It is only when they discover an old priory with a magical atmosphere that their chance for happiness become a reality.

A Bantam Paperback
0 553 50717 6

LOVE SONG
by Charlotte Bingham

'A perfect example of the new, darker romantic fiction
. . . a true 24-carat love story'
Sunday Times

Hope Merriott has always thought of herself as truly blessed with her three daughters, Melinda, Rose and Claire, until, that is, the arrival of a fourth daughter, Letty. Loved though she will be, the baby's birth coincides with the failure of her husband Alexander's newest business venture.

Neverthless, life at West Dean Avenue continues on its usual cheerful – if improvident – course, until Alexander's Great Aunt Rosabel comes to stay for Christmas. Unaware that a considerable inheritance was dependent upon her fourth child being a boy, Hope is full of seemingly unreasonable foreboding when the old lady offers to gift Alexander her large, elegant house, Hatcombe, in Wiltshire.

Overnight, Alexander moves the family from what Hope sees as their cosy life to the loneliness and isolation of Wiltshire's rolling acres. Indeed, once at Hatcombe, many of Hope's premonitions seem about to be realized when Jack Tomm, a neighbour, comes to call on her. Although they intend only to introduce their teenage children to each other, all too soon Jack and Hope fall passionately in love . . .

A Bantam Paperback
0 553 50501 7

A SELECTION OF FINE NOVELS
AVAILABLE FROM BANTAM BOOKS

THE PRICES SHOWN BELOW WERE CORRECT AT THE TIME OF GOING TO PRESS.
HOWEVER TRANSWORLD PUBLISHERS RESERVE THE RIGHT TO SHOW NEW
RETAIL PRICES ON COVERS WHICH MAY DIFFER FROM THOSE PREVIOUSLY
ADVERTISED IN THE TEXT OR ELSEWHERE.

50329 4	DANGER ZONES	*Sally Beauman*	£5.99
50630 7	DARK ANGEL	*Sally Beauman*	£6.99
50631 5	DESTINY	*Sally Beauman*	£6.99
40727 9	LOVERS AND LIARS	*Sally Beauman*	£5.99
50326 X	SEXTET	*Sally Beauman*	£5.99
40163 7	THE BUSINESS	*Charlotte Bingham*	£5.99
40497 0	CHANGE OF HEART	*Charlotte Bingham*	£5.99
40890 9	DEBUTANTES	*Charlotte Bingham*	£5.99
40895 X	THE NIGHTINGALE SINGS	*Charlotte Bingham*	£5.99
17635 8	TO HEAR A NIGHTINGALE	*Charlotte Bingham*	£5.99
50500 9	GRAND AFFAIR	*Charlotte Bingham*	£5.99
40296 X	IN SUNSHINE OR IN SHADOW	*Charlotte Bingham*	£5.99
40469 2	NANNY	*Charlotte Bingham*	£5.99
50501 7	LOVE SONG	*Charlotte Bingham*	£5.99
40117 8	STARDUST	*Charlotte Bingham*	£5.99
50717 6	THE KISSING GARDEN	*Charlotte Bingham*	£5.99
50718 4	THE LOVE KNOT	*Charlotte Bingham*	£5.99
40973 5	A CRACK IN FOREVER	*Jeannie Brewer*	£5.99
17504 1	DAZZLE	*Judith Krantz*	£5.99
40732 5	THE JEWELS OF TESSA KENT	*Judith Krantz*	£5.99
17242 5	I'LL TAKE MANHATTAN	*Judith Krantz*	£5.99
40730 9	LOVERS	*Judith Krantz*	£5.99
17174 7	MISTRAL'S DAUGHTER	*Judith Krantz*	£5.99
17389 8	PRINCESS DAISY	*Judith Krantz*	£5.99
40731 7	SPRING COLLECTION	*Judith Krantz*	£5.99
17503 3	TILL WE MEET AGAIN	*Judith Krantz*	£5.99
17505 X	SCRUPLES TWO	*Judith Krantz*	£5.99
81287 4	APARTMENT 3B	*Patricia Scanlan*	£5.99
81290 4	FINISHING TOUCHES	*Patricia Scanlan*	£5.99
81286 6	FOREIGN AFFAIRS	*Patricia Scanlan*	£5.99
81288 2	PROMISES, PROMISES	*Patricia Scanlan*	£5.99
40941 7	MIRROR, MIRROR	*Patricia Scanlan*	£5.99
40943 3	CITY GIRL	*Patricia Scanlan*	£5.99
40946 8	CITY WOMAN	*Patricia Scanlan*	£5.99
81245 9	IT MEANS MISCHIEF	*Kate Thompson*	£5.99
81246 7	MORE MISCHIEF	*Kate Thompson*	£5.99

All Transworld titles are available by post from:

Book Service By Post, PO Box 29, Douglas, Isle of Man, IM99 1BQ

Credit cards accepted. Please telephone 01624 675137
fax 01624 670923, Internet http://www.bookpost.co.uk
or e-mail: bookshop@enterprise.net for details

Free postage and packing in the UK. Overseas customers: allow £1 per book